Bitter Quadrille

For Denise,
with my thanks &
best wishes,

Sheila

Bitter Quadrille

A Novel

by

Sheila Heywood

THE CHOIR PRESS

First published in the United Kingdom in 2023 by
The Choir Press

ISBN 978-1-78963-413-6

Prologue

We haven't chosen a name for him yet, this wonderful brand-new addition to our family. In fact, there is no 'we' – my better half and I – about it. Before our firstborn came along, my wife bought one of those baby-naming books and after poring over the pages, ploughing through from A to Z, enthusing over many and eliminating many more, we finally shortlisted the chosen ones to three. To be honest, my interest had well and truly waned by then, and as our firstborn was a girl, I concluded that my wife should be the one to decide; with the co-operation of other females, naturally: sister, mother, best friend. And so I valiantly (as they thought) opted out of the equation and our baby daughter was baptised a suitable, feminine, floral name and with my blessing.

Our second progeny, three years later, was also a girl, and we went through the same procedure with the same book – a little dog-eared by this time – and with the same result. I had no say in the choice of our second daughter's name but, surprisingly, this time it rankled a bit. I felt – perversely, I suppose – unimportant, as though my opinion didn't count. Which it obviously did not.

This time, however, it is going to be different. Oh yes, this time, it's my say, my choice. I look down and smile as I wheel him down the garden path towards the large wooden gate and, as I leave the path and turn left across the cobbles, an elderly neighbour I know by sight stops in his tracks and bends over to have a look. He pats my shoulder and winks, tells me how fine, how beautiful he is. His companion comes puffing and panting up the hill and she has a look, too, and nods her approval together with a womanly, knowing smile.

I almost tell them that he hasn't got a name yet but manage to bite my tongue. They are another generation and would probably think it was odd – that I was odd. So, I nod and smile, give them the thumbs-up and we go our separate ways.

The hill where we live is quite steep so I'm very careful and cling on tightly to avoid any mishaps, but my active brain is still focused on what I – ostensibly we – are going to call him. Something unforgettable, easily pronounced, preferably two syllables – not too short, not too long ...

We have come quite a distance and turn right onto the busy main street where the market takes place every Saturday morning ... today is Saturday. We're bound to meet more people who know me and who'll want to give him the once-over ... I swing myself onto my beautiful red and silver Triumph, turn on the petrol tap, turn on the ignition and kick-start my fine and beautiful motorbike. I put him into first gear, release the clutch and we roll together down the road. I feel the warm breeze on my face and want to shout out my exhilaration to the world – or at least to the small crowd of people just coming out of the market square ... I look down at the speedometer and, just as I – we – approach the shopping-laden flock, the name comes to me in a flash and, exhilarated, enervated, *relieved*, for God's sake, I accelerate again and yell the unforgettable, easily pronounced two-syllable name to whoever cares to listen ...

Chapter One

Few people would deny that autumn is the most stunning season of the year. Autumn, with its rich reds and golds and gentle mists. Of course, there are those who would argue that autumn is miserable because of its nearness to winter, or because of this, that and the other. They would also argue that black is really off-white and that Adolf Hitler was a Jew. They don't really believe in what they're saying, they just enjoy contradicting the other person's point of view; picking and poking at their words, making that other person feel foolish and not worth listening to. About anything. Fabricating incompatibility.

Catherine Jarvis was married to one of those people.

Catherine loved the autumn, she always had. Even on this Monday morning in early October 1983, when there was more than a slight nip in the air, she could feel the almost ethereal beauty of the season. A sudden chill ran through her slim body and she speeded up her steps, hurrying through the damp leaves until she reached the red-brick semi-detached house on the corner. She shivered as she fumbled for her keys and mentally promised herself a large mug of milky coffee as soon as she got in, a rare treat. She slammed the door behind her and was glad she'd persuaded Brian to turn the central heating on the night before. 'Persuaded' was putting it mildly. If it had been up to Brian, they would have made do with the two-bar electric fire all winter, which was neither use nor ornament. He wouldn't have approved of making coffee with milk, either. It would have been an unnecessary extravagance. Well, Brian wasn't here and she'd make the most of his absence.

The postman had called while she was out; there were two envelopes on the doormat. One plain, brown and official-looking was obviously a bill and Catherine inwardly groaned. That meant another post-mortem on their expenditure over the last quarter and great, lengthy discussions on 'how they could economise'. So, she already knew what their after-dinner conversation would be; not exactly something to look forward to. The other envelope was pink and, Catherine noticed with mild amusement, slightly perfumed. Addressed to Mr and Mrs B Jarvis and the postmark was London.

Catherine dropped the two envelopes on the bottom step together with her well-worn shopping bag and ran upstairs to hang up her raincoat and comb her damp, matted hair. Not that she needed to. At one time, she'd have flung her raincoat across a convenient chair and to hell with her lanky locks for the time being ... she was in desperate need of a reviving hot drink and everything else could wait ... However, for the past three years she'd been conditioned. If there was anything that Brian couldn't stand, it was slovenliness. A woman should be proud of her appearance; her clothes, her hair; she should always make the most of herself. Fine. But when Catherine occasionally bought a new dress or splashed out on an expensive perfume ... well, it just wasn't worth the inquisition afterwards. Catherine looked at her face in the dressing-table mirror. She didn't like herself; she hadn't liked herself for the past three years. She wearily examined her sallow skin that had once been so fresh; the sad brown eyes that had once been so clear; now you didn't notice her eyes for the dark shadows underneath. And her hair – her once-upon-a-time crowning glory. Reddy brown like the autumn leaves, shining with life and bouncing down her back. It was still reddy brown, but the life and bounce had long since gone.

She plodded down the stairs and, picking up the dropped envelopes, went into the kitchen at the back of the house. She opened the fridge, took out a carton of milk, poured a small measure into a red non-stick pan and turned on the electric ring. She spooned coffee into a red and white striped mug and thought about the pink envelope from London. She was curious, to say the least. She and Brian didn't know anyone in London. Well, Brian had business contacts there but this was obviously a personal letter and, what was more to the point, from a female ... Good God, *of course*, Brian's sister, the beautiful rich bitch, Melanie Jarvis. Of course. It had to be from her; Catherine couldn't think of anyone else they knew in London. And a perfumed pink envelope would certainly be her silly style. So why had *she* suddenly turned up out of the blue? If it hadn't been for the magazines and the odd television commercial when Brian was capable of throwing a brick through the screen, she could have been dead. Well, as far as Brian was concerned, Melanie *was* dead. Catherine examined the frivolous envelope; it was addressed to Mr and Mrs B Jarvis; she could open it without feeling riddled with guilt. No, on second thoughts, she'd leave it for Brian to open. Better to be safe than sorry. If the letter was from Melanie – and Catherine

2

was sure that it was – then Brian would expect to read it first. She left it on the kitchen table next to the bill. She didn't open that, either.

According to the clock on the kitchen wall, it was ten-thirty and the day stretched ahead of Catherine like a big blank, as usual. She'd spend her Monday cleaning, kicking her heels and killing time until Janine came running, flushed and giggling, through the door at three-thirty, her words unfathomable because of her general zest for living. Janine. If it wasn't for that beautiful five-year-old godsend, Catherine would have cracked up before now. She unconsciously smiled as she thought about her daughter and then remembered the long empty hours she had to fill before she saw her again and her smile faded. And then she thought about Brian walking through the door at six o'clock and her smile disappeared.

She decided to go for a walk, to lose herself in the season's glory. Catherine had always loved the autumn. For some reason that she couldn't explain, it was a magical, mysterious time. A time to reminisce on the dying year before it was completely buried under the snows of winter. Autumns in the past had always been significant somehow, especially when she and ... Catherine slammed he empty mug into the sink and ran upstairs to recover her coat.

She needed a real job, of course, she was vegetating, becoming dull and undynamic, as Brian more than subtly hinted. So, what was his objection to her finding a job outside the home? Because he provided her with enough translations to keep her busy several hours a week and his company paid her well for doing this important work. Fair enough, but translating was laborious and solitary work and Catherine liked people; she craved company. Lively, interesting conversations with like-minded people. She'd rebelled, of course, and registered with an agency to do part-time secretarial work. The agency had kept her reasonably busy during the summer months but jobs were very scarce at this time of year and Catherine was finding herself at home more and more. Anyway, Brian preferred his wife to stay at home, to make a comfortable place for him, and he also expected her to be a sparkling, lively hostess when he brought people home for dinner or drinks in the evening. Well, she'd be a sight more sparkling if she was out of the house, doing an honest-to-goodness job and meeting stimulating people ... Catherine kicked at a pile of dried, ruddy leaves without realising what she was doing. An elderly man walking his West Highland terrier turned and stared and the dog stopped trotting and pricked up its ears. Catherine didn't notice. She hardly even noticed the autumn around her.

*

Janine tornadoed through the door at three-thirty, her black curls flying behind her, her cheeks flushed with the cold, her mouth and eyes laughing. Catherine looked up from the crossword puzzle that she was tackling at the kitchen table.

'Hello, Mummy.' Kiss, kiss.

'Hello, sweetheart. Did you thank Mrs Wainwright for bringing you home from school?'

The children's mothers took turns to collect them at three o'clock, an idea that Catherine secretly objected to. She hated the days when someone else met Janine. Not because she was possessive; she just appreciated the short walk to the school and back.

'Now then, how about a nice glass of orange juice and you can tell Mummy all about school.'

'Okay.'

Janine grinned and, throwing her small plastic schoolbag on the floor, she scrambled onto a white kitchen stool. Her sharp eyes immediately fell on the bright pink envelope, still unopened. She picked it up and said,

'Who's this pink letter from, Mummy? Ooh heck, it smells!'

Catherine burst out laughing at her daughter's screwed-up face, but she didn't really know how to answer the question. Janine had no idea that Aunty Melanie Jarvis existed.

'I don't know yet, darling. Daddy's going to open it when he comes home.'

The child quickly lost interest and began to tell her mummy all about school and the horrible, yucky shepherd's pie she'd had to eat for lunch and the lumpy custard that had made her feel sick.

'Why can't I come home for lunch, Mummy? My friends do.'

Catherine tensed as she placed two glasses of orange juice on the table.

'You know why, darling. Let's not start that again.'

There was nothing that Catherine would love more than to have Janine home at lunchtime. But Brian, being Brian, said no. It would do the child good to stay at school and suffer the 'awful' food so that she'd learn to appreciate her meals at home. But she already did, for God's sake. She must learn to be a stoic. At five years old? Anyway, Catherine had rationally argued, if Janine stayed to school lunches, it was pointless her – Catherine – being stuck at home all day. She could – and should – find a job. But Brian wouldn't discuss it. The subject was closed. And Janine stayed at school for lunch.

*

Catherine thanked God that she'd decided not to make shepherd's pie that evening. It had run through her menu-conscious mind. However, while she'd been standing in the butcher's queue, debating between the mince and the nice, thick pork chops, she'd realised that they hadn't had chops for about three weeks and that, of course, had decided her. Congratulations, Mrs Jarvis, on such commendable perspicacity. Oh, what an exciting, mind-blowing, challenging life she led. And when she thought, as she occasionally, no, very often, did, of what her life could have been ...

She was just dishing up the juicy pieces of meat, together with roast potatoes and apple sauce, when Brian walked into the kitchen. It was six o'clock. Bang on. Timing had, for a long time, been the only good thing about their marriage.

'Hello, Daddy!' Janine yelled and, leaping off her stool, threw herself into Brian's arms.

'Steady on, girl, steady on,' Brian Jarvis frowned. 'I wish you'd learn not to be so sloppy, Janine. Not as soon as I walk through the door, for goodness' sake. I can't do with it, I'm afraid ... no, get down. Go sit down or go play or ... something. I'm too tired; bloody exhausted.'

He pushed the bewildered child away, sat down at the kitchen table and, without acknowledging his wife, picked up the two envelopes. Janine, her rejection quickly forgotten, excitedly cried,

'That pink envelope smells, Daddy! Honest, it does! Go on, have a pong!'

Brian breathed in through his nostrils and threw the envelope back onto the table. He folded his arms across his chest and leant towards the little girl, his small grey eyes tearing at her face.

'What did I hear you say, young lady?'

Catherine, dishing out vegetables, tensed.

'Oh, for goodness' sake, leave her alone, Brian.'

Brian ignored the woman standing by the cooker, as usual.

'"Go on, have a *pong!*" What kind of remark is that, d'you mind telling me? Eh? I don't know what they reckon to teach you at that school but it's certainly not good manners.'

Janine's eyes had filled up and she was holding her breath to stop herself from crying, a habit that, over the years, she'd had to get used to.

'It's time we started thinking about sending you away to a decent school, somewhere where they'll teach you how to behave ...'

'Brian!'

Catherine pushed her husband's dinner in front of him and glanced at her daughter. Her expression was one of sheer terror and Catherine wanted to take her in her arms and give her a big bear hug and say, *He doesn't mean it, darling, he doesn't mean it.*

But she knew that Brian did mean it. If he had his lousy way, Janine would be sent away to boarding school as soon as possible; it didn't matter which, it didn't matter where. Anywhere, as long as she was away. And paradoxically ... sod the expense.

The meal was eaten in stony silence and the envelopes were temporarily forgotten. Brian ate slowly, examining every forkful as though it were vitriol, as though his wife were planning on poisoning him. *Come to think of it,* Catherine mused, *that wasn't such a bad idea.* Janine gobbled her food, eager to leave the miserable table, her moist eyes darting from one adult to the other. Catherine only picked at her pork chop because her already small appetite had disappeared. When Janine had quickly left the table, after quietly begging Brian's permission, he picked up the brown envelope. The expression on his face as he slowly slit the paper reminded Catherine of a high court judge about to give his sentence. She began to pile the dishes into the sink, so that her back was turned.

'Christ Almighty, woman, I don't believe it.'

Catherine's blood drained away and her stomach turned over. She turned on the hot tap and concentrated on squeezing Fairy Liquid into the water. Brian's chair scraped along the red and white tiled floor and she suddenly felt his hot breath on the back of her neck. She pulled on her yellow rubber gloves.

'Eighty-five bloody quid? For the summer quarter! What d'you think you're playing at, woman?'

6

Catherine, trying to behave rationally at a very irrational moment, slowly turned to face her husband.

'What am *I* playing at, Brian? Correct me if I'm wrong but I think you live here, too.'

'I can't deny that – but I'm not in the house all day, am I?'

Catherine's equilibrium snapped.

'And neither would I be if I had my way. You know damn well I hate being stuck at home all day and—'

Brian's right hand slammed against her left cheek and she reeled.

'Don't you dare raise your voice to me like that. I've no desire to be married to a fishwife.'

Catherine tentatively touched her stinging face with her rubber hand. She looked up at him, her brown eyes bewildered and accusing at this unprecedented physical attack.

'Then please don't treat me as though I were a fishwife. I have to use the electricity when I'm at home all day, don't I. And just remember you're the one who goes out every night, using the hot water for your shower, not me ...'

She'd had to get that in. Brian's small grey eyes didn't leave her face. He was unrepentant.

'It's ridiculous. I'm going to put a stop to this bloody extravagance. If this is the bill for the summer quarter, what the hell's it going to be at Christmas? Anyway, I'm going to turn the central heating off, that'll teach you. I can't trust you, Catherine ... I just can't trust you to think and act like a grown woman with responsibilities. You need me behind you for every little thing.'

And then his hands began to tear at the pink envelope from London and a long silence followed. Catherine finished the washing-up, emptied the red plastic bowl, pulled off the rubber gloves and tried to ignore her still-stinging cheek. She slowly turned to look at Brian. There was some kind of card on the table and he was reading a letter, written on pink paper.

'Who is it from?' Catherine asked, her voice almost a whisper, resenting the need for communication. She reached out and picked up the card. It was an invitation to an engagement party in Hampstead, north London, the last weekend in October. From Melanie.

'So, my bitch of a sister's finally decided to take the plunge,' Brian said. He threw the letter onto the table. 'Well, God help him, whoever he is. She hasn't said, you know. She hasn't had the decency to tell us who she's bringing into the bloody family. "It's a secret." Typical of her. Who does she think she is? Mind you, he's probably some half-wit she's picked up on the streets. He'll have to be some kind of a nutter to marry her. When he sees under all that glamour, he'll soon realise his mistake.'

Catherine blinked and bit her lip. She didn't know how he had the bloody nerve. He was a fine one to talk about anyone making a mistake. He had to look no further than his own wife.

'Shall we accept the invitation?' she asked.

'Well, what do *you* think? I'm surprised you need ask. Of course we're not going to accept the invitation.' The last three words were a mimicry of her own voice. 'After all she did to us, all the bloody upset she caused us. You must be joking. And if she can't even be bothered to tell us who the bloke is ...'

'I'd like to go.'

'Well, hard bloody lines.' Brian raised his voice. 'It'll be a pantomime, anyway. You know how she carries on, queening it over everybody. I'm not going to give her that satisfaction. And you can bet your life there'll be some kind of scene. Wherever Melanie Jarvis puts in an appearance, there's always a drama. You of all people should know that. Or is your memory fading with age?'

'Please, Brian, let's go. We could make it a weekend in London. It'd be a ... a lovely change.'

Apart from anything else, Catherine was curious about the fiancé; there must be something special about him for Melanie to be so secretive. Maybe she'd landed herself someone very famous, or better still, infamous. It was more than possible, her being so successful and leading the lifestyle she did. Janine chose that moment to come back into the kitchen, the dinnertime troubles forgotten, her small round face smiling and happy. Here was another good reason to go down to London for a weekend. Catherine's mother was always complaining that she didn't see enough of her only grandchild, and she'd love to have Janine to herself for a couple of days. It would be good for Janine, too. It would be good for her to get away from Brian.

'Come here, sweetheart.'

Catherine pulled her daughter into her arms and squeezed tight.

'Now then, how would you like to go and stay with Grandma for a whole weekend?'

8

Catherine, her heart hammering, her voice barely audible, sat down and pulled the little girl onto her lap.

'Ooh, yes please, Mummy, Grandma makes the bestest ever chocolate cake! When can I go?'

In spite of herself, Catherine couldn't help laughing.

'At the end of this month.' She swallowed hard and took her chance. 'Mummy and Daddy are going to a big party in London and you, darling, won't be able to come. But Grandma will be really looking forward to you staying with her. And that's a promise, darling.'

The child yelled with delight, hugged her mother, kissed her still-sore cheek and disappeared out of the room. The atmosphere in the previously oven-hot kitchen was now frigid. To say the least.

'I suppose you think you're very clever.'

Catherine returned Brian's steely glare.

'We can't break a promise to a child.'

'Oh, can't we now?'

'No! No, no, no!'

'Well, let me remind you, my lovely wife, that little half-breed out there belongs to you. She's got nothing to do with me, or had you forgotten? And it wouldn't hurt me one little bit to break a—'

Catherine stood up; she couldn't let him go on. He'd already upset her child too much; he wasn't going to do any more damage.

'Please, Brian, let's go to this party. Let's have a nice weekend in London. Janine will enjoy herself with my mum and it'll give us a break ...'

Her enormous once-beautiful eyes were looking up at him, imploring. Her voice was pleading, placating, and she hated herself and told herself she was doing it for Janine. The silence was long and Catherine knew she was bashing her head against a brick wall. When Brian said no, he didn't mean yes. So, she was more than a little stunned when he finally barked,

'Okay, if that's what you really want, we'll go to the damned engagement shindig. We'll accept this ... this ridiculous, nauseating pink invitation. But don't blame me if it's a fiasco. And for God's sake, don't expect me to be the life and soul of the party.'

Catherine began to breathe again and secretly smiled to herself at the thought of her husband being the life and soul of any party. Brian briskly turned away from her and headed out of the kitchen, no doubt to shower and change before his nightly trip to the pub, or Belinda's bed, or wherever it was he went. At the foot of the stairs he suddenly spun round, and the look on his face sent shivers of apprehension down Catherine's spine.

'Oh, by the way, my love,' he smiled, 'when we leave the half-breed with your mother, do you think we could forget to pick her up?'

Chapter Two

Why didn't she leave him? Catherine had asked herself that question time and time again and always got the same answer. It was a classic case of hope springing eternal. At the beginning of their marriage, when Brian's Jekyll and Hyde character had first come to light, Catherine had been mystified but hadn't worried too much. Most men were bad-tempered after a hard day's work; most men, in such circumstances, had to adjust to suddenly becoming a stepfather; most men were critical of their wives occasionally, weren't they? But Catherine had never confided in other wives so she never found out. She constantly told herself that they were having teething troubles, that in time they would sort themselves out; it was only a matter of time and adjustment. Even now, three years later, she still clung to the dim hope that their marriage would improve with time, rather like a good bottle of wine. Although her feelings for Brian had long ago died – brutally killed by the man himself – there was something about him, a kind of monstrous magnet that drew her and kept her there, day after awful day. Other than the idea that maybe her husband was mentally ill and needed help, she hadn't a clue what this magnet was. She wasn't weak nor was she a fool and she knew that her life, or existence, as she'd come to think of it, couldn't continue like this for ever. It was ridiculous, out of the question. Catherine, sooner or later, and preferably sooner, had to sort out her life – existence – assert herself, take charge of her own life and that of her daughter.

Why don't I leave him? Catherine was asking herself this question now, sitting beside Brian in the blue Ford Escort, on their way to her mother's house in Harrogate. *Why the hell don't I leave him and find a decent, kind man who'll love both me and my child? Or do those men exist only in fairy stories and badly-done-to wives' imaginations?* She briefly glanced at her husband driving. His face was set; it had been 'set' for the past three weeks, ever since the pink invitation had arrived. And when Brian set his face, nobody on God's earth could move him. Make him smile; create a crinkle or two around those grey steely eyes. Nobody. It had to be in his own good time, when he was ready to behave like a human being again. He hadn't behaved like a human being for three weeks. His hands were now gripping the steering wheel until the knuckles showed white, as though he were struggling with some kind of mechanical demon. He was taking his stepdaughter to stay with her grandma for a weekend and then he was going to London, to a big party, a celebration ... but nobody would think so. He could have been going to the electric chair.

Oh God, please give me the strength, the whatever is lacking, to improve my life.

*

Molly Carter was in for a real treat. She didn't see enough of her granddaughter; she didn't see enough of her by far. She worshipped that child, spoilt her rotten, probably, but she didn't care. She didn't get as many opportunities as she'd have liked to see the little girl, not with that so-called son-in-law being as he was. It wouldn't upset her if she never laid eyes on that one again, but as for Catherine and Janine, it nearly broke her heart to think how little she saw of them. And it wasn't as if they lived a million miles away because they didn't ... Leeds was no distance at all from Harrogate, but Brian being as he was ... Ooh, it wasn't worth thinking about. Anyway, she had the weekend to look forward to. Janine all to herself. She was delighted, thrilled to bits. She'd baked all day Thursday and spent most of Friday shopping and making the spare bedroom cosy. Molly looked at the old mantel clock on the even older mantelpiece. Four o'clock; they'd be here soon. She'd better put the kettle on.

The blue Ford Escort pulled up rather sharply outside the stone-built terraced house in the centre of Harrogate, a stone's throw from the main shopping district. Molly opened the door, not noticing the cold air that rushed in together with her granddaughter.

'Hello, Grandma!'

'Hello, me little sugar plum, it's so lovely to see you again. Come and give your grandma a big kiss!'

There were tears in Molly Carter's eyes as she swept the child into her ample arms and squashed her to her large soft breasts. Tears of joy at holding her again and tears of anguish at what might have been ... at what nearly was.

'Hello, Cathy, love – Brian – come in, come in, I've just made a pot of tea.'

Catherine gave her mother a brief hug and tried to look as though everything was hunky-dory as she and Brian followed Molly into the house. Janine had already helped herself to one of the scones that were piled on a tea plate on the low coffee table in front of the gas fire. Had she done that at home without asking, Catherine would have remonstrated with her in no uncertain terms, but she knew it was no use in her mother's home. She knew that her kid would get away with blue murder over the next couple of days. And she was so pleased; it would be a bit of light relief after Brian.

'We can't stay long, Mum, we're driving straight down to London so we'll have to be off soon.'

'Surely you've time for a cuppa?'

'No,' Brian interrupted, 'we don't have any time to waste. We've had to come miles out of the way as it is.'

Molly didn't want to argue. Well, she did want to argue with Brian – quite often, in fact – but she always kept quiet for Cathy's sake.

'Aye, you don't want to leave it too late, I suppose. It's an engagement party yer goin' to, isn't it?'

Molly felt she'd been left a bit in the dark about this engagement party but she'd kept quiet about that, too. Brian shoved his hands into his jeans pockets and walked to the window, looking out at the small garden and the almost naked bushes that lined the short footpath.

'Yes, it is. You remember Brian's sister, Melanie, don't you? We haven't seen her since ... since our wedding.'

How could anybody *forget* Melanie? Not after her performance at Cathy and Brian's wedding reception. Well worth an Oscar it was, somebody had quipped, for Best Bitch or witch, or something. Molly's expression remained bland. She answered Cathy's question in the affirmative, her face showing no emotion, and she asked who Melanie's new fiancé was.

'We don't know, Mum. She's keeping him a secret till the party.'

Molly grinned wickedly.

'Oh aye? There must be summat up with 'im then, I reckon. Maybe he's got two heads or less than two—'

'Mum, don't be rude!' Catherine laughed. 'I think it's somebody really famous and rolling in money. Melanie, erm, moves in those sorts of circles, as you know. She's probably going to make a great announcement and it'll all be a bit theatrical. I think it'll be very romantic.'

13

Brian turned from the window and looked at the two women.

'Well, I think she needs her arse tanning like the spoilt, silly brat that she is. I shall tell her so when I see her and I'll make no bones about it. Right, come on, it's time we were moving.'

Catherine mechanically got up and hugged and kissed her child.

'Now, I hope you're going to be a good girl and help Grandma and try not to eat her out of house and home.'

'Go on with you!' laughed Molly. 'She's goin' to enjoy herself, aren't you, me little sugar plum? And if that means eatin' me out of house and home, then so be it.'

*

They had decided to spend Friday night in a hotel in north London; the party wasn't until Saturday evening. They hadn't booked anywhere. Brian knew that they'd have no trouble finding accommodation at that time of year and, of course, Brian knew best. So, Catherine had agreed with his suggestion. Deep inside her, she was desperately hoping that this short stay in the capital would in some way help to reconcile them; help to salvage what little was left of wedded bliss. She was wondering if maybe a night in a hotel, in a strange bed, the freedom of a weekend away from home and, she had to be honest, away from Janine, would somehow rekindle a spark of their old passion, their used-to-be togetherness. Neither Brian nor Catherine attempted to speak on the long journey. Catherine knew it would be a waste of time and she'd rather behave like a deaf mute than risk being barked at. She kept glancing at Brian out of her eye corner but although he noticed, he pretended to be concentrating on his driving and ignored her. At Leicester Forest service station, however, he told her they were stopping for a meal and a short rest. Catherine wasn't hungry and the thought of eating in one of those places practically turned her already churning stomach, but she acquiesced. Why bother causing more friction? Dinner was ham salad, a cup of tea and total silence. They sat facing each other across the not-very-pristine table and both may as well have been eating with a stranger. As soon as the meal was finished, Brian looked at his watch, frowned, stood up and pushed himself away from the table.

'Right, come on, let's get going,' he muttered. 'We've wasted enough time in here.'

Catherine felt as though it had been her unacceptable idea to stop, rest and consume. She let it go. They arrived in London about nine o'clock and, as Brian had predicted, found a bed and breakfast place with no difficulty whatsoever. Nothing special but it was only for two nights, so it didn't matter, did it? No, of course not, Brian. Bang went Catherine's visions of rediscovered erotica in an opulent five-star. Their room was small and although not exactly scruffy, hardly the Ritz. There was a tiny adjacent bathroom, a fusty-smelling wardrobe and an uncomfortable-looking bed from which Catherine could imagine every twinge and turnover would echo throughout the building. She inwardly shrugged. She probably wouldn't have to worry about that. After they had unpacked, Brian said he was feeling shattered after the long drive and told his wife they were going to have an early night. His wife knew better than to interpret a sexual connotation in the remark.

'Oh, Brian, can't we go out for a drink or something? Just a quick one ...'

Well, it wasn't every weekend they came to London and ... Brian shook his head, yawned and started to unbutton his grey checked shirt.

'Don't be so selfish, Catherine, think about somebody else for a change. You haven't been working all day and driving down the bloody M1. If you did any driving, you might have a bit more sympathy.'

She took a deep breath and didn't remind him that she'd desperately wanted to take driving lessons when they were first married and he'd told her that they couldn't afford the expense at the time; anyway, one driver in the family was quite enough. No, there was no point in reminding him of that.

Brian tossed his clothes onto a chair, had a quick wash, brushed his teeth and got into bed. Catherine sighed. She didn't feel a bit tired and had no desire to sleep but Brian had a point. He'd had a long day. Why hadn't she thought to bring a book? Well, that was a daft idea, anyway. She wouldn't have been able to read in bed. Brian wouldn't be able to sleep with the light on, and she certainly couldn't read with the light off. So that was that, as usual. She slowly undressed, switched off the lamp and slid into bed beside her husband. They both lay awake in silence, not touching, of course. How long was it since Brian had touched her, really touched her? With affection, passion, desire? She couldn't remember. She accepted his sexual indifference now; she accepted that the physical side of their marriage was dead, never likely to be resurrected. But because Catherine was a naturally sensitive, passionate woman who found love-making one of the greatest pleasures in life, she often lay awake at nights, aching for her husband's marble body. Sometimes, she had to admit to herself, she ached for just a body, preferably complete with heart and kindly mind. And, tonight was no exception. But it *should* be, surely? Wasn't that one of the reasons why she'd wanted to come away? An intimate, romantic weekend away in a hotel, just the two of them ... She closed her eyes, took a deep, nervous breath and tentatively reached out her hand, gently stroking Brian's arm, his chest with the fine, fair hairs; his belly. For a few seconds, nothing, and then he brusquely turned away from her, his back in her face.

'Good night,' he said.

*

Autumn in London was much warmer than autumn in the north. On Saturday morning, after an inadequate breakfast of thin toast, jam and weak coffee, Catherine suggested going for a nice walk, a look round the shops and maybe a pub lunch later. She was determined to enjoy her short stay in London and if Brian intended to be awkward then she'd just have to amuse herself. However, that wasn't necessary.

'Well, I hadn't planned on spending all day in this godforsaken place.'

And so, they walked out of the far-from-perfect B&B into the cosmopolitan vortex that was London. Surprisingly, the day passed quickly and rather pleasantly. They talked to each other more than they had done for a long time, about nothing in particular, just normal chatter, and even shared jokes between husband and wife. They ate a delicious ploughman's lunch in a noisy pub off Oxford Street and looked for small gifts to take back for Molly and Janine. A large souvenir mug for Molly's ubiquitous tea, a pearly queen doll for Janine. It was six o'clock when they returned to their lodgings to rest and change for the evening. Catherine, enervated by the small pleasures of the day, was beginning to feel excited, a little optimistic about the evening and even her future. She had been right. This weekend away from home would be oh-so-good for them, for their marriage, for Janine. She was looking forward to the engagement party even more and chatted happily as they both dressed.

'I wonder who'll be there this evening, Brian. I bet Melanie's flat will be bursting at the seams, don't you? I tell you what, I'm dying to meet this mysterious fiancé – especially if he's somebody famous. Do you fancy having a celebrity for a brother-in-law, Brian? You never know ...'

Catherine wasn't looking at Brian; she was studying her reflection in the cracked wardrobe mirror and, for once, liked what she saw. The turquoise and black dress she had found in a small boutique that morning really suited her. She'd also found some turquoise hair ornaments to match and had pinned back her hair at either side of her face. She looked ... okay. Good. Then Brian's voice on the other side of the room arrested both her positive thoughts and her happy prattle.

'For God's sake, woman, I've had to listen to your monotonous voice all day. Just give it a break, will you?'

Catherine's chatter choked in her throat.

*

Melanie Jarvis lived in a small but exquisitely beautiful flat in Hampstead, not far from the heath. It didn't take Brian long to find the address and when they saw the stream of vehicles lining the street, they knew they had arrived. Catherine clung on to the humble engagement gift (a small crystal vase) and card and followed Brian up the flight of stone steps leading to the front door. Brian pressed the doorbell marked 'Jarvis' almost savagely, his jaw set again, his mouth a tight line in his face. *He's come intending to have a lousy time*, Catherine thought, and she suddenly began to feel very nervous. A wave of nausea swept through her insides, making her slightly dizzy. *God, please don't let anything awful happen. I don't think I'll be able to take any more ...* The door was finally opened and they followed the good-looking stranger and his glass of wine up two flights of carpeted stairs and into Melanie's home. There were people everywhere; people standing talking to each other; people squeezing and bumping into each other; people dancing to the reggae music; people kissing, shrieking and laughing. Melanie's kind of people.

Melanie stood in the centre of the room, radiantly observing her realm. Her long blonde hair was piled in a knot on top of her head with long, curling tendrils around her face. She wore a black cocktail dress that clung to her body, showing every curve to its advantage, and finished just below the knee. She held a glass of white wine and chatted, radiating warmth and joie-de-vivre like the perfect hostess that she obviously was. The man who

17

had opened the door elbowed his way across the room towards her, whispered something in her diamond-studded ear and nodded towards Catherine and Brian, who were still standing in the doorway. Melanie's social smile disappeared. Like a trapped mare, her eyes flashed and her nostrils flared. She handed her half-empty glass to the man, excused herself and pushed her way through the crowd.

'Well, *hello,* you two. How wonderful to see you both again after all this time. I'm absolutely *delighted* you could come.'

She kissed the air around Catherine's cheeks and held out her perfectly manicured hand to her brother. The smile was in place on her face again. Her well-rehearsed greeting left Catherine feeling tongue-tied and inadequate. She already felt out of place here. Maybe Brian had been right after all; maybe they shouldn't have come … She glanced at her husband. His face gave nothing away and he didn't look in her direction. She almost timidly held out the gift-wrapped box and card.

'Thank you for inviting us, Melanie. You … you look lovely. And congratulations. This is just a little something …'

Melanie gushed her thanks at the unopened gift and ostentatiously held out her left hand for Catherine to inspect. The white-blue diamond set in white gold sparkled under the disco glitter ball that hung temporarily from the ceiling. Brian, who hadn't yet spoken to his sister, averted his eyes, as though the gem was hurting them. Catherine drooled and murmured all the right things.

'Thank you, Catherine, it's so nice of you. And now you must meet the man who gave it to me. My Mr Wonderful. I honestly can't believe how lucky I am. I must admit, we haven't known each other very long but I just know he's the right man for me. I've never known anyone like him and I've certainly never felt like this about anyone in my life. And the crazy thing is—'

'And when are we going to meet this paragon?' Brian's humourless first words cut into Melanie's monologue and she glared at her brother, her true emotions finally showing on her face.

'Right now.'

He was standing by the ornate, pink marble fireplace. A tall, tanned man with thick dark hair turning grey at the temples and brown eyes that danced with warmth when he smiled. Melanie moved towards him, politely released him from the obvious verbal tenacity of his companion and gently pulled him towards the newcomers who, she said, were so looking forward to meeting him.

'Brian. Catherine. I want you to meet my fiancé, Jean-Marc de Bergier. Darling, this is my beloved brother … and his lovely wife.'

Catherine's mouth dried up and her skin began to tingle. She felt her knees buckle and a tiny, inaudible cry of disbelief and sheer panic strangled in her throat. She watched in stunned silence as her husband shook hands with the French fiancé. Janine's father. The only man she had ever really loved.

Catherine

Chapter Three

Sunday, 2nd September, 1973. The large stone-built terraced house in the centre of Harrogate had not seen so much life for over a year. The telephone hadn't stopped ringing for seven days and Molly Carter could have sworn that the doorbell must be wearing out by now. And she'd brewed more tea and baked more cakes and what-have-you over the last week than she had in her entire life. Not that she minded, of course. Far from it. The house had been too quiet by far over the past twelve months. There hadn't been any girlish giggling and chatter; no young voices to liven the place up. No strange-looking but pleasant young men sheepishly standing at the door, asking for Cathy. But Cathy was back now and the house would be a home again.

Molly kicked the living-room door shut with her slippered heel, balancing a tray of freshly brewed tea and coffee in her hands. Her eyes travelled around her living room; there wasn't a seat to spare. Young bodies were sprawled along the cream three-seater sofa; other young bodies occupied the two matching armchairs at either side of the unlit gas fire and two youngsters were – believe it or not – managing to balance on the brown and beige pouffé in the corner. Molly looked at the eager young faces looking at Cathy and she smiled to herself. At this rate, she'd have to start telling folk to bring their own mugs. She set the blue and white plastic tray down on the coffee table and told everybody to help themselves. Cathy, sitting in her usual position on the floor, her legs curled underneath her, looked up at her mother and smiled her thanks.

Paris has been good for her, Molly thought for the umpteenth time, *she's growing up into a sophisticated young woman. She's got a bit of class and polish that she'd never have had otherwise and, even if she is me own daughter, I must admit she's gettin' to be a beauty. And by God,* she added, *it's good to have her back.*

'So, did you actually *enjoy* au pairing?' one of Cathy's friends asked, hugging her coffee mug and helping herself to a biscuit. 'I mean, well, I always thought it were too much like being an 'ousewife wi' none of the pleasures thrown in!'

Cathy smiled at the pretty bottle-blonde and, Molly couldn't help thinking, rather gormless old school friend.

'Well, I never felt like a housewife, Jane. I only had to do a bit of dusting and polishing and washing-up every day. I mean, it was hardly slave labour. I spent every morning studying French at the college and, of course, I had to look after the little girl every afternoon. But that was fun.'

'What was she like?'

'What was *monsieur* like?' another girl giggled, 'that's more to the point.'

Cathy laughed. Why did Frenchmen always have a reputation for being handsome and sexy? Monsieur de Bergier, kind and comical as he was, was hardly the answer to a maiden's prayer. He was far too short and round and thin on top. In fact, during the entire year she had lived with the French family on the Left Bank in Paris, she hadn't fallen in love, or even 'fancied' one Frenchman. Not one. She had met a lot of kind, charming and amusing young men but her own preconceived ideas of the gorgeous, sexy Frenchman had certainly been kicked into touch. They were just ordinary human beings like everybody else.

'Did you take many photos?' asked one of the lads, struggling to keep upright on the pouffé, an enthusiastic amateur photographer himself.

'Thousands! Well, quite a lot. Don't worry, when I've sorted them out, I'll bore you all stiff for hours on end.'

'How many times did you go up the Eiffel Tower?'

'I bet you never walked up!'

'Where did you buy all your clothes? Did you ever go to a fashion show?'

'Are those pavement cafés as romantic as they're made out to be? Are they really expensive?'

'Hey, Cathy, how did you celebrate your twenty-first birthday?'

Molly's maternal smile temporarily disappeared. That was the only thing that had upset her, really. Cathy celebrating her twenty-first away from home. She'd been thinking about her on that lovely August day, only a month ago. She'd been hoping that Cathy would manage to get home for her birthday but it wasn't to be. She'd spent the whole month of August in the South of France, somewhere near the Pyrenees, having a whale of a time. Molly didn't begrudge her that, of course, but it would have been nice … Cathy twenty-one, she could hardly believe it and such a lovely-looking girl – woman – now. What would her dad have thought of her if he were alive? *He'd 'ave idolised her, he would that …*

Sitting on a hard-backed chair at the back of the room, Molly swallowed hard and blinked away a forbidden tear. She mustn't start thinking like that, not now. She forced her ruminations back to the present and heard someone say. 'And what are you going to do with yourself now, Cathy? Have you got anything in mind?'

Cathy took a bite out of a chocolate digestive and concentrated on munching for a few seconds. She finally shrugged her shoulders and glanced at the girl who'd asked the question.

'I suppose I'll stay in Harrogate and look for a job.'

'Doing what?' This was Jane. 'Looking after somebody's kid and vacuuming their carpets?'

Molly flinched. Sour grapes. Resentful as well as gormless, that one. She stood up, put her empty cup and tea plate back on the tray and listened. What *was* Cathy thinking of doing now? They'd had neither the time nor the inclination to discuss this important business since Cathy arrived home.

'I've not really thought too much about it. I wouldn't mind doing some translating if I could find that kind of work in Harrogate. I definitely want to use my French. Otherwise, it's all been a waste … Well, not a waste exactly but … well, you know what I mean.'

'Ooh, Cathy, I don't think you'll find a translating job that easily around here. Not in Yorkshire. Not in the *north*. All that kind o' work's done down south … In London. Makes sense. You might 'ave to move down there. Otherwise, you'll forget all that French, if you're not using it.'

Sour Grapes herself again. Molly wondered what kind of work this little madam did; nothing to write home about, she wouldn't mind betting.

'Didn't you say summat about a Frenchman giving lessons around here somewhere?'

Molly's voice ricocheted around the room and several pairs of eyes turned to look at her. Molly flushed a little; maybe she'd spoken out of place. Maybe mothers were supposed to only provide refreshments and keep a low profile? *What a load of tripe*, she then admonished herself. *These are my Cathy's friends and they're all decent kids. Well, most of 'em. I'm getting paranoid in me old age.* Cathy's shoulders were being shrugged again.

'Oh, Monsieur de Bergier gave me a phone number to ring if I was interested in private French lessons – some relative of his who teaches at home. He lives in north Yorkshire but I've no idea where. To be honest, I didn't take that much notice at the time. I was too busy packing and getting ready to come home...'

'If *you're* not interested in taking private lessons from a dishy Frenchman, Cathy Carter, maybe somebody else is! What's his name, address and phone number and how much does he charge? If he's tall, dark and sexy, who cares how much he charges?'

There followed a squeal of youthful ribald jokes and a lengthy fit of giggles. While her friends were indulging in their own fun and nonsense, Cathy's mind was starting to tick over. Maybe getting in touch with this French teacher wasn't such a bad idea; the last thing she wanted to do was lose her proficiency and fluency in the language – and maybe the chance of landing an interesting job. She suddenly jumped to her feet, left the room, ran upstairs and a good ten minutes later reappeared, holding a brown leather address book. She pulled out a scruffy piece of paper and waved it in the air. Everyone stopped chattering and looked at her, expectantly.

'I've found it. Here we are. Jean-Marc de Bergier ... Oh goodness, he lives in Russetlea, that gorgeous little village about five miles from Harrogate ... You know, going towards Ripon. Wow! Well, that'll be handy for me, anyway.'

*

For the next few days, Cathy Carter was too busy accepting invitations from various friends and acquaintances and settling down in her old environment to think about anything else. She was happy to meet her mates again, of course, although some of their interests and projects had changed and she found that she now had little in common with most of them. She still missed her best friend, Diana, the girl next door whom she

23

had grown up with, been through school and college with and who she thought would always be there. Always. Through life. Like the sister she'd never had. Diana had felt exactly the same; they were 'the inseparables' for many years. They enjoyed being 'the inseparables'; it was fun, it was warm and cosy, it was right. And then, two years ago, Diana's parents had decided to join some of their family in Australia and, of course, Diana had disappeared, too. A wrench, to say the least. For the first year, letters and postcards had been frequent and much looked forward to and then ... inevitably, maybe, they had become scarce, less affectionate, and then they stopped. Cathy had told herself that it was normal that Diana – thousands of miles and a whole different life away – would have new interests (was she still interested in languages? maybe not) and make new friends. And eventually forget Cathy and their closeness, oneness. Cathy's acquaintances, pals, mates, remained the same but there hadn't been another really close friend since Diana left her life. And Cathy missed her so much.

A couple of weeks after her return, however, the excitement and novelty of living in Harrogate and all that meant was beginning to wear thin and she thankfully found she had more time to herself. Time to organise her bedroom into something more lived in and time to catch up on some lost sleep. And she finally settled down to writing a long letter to Mr and Madame de Bergier. They were a lovely couple and had been so kind to her and had made her life in their home so special that she'd promised herself she would never lose touch. At her morning French classes, she'd met a lot of other au pair girls and heard some very different stories and knew how very lucky she was. And she had loved the de Bergiers' daughter, Nathalie, her protégée. Oh yes, she had loved that three-year-old bundle of French fun and now she was missing her, very much. Cathy ended the letter by sending a thousand kisses to Nathalie and signed her name with lots of crosses underneath, which she knew amused the French. And as an afterthought, she wrote a short PS: *I am going to phone your cousin Jean-Marc this evening.*

And she did.

*

'Russetlea 4327.'

The masculine voice was deep and mellow with only a hint of an accent.

'Oh hello. Is that Jean-Marc de Bergier? The ... erm ... the French teacher?'

'It is.'

'Oh hello. My name's Catherine Carter and I've just come back to England. I lived in Paris for a year until very recently. With your cousin, in fact, Henri de Bergier.'

Cathy was beginning to feel tongue-tied. There was no response.

'And his family, of course. I was their ... their au pair girl. I looked after little Nathalie every day. Did a bit of housework. Mr de Bergier gave me your telephone number. In case I wanted to take French lessons ...'

'Ah. And *do* you want to take French lessons?'

'Oh yes. Well, I'm thinking about it ...'

'You're thinking about taking French lessons. I see. Where do you live?'

'Harrogate.'

'Hmm. And when would you be able to come and see me, to talk about these French lessons?'

'Oh, any time, Mr de Bergier. I'm unemployed at the moment so I'm free during the day and—'

'Unfortunately, I'm not. And my only free evening next week is Thursday. Would that suit you?'

'Thursday next week? Oh, well, yes ... yes, I think so.'

'Good. Do you have my address? You do? Then let's say next Thursday at seven-thirty. And please be on time, Miss ... What did you say your name was?'

'Catherine. Catherine Carter.'

'Next Thursday, then. And please be on time, Miss Carter. Goodbye.'

Catherine changed her mind a hundred and one times before the following Thursday and for almost as many reasons. She wasn't going to like Jean-Marc de Bergier; she wasn't going to get on with him, she knew that before she even met him. He sounded so arrogant, self-opinionated and had made her feel foolish and inadequate even on the telephone. If he was capable of that, how would he make her feel if she was his student? And on a more practical level she didn't have her own transport, and buses to Russetlea and other small villages around Harrogate weren't too reliable after six o'clock. He'd told her – *commanded* her, almost – to be on time.

What if, through no fault of her own, she was late? And what about getting home? She hadn't thought of that. She was going to cancel her appointment. No, she wasn't. She had just spent a year living in a foreign country with a family she'd never even met before. She'd learnt a lot about life and she'd passed her exams with flying colours. She had absolutely nothing to be ashamed of. She wasn't going to be intimidated by anybody … least of all this arrogant, quite impolite … person.

Green, Cathy decided after an extensive search of her not-very-extensive wardrobe on that Thursday afternoon. She'd been told many times that green suited her more than any other colour. Her initial apprehension had returned and reached new heights over the past couple of days. Not because of the French lessons; she wasn't worried about them. She was really looking forward to the lessons. It was the man. There had been something about his voice on the telephone; arrogance, yes, but something more than that. Something she couldn't quite put her finger on but which gave her cause for concern. He didn't sound at all like his cousin in Paris, that was for sure. Henri de Bergier had a light, sing-song voice that people warmed to. Yes, green. The colour suited Cathy's beautiful red-brown hair that tumbled around her shoulders, and her large, sparkling brown eyes. She chose an emerald green cotton jumper with a black skirt and black tights. Somehow, Cathy didn't know why, she felt that she had to make an impression on Jean-Marc de Bergier. A very good impression. And some of it was nothing to do with her knowledge of his native tongue.

Seven-thirty, he'd said, and he expected her to arrive on time. She was in two minds whether to leave home in time to catch the seven-thirty bus from Harrogate bus station … But her own pet hatred of tardiness overcame this. Anyway, it would have been foolish to deliberately annoy her tutor, a man whom she needed on her side. Foolish and very immature. And not helping towards the good impression. She very sensibly left home in time to catch the earlier bus.

*

The only bus stop in Russetlea was actually an oak tree standing on one corner of the village square, at the side of which stood a small rustic wooden shelter. Cathy got off the bus at seven-fifteen and, pulling her

26

black jacket collar tighter around her neck because of the cool evening breeze, she looked around her. The road leading out of Russetlea was now behind her, lit by soft pink lamps almost hidden among the rowan trees. The village square lay ahead of her, complete with ancient stocks, and to her left the fifteenth-century church, its floodlit stone tower glowing green in the September dusk, creating an eerie, almost sinister, atmosphere. Cathy shivered and, as she began to walk across the cobbles, the church clock, luminous in the fast-fading light, began to strike the quarter-hour. On the opposite side of the square was a row of stone-built cottages with leaded mullioned windows, their curtains drawn against the outside world. The doors opened straight onto the cobbles but each cottage boasted a large well-kept garden at the back. Cathy, unsure where the house she was actually looking for was located, walked slowly, paying attention to her whereabouts, ready to ask the first person she met if they knew where the Frenchman lived. But she met no one. A dog barked somewhere and there was a distant sound of a car speeding along, and then nothing. She began to hasten her steps. She wasn't frightened exactly but she suddenly began to feel very alone. And she was going to be late. After the row of cottages, a long stretch of unkempt land led to a couple of shops, closed and shuttered now, of course. Under the faint but pretty pink lighting Cathy could make out a baker's sign, a butcher's sign and what looked like a general store. All shuttered, all very quiet. She hurried on and suddenly stopped in her tracks. In front of her, looming out of the quickening darkness, stood a mansion, a kind of stately home. Magnificent and, like the church, eerie in the fading light. Made of stone like the cottages and also with leaded mullioned windows but grand, imposing, with tall chimneys reaching to the sky and lawns leading down to the large black iron gate where Cathy was now standing. And beyond, nothing. Only fields and woods and, yes, she could hear the sound of water; a stream, and she could also make out a wooden bridge disappearing into the darkness. Cathy shivered. She looked through the bars of the gate at the house, floodlit like the church but golden, not green. Surely Jean-Marc de Bergier didn't live here at Mullion Hall. It wasn't possible. She'd heard that since the owner died a couple of years ago, the Hall had been up for sale but she didn't know of any buyers. She stood gazing at the building for a long time and then the church clock chimed the half-hour. Oh, crikey. If this wasn't his house, she still had to find it … She opened her handbag and took out her address book. *Surely, if his address had been Mullion Hall, I'd have remembered* … At that precise moment, a door behind her opened and a voice rang out in the silence.

'Good evening. I imagine you're Miss Carter.'

Cathy whirled round. She had paid little attention to the small, somewhat insignificant building just behind the iron gates and to her right. Built with the same materials as the Hall, with similar windows and one huge chimney at the end of the low tiled roof, it looked like a colossal and quaint doll's house. A man stood in front of the oak door, his arms folded across his chest, his dark hair blowing slightly in the breeze. For a moment, Cathy didn't move. They looked at one another through the iron bars and then the man stepped forward and unlocked the gate. It scraped loudly along the gravel as he pulled it and impatiently beckoned Cathy to enter.

'You're late,' he said, and ushered her into the doll's house, the lodge of Mullion Hall.

Cathy didn't reply. She stood mute in the tiny entrance with its creaky wooden floor and uncarpeted stairs leading to who knew what. Jean-Marc de Bergier pushed open an interior door and motioned for Cathy to go through. She almost gasped aloud as she entered what was obviously the Frenchman's living room and study. The room was not very large and two of the walls were lined with books. A huge fire crackled and glowed in the handsome stone fireplace and two maroon leather chairs stood on either side bearing cosy-looking cushions. A small mahogany desk stood in one corner displaying more books and a green shaded lamp. Another, larger, lamp with a soft pink shade stood by the fire and the mixture of lights sent mysterious shadows along the walls and the long green velvet curtains, which were drawn. On the parquet floor, a maroon, pink and green Persian rug filled the centre of the room.

'Let me take your coat.'

It occurred to Cathy that she hadn't actually spoken yet. Jean-Marc de Bergier was standing behind her, holding out his right hand in anticipation of taking her jacket. She quickly unzipped it and the zipper stubbornly stuck at the bottom. Cathy pulled and tugged and fiddled with it for what to her seemed an interminable time, and finally the fastener gave way. When she lifted her head, she found herself gazing at her reflection in a gilt-edged mirror over the fireplace, and she caught Mr de Bergier's eye. He looked exasperated, to say the least.

'Thank you,' he said, when the offending garment was finally handed over. 'I'll hang it up. Have a seat.' He indicated one of the maroon leather chairs near the fire.

'Thank you.'

'Ah,' he said, 'you do speak. I was beginning to think you'd lost your tongue. The English usually use that expression with children, don't they?'

He was looking at her with raised eyebrows and Cathy, furious with herself, found nothing to say.

'I do hope you're going to be a little more voluble during the lessons, Miss Carter, or there really won't be any point in your coming here.'

Cathy sat down, willing herself to find the words and the wit to reply to this supercilious and arrogant Frenchman. She wondered if he spoke to all of his students this way. If so, he didn't deserve to have any students. While he was out of the room, Cathy warmed her very cold hands in front of the bright orange flames and her eyes wandered again around the room. It really was cosy ... but it was also a bit eerie in an odd sort of way. Cosy and eerie; was that possible ... ? Suddenly she heard the sound of pots rattling and water running and then Jean-Marc de Bergier strode back into the room carrying a pot of freshly percolated coffee and two mugs. He handed a mug to Cathy.

'Sugar?'

'No. No, thank you.'

'I don't spoil all my students, you know. They usually get a glass of mineral water if they're lucky. But you look as though you need warming up.'

'Thank you.'

The steaming coffee burned her too-eager lips and Cathy coughed as the liquid reached her throat, and she had to put the mug on the floor and quickly look for her handkerchief. She coughed into it and then blew her nose rather loudly. Jean-Marc de Bergier, blast him, witnessed everything.

'You've not had much luck since you arrived, have you? Would you like to go outside, come back in and start again?'

Normally, Cathy would have laughed, both at herself and at her companion's poor attempt at humour, but at that particular moment, laughter couldn't have been further from her mind. She glared at him, picked up her mug and took another, slower, more elegant sip of coffee.

'Well, Miss Carter, I'll start by introducing myself.' The teacher sat in the chair opposite hers. 'As you know, I'm Jean-Marc de Bergier, cousin to Henri de Bergier, whom you probably know much better than I do, having lived with him for a year.' He paused, one eyebrow raised, but Cathy passed no comment. 'I'm thirty-five years old. I've been living in England for quite a few years and I teach French full time at a business college in Knaresborough. However, very soon … no … no … that doesn't matter. I give private lessons at home on Tuesday and Thursday evenings and I charge £2.00 an hour. Does that suit you?'

Cathy nodded and asked how many hours each session would take.

'Two, if you like.'

'Yes, that's fine.'

'Excellent. Well, I know that your level is already very high and you don't need tedious grammar lessons. I suggest we study French literature for one hour and have an hour's conversation. I'll also expect you to study at home, read as much as you can; write. I'll be giving you plenty of exercises to do and I shall insist that you do them, Miss Carter. Two things I never tolerate either in my private or professional life – unpunctuality and laziness. If someone wants me to be his or her tutor then that person must expect to work and to work hard. And you don't need me to tell you, Miss Carter, that language is a living thing. It changes all the time … new vocabulary, new jargon. Words become obsolete, extinct. Dialects are also very interesting to study … accents … and phonetics, of course. A language student can't afford not to work hard, Miss Carter. Have you finished your coffee?'

Cathy hadn't given her coffee a single thought. She'd been hanging on to every word, interested, fascinated, wanting to talk to him, discuss with him. She looked down at her almost full mug.

'Not yet, Mr de Bergier, I …'

Her tutor looked impatient, drained his own mug, stood up and walked to his desk in the corner of the room.

'Well, I suppose you can drink coffee and speak French at the same time. Now, tell me, what French authors do you know?'

Cathy watched him rummaging through the pile of books on his desk.

'Oh … Maupassant, Zola, Balzac, Hugo. The usual …'

'Ah, the *usual*. I see. So, if I suggest, for example, our studying *Germinal* together, or *Bel Ami* or, dare I say it, *Les Misérables*, you will probably pooh-pooh me and tell me you know these masterpieces back to front,

30

upside down, inside out and, please, *monsieur* (at least I hope you would say "please", Miss Carter), may we read something a little more *unusual*?'

'I didn't mean …'

Jean-Marc de Bergier was walking back to his chair by the fire, carrying an armful of French literature and Cathy's greedy eyes fell onto the precious bundle as he laid it carefully on the floor. Her fingers were itching to pick up the books, turn the pages and devour them. She could see that they were old and, if not exactly priceless, they would not have been cheap, either. She eventually dragged her eyes away from the literature and felt Jean-Marc's eyes on her. She looked at him and the shadows from the fire and the lamps made strange patterns on his slightly tanned face.

'So, tell me, Miss Carter, what *unusual* French literature did you have in mind? The *Michelin Guide*, perhaps, or *Astérix le Gaulois*?'

Right. Cathy had had enough. If this was his idea of humour, of being amusing, then it wasn't hers. Apart from making her a cup of coffee, he'd done absolutely nothing to make her feel welcome, nothing to put her at her ease, to make her want to take French lessons with him. She'd never met such a rude, arrogant, sarcastic man in all her life. That's what she couldn't stand more than anything – his sarcasm. Well, if *he* wouldn't tolerate unpunctuality and laziness, she certainly wouldn't tolerate arrogance and sarcasm. She stood up.

'I'm sorry, Mr de Bergier, I'm not a child and I refuse to be treated like one. I don't think I'll be able to … to take French lessons with you. I'd like to leave now, if you'll give me my jacket.'

Jean-Marc looked at his watch and then at her, eyebrow raised.

'It's eight o'clock.'

As he said this, the church clock began to chime the hour and Cathy imagined the old stone building glowing a sinister green in the darkness. She shuddered.

'What time is the next bus to Harrogate?' Jean-Marc asked her.

Cathy cursed and her voice was small as she replied, 'Nine o'clock. They only run once an hour now.'

'Then you have an hour to wait. You may as well wait in comfort in front of the fire. I'll walk you to the bus stop when it's time to leave.'

'No, thank you.'

'I don't think it was a question, Miss Carter.'

Cathy, not trusting herself to speak, stared into the fire.

31

'Better still, I'll run you home in my car.'

'I prefer to take the bus, thank you.'

'As you wish. Would you like another cup of coffee while—'

'No. Thank you.'

Jean-Marc bent down and picked up the assortment of books and quietly handed them to her.

'You may like to have a look at my book collection, then. My very precious book collection, I might add. Miss Carter.'

Cathy bit her lip, avoided the Frenchman's ironic gaze and wordlessly took the books out of his large square hands. Well, she couldn't sit and do absolutely nothing for all that time, could she? For the next twenty minutes, her head bent low, she fingered and read and re-read the titles, glanced at prefaces and introductions and, in some cases, looked at beautiful illustrations. They were magnificent and obviously valuable books. Some of them she had read and studied; others were new to her and her eager eyes longed to devour the words, the chapters, the stories.

'It's eight forty-five. Maybe you should start to think about leaving.'

Jean-Marc's voice cut into her thoughts and she quickly put down the books and stood up. Jean-Marc stood by the door, holding her jacket. He handed it to her without offering to help her into it and Cathy was relieved. Courtesy would have been inappropriate and she couldn't have coped. She walked through the narrow hall and Jean-Marc opened the front door. A gust of now very strong wind whipped their faces. Cathy knew she had to say something before she left him and the only thing she could think of was,

'Thank you for letting me look at your books.'

He smiled and bowed his head rather foolishly.

'If you were coming back to me for lessons, Miss Carter, I would lend you all these books with pleasure.'

Their eyes met and Cathy interpreted in his laughter, derision, a challenge.

'I won't be coming back to you for lessons, Mr de Bergier. Goodbye.'

Fortunately, Cathy didn't have long to wait for the bus and when it arrived it was almost empty. She fell into a seat behind the driver and was horrified to suddenly feel tears pricking her eyes. She *wasn't* going to cry ... she wasn't. Jean-Marc de Bergier was not worth weeping over. Just who the heck did he think he was? Did he treat all his students the same way or only a chosen few? Maybe she'd been hand-picked for special treatment and ...

oh, she didn't know and she didn't care. Jean-Marc de Bergier was a thing of the past.

*

Cathy knew that she had to do something with her life; she was getting very bored. She missed the excitement of the Left Bank and her mornings spent at the college and her shared interests, discussions and laughter with the other students. And yes, she missed the de Bergiers and especially little Nathalie. But she mustn't think like that, not anymore. She was home now. She had a comfortable, safe home and a wonderful mum to share her life with. Her mum was really her best friend now, which she supposed was a rather sad reflection. How she would have loved to come back to a life with Diana as her best friend; how things would have been different. She missed Diana; she still missed her so very much. Nobody had replaced or ever could replace her and although Cathy had more than her fair share of pals and acquaintances, there was no special person in her life now. Only her mum.

But she needed something else; of course she did. She needed to work. She hated being idle and longed for a career that would engross her and use what few talents she had. But she hadn't found anything suitable, or even unsuitable, yet.

Wednesday evening. The television was turned on, talking to itself. Molly was dozing in front of the gas fire which was turned up full – autumn was well and truly established now and the nights were cold. October already. Cathy, curled up on the sofa, her head in her mother's weekly magazine, was mulling over her life, as usual. She'd been back in Harrogate almost six weeks and she was no further— The telephone suddenly interrupted her thoughts. She heaved herself off the sofa and dashed into the hall where the two-tone grey phone stood on a small wrought iron table.

'Hello?'

'Good evening. Would it be possible to speak to Miss Catherine Carter, please?'

'Yes. Speaking.' The gas fire had made Cathy sleepy too and she stifled a yawn.

'This is Jean-Marc de Bergier, Miss Carter. When are you going to come and start your French lessons with me?'

33

Cathy was abruptly shaken out of her drowsiness. A month had passed since that awful 'rendezvous' and she had hardly given him a thought over the past couple of weeks.

'I ... erm ... I told you I wasn't interested ...'

'Look, Miss Carter, why don't we pretend our last meeting never happened and start again? Would you please come back to Russetlea tomorrow evening? At seven-thirty?'

*

She arrived at seven twenty-five, a little breathless after hurrying rather than strolling through the village square. The gate had been unlocked and as she walked through, Jean-Marc opened the door of his quaint home.

'Good evening, Miss Carter.' He greeted her with the slightest smile on his lips and relieved her of her jacket. He motioned for her to go through to his living room/study and told her to sit down in one of the large maroon leather chairs. He walked to his desk and concentrated on looking at some papers for a while. Then he said,

'Have you been practising French since our last meeting?'

'Of course not; because I've nobody to practise on.'

'And whose fault is that, Miss Carter? You chose not to come back. You have only yourself to blame.'

Oh God, was it all going to start again? Why couldn't he speak to her in a normal tone of voice, like a normal human being? Why did she allow him to ruffle her feathers so easily?

'As I told you before, young lady, a foreign language is something that must be worked at, practised as often as possible. Otherwise, one forgets very quickly and loses one's fluency – both in speech and in the written word. We can't allow that to happen to you, can we?'

Cathy, feeling somehow small and insignificant in the imposing chair and listening to his patronising words, glared at him.

'I'd prefer to lose my fluency in French than to lose my good manners, Mr de Bergier.'

For the first time, Jean-Marc laughed. His face suddenly seemed to come alive; his brown eyes sparkled and danced with mirth. But Cathy couldn't join in; the joke was lost on her.

'Look, Miss Carter, if you're going to continue your evening classes with me – and I sincerely hope you are – you must learn to develop a sense of humour. The ability to laugh at oneself is essential in this wicked world, and the ability to promote one's own skills and accept one's limitations is also very important. If I didn't think you weren't worth tutoring, I wouldn't have encouraged you to continue. And if I thought you didn't have a sense of humour, I certainly wouldn't have invited you back. Shall we start with a cup of my delicious coffee?'

As they sipped the, as far as Cathy was concerned, far too strong coffee, Jean-Marc talked about the forthcoming lessons with great enthusiasm. He would provide her with a good text book but she would be expected to buy her own exercise books and he would also expect her to read lots of French novels whenever she had the opportunity. His eyes slowly travelled around the bookshelves that monopolised this room.

'I'll be happy to lend you my books but I'll have to insist that you keep them in perfect condition. If you return them to me covered in coffee stains or with torn pages or dog-eared, I'll be furious. Absolutely furious. I'm warning you in advance, Miss Carter.'

Cathy felt the blood draining from her face. The antagonism she had felt towards him on their first meeting was nothing compared to how she was feeling now. Her stomach did a double somersault and she involuntarily clutched the leather arms of her chair.

'Mr de Bergier, I've got books at home that I've had since I was a little girl and they're in almost perfect condition. I'd no more think of spilling coffee on a book, tearing the pages or folding them over than …'

'I'm very pleased to hear it. Now, would you like to repeat what you have just yelled at me – in French, please?'

Words, French or otherwise, stuck in Cathy's throat.

'Right,' Jean-Marc almost smiled at her, 'if you've calmed down, perhaps we might begin the lesson.'

*

Cathy hated Jean-Marc de Bergier. During the long empty hours that she spent in her bedroom or wandering around the town trying to look for work, she thought about her tutor, and the more she thought about him, the less she wanted to continue her studies. And if she didn't find work soon, she would have to give up her lessons, anyway. She wouldn't be able to afford them. Her limited savings were dwindling away and the unemployment benefit that she received contributed to very little. Oh, her mum helped her out financially, of course, when she could, but Cathy hated relying on other people's benevolence, including her mum. She wanted to be independent. She wanted to find an interesting job that paid well so that she could move into a place of her own. Nothing fancy; a small flat or even a bedsit would do. Not that she didn't enjoy living with Molly. Her mum was good to her in many ways – her new best friend – but after a year living away from home, she now felt trapped, a bit smothered. If she didn't find work soon, she felt she'd go totally bonkers. Her days were wasting away. No, they weren't, not entirely. She spent hours reading the French novels loaned by Jean-Marc de Bergier and practised the written exercises until her head ached … but it wasn't enough. She desperately wanted and needed to work.

*

In the past, Cathy had always looked forward to Christmas. She loved to wander around Harrogate, taking her time choosing special gifts for special people – her mum and Diana – and anticipating the coming festivities. There was always something exciting happening. This year, of course, was very different. She had no money. There was really no point in looking round the shops because it only depressed her. Christmas would be a very sad affair this year; she accepted that. Oh, her mother would do her best, obviously, but Molly was no Lady Bountiful; she couldn't afford to be. And there were no other nearest and dearest whose company would be enjoyed. No, Cathy thought, coming out of an exclusive gift shop on Parliament Street, empty-handed, she wasn't looking forward to the festive season, not this year. And when she thought of last December, shopping in Paris … oh no, it was starting to snow. She wasn't surprised, though. It had been threatening all day. She pulled her collar up and with her head bent against the heavy snowflakes, she headed for home. She wasn't looking forward to her French lesson that evening, either. It would be no fun waiting for the irregular buses in this weather. But it was her last lesson before Christmas so she must make the effort. Anyway, she had a Christmas card for Jean-Marc de Bergier. Not that he deserved one.

'Yer French tutor rang while you were out,' Molly greeted her as she tugged the damp raincoat from her daughter's shoulders. 'He said he realised it was a bad night but he'd be pleased if you went for your lesson. Said he had summat important to tell you.'

They shuffled into the kitchen together and sat down to a plate of very welcome steak and kidney pie.

'But you won't be goin', will you?' Molly frowned across the table. 'Not in this weather. Yer barmy, lass, if you do. You could be sittin' in front of a nice fire, watchin' telly instead of going out in the cold and dark … you'll catch yer death …'

'Mum, I've been out in much worse weather than this and survived to tell the tale. And anyway, you said he'd got something important to tell me. Did he give you a clue?'

'No, he didn't and I'm sure it's not that important that it can't wait until the new year. It's probably just a new book he's bought or summat like that. Nowt that can't wait, I'll be bound. Stay at 'ome, lass, and …'

Cathy carefully put down her knife and fork and looked steadily at her mother.

'Mum, I'll be going to Russetlea for my French lesson and I'll be catching the seven o'clock bus, as usual.'

'You will if it turns up. I wouldn't be surprised if …' She shrugged her heavy shoulders. 'Anyway, don't blame me if you end up wi' pneumonia.'

Cathy was curious. What did Mr de Bergier have to tell her that was so important? It was nothing to do with buying books, that much she did know. She looked up at the curtainless kitchen window into the blackness outside; the snowflakes now looked like large balls of cotton wool. She inwardly groaned and hoped her mum's prophecy about the bus service didn't prove to be right. Ten minutes later, the telephone rang and it was her tutor.

'I'll pick you up at seven o'clock,' he told her.

Cathy started to protest.

'Just give me your address and brief directions … okay, thank you. I know the street very well. I'll pick you up on the corner at seven o'clock.'

'Well, thank you …'

'And please don't be late.'

He was obviously desperate to see her that evening, for some reason.

The snow was thick on the ground and still falling when Cathy left the house and tried to hurry towards the silver Peugeot 404 waiting for her on the corner. She pulled open the passenger door and sank into the grey seat, pulling off her hood and shaking her hair around her shoulders.

'Hello. Thanks ever so much for coming for me ... it's really good of you. Have you had any trouble getting here? I hope we'll get back to Russetlea okay because it's still coming down fast, isn't it? I think we're going to have a white Christmas. What did you want to tell me?'

Jean-Marc checked the road behind and turned on the engine. The Peugeot moved forward, very slowly. Cathy looked at him.

'Mr de Bergier?'

'Hmm?'

'What did you have to tell me that's so important?'

'I don't discuss business when I'm driving, Miss Carter. And especially not in these conditions.'

Business? Cathy stared at him and he continued to stare at the white world in front of him. Neither of them spoke again on the short but hazardous journey.

The living room/study emanated a warm, seasonal glow. The huge fire was crackling in the hearth and Jean-Marc lit several scented candles and placed them strategically around the room. There was even a small Christmas tree standing in the corner next to his desk, twinkling with multi-coloured fairy lights. The effect was magical, delightful. Instead of the usual pre-tutorial coffee, Jean-Marc offered Cathy a glass of wine as she sank into her usual chair. She thanked him as he handed her the glass.

'Hardly the ideal drink on a freezing cold December evening but much more seasonal.' Jean-Marc took a sip. 'And very French. Cheers.'

Instead of taking his usual place either behind the desk or seated in the other chair, Jean-Marc sat cross-legged on the Persian rug in front of the fire, obviously enjoying his Châteauneuf-du-Pape.

'Far too cold to be sitting in a corner this evening. And in the candlelight far too dim. What do you think of the wine, Miss Carter?'

Cathy didn't give a damn about the wine. All that interested her right then was the 'business' he had to talk to her about. He'd said it was important but nobody would think so ...

'Il est très bon, Mr de Bergier.'

'Parfait! And the glasses. Have you noticed the texture of the glass, Miss Carter? Crystal, of course, and many years old. Worth a fortune ... they've

been handed down in the family for generations. They're quite exquisite ...
don't you think?'

'Yes, they're lovely, Mr—'

'You probably drank out of identical glasses at my cousin's home. Henri,
I believe, inherited the sister set. And I know his wife is very fond of—'

Cathy coughed and unconsciously twisted the wine glass around in her
trembling fingers. She didn't remember seeing any glasses like these in
Paris and, if she did, she probably wouldn't have remembered them.
Glasses were glasses, end of story. Why didn't he shut up and tell her what
he wanted to tell her, for goodness' sake? This was wasting precious time
and, anyway, she wanted to get on with her French lesson and then get
home before she was snowed in.

'Mr de Bergier ...' She didn't mean to sound impatient and rude but she
did.

'Yes, Miss Carter?'

He took another long sip of wine, carefully put down his glass on the
rug and looked up at her, the firelight dancing on his face. His eyes were
shining, creasing at the corners, and the hint of a smile played on his lips.
He was *teasing* her, for goodness' sake! Cathy would never have believed
that he'd be capable of teasing anybody. Especially her. She suddenly felt
confused. She had learnt how to cope with him when he was arrogant,
sarcastic, downright rude. But now he was making her feel foolish, girlish,
gauche. She sipped her wine, swallowed loudly, bit her lip, blushed and
continued to play with her glass, racking her brains to think of something
appropriate to say. Something sparklingly witty and clever.

'Please tell me ...'

So much for sparkling wit and cleverness. Jean-Marc laughed, leapt up
and walked over to his desk. He pulled open a drawer and took out an
envelope. He sat down again, cross-legged in front of the fire, and looked
up at Cathy's eager but mystified face.

'For the past two years I've been acting as an external translator and
interpreter for a large international company based very near Harrogate,
called William Kaye International. Maybe you've heard of them. They
manufacture industrial sewing machines and have a lot of business
interests in France, Belgium and Switzerland and therefore a lot of
correspondence, and often their meetings are in the French language.
Letters, telexes, legal documents, and so on. Over the past year or so, the

company has been expanding even more, so much so that I'm afraid I can no longer cope with all the extra work as well as my own teaching commitments. I haven't mentioned it before but I'm negotiating with lawyers at the moment for the purchase of Mullion Hall. My idea is to open my own language school. However, that's far away in the future and beside the point. William Kaye International has decided to employ someone who's capable of managing these translations and who also has secretarial skills. In other words, they're looking for a bi-lingual secretary to work for the export manager. Now, Miss Carter, I believe you're looking for a job?'

Cathy stared at the Frenchman. Wow! This sounded like a real gift from the gods, unbelievably so, but the first thought that crossed her mind was, *am I up to it?* The technical words, the legal jargon and … yes, she had excellent secretarial qualifications but, well, she hadn't used them for well over a year now and …

'Well. Well, thank you for thinking of me, Mr de Bergier, but …'

The unexpected 'but' hung in the air between them. Jean-Marc raised his black eyebrows and stared at her.

'But what?'

'Well … don't you think it would be too much for me? I mean, I don't know much – if any – technical French and I don't think I'm fluent enough to cope with interpreting and it's so long since I've done any shorthand and typing and … oh, Mr de Bergier, I really don't think I'd be up to it.'

The pleasant expression had completely disappeared from Jean-Marc's face. He leapt off the floor again but this time slammed his wine glass and the piece of correspondence on the desk. He turned round and, as he headed towards the door, the candlelight played on his rigid, furious face.

'I can see I've been wasting my time with you, Miss Carter. You've been coming here every Thursday evening for the past three months and totally wasted my precious time. Normally, when I meet students for the first time, my intuition serves me well. I recognise talent and determination, and when I met you, I thought these qualities were very obvious. I couldn't have been more wrong. Miss Carter, you are a coward and unworthy of my time. I've tried to help you and you've disappointed me. I shall take you home now and I suggest you discontinue your lessons in the new year.'

Cathy trembled. She watched him leave the room and she trembled with humiliation and self-pity. Tears sprang to her eyes and although she tried to choke them back, they fell down her face and she wiped them away with the back of her hand. How could one human being speak to another in such a despicable manner? She didn't deserve to be spoken to like that ... did she? Her weeping suddenly stopped on a loud sob. She had been looking for a job all these months, an interesting, exciting job where she'd be able to use her knowledge of the French language and here it was, more or less handed to her on a plate. And what had she done? She walked over to the desk and picked up the sheet of paper. The letterhead was William Kaye International and it was addressed to Jean-Marc de Bergier.

Dear Jean-Marc,
Thank you very much for your letter of 4th November 1973. I can quite understand your difficulties in being able to cope with our increasing translation requirements as well as your teaching duties. Although we shall obviously regret losing your excellent services, we have now decided to advertise for a bi-lingual secretary (fluent in French) to work for our export manager, Mr Samuel Morrison. Now that our relations with Europe are escalating, it will be more suitable to have a translator/interpreter working on the premises. The post will be advertised in the *North Yorkshire Gazette* early in 1974.

Once again, Jean-Marc, allow me to express our thanks for all your help in the past and may our friendship continue. If you happen to know of any bi-lingual young lady who may be suitable for the above post, please do not hesitate to contact me.
Yours sincerely,
James McMichael
Personnel Officer

Cathy was reading the letter for the second time when Jean-Marc came back into the room. He was holding her coat over his right arm. The French lesson hadn't even begun.

'Allow me to help you on with your coat, Miss Carter.'

He walked towards her and Cathy placed the letter on the desk. She couldn't look at him as he draped the garment around her shoulders. Oh, dear God, what had she done? This might be the chance of a lifetime that she was throwing away, along with her Thursday evening classes and her self-respect.

'Mr de Bergier?'

Cathy looked up at her tutor, her huge brown eyes pleading with him to listen to her. He was now blowing out the candles and soon the only light that remained came from the embers of the dying fire and the small winking fairy lights. The long shadows played on their faces, magnifying their emotions.

'Mr de Bergier, I want to change my mind. I hadn't had time to think, it was all so sudden and unexpected. I *am* interested in the job, honestly.'

'Come along, Miss Carter. I'm taking you home before the snow gets any worse.'

It took quite a while to get the silver Peugeot started and when it finally began to move, oh so slowly, through the village square, the windscreen wipers working vigorously, they were both as silent as the still-falling snowflakes. Cathy desperately wanted to say something to him; she wanted to ask him to forgive her for being so stupid. She wanted to ask him to turn around and take her back to his home to talk, discuss. But she didn't, of course. Her pride got in the way. They both sat in stony silence until, after what seemed an age, Jean-Marc pulled up at the corner of Cathy's street. He didn't look at her.

'Good night, Miss Carter. I hope you have a very happy Christmas.'

No, he didn't. He didn't give a damn what sort of Christmas she had.

'Mr de Bergier?' Cathy's voice was barely audible. 'I'm sorry. Really, really sorry. I reacted badly ... stupidly ... and I'm ... well, I'm ashamed of myself. I *would* like to apply for the job in January. It's exactly the kind of work I've been hoping for. Well, you know that. And ... and if I'm lucky and they offer me the job then, well, I'd like to continue my Thursday classes. I really, really would.'

They still didn't look at each other. They both looked straight ahead, watching the snow and listening to the silent street.

'I'll be very happy to give you a reference,' Jean-Marc finally said, 'and your next lesson will be on the second Thursday in January.'

'Oh, thank you! Thank you so much, Mr de Bergier. And thanks for bringing me home. Oh, and happy Christmas!'

It wasn't until the following morning that Cathy discovered her Christmas card to Mr de Bergier at the bottom of her bag. She threw it in the bin.

*

Christmas 1973 was a quiet affair for Cathy and Molly Carter. Molly spent most of her time reminiscing about past Christmases spent as a married woman. It had never been the same after Norman died. No matter how much she loved her daughter, no matter how many visitors came and went, the festive season was never the same. And as for last year, when Cathy had been in Paris – well, that didn't bear thinking about. Cathy had been torn in two, God love her. She didn't want to be away from her mum at such a time but, on the other hand, she'd wanted to experience a French Christmas and Molly had encouraged her to do just that. She didn't want Cathy to feel she'd missed out on anything during her year in France, especially something as important as Christmas. So, Cathy had stayed in Paris and Molly hadn't been alone at all. Her sister-in-law in Sheffield had invited her to stay with her and the family and Molly had given a small 'do' for a couple of close friends and neighbours on New Year's Eve. She'd enjoyed both occasions but, she had to admit, without Cathy (not to mention Norman, but it certainly wasn't her first Christmas without him), it hadn't been the same.

Cathy was also thinking about her previous Christmas. It had certainly been different from what she was used to but she'd enjoyed it all the same. Buying gifts for little Nathalie and watching her open them. Receiving suitable gifts from Monsieur and Madame de Bergier. Suitable in that she was the au pair girl, but a much-valued one and dear to the family. What would they be doing this year? she wondered. What culinary delights would Madame have produced? She was an excellent cook and last Christmas Eve (for that was the most important time for the French), she had excelled herself. Oysters, smoked salmon, turkey and chestnut stuffing with tons of vegetables in delicious sauces; many different cheeses and the French Christmas dessert, the *bûche*, the chocolate log. All accompanied by good vintage wines from the de Bergiers' cellar. A table set for twelve people and beautifully decorated. Christmas Day was much less extravagant as far as food and drinks were concerned, but it was the day on which to relax. It was a shame that Boxing Day didn't exist in France; most people were back at work on the 26th of December, which had seemed a bit cruel to Cathy at the time! But it was all part of experiencing a foreign Christmas, of course. Cathy suddenly wondered whether Jean-Marc would be spending the holiday in Paris with his family this year. She knew he was going to France but he hadn't told her any details. He hadn't been a guest at the table for twelve last year, nor had he been a fleeting visitor.

In fact, this time last year, Cathy suddenly realised, she had never even heard of Jean-Marc de Bergier.

*

When the New Year festivities were over and 1974 was into its third day, Cathy wrote to William Kaye International. Her initial doubts and fears were now a thing of the past and she felt embarrassed and ashamed when she thought about her reaction. How could she have made a fool of herself like that when it was just the job she'd been dreaming of? No wonder her French teacher had reacted the way he did; she couldn't blame him in retrospect. Now she was just hoping and praying that she would be the successful applicant.

She was invited for an interview at William Kaye International on the third Monday in January. Molly had taken her shopping at the weekend and bought her a coat in the sales; air force blue, which suited her colouring, and a woollen dress in almost the same shade. Cathy knew she looked good in the outfit and it gave her confidence. *If you feel good, you look good*, she told herself, after recently reading that in a woman's magazine.

William Kaye International was a large, sprawling modern building that stood on the edge of a small but busy trading estate a couple of miles south east of Harrogate. It consisted of two office blocks and a factory. Cathy walked through the plate-glass double door and approached a young over-made-up receptionist who greeted her with a radiant smile. Ah yes, Mr McMichael was expecting her at two o'clock. Would Cathy like to take the lift to his office on the first floor?

James McMichael stood up when Cathy walked into his office and warmly shook her hand.

'Have a seat, Catherine. May I call you Catherine? Would you like a cup of tea or coffee?'

Cathy could have murdered a cup of coffee but she declined with thanks. She'd probably spill it or need to pee during the interview, knowing her.

James McMichael immediately picked up Cathy's application letter together with the very important reference from Jean-Marc. He was

44

obviously impressed with her qualifications and the fact that she was a student of Mr de Bergier.

'You couldn't have a better recommendation.' He smiled and then invited Cathy for a second interview three days later, on Thursday of that week.

'To meet Samuel Morrison, our export manager.'

Sam Morrison's office was two doors down from the personnel officer's. He, too, beamed when she entered his domain and shook her hand vigorously, after which it ached for quite a while. He was an elderly man and he informed Cathy that he'd been with the company for forty years. He leant forward and, the smile still on his face, said,

'I started on the shop floor, y'know, a young whippersnapper I was, wi' nowt much on top. But I was a quick learner. The company and me, we've grown together, Catherine, we've seen some good times and we've seen some bad, but I wouldn't want to be anywhere else; no, thank you. I've been export manager for a good few years, an' I've done a fair bit o' travelling, I can tell you. It's all gettin' a bit much for me now, though. D'you like travelling, Catherine? I reckon you must do if you've lived in France. Gay Paree, no less. Well, that's 'alf the battle in this job. You've done a translation for us, haven't you, love, to give us an idea, like? Righto then, I'll just give you a quick shorthand test and we'll take it from there. Do you prefer to write with a pen or a pencil?'

*

Jean-Marc finished his coffee, banked up the fire and pulled his leather chair closer to the hearth. France had been cold but nothing like this – but he was glad to be back. He frowned as memories of his brief holiday in his homeland came rushing back to him, and took in a deep breath. Well, he was back home now ... He opened his book and flicked through the pages; he'd found one of Emile Zola's lesser-known short stories on his bookshelves that he wanted Miss Carter to begin reading with him that evening. He knew that Zola was her favourite French writer but he was sure she'd never read this. *Les Coquillages de Monsieur Chabre*. It would amuse her, too, he was sure of that. The doorbell rang.

'Hello and a happy new year.'

They shook hands rather formally. Cathy followed Jean-Marc into the living room/study. He said he would make a fresh pot of coffee, picked up his empty mug and turned round. He almost bumped into his student. She was standing in the middle of the room, her air force blue coat unbuttoned, her hair loose around her shoulders, her face flushed and her mouth a melon-slice grin.

'I got the job.'

Jean-Marc found somewhere to put his mug and clasped Cathy's hand firmly in his own. He smiled warmly at her.

'Well, that's excellent news. I'm absolutely delighted for you. Congratulations, Miss Carter. When do you start?'

'Next Monday.'

'So soon? That's wonderful! And what do you think of Sam Morrison?'

'He seems really, really kind and warm and funny. In fact, everyone I've met so far has been fantastic.'

Jean-Marc laughed.

'Well, I'm very pleased and I know you'll do well. I think this post was created at just the right time as far as you're concerned. And the salary – it's okay?'

'It's much more than okay – I'm going to be rich!'

'Excellent! I'll know where to come when I'm …' he hesitated over the expression, 'broke?'

Cathy laughed, nodded and told him, with a little blush, that his English was very good.

'No coffee this evening, I think. This evening, we're going to celebrate. We're going to open a bottle of Champagne.'

Several minutes later, sitting in the maroon leather chairs on either side of the fire, they clinked glasses and Jean-Marc said,

'And on Saturday evening, I would like to take you out for a meal. A real celebration à la française!'

Les Coquillages de Monsieur Chabre didn't get opened that evening.

Chapter Four

The Old Windmill in Harrogate was one of those exquisite little restaurants frequented and loved by couples celebrating engagements or wedding anniversaries, businessmen entertaining important clients and off-the-rails married men hoping to impress their mistresses. It stood on the banks of the River Nidd, just north of Harrogate. Stone and virginia-creepered on the outside and mahogany, red velvet and candlelit inside. The service was always impeccable, the food delicious and the wines vintage. Jean-Marc de Bergier had booked a table at the Old Windmill.

Cathy wore a green jersey dress that she'd bought in Paris and had had the opportunity to wear only once in that city. Mr and Madame de Bergier had invited her to their own favourite restaurant in the fashionable sixth *arrondissement*, the evening before her departure, and she'd wanted to look her best. She wanted to look her best for the Old Windmill, too. It was a restaurant that she'd heard about and always very favourably and she'd dreamt of being taken there one day. She and Diana had often imagined romantic evenings there – not together, of course – with their respective desirable dates for the evening ... maybe one day ...

Jean-Marc had booked a table in the corner; comfortable, warm and intimate. At one time, it would have been a little intimidating, Cathy thought, settling herself into the red velvet chair, but thanks to her year in the French capital, she didn't feel conspicuous in elegant restaurants anymore. She'd been educated in that respect, too, as well as many others. *Thank goodness*, she thought now, looking across the table at Jean-Marc. She'd have died rather than show herself up in front of *him*. The waiter, smart and smiling, headed towards their table with menus. He bowed slightly, first at Cathy then at her companion.

'Good evening, Mr de Bergier. How *very* nice it is to see you here again.'

'Hello, John. I hope you're well?'

'Very well indeed, thank you. I hope it's not too late to wish you – both – a very happy new year.'

Cathy watched the waiter bowing his way from the table and stifled a giggle. She wanted to say, *What a twerp!* or something like that but, of course, she didn't. Not to Jean-Marc; he'd soon put her in her place. She opened the large green leather menu and glanced at her companion over the rim. She jumped. He was looking at her, smiling at her.

'I can see you're not impressed with our waiter, Miss Carter. I don't blame you. He's an old groveller and he makes me want to ... throw up.'

Cathy gaped at him and then laughed. The unexpected and tasteless turn of phrase, together with the hint of a French accent, delighted her. The smile was still playing on Jean-Marc's lips as he studied his menu and Cathy looked at her own. She inadvertently caught her breath. There were far too many dishes to choose from and every one made her mouth water. Why couldn't she have a little bit of everything ...? After a couple of minutes, Jean-Marc said,

'Have you decided what you're going to eat, Miss Carter?' and he beckoned the ebullient waiter.

Cathy suddenly wished he'd stop calling her Miss Carter. It was all right during a French lesson on Thursday evening when they both had their heads in a book or whatever but, well, it seemed silly somehow, here in this gorgeous restaurant, and anyway ... it made her feel sort of prim and ... elderly ... a bit Miss Marple-ish ...

'Oh, Mr de Bergier, no, I haven't. Everything looks so delicious.' *And expensive*, she added to herself.

When they had both finally made their decision, John took their order and reappeared bearing lobster pâté and salad with thin wedges of toast as the starter. Jean-Marc, helping himself to butter, smiled and said,

'Oh, by the way, Miss Carter, before we begin our meal, would you mind very much calling me Jean-Marc? I would prefer it, you know. I'm likely to choke on my roast duckling if you say "Mister" or even "*Monsieur*" this evening. Will you allow me to call you Catherine?'

Cathy grinned at him and started to spread pâté on her toast.

'Cathy, please.'

Jean-Marc shrugged and pulled a face.

'No. No, I don't like "Cathy". I prefer Catherine. I'll call you Catherine. And now let's talk about your job. Are you getting excited?'

No, Cathy, don't let him ruffle your feathers, keep calm. If he wants to call you Catherine, let him get on with it. Arrogant devil.

'Yes, I'm really excited but I'm more nervous than anything. Oh, Mr de

Bergier, do you honestly, *honestly* think I'll be able to cope? With the translations, I mean. Come to think of it, with anything. It's so long since I did any secretarial work ... changing nappies and singing nursery rhymes is more my line now ...'

'Well, I'm sure if you asked Sam Morrison nicely ...'

They looked at each other and smiled.

'Catherine, if I didn't think you could do the job, I wouldn't have suggested you apply and I certainly wouldn't have given you a reference. Please, stop worrying. You'll be absolutely fine. I have every confidence in you.'

'Another thing that's worrying me, Mr de Bergier.'

'Do you really want me to choke?'

'What? Oh, sorry. Seriously, Jean-Marc, Mr Morrison was very nice to me but he's been with the company such a long time that he's bound to be set in his ways, isn't he, and his last secretary was with him for donkey's years. Oh, you know what I mean ...'

'For God's sake, Catherine, don't worry at all about Sam Morrison. He's a decent man, the salt of the earth. He works very hard, he travels a lot and he appreciates all the help he can get. He's also very human and, believe me, you'll have no problems with him. However, I don't think he'll be there for much longer.'

'What do you mean?'

'Well, he must be coming up to retirement age, if he's not passed it. But don't worry about that. Get yourself established, it's a good company to be with, and I know they're always looking for fresh young talent. You never know where this job will lead to ... managing director? Chairwoman?'

'Chair- or *char*-woman?'

Jean-Marc made a semi-frown and Cathy giggled and shrugged her shoulders.

'Don't get too ambitious, I'm only twenty-one. Give me at least two years.'

'And, Catherine, if you do need any help ... I'm not saying you will, but if you do, please get in touch with me. Any time. You have my home number and I'll give you my number at the college, just in case. You will have a lot to learn, there's no doubt about it, but I'm convinced you can do it. And you've got me behind you. Okay?'

'Thank you, Jean-Marc.'

They left the Old Windmill at ten-thirty and were greeted by the crisp, cold January night. The ground was slippery with decaying snow and ice and Jean-Marc gently guided Cathy to the Peugeot waiting at the far end of the small car park. It wasn't easy walking on the uneven icy cobbled stones and Jean-Marc took Catherine's arm. She smiled her thanks.

'Thank you for a really lovely evening,' she said when she'd warmed up a little inside the car. They were driving towards her home.

'It was my pleasure, *mademoiselle*.' Jean-Marc grinned but his eyes didn't leave the road. They didn't speak again until he'd pulled up outside the terraced house.

'*Voilà, mademoiselle*! The young lady is returned safe and sound and without a mark on her!' Jean-Marc smiled. 'The young lady also looked very lovely tonight. Green suits you, Catherine. It enhances your beautiful hair.'

Catherine didn't know what to say. Compliments from men usually left her feeling tongue-tied and foolish; but a compliment from this man had twice the effect. Jean-Marc ignored the lack of response, got out of the vehicle and opened the door for her. Cathy thanked him again and he replied,

'If you enjoyed yourself so much, *mademoiselle*, I'll have to think about inviting you out again. And now may I wish you good luck, or rather *bonne chance*, for Monday morning and I'll see you next Thursday evening.'

He walked around the car to the driver's door.

'And don't be late.'

*

William Kaye International had started life in 1925, a small scruffy room that passed as a workshop and an even smaller space that was known as the 'clerical room', plus a handful of enthusiastic staff. At that time, of course, it wasn't known as William Kaye International; there was nothing international about it. The company, manufacturing sewing machines and parts, had been born in Harrogate and its employees were all natives of the town; employees who either stayed and helped the company to expand or flew from the nest to pastures new. The ones who stayed lived to be thankful. Within a decade, the nondescript workshop was sold and William Kaye, the 'daddy' of the small firm, bought a warehouse on the outskirts of the town, invested in more modern, more expensive machinery and gradually employed more staff. The shop floor was full of bright young lads, eager to get on in life and more than willing to work overtime; evenings and weekends, too. The 'clerical room' began to take shape as a busy office, crammed with desks and cupboards and shelves and cabinets. More staff were needed, the building was overcrowded and the money was flowing. William Kaye sold his 'warehouse' and purchased yet another, bigger and better property, on what was later to become a trading estate. Then came World War II. Tailoring factories were hives of activity, churning out uniforms for the armed forces, and more and more machines were needed. William Kaye thrived. William Kaye himself was now a very rich man.

Samuel Morrison was no pauper, either. He was what was known as a grafter, working all hours God sent on the factory floor, never taking days off sick, never shirking his duties. By the time the war ended in 1945, he was thirty-two years old and had become office manager. He was a married man by then, and in December of that year became a father for the first time. He took his first day's leave when Alice produced their son; he hadn't taken any time off after their wedding. They were married on Saturday and Sam was back at the office on Monday morning. A war was on, he told everyone, and work came first. When his child was born and he took the day off, William Kaye told him to take the whole week as paid leave but Sam refused. Alice had her mother at home with her and there were plenty of good friends and neighbours to help; it would be daft him getting in the way. He'd rather be where he was needed.

When William Kaye retired, it was a foregone conclusion that Sam Morrison would take over as director. Nobody actually talked about it; it was simply taken for granted. Nobody else would be able to do the job and keep the company on its feet like Sam Morrison. And by the time William Kaye retired, Sam would be getting on for fifty, a well-established pillar in the firm, a respected and admired veteran. A must for the job. But William Kaye didn't retire. He died of a massive heart attack in 1960, aged sixty-three. After the initial shock, everyone confessed they weren't really surprised. William Kaye had literally worked himself to death. He left behind a grief-stricken wife, two daughters and a panicking company. A meeting of the board was held shortly after the funeral and, as anticipated, Sam Morrison was elected to take over the deceased's post. But the boss's early and untimely demise had set Sam thinking. Seriously. He was almost fifty years old, not much younger than the founder of his company and living much the same lifestyle. He didn't want the job.

'In fact,' he told the dumbfounded board, 'I'm going to take a long holiday. I think I deserve one.'

He took Alice and their fifteen-year-old son to Europe but, although he enjoyed his tour, work was never far from his mind. He talked to people, casually called in tailoring factories and offices (much to Alice's chagrin) and managed to establish contacts in France, Belgium and Holland. Two years later, he was promoted by the board to export manager, handling foreign customers, travelling extensively and, thanks to his determination and expertise in dealing with the human race, William Kaye International was created, and enjoyed a thriving market. Although Sam's new and exciting position was demanding, he compensated by taking more holidays and occasional days' leave.

Sam's very efficient secretary, Joan Little, had been with him for twelve years when he managed the sales office, and was promoted with him. Although he had always found her almost faultless at her work, Sam soon began to realise the need for someone who was competent when working with foreign contacts. And Joan wasn't. She had no knowledge of any other language and was, quite frankly, intimidated by anyone who wasn't born in the United Kingdom. As European correspondence increased, so did Sam's frustration and new feelings of inadequacy. He gently suggested that Joan take a beginner's course in French at night school but she was horrified.

'I'm far too old for that sort of thing!' she cried.

Sam accepted the situation and advertised in the *North Yorkshire Gazette* for a translator/interpreter to do several hours' work per week for the company, fee negotiable. He wasn't exactly inundated with replies. He received two – one from a rather overambitious schoolgirl studying for A-levels, to whom he sent a courteous refusal; the other from a Mr Jean-Marc de Bergier, a French national living in a village not many miles from Harrogate and teaching in nearby Knaresborough. He telephoned Mr de Bergier, invited him for an interview and immediately employed him. The liaison was extremely satisfactory to both parties and lasted two years. During that time, William Kaye's business with France expanded; more clients were found in Belgium and Switzerland and thus the correspondence and all it entailed grew to vast proportions. To the extent that Mr de Bergier was no longer able to cope with these and his teaching commitments. He also intimated to Sam that if a certain project he was working on at the moment worked as he hoped it would, then his whole professional life would have to be reconstructed, leaving no time at all for other outside interests. This was unfortunate but understandable and, as Joan Little was making noises about taking early retirement, Sam Morrison decided to advertise for a bi-lingual secretary to replace her. In addition to James McMichael's official letter to the Frenchman, Sam telephoned and asked him to keep his eyes and ears open. If he found anybody who'd fit the bill, he should let Sam know immediately.

*

'Good morning, Mr Morrison.'

Catherine Carter was hovering rather uncertainly in the doorway of Sam's office, looking very wintry in her calf-length sheepskin coat, covered in snow, and matching mittens.

'Eeh, Catherine, hello. Come in, come in. What a blinking lousy morning to start a new job, eh? Never mind, the day can only improve. I'll show you where to put yer coat and then I'll show you where kettle is and we'll have a nice cup o' coffee. What d'you say?'

Catherine knew that she was going to like Mr Morrison; she felt she was a good judge of character and her first impressions were usually right. At the interview, in spite of his high position, he seemed quite a fatherly type, and the fact that he didn't try to disguise his thick Yorkshire accent endeared him to her. And now, on this freezing January morning when she was feeling sick with cold and anxiety, he'd put her at her ease just by smiling at her and with a few friendly words. Oh yes, she was going to like Mr Morrison.

Over the very welcome hot drink, Sam talked to Catherine about the company and encouraged her to talk about herself. When she had finally warmed through and her fingers felt like flesh and blood and not icicles anymore, he took her on a long tour of the premises, introducing her to people whom she needed to know and machines that she needed to use. Most people seemed friendly, Catherine was pleased to notice, and, as the day wore on, her initial nervousness and lack of confidence began to evaporate. She didn't do much on that first day; she typed a couple of letters and translated a brief telex from a firm in Lille. She spent her lunch break in the canteen, eating a satisfying if unexciting meal and getting to know her colleagues on a more personal basis. She left the building at five o'clock feeling fulfilled and happy with life and looked forward to going back on Tuesday morning.

*

By Thursday evening, Catherine was bursting to see Jean-Marc. If it hadn't been for him, she would never have got this super job and, oh, there were so many things she was longing to tell him! However, after working a little later than usual that evening and spending longer than usual looking for something decent to wear, she missed the bus and arrived at the lodge of Mullion Hall at seven-fifty. In spite of the cold, Catherine's eyes were sparkling and her lips smiling when Jean-Marc opened the door. However, the visible signs of happiness on her face were very quickly wiped away.

'Ah! My seven-thirty student! Well, it seems that whatever I say to you goes straight in one ear and out the other. I thought you'd understood that I absolutely do not tolerate unpunctuality.'

Without waiting for a reply, Jean-Marc turned round and walked into his home, leaving Catherine standing on the doorstep, frozen stiff and furious. It was obvious he was expecting her to follow him and no doubt apologise and beg his bloody forgiveness. Well, she'd show him; she wouldn't apologise to a ... a pig ... like him. He ought to be thankful she'd put an appearance in at all on a night like this – and paying him, too! *He* should be paying *her*! The pig! She turned round and under normal circumstances would have quietly walked up the path into the village square and jumped on the next bus (even if she had to wait an hour) and never be seen again. That evening, however, the circumstances were not normal. The snow and ice were against her and dignity was transformed into calamity as she slipped, screamed and sprawled on the uneven cobbled path. She couldn't get up. Her knees hurt, her right elbow hurt, but most of all her pride hurt. *Oh, dear God, please let me get up and get away* ... Jean-Marc then reappeared in the doorway. He leant against the door jamb, his arms folded, watching her struggling to her feet. And then he laughed. He laughed! The pig! And then he pulled her to her feet, lifted her up and carried her into the lodge, kicking the door shut behind him. He carefully lowered her into one of the leather chairs and knelt in front of her, grinning. Catherine wanted to spit at him.

'Where does it hurt the most?' he asked.

'It doesn't hurt at all,' Catherine croaked. 'It was just a bit of a shock.'

'Then I suggest a large glass of brandy rather than a bandage.'

He left the room and returned with the promised medicine and one for himself.

'Feeling better?' he asked after five minutes' silence. Catherine nodded. She was beginning to thaw out physically and emotionally. There were no bones broken and the places that hurt didn't hurt quite so much. She handed her empty glass to Jean-Marc.

'You're mean and miserable, Jean-Marc. How could you be so obnoxious when I was twenty minutes late on a freezing cold, disgusting night like this?'

'Frankly, I didn't expect you at all. I'd been waiting for a phone call. You're crazy coming out this evening. You should really have cancelled and we'd have done extra hours another time. Anyway, where's your sense of humour? A sense of humour is very important, you know, never forget that. You must learn to recognise when I'm serious and when I'm joking. If you don't, our relationship won't stand a chance.'

Sense of humour? Well, falling flat on your face in the freezing snow might be his idea of ... relationship?

'And William Kaye International, Catherine? Are you enjoying your work so far or has it been the biggest mistake of your life?'

'Oh, I love it! It's the best thing that's happened to me since I came back from Paris. It's so interesting and the people are so friendly and Mr Morrison's so lovely, just like a ... just like a second dad.'

Jean-Marc, now standing with his back to the blazing fire and looking down at her, smiled.

'I'm rather disappointed, Catherine. I was hoping I was the best thing that'd happened to you since you came back from Paris. Oh well, never mind. Is this the same young lady who thought she wouldn't be able to cope and who was going to refuse an interview? I can hardly believe it.'

Catherine laughed. 'Neither can I. I must have been mad. Oh, and thank you, Jean-Marc. Thank you *so* much. If it wasn't for you—'

'If it wasn't for me, you wouldn't be the brilliant career girl that you are now and the future chairperson of the board. Yes, I realise that. So – how are you going to thank me?'

He was grinning at her, his eyes dancing, his face golden from the glow of the fire. Catherine blushed and looked away. He was teasing her again; he enjoyed making her feel foolish and gauche. Like a little girl. Well, she wasn't a little girl, she was twenty-one years old, a fully-fledged adult, a woman. She'd make this … this *pig* treat her like a woman if it was the last thing she did. Right then … okay … She raised her head and looked up at him, her eyes holding his and not letting go. She slowly began to lick her lips.

'I really don't know.' She made her voice low, throaty and, she hoped suddenly, seductive. 'What do you suggest, Jean-Marc?'

Jean-Marc smiled at her, walked to his desk in the corner of the room and sat down behind it.

'I suggest a solid hour of interesting, thought-provoking French literature, Catherine. That's what you came for, isn't it?'

Oh, she hated this man; she really, really hated him.

*

The following Saturday, Jean-Marc invited Catherine out again. They went to a cosy pub in the centre of Harrogate, overlooking the Valley Gardens, looking majestic under the blanket of snow and illuminated by pink lights. Catherine sat at a table by the window and watched Jean-Marc walk to the bar. It was still quite early; there were few customers as yet and Jean-Marc was served immediately. He came back to the table with a gin and tonic for himself and a Pernod and lemonade for Catherine.

'How did you know I like Pernod?' she asked.

'Most people who live in France for any length of time develop a taste for Pernod.' And then he added, 'And, of course, it's a wonderful aphrodisiac.'

Catherine grinned at him and decided against a witty reply. She couldn't think of one, anyway.

They never seemed to stop talking that evening. About everything and yet about nothing in particular. Jean-Marc's wit made Catherine laugh a lot and occasionally he annoyed her with his teasing, but the threatened fights always dissolved into giggles. And later they strolled back to the car, seemingly unaware of the biting cold, and Jean-Marc drove Catherine home, and they talked and laughed all the way. When he stopped the car outside the house, he left the engine running and told her he would see her the following Thursday at seven-thirty – on the dot. Feeling strangely disappointed, Catherine opened the door.

'I'll probably phone you before then,' Jean-Marc added.

*

The winter was beginning to die. March was cold and very windy but fresh and free from the ravages of snow and ice. Life became easier as spring arrived; getting out and about was no longer a headache and neither was getting to work on time. Work. How Catherine loved her work. She thought when she'd started this job in January that her professional happiness and satisfaction couldn't improve. But as her knowledge of the company increased and she became more self-reliant and less dependent on her colleagues' know-how, as she gradually got to know members of the female staff and as her initial, warm relationship with Sam grew even closer, so her happiness and satisfaction escalated.

She looked forward to every working day; to the challenges, the achievements, the lively conversations, the laughs. Most of all, she looked forward to the foreign correspondence that she was required to translate or, better still, when she was needed to interpret. That was what she enjoyed the most. The feeling of satisfaction and pride when Sam Morrison expressed his thanks and approval was quite overwhelming and made her even more determined to climb to the top of her professional ladder. With Jean-Marc's help, of course. He was behind her all the way, pushing her, pumping her, testing her and, occasionally, slating her. Their Thursday evenings developed from two-hour French classes into lengthy, heated discussions on politics, religion, current affairs, sex. Discussions punctuated with laughter, profanities and sometimes even tears. Discussions that were helped along by the odd glass of wine or beer and a light supper. Discussions that began at seven-thirty (on the dot) and often finished at ten-thirty, eleven-thirty, on one occasion, midnight; whenever. Discussions that began in perfect French and often ended in very bad English in the Peugeot 404 on the way home.

*

It was drizzling when they came out of the cinema and the wind lashed their faces.

'You're not in a hurry to get home, are you?'

'No, not particularly.'

'Right, let's make for the nearest pub. First one there buys the first round.'

Cathy pushed open the pub door, wiped her feet on the mat and made her way to the bar. She caught the barmaid's eye as she finished pulling a pint and was instantly acknowledged. Drinks in hand, she then shuffled her way to the chosen table.

'Cheers!'

'So, what did you think of the film? It scared me witless.'

'Rubbish! I could have laughed all the way through.'

'Me, too. In fact, I did. I couldn't take it seriously and can't imagine how it got such a good write-up. Anyway, at least we've seen *The Exorcist* and that's that.'

'And I for one won't want to see it again.'

'Hey, how's the job going, Cathy? We haven't had time to ask you.'

Cathy smiled and wrinkled her nose. She sipped her glass of wine and licked her lips.

'It's absolutely fantastic. I love it. I really, really feel at home there.'

'Bloody 'ell. That's saying summat. Have you met the Frenchman of your dreams yet, then, with all this interpreting?'

Catherine looked across at Jane, or Sour Grapes as Molly had baptised her, and smiled.

She smiled and winked at the same time. 'That'd be telling.'

Her friends all gazed at her, glasses held in mid-air, but Catherine offered no more information.

'I don't suppose you've heard any more from Diana? I reckon she's disappeared off the face of the earth. Shame really, she were all right, were Diana.'

Cathy didn't offer a reply to that remark, either. She would have given anything … absolutely anything … to be able to sit and talk to and tell her best friend everything that had happened over the past few months. Jane was looking at her with a jeer on her thin lips. Maybe Cathy should feel sorry for her, really; she was obviously a very unhappy person.

*

April arrived with its showers, buds and blossoms and a beautiful spring. One lovely warm evening, Jean-Marc looked up from his desk and watched his Thursday evening student working on the floor. Catherine often did this now. She no longer sat rigid and intimidated in the big leather chair. She curled up, or lay on her stomach, silently reading whatever French masterpiece was at her disposal and occasionally asking Jean-Marc for his opinion, or his help. In this way, he could get on with correcting his other students' written work and it was a rare and pleasant respite from their heartier, rowdier Thursday sessions. Jean-Marc watched Catherine for a long time. He watched how her facial expressions changed as she studied her book; the placid, indifferent look of the tired student would suddenly be transformed into a vision of sheer joy as she read something that amused her. And just as quickly, it would change to confusion or frustration when there was something she didn't quite understand. Then, after a while, she would give in and look up at him and wait for a convenient time to speak and ask for his help. She looked up now. Jean-Marc was watching her and Catherine somehow knew that he'd been watching her for a long time. She wasn't surprised because he often did. In the study on evenings like these, in pubs or restaurants when they sometimes went out together at the weekends. Even at her mother's home, when Molly left the room, she'd feel his eyes on her, as though he was wanting to say something important to her ... but he never did.

All at once, Jean-Marc stood up and, not taking his eyes off Catherine's face, he moved around the desk and slowly walked towards her. Catherine felt a warm shiver run through her body. She pulled herself into a sitting position, her legs tucked underneath her, in the usual way. She smiled at Jean-Marc as he squatted beside her on the floor.

'Hello,' she said, softly.

'Hello, *mademoiselle*.'

His face moved towards her, his eyes holding hers, questioning, searching. His lips briefly touched her cheek and he heard the small gasp catch in her throat. He pulled himself away and looked at Catherine. Her eyes were closed, her lips slightly open. He touched her face with his right hand, running his finger down her cheek, across her mouth, through her beautiful hair. Catherine blinked open her eyes and they smiled at each other.

'Time to go home, *mademoiselle*,' Jean-Marc murmured.

59

Chapter Five

If Catherine Carter had been asked to describe in one word the following year or so her life, she would have had a desperate struggle to find one that was complete enough. Idyllic perhaps, blissful maybe, perfect. Even that superlative didn't seem adequate to describe her life. Could anyone be so ecstatically happy and contented with life without a deep feeling of impending doom? No one should be entitled to such euphoria when there were millions of people suffering in the world. People who were starving, people who were desperately ill, people whose lives were, for one reason or another, a kind of living hell. Why should she, Catherine Carter, be singled out for real happiness? It wasn't fair and it wouldn't last, it couldn't last for ever; nothing did. According to the law of averages, her life would suddenly take a nasty turn and one part of her perfect little world would disintegrate, disappear and there would be sadness. But not yet, dear God, please not yet.

*

A delegation of engineers and draughtsmen from a company in Brussels were visiting William Kaye International for two weeks in May 1974. There were eight of them, two of whom spoke a little English but not enough to put Catherine out of work. It had been a hectic week for her. As well as typing long reports on various aspects of the visit, she was constantly being called into the factory or wherever the visitors happened to be, to help with the linguistic difficulties, of which there were many. She was also being taken out to lunch every day and once or twice in the evenings, strictly business but, for Catherine, also great fun. Sam expressed his gratitude every morning when she arrived at the office early, and every evening when she left late.

'Yer a grand lass, you know,' he grinned at her on the Wednesday evening of the second week, 'and I do appreciate everything yer doing. And don't worry, I'll see that yer well remunerated at the end o' this month.'

'Thanks a lot, Sam,' Catherine smiled. 'I'm enjoying every minute, honestly. Would you like me to come in early tomorrow?'

Sam frowned, scratched his grey head, a frequent habit of his, and looked in his diary.

'No, lass, there'll be no need. There's nowt happenin' tomorrow morning. But I'd be eternally grateful if you'd join us tomorrow evenin' for a meal and a few drinks. It'll be the Belgians' last night in 'Arrogate, as you know, and I'm takin' 'em out. I'd like you to be there, just in case. I'll need you, that goes without sayin', but I know they'll want you to be there for social reasons. To say goodbye properly, an' all that.'

'Well, thank you, Sam. I'd love to come. No problem at all.'

No problem, she'd said. Of course there was a problem; it was Thursday. She couldn't cancel her evening with Jean-Marc. Well, she could, of course she could, but she didn't want to and she knew he wouldn't want her to. Thursday was the one evening in the week that she anticipated, looked forward to, sometimes got nervous about. Wondering whether, well, ever since that night last month when Jean-Marc had kissed her cheek and touched her and looked at her sort of … well … affectionately … she'd thought it had been a prelude, a kind of apéritif, but she'd been wrong. Oh, he was kind to her, helpful and amusing … but now there was something missing. There was a lot missing.

She rang Jean-Marc as soon as she got home.

'Russetlea 4327. Hello.'

'Hi, Jean-Marc, it's me.'

'Me. *Me.* Who the devil is "me"?'

She heard the teasing in his voice; she could almost see the sardonic smile playing on his lips. He damn well knew who 'me' was.

'It's Catherine Carter. Your Thursday evening student. And I'm afraid she won't be coming this Thursday evening.'

'What do you mean you won't be coming? Are you ill?'

'No, I'm not ill, but—'

'If you're not ill, Catherine, there's no excuse. I'll expect to see you at seven-thirty.'

'On the dot.'

'Exactly.'

'Well, I'm sorry to disappoint you but I won't be coming tomorrow evening. I'm going out for a meal with Sam and the Belgians … it's their last night in Harrogate and—'

'Thank God for that, they're a bloody nuisance. They've monopolised you for the last fortnight.'

'*Monopolised* me! Jean-Marc, what are you talking about? It's business …'

'Exactly. You've got no life of your own. Your whole life revolves around your work now …'

'Aren't you proud of me, Jean-Marc?'

Silence. Jean-Marc de Bergier could not see the amused little smile, the teasing little smile on Catherine's face. He heard only words, and they confused him.

'Yes, of course I'm proud of you. Professionally. But there's more to life than work.' Pause. 'Where are you going for this meal?'

'I've absolutely no idea.'

'I see. I hope to see you *next* Thursday then. Unless, of course, you have another priority. For example—'

'Good night, Jean-Marc.'

*

Sam decided to invite the Belgians to an Italian restaurant with wide windows overlooking the Stray, an expanse of green, flowers and trees that looked particularly beautiful on that warm May evening. The meal was no doubt cooked to perfection, but Catherine had difficulty eating the lasagne that she normally devoured. Her appetite had gone and her enthusiasm had gone with it. She'd been expecting a telephone call from that ridiculous, unreasonable Frenchman all day, but none had come. What was wrong with the man? She really wished she could understand him, get through to him, poke around in his brain a bit and see what she could find in there. Was he angry that she'd missed a valuable lesson? Could he possibly be jealous? Or was he just being downright childish because she'd prioritised the visiting Belgians? The stupid man.

'You look a little sad this evening, Catherine,' observed Bernard, one of the English-speaking men. 'You are no doubt sorry that we are leaving, yes?'

Catherine smiled.

'Of course I'm sorry. You've kept me very busy for two weeks! Whatever am I going to do now?'

Sam swallowed the last of his pizza and winked at her. He looked around the table and grinned at everyone.

'Well, I think it's a man who's upset 'er,' he said, 'I can feel it in me bones.'

Everyone laughed politely, although no one understood a word, even the ones who knew English. But Catherine understood perfectly. Sam winked at her again. She blushed and gazed at her empty plate. At the end of the evening, she expected to say goodbye to the Belgian team outside the restaurant and be given a lift home by Sam. But it didn't quite work out like that. She was sipping her coffee and trying to make pleasant, easy conversation with the young man on her left, when a shadow suddenly fell across the table. Sam looked up and smiled.

'Well, well, well ... If it isn't Jean-Marc de Bergier. What a surprise! Come and 'ave a drink with us, Jean-Marc, an' meet our Belgian friends.'

Catherine felt the colour rising to her cheeks and she almost choked on her coffee. She slowly turned around. Jean-Marc was standing behind her, his hands clutching the back of her chair, his eyes acknowledging the whole party. He was introduced to, shook hands with and spoke politely in French to the foreigners for a few minutes and then he turned his attention to their interpreter.

'If you've finished your meal, Catherine, I should very much like to take you home.'

Catherine looked first at Sam, who silently nodded, and then she looked at the Belgians, who were already talking among themselves. She made a show of finishing her coffee and stood up. Her legs wobbled; her hands were clammy; her throat felt dry. Did she feel totally humiliated or thrilled to bits? She didn't know.

'*Alors, messieurs,*' she addressed the table, '*il faut que je m'en aille. Au revoir et je vous souhaite un très bon voyage.*'

She shook hands with each one and was volubly thanked for all her help. Sam caught her eye and winked at her again.

'See you tomorrow, Catherine,' he beamed. '*Bonne nweet.*'

Catherine walked out of the restaurant into the soft warm May evening and she turned to face the Frenchman. He was grinning at her.

'You look like the traditional Cheshire cat,' she almost spat at him. 'What d'you think you're playing at? Who ... who d'you think you are, Jean-Marc de Bergier, bursting in like a ... like a bull in a china shop and showing me up like that? I felt like … humiliated. You've no business to … anyway, how did you know where to find us?'

Jean-Marc threw back his head and laughed and then pulled her towards him.

'Ask Sam Morrison tomorrow,' said the Cheshire cat-cum-bull-in-a-china-shop. And then he kissed her, holding her body close to him and feeling her responding slowly, but so very, very surely.

The study was almost in darkness when they arrived. He switched on the lamps and drew the curtains. Then he moved towards Catherine, who was standing by the fireplace, watching his every gesture, and he took her in his arms. He kissed her and Catherine felt her fingers, her face, her thighs begin to tingle. This was a very new sensation for her; no one else had made her body feel this way. She knew she was completely out of control and she didn't care. Jean-Marc pulled away. He looked down into her eyes and he touched her face, gently running his fingers around her cheeks, down her neck, across her lips. Catherine kissed them slowly, one by one.

'Catherine …'

No, she didn't want him to stop; she didn't want him to talk to her, not now. She gazed up at him, still caressing his fingers with her mouth. His arms folded around her, his lips covering her face, her neck, her eyes with kisses, his hands gently stroking her aching breasts. Catherine felt that her body was about to burst into flames. She kissed the man that she'd hated and despised and admired and loved, and every feeling that she'd ever experienced was in that kiss. Jean-Marc pulled away again, took her face in his two hands and his brown eyes looked into hers.

'Catherine, you know that I love you, don't you?'

And later, in Jean-Marc's small but tastefully furnished, male-orientated bedroom, Catherine's body slowly burst into flames.

*

How could hate develop into love so quickly and so completely? Catherine often wondered. How could your feelings for another human being be so capricious? And why should she, Catherine Carter, have so many blessings poured onto her when there were people in the world … oh, she could go on for ever trying to analyse her thoughts, her feelings, her life. When, really, she should just be thanking God that she had a super job, a mum in a million, good mates and Jean-Marc. The best mate of all.

Her days were spent working hard and getting to know and admire Sam more every day. He had his little quirks – what boss didn't? – but he was an intelligent, kind and humorous man and, in a way, Catherine loved him like the father she had lost so young. He taught her many things, not only about the company and her work but also about life. Catherine could feel herself expanding, growing under his guidance. She looked forward to her days at the office, and certain professional trips away with Sam, but most of all now she looked forward to her evenings and weekends with her wonderful Frenchman.

In spite of their new and developing relationship, Thursday evenings were still spent deep in French conversation, French literature or French whatever. From seven-thirty until nine-thirty. And after nine-thirty, the tutor and his student once more became friends, and upstairs in the tastefully furnished and male-orientated bedroom, ardent and passionate lovers.

Their weekends were spent shopping in Harrogate, seeing films and eating out in Harrogate, sleeping at the cottage and, as the warm mellow spring developed into a blazing hot summer, driving into the Dales or to the Yorkshire coast. Even during the summer months, Jean-Marc dedicated quite a lot of his evenings to working in the study. Long, quiet periods when Catherine would curl up in one of the chairs or on the floor, contentedly reading. And when Jean-Marc decided he'd laboured enough, they would chat over a drink, listen to either soft classical music, jazz or Abba, the Carpenters, Rod Stewart and reggae on his stereo system, and Catherine learnt the word 'eclectic'. Later, they would make love in the bed that creaked and groaned with their passion.

*

'Catherine, sunshine, you've been a little godsend to this office,' Samuel Morrison said to her one Friday afternoon in late September, just as autumn's glow was beginning to decorate the town. He was reading Catherine's translation of a telex from a tailoring factory in the north of France, the confirmation of a sale of four machines, totalling over £15,000.

'I can 'onestly say, love,' he added, 'if it hadn't been for your help when their MD visited last month, I doubt very much we'd 'ave made this sale.'

Catherine glowed with pride.

And the same evening when she lay in Jean-Marc's arms, her head resting on his naked chest that was covered with dark hair, just before he slipped into a deep sleep, he whispered,

'Catherine, I want to spend the rest of my life with you.'

Catherine glowed with love and deep contentment. She closed her eyes and clung to the beloved body at her side.

But life is far too brutal for deep contentment to last very long.

Brian

CHAPTER SIX

You couldn't see the house from Harrogate Road. You had to turn left after the crossroads in Heaton Brow, a village consisting of several cottages, one general store and a small hotel, and then take the narrow lane to the right until a dark clump of sycamore trees came into view. The house stood, rather grandiose and very much alone, at the end of a long and winding stony path, lined with beech trees.

Greystones, the house with its few acres of land, had been built in the early nineteenth century and its architecture typified the era. The stony path eventually led to a flight of wide stone steps, uneven now, cracked and perhaps not as safe as they should be, and at the top a thick oak door with small stained glass windows in the upper half. Virginia creeper trailed around the tall red chimney stacks, down the grey tiled roof and coiled around the many small leaded windows. The door opened into a cold, draughty hall with a tiled floor on which the softest footfalls echoed, and high wood-panelled walls. The rooms, many of which were no longer in use, were all spacious and, although architecturally charming, they were also cold and uninviting. Log fires always blazed in rooms which were occupied but these never seemed to compensate; the house was too big, its history too old. At the side of the vestibule a wide and winding red-carpeted staircase led to rooms and corridors upstairs, corridors decorated with many fine original paintings; portraits, landscapes, still lifes. These beautiful and, in some cases, priceless works of art had, at one time, been a source of great pride to the owner of Greystones.

Vincent Jarvis, after spending several years stationed in Holland during the Second World War, returned to Yorkshire with a Dutch bride whom he had met, wooed and wed within three short months. He was passionately in love with the fragile, blue-eyed blonde girl who had been only too willing to give up her grim, impecunious existence in the back streets of Amsterdam and accompany her new husband to … anywhere he chose to take her. For two years, the couple lived with Vincent's wealthy, widowed and rather eccentric father, Thomas Jarvis, whose two passions in life had been extensive travel and the collecting of rare, ugly and beautiful and often priceless pieces of art and objets d'art. He had loved his wife in his own way but had thought nothing of leaving her alone on a whim to take off to distant lands. He loved his son, too, but his frequent absences rendered a close father-son relationship impossible. As Vincent grew older, he appreciated the times when his father was away so that he could have his mother to himself. When his father was present in the big house, his mother's time was divided and it was obvious, even to Vincent, that the time she spent with her husband was rewarded with indifference. He, in his young, clumsy way, tried to make up for his father's lack of affection, but Sarah Jarvis, not being used to physical demonstrations of love, was unable to return the tenderness that Vincent craved. After her death, he and his father continued to live in the same house but were merely two men existing under the same roof. The two women who came every day from the village to clean and cook for them became go-betweens, giving occasional messages from father to son; son to father. On their rare moments in each other's company, there was such an uneasiness between them that they both preferred to keep their solitude and their privacy. Vincent, also a lover of art, organised a studio in one of the upstairs rooms and spent most of his free time at home locked inside there. His paintings, in the beginning, were described as average, but with time and experience his style developed and became pleasing. His artwork had a style, a character of its own, and he began to sell. The Heaton Brow Arms, the small hotel on Harrogate Road, bought two of his local landscapes to hang in their lounge bar. A dealer in Harrogate and a small gallery in Knaresborough also showed an interest in Vincent Jarvis's work and he began to achieve a certain reputation. If his father, the great art lover and proud possessor of priceless paintings, was proud of him, Vincent was never aware of the fact.

Vincent and Anna Jarvis lived at Greystones with the eccentric and increasingly remote old man for two years. His presence in the austere house was so unapparent that Anna never felt that she was living with her father-in-law. There were no feelings of intimidation, inhibition. She felt completely at ease – at home – in her new home; after a childhood and adolescence of poverty and endless economising, she relished this fine and somewhat grand English house. The time passed quickly. Anna spent several hours a week improving her already adequate knowledge of the English language. She bought books and read and wrote and asked her husband, when he wasn't painting, to be her teacher. She helped Mrs Wakefield to clean the many rooms, all the time chatting to her; she helped Mrs Sutton in the kitchen, all the time chatting to her. How the two domestics felt about the lady of the house infiltrating their domain, she didn't care nor did she find out. In the spring and summer, she spent hours walking in the woods and hills surrounding her home. And, of course, she sat for her husband, whose joy it was to draw outlines of her beautiful face and paint her in pastel because that was how he thought of her. His pale, pastel, perfect Dutch wife.

In the autumn of 1947, Vincent's father became victim to cancer of the pancreas and died in his room at dusk one Sunday evening. The tragedy was that he had been dead for four hours before anyone knew. Anna discovered the cold, stiffening body lying in the lumpy old bed when she tentatively went to ask him if he'd like to eat a light tea. She received a slight shock but nothing more; no tears were shed, no heart was broken. Nor were any tears shed at the funeral, which took place in Heaton Brow church a week later. There were four mourners. Mr and Mrs Vincent Jarvis; Mrs Betty Wakefield, the deceased's cleaning lady of many years; and Mrs Irene Sutton, the deceased's cook of as equally many years. Mr Mackley, the gardener of two years, had been unable to accept the invitation. The reading of Thomas Jarvis's last will and testament was a very simple affair. Vincent and Anna were required to attend the offices of Messrs Heptonstall, Dunn and Jones in Parliament Street, Harrogate, where they discovered that Vincent's father had bequeathed the young couple, whom he knew so little and seemed to care even less about, his entire estate and what was left of his fortune after all necessary outgoings had been finalised.

A long period of mourning would have been hypocritical. The old man had lived his life as he'd wanted to live it with little thought for those who loved and needed him. He died as he probably intended to, alone and with no one dancing attendance at his bedside. If, lying in his grave in the ancient churchyard, he thought his small family was grieving, he would have scorned them. The atmosphere of Greystones changed almost overnight. The new owners sold some of the older, formal and stark furniture and replaced it with modern, bright and homely items. Vincent was eager to completely renovate the 'museum' but Anna wouldn't hear of it. It would have been an absolute sin to destroy the history and grandeur of Greystones and, therefore, the basic style, structure and essence of the building remained. Now, however, there was light, there was warmth, and there was the constant and welcome sound of laughter.

Their first child arrived in 1951 when Anna and Vincent were beginning to despair of ever becoming parents. The baby boy was plump and blond, the latter quality inherited from his mother. Both parents were delighted that their firstborn was a male, and Vincent showered his 'clever little wife' with flowers, Champagne and the promise that their son would have a Dutch forename. Anna refused.

'Our son is going to be a British citizen – and anyway, a Dutch name would sound ridiculous with Jarvis.' She smiled, relaxing against the soft white pillow, and she told her husband to choose a good, solid English name. Vincent didn't consider himself a connoisseur of good, solid names, English or otherwise. His going through the alphabet didn't get very far.

'Brian,' he announced. 'A good, solid, no-nonsense English name.'

Brian was thenceforward the centre of their world. A blond-haired, grey-eyed little minx; a minx who could do no wrong. Whatever Brian wanted, Brian got. Wherever Brian wanted to go, Brian went. By the time Brian was three years old, Anna had devoted almost every second of every day to his needs and desires, at the renunciation of her own social life. Anna had never worked outside the home but she'd always enjoyed participating in the household chores, and had occasionally done voluntary work for the elderly or infirm who lived in the neighbourhood. Among the many rewards of these services was the knowledge that she was improving her abilities in the English language. Now, she decided, it was time to reinstate herself in society, maybe even enrolling as a registered voluntary worker in the Harrogate district in order that she could render services to the needy further afield.

It became necessary, therefore, to search for a resident nanny and, after much heart-searching and hair-tearing, one was found. Miss Frances Duke, a highly qualified and experienced lady of that profession, moved into Greystones in April 1954. But Brian wasn't keen on his nanny and at the beginning of May 1954, she had to go. Brian was delighted.

Unfortunately for him, however, the next female to become resident at Greystones wasn't to be so easily got rid of.

When Brian was four years old and king of the castle, Anna gave birth to her second and final child, a very welcome daughter.

'She's the most beautiful, perfect baby in the world,' Vincent pronounced, once more providing flowers and Champagne. 'Her name is Anna.'

'No, it is not,' Anna firmly contradicted, cuddling and stroking the newborn. 'This time, I'm going to choose our baby's name. She will be called Melanie.'

An old and well-worn copy of *Gone with the Wind* was lying on her bedside table and Vincent smiled indulgently at his wife.

When Brian Jarvis was introduced to his new sister, his enthusiasm left a lot to be desired. He didn't want a sister, he told his gently cajoling parents. He didn't want anyone else in the house. No nannies, no sisters, nobody. They must send her back. But they couldn't send Melanie back, of course. Brian's baby sister was here to stay.

*

It didn't happen overnight; it was a slow, gradual process. The not answering when Brian asked a question and Melanie was being attended to. The ignoring when Brian wanted to talk to Mummy and Daddy and Melanie was being attended to. The gentle pushing away, the being told to 'Go play now, there's a good boy'. The unprecedented smacks and hard tongues for mischievousness that he'd previously got away with. When Melanie was being attended to.

Brian started school when he was five years old. This was appreciated because he could escape from his sister for nearly a whole day, and at the small select village school he came into his own. Although plump as a baby, Brian was a sturdy but slim little boy and tall for his age, so other children had to look up to him. And not only physically. He was determined in his own childlike way that if he was getting his nose pushed out at home, he'd be kingpin in the classroom. And so, he was. He was a clever boy with a lively mind and a high capacity for learning. As the years went by, he excelled in most subjects, and in those where he was less than perfect, he made up for it with a glib and witty repartee in class. A repartee that earned him admiration from his peers and a grudging kind of respect from his teachers. In the playground and in later years on the sports field, he also reigned supreme. If his love of attention and esteem was not being realised at home, he certainly made up for it elsewhere.

Vincent and Anna, meanwhile, unwittingly poured all their attention and adoration on to the fortunate little Melanie. There were times when they seemed to forget that they had a son and how much their firstborn had once meant to them. But Melanie was such a beautiful infant that nobody could help doting on her – could they? Petite, with long, shining blonde hair normally worn in pigtails; big blue eyes just like her mother's; soft, rosy cheeks. Usually dressed in short frilly dresses, ribbons and pure white ankle socks. The epitome of perfect little girlhood.

Everyone loved little Melanie except Brian, her brother. Brian was totally indifferent to her childish, coquettish charms. When Melanie played up to him, as she played up to all her acquaintances, he snubbed her. At first, the idolised little Melanie was stunned and hurt and bewildered. She didn't understand. She tried again. And again. She endeavoured to make Brian, her beloved older brother, talk to her, play with her, cuddle her. But Brian wouldn't talk, wouldn't play, and certainly wouldn't cuddle. Brian closed his ears, turned his back, pushed her away. Over the years, as Melanie tried and tried again to win her sibling's attention and approval, her initial shock turned to pain and finally to an equal feeling of animosity. Melanie was adored by everyone except the one person she ached to be adored by. Her older brother.

*

In May 1970, Vincent and Anna Jarvis celebrated their silver wedding anniversary. Twenty-five years of married life. Twenty-five years of almost perfect togetherness. Where had those years gone? Their children, Brian and Melanie, were nineteen and fifteen years old respectively and quite of an age to be left alone for a week, Vincent decided, while he took his wife away to celebrate. Where should he take her? he asked his children, after swearing them to secrecy. This was to be a surprise for Anna, who was in Harrogate on one of her voluntary work missions that evening.

'You obviously have to go somewhere very romantic, Daddy!' Melanie grinned, hugging her knees as she curled up in one of the deep, comfortable armchairs. 'I think he ought to take Mummy abroad, don't you, Brian?'

Brian, lounging on one of the three sofas, stifled a yawn and shrugged.

'Why should they go abroad? Just because you've got fancy ideas about travelling doesn't mean to say that's what Mum wants. Knowing her, she'd prefer a weekend up in the Dales, at a good hotel ...'

Melanie giggled, thoroughly enjoying the cloak and dagger element of the conversation and secretly wishing she could go, too. Especially if they were going abroad.

'You're not very romantic, are you, Brian? I'm *so* glad I won't be spending my wedding anniversaries with you.'

Brian glared at his sister across the room and watched the evening sunlight playing on her lovely young face. He had to admit she had a lovely face.

'Well, I can't imagine *anyone* wanting to spend his anniversary with you, Melanie, dear, because I can't imagine *anyone* wanting to marry you.'

He saw the hurt in her eyes and quietly congratulated himself. She cut no ice with him, the spoilt, silly little brat.

Vincent stood up, sighed and rubbed his thin, lined face. They were at it again; he was sick and tired of the constant bickering and feuding between his two kids. They weren't normal. He was convinced they weren't normal. All siblings quarrelled at times, he knew that, and especially at their difficult ages. But not as often and as bitterly as this pair. And it was Brian who was always at the bottom of it; Brian who should have known better. Melanie couldn't open her mouth without the lad jumping down her throat, pulling her up, tearing her to pieces. And, naturally, Melanie bit back, defended herself. But Brian always had an answer ready – and so it went on. Vincent was bewildered, and so was Anna. Why, for God's sake, did their two children always behave so abominably to each other?

'Maybe it's not such a good idea to spring a surprise on your mum,' Vincent murmured, wanting to close the subject and flee from the room. 'I think I'll ask her how she'd like to celebrate and take it from there.'

I don't think it's such a good idea to leave you two alone together, either, he could have added. But he kept that thought to himself.

Vincent left the room and was immediately followed by Brian, leaving

Melanie curled up alone in her chair. She sat for a long time staring out of the window, wondering why Brian had always been so hostile, so mean to her. She wished she didn't care but she did. And the caring that had once made her cry and feel humiliated and love him all the more was slowly changing, developing into a fight for her own self-respect and a mutual feeling of aggression towards the brother she had once loved so deeply. She watched the sun slowly sinking on the horizon and choked back her frustrated tears.

*

The same evening, alone in their bedroom, Vincent watched Anna brushing her short, still-lustrous blonde hair in front of the dressing-table mirror. His love and admiration of her had not diminished in any way since the day he first saw her in her native city. If anything, their years of married togetherness, with all its ups and downs, had helped to increase his feelings for his much-cherished wife. Twenty-five years already.

'Anna, you know that in two weeks you will have put up with and made me a very happy man for twenty-five years? I *know*, I can't believe it, either. And I want us to do something ... go somewhere very special to celebrate. I want you to choose. Anywhere in the world that takes your fancy. Do you want to think about it and let me know later?'

Vincent had started to undress and was hanging his suit up in his side of the walk-in wardrobe.

'I don't need to think about it, Vincent. I know where I'd like to go. And it's not a million miles away from here.'

Vincent turned round, curious.

'I'd love you to take me to the Old Windmill. You know the chic, supposedly exquisite restaurant in Harrogate? I've heard so much about it and we've never been there ...'

'But why on earth haven't you said something before? Of course we can go to the Old Windmill .... We don't have to wait until our wedding anniversary to do that. We'll have dinner there next weekend, and you can think about a trip for our silver wedding ... Paris, Rome ... Lake Baikal. Wherever's your heart's desire, my darling.'

Anna smiled up at him as he walked across the room and kissed her shoulder.

'The Old Mill is honestly my heart's desire for our celebration, Vincent. I don't want to go on any long trips with all the hassle that's involved. Just a good meal in a beautiful place, lots of candles and soft music and it will be very romantic. Thank you. And as it's our wedding anniversary,' Anna took hold of his hand, 'why don't we make it a family affair? Why don't we take Brian and Melanie along? I'm sure they'll—'

Vincent pulled his hand away from her shoulder and turned away. No, he told her, this was *their* wedding anniversary, no one else's, and that included their children. *And I don't want our special evening to be ruined*, he added to himself.

Their silver wedding anniversary was also their last anniversary. On their way home from an idyllic evening at the Old Windmill, a drunken driver coming home from a night out in Leeds hit their car head-on at the crossroads in Heaton Brow. Anna, sitting in the passenger seat, was killed instantly. Vincent spent several months in the hospital in Harrogate at the end of which time he insisted on returning to Greystones, the bottom half of his body not working. His heart had also stopped functioning.

Needless to say, Vincent needed twenty-four-hour medical attention. A private residential nurse named Margaret Farrar moved into Greystones and proved to be a warm-hearted, humorous woman as well as efficient. Margaret was happy, in her middle-aged spinsterhood and solitude, to dedicate the rest of her working life to the needs of the handicapped Mr Jarvis. Unfortunately, however, Margaret's presence wasn't enough to cope with the now undesirable circumstances at Greystones. There was no lovely, lively, willing and very capable Anna to run the rambling old house. Vincent called both his children to his now solitary bedroom where he sat up in the double bed, his head propped against several pillows, his face lined and bitter.

'Well, sit down, the pair of you. Don't stand there like two sentries. What? I didn't hear what you said … well, bring that wicker chair over to the bed, Brian, frame yourself for once. No, Melanie, don't sit on the bed, for God's sake, you know I don't like that, it … Brian … fetch a chair for your sister out of one of the guest rooms … Melanie, I need more water in this jug. Ask Margaret to fill it up for me, will you? Well, get on with it, don't just stand there like …'

When Vincent's desires had been granted and Margaret had left the room, there was a brief silence while the siblings waited for their father to speak. His head moved slowly from side to side, in an effort to look at both his children sitting on either side of his bed; to give them equal attention.

'Right, Melanie ... Brian. Your mother is no longer with us, she's no longer here to run the house and look after me, the damn useless invalid that I've become. Margaret, as you both know, is a good woman and efficient, in her own way. But that's not enough. Greystones is a big house; it's my home and I'm determined to end my days here. And you're my children and I'm going to need you. You're going to have to get your act together, the pair of you, and help as much as you can in the house. I don't want to employ any more women; one stranger in the house is more than enough. No more Mrs Wakefields and Mrs Suttons – your mother cooked and cleaned and looked after us far better than that pair ever did. So, I've decided – and I don't want any arguments – that Margaret will be my nurse and maybe help a bit in the kitchen but I want you two, my son and my daughter, around me, working together to keep our family and Greystones in the manner ... What I'm saying is, if either of you have any fancy ideas of moving away, finding jobs anywhere but in Harrogate, finding places of your own to live in ... please forget them. Now. I need you and I want ... expect you to take care of me and our home until I join your mother in Heaton Brow churchyard.'

The colour had drained from Brian's face and his knuckles were white as he grasped the arms of the green wicker chair.

'Well, that's a bit much, Dad. There's nothing I can do around the house that Margaret and Melanie can't, is there? I work all hours God sends during the day and I have to travel around the country, as you know. And this is just the beginning. I'll be spending a lot of time away from home in the future, travelling on a more regular basis. So, I do what I can now and I always will, but you can't expect any more from *me*. My work's important and so's the salary. I'm afraid it's up to Melanie to prove what a good little *hausfrau* she can be.'

Melanie, sitting on Vincent's left, was studying her nails, or rather the colour of the new varnish she'd painted on that morning. She slowly lifted her head and her eyes held Brian's across the bed.

'What do you mean "*hausfrau*"? What are you talking about?'

'It's German, Melanie. *Hausfrau*. Housewife, stay-at-home wife, or in your case, stay-at-home daughter. So, if you really want to work when you leave school in July, you'll have to find something in the village. A job that's

76

not too demanding so you can concentrate on being the housekeeper at Greystones, and you can spend most of your time with Dad. You'll enjoy that, won't you, Melanie? Daddy's girl.'

Melanie glared at her brother and a furious flush appeared on her cheeks. She looked pleadingly at her father.

'He's not serious, is he, Daddy? You wouldn't expect me to stay at home with you, would you? You don't need me. You said that Margaret's efficient, and the house—'

'We can't expect Margaret to do everything,' Vincent snapped. 'It's not her home. But it is yours. Ours. And you know how hard your mum used to work ... No, of course I won't expect you to stay at home all day but as Brian says ... A nice little part-time job in the village. Maybe something at the Heaton Brow Arms a few hours a week, just to get you out and about, meeting people ...'

'Out and about and meeting people in the Heaton Brow Arms! You've got to be joking! Daddy, you know what I want to do, don't you? You know how much I want to go to London and maybe ... train to be a model. I know it's not easy work to get into but at least I can try. I've written to loads of agencies and sent all those photos you took last year ... and I've even sent a photo of the painting you did when ...' Her voice was rising now, pleading; there were tears ready to fall down her red cheeks. 'Oh, Daddy, you know how much I want to travel, see the world ...'

Vincent squeezed his daughter's hand, lying back on his pillows, and closed his eyes. What Brian said made sense. His career was just beginning and he'd already made an impression in the company. In fact, he was coming on in leaps and bounds, making a bit of a name for himself, as well as earning a decent salary. And he was young; the future looked bright and rewarding. No. Brian couldn't be expected to sacrifice a career for the sake of a handicapped father and the needs of a rambling old house. He was being selfish. Melanie, on the other hand, was a very different kettle of fish. She had no career to think of and, as far as Vincent was concerned, this modelling idea wasn't even worth thinking about ... She was a beautiful kid but he didn't like the idea of his daughter earning her living through her face and her ... her body. It didn't seem right somehow; it seemed cheap, lowly work and not worthy of his daughter. He'd prefer her to do some voluntary work, like her mother before her, or give a helping hand in the local hotel; something at least worthwhile ... not flaunting her face and figure off to the world and his wife. If she wanted to show off her good looks, he could still paint her; there was nothing wrong with his hands. And as for travelling the world, which he knew had always been her big ambition – well, there'd be plenty of time for that when he, Vincent, was lying under the ground, beside his wife. Anyway, he wanted his daughter, his Melanie, to stay here with him; to be there when he needed her; to look after him, as a daughter should … He turned and smiled at Melanie and gently took her hand.

'You know I'm not going to live for ever, my darling daughter. Nor do I want to, not like this.' His arm swept the bedclothes and the lower part of his body. 'I would just like you to be as close to me as possible until your mum and I can be together again. And then you'll be as free as the proverbial bird.'

Melanie knew she was trapped. She looked from the quiet, passive face of her father – the post-accident irascibility temporarily absent – and into the mocking eyes of her brother. She knew he was rejoicing. She burst into tears and ran out of the room. Ten minutes later, Brian left his father's bedside, walked along the corridor and opened his sister's bedroom door, without knocking. He looked down at her, lying on her bed, her damp blonde hair covering her face, her young body heaving with sobs.

'Dad's so pleased that you're giving up your life to look after him, Melanie. And the house, which really does need a *hausfrau*. He's very, very grateful to you.'

Melanie sat up and stared at her brother. Even now, she couldn't believe that Brian could be so cruel, so vindictive. Brian, her own brother. Brian, whom she'd once idolised.

'What about *you* giving up your life, Brian? What about *you* looking after Daddy and Greystones and giving up *your* wonderful career?'

Brian grinned at her before turning away and quietly closing the door behind him.

'I'm not sacrificing my life for anybody,' he laughed. 'Not even our dad. And, as for my career, well, I really don't think William Kaye International could function without me, now.'

Chapter Seven

Melanie saw the postcard as soon as she walked into the kitchen. Margaret had propped it up against the cereal boxes on the worktop, ready for breakfast. She picked it up. Cairo. She turned it over.

Cairo, Sunday, 2nd September, 1973. Arrived here yesterday morning and am staying in super hotel in city centre. At the moment, sitting in a restaurant and trying to keep cool. Start work tomorrow and afterwards will do some sightseeing. Pyramids first. Brian.

Melanie tore the card into four pieces and dropped it on the floor. Cairo. Three months ago, it had been California, and this time last year, he'd travelled around Europe. This should be her, Melanie Jarvis, bombing around the world, sending blasé little postcards to the 'folks back home'. Instead, she *was* the folks back home and she had been for two years. Two bloody years; she couldn't believe it. Two years stuck in this mausoleum with an increasingly difficult-to-please invalid father and a taciturn, goody-two-shoes nurse for company. And a brother who came home when he felt like it. Two years cooking, cleaning, keeping house and trying her best to care about her once-beloved daddy. She'd had jobs, of course, in those two years. Jobs that had kept her close to home; helping out behind the bar and in the kitchen at the Heaton Brow Arms; running errands for housebound or lazy women in the village and not getting paid, either. How her mother had put up with it all those years, Melanie would never understand. Jobs that drove her round the bend and that she either lost or resigned from. Now she didn't see the need to work, not unless she was doing what she really wanted to do. And there was no chance of that, was there? Not yet. But one day, one day… She still hadn't given up that girlhood dream. Her eyes fell upon the pieces of postcard where she had dropped them. Her feelings for her brother had changed very gradually over the last two years. While he was globetrotting and making money for himself and William Kaye International, she was a prisoner in her own home. She hated him, despised him. Her deepening frustrations were slowly swelling into enmity towards the human race in general, but in particular towards the brother whose love and admiration she had once craved.

*

'I've never seen anything so magnificent.'

Brian carefully put his Pentax back into its case and turned to Mr El Sayed, his Egyptian client and host, standing on his right. The sun was blazing and Brian had had enough; he was beginning to feel sickly and feverish and was ready to go home. He'd seen all the sights, taken God knows how many photographs, spent a hell of a lot of William Kaye's generous expenses and willingly accepted Mr El Sayed's continued hospitality. But two weeks was enough. He'd clinched three big sales and now he was ready for some English beer, English women and even some English rain.

'Come,' said his client, politely guiding Brian to his British-made car standing on the road winding to the Great Pyramid, 'I will take you back to your hotel. Will you dine there this evening?'

Brian turned to take a last look at the three pyramids outlined against the most beautiful sunset he'd ever seen. He just hoped he'd captured it on film and his new, specially purchased camera wouldn't let him down. He had to have photographs to display at home.

'Yes, I'll be eating at the hotel this evening, Mr El Sayed, but I know the food won't be as good as what your wife cooks. My flight leaves at eight o'clock tomorrow morning so I must go to bed at a reasonable time.'

'Of course, Mr Jarvis, you must rest well. It is very important.'

On the way back from Giza to Cairo, the Egyptian offered to drive Brian to the airport the following morning. Brian refused as graciously as possible without offending. This chap seemed to want to spend twenty-four hours a day with him and it was getting to be a strain, to say the least. He was desperate to have a bit of a rest in his own company. Anyway, Mr El Sayed had been useful, showing him around, introducing him to the right people, buying £25,000 worth of industrial sewing machines for his new factory. Sam Morrison would be glowing.

Back in his hotel room, after a much-needed shower – God, he needed to shower every hour in this country – he lay naked on his single bed for a while before dinner and re-read the telex from Sam, which had arrived at the factory that morning.

Report to office on arrival in Harrogate. Hopeful new client in Sofia, Bulgaria. Prepare to depart next week. Sam.

Brian sank back against his pillow and closed his eyes. Great, but I hope the old bugger'll give me a couple of days off before I leave ... he fell asleep.

*

Sam Morrison didn't give him any days off. Brian arrived at Greystones late on Sunday evening and he was in the office at eight o'clock on Monday morning. He hadn't seen anyone at home but they'd know he was back because he'd left a note on the kitchen table.

Sam beamed when Brian walked into the export department.

'Come in, lad, sit down. Joan, please make our wonder boy a cup o' your special coffee an' I'll have tea. By God, lad, you've done well, you've really got what it takes, I'll say that. Twenty-five thousand quid ... I was staggered when I read yer telex. When do they expect these machines?'

'Within three months.'

'That's cuttin' it a bit fine, lad.'

'I promised.'

'Then it shall be done. 'Ow were Egypt?'

'Bloody hot.'

'Well, you can cool down in Bulgaria. Yer goin' tomorrow night.'

'What! Tomorrow night? What the hell, Sam, I'm knackered ...'

'An' so will this sale be if you don't go. I'm relyin' on you, Brian. Wonder Boy.'

Sam winked and Brian groaned.

*

Melanie felt much older than her eighteen years and thanked God she didn't look it. In spite of the monotonous, soul-destroying life she was leading, she had managed to preserve her good looks, even though every time she gazed in the mirror, she expected to see a different face looking back. An older, less attractive, bitter face. Because Melanie was bitter. She hadn't always felt this way; it had been a slow process. A combination of prolonged anger and frustration at what she thought of as her life sentence. She could take off, she supposed; pack her bags and

81

make a new life for herself. But what with? She had no money of her own and, of course, she couldn't ask her father for money; not for what she wanted it for. And she couldn't run away on thin air. Anyway, where could she go and who with? Over the past two years her few schoolfriends had slowly drifted out of her life; gone their own, more exciting ways. There was nobody in her life she could call a special friend, nobody she could have a heart-to-heart chat with, whose shoulder she could cry on. Nobody. Margaret goody-two-shoes didn't count. She'd almost forgotten what it was like to have a giggle with a girlfriend. And as for boyfriends, what were they? Would she ever know what it was like to have a relationship with the opposite sex? Oh, she'd met young blokes when she was barmaiding at the Arms, but she wouldn't have looked twice at any of them. She'd only been polite because she had to. Melanie walked again to the long wardrobe mirror in her room and studied her semi-naked body. She was beautiful; she knew she was beautiful. But she also knew that her beauty was being totally wasted. Oh yes, Melanie was beginning to feel very, very bitter.

There was a knock at the door.

'Melanie, dear, it's Margaret. Your daddy wants to know why you're not having breakfast with him. Aren't you feeling well? he's asking. And there's a postcard from Brian.'

The nurse's voice trailed away. Melanie sighed, not really wanting breakfast but knowing she'd have to visit her dad's room and talk and listen to him. He was like a leech. Over the last couple of years, he'd become more and more like a leech, clinging to and sucking the life out of her. She slowly dressed in jeans and a blue sweater and brushed her long blonde hair over her shoulders. A postcard from Brian – Margaret announced it as though it was a major event. And it wasn't. It was regular, customary, normal to receive postcards from Brian. This one would be from Bulgaria. She sighed again and felt a stab of something deep inside her. Jealousy. Plain, simple, ugly jealousy.

Vincent was propped up against his pillows, a tray in front of him, when Melanie walked into his room. He looked at her reproachfully; there was no smile or light in his eyes to show his pleasure at seeing her. He transferred his gaze to the food in front of him.

'I was beginning to think you'd fallen out with me.'

Melanie didn't reply. Brian's postcard was lying on the blue silk eiderdown at the side of the breakfast tray. Melanie sat down, helped herself to toast and coffee and chose to ignore the childish, silly reprimand. Neither of them spoke for several moments and it was Vincent who finally broke the silence.

'Brian seems to be having a good time. Difficult client, though, he says. Not as amiable as that Egyptian chap.'

Melanie continued to munch her toast. She didn't offer to reply or look at the postcard.

'Well, go on, love, read what your brother has to say. It's meant for both of us, you know.'

Oh, for God's sake ... She picked it up and scrutinised it. Yes, Brian was having a good time. Her eyes wandered to the window at the far side of the long room and for a while she watched the early October rain. She shivered.

'What are we going to do today, Melanie? Have you got anything planned for us?'

Vincent was almost smiling at her, but his indulgent father's smile had long since disappeared. It was a don't-you-feel-sorry-for-me kind of smile these days, and Melanie could never respond to it because she was too busy feeling sorry for herself. She didn't find it easy to smile very much at all anymore, and their conversations were more often than not a strain. And then Melanie felt riddled with guilt – it wasn't her father's fault, not really. He deserved better treatment than this. But she couldn't help it; she really couldn't. It was something deep inside her; jealousy, frustration, resentment. She picked up the postcard again. Brian did it on purpose. He didn't have to send postcards from business trips; it was his idea of rubbing salt into her very painful wound. Oh, why did her brother hate her so much? What had she done to deserve this totally miserable existence?

Vincent was still looking at her, eagerly waiting for an answer to his inane question. His breakfast was finished, his medicine taken, and now he expected to be entertained.

'Why don't you listen to the radio for a bit, Dad?' Melanie suggested, 'I've got things to do downstairs. Maybe later ...'

'Aw, listen to the radio! I'm fed up of listening to the radio, I want company. I want *your* company, Melanie. I want you to sit next to me and talk to me and ... Can't you understand that?'

Her father's thin, trembling hand groped for hers and she swallowed repulsion as she took hold of it.

She'd had the same response when she had suggested that he draw, sketch, paint ...

I'm fed up of ... I want your company.

'Okay, Dad, I'll take these things downstairs, do the washing-up and then I'll come back.'

'That's my girl.'

The rain splashed on the kitchen windows and tears splashed down Melanie's face as she took her time washing the breakfast dishes.

*

Bulgaria had been exhausting. Hard work without the usual luxuries thrown in. The hotel had been basic to say the least, the nightlife almost nil and the client not very cooperative – and that was putting it all mildly. Brian didn't even know if the extended trip had been worth it; there had been no promise of future correspondence. Sam had warned him it wouldn't be easy but Sam was always open to challenge; he was very much like Brian in a lot of ways. Maybe that's why they got on so well. Brian unfastened his safety belt and stretched his legs as best he could in the cramped space. At least the old bugger hadn't sent him a telex this time, sending him off to more foreign parts.

'Excuse me.'

Brian turned to look at the woman sitting on his left. The 'Excuse me' gave away a foreign accent and one that he couldn't identify. He raised his eyebrows in response but didn't smile at her. The woman indicated an unlit cigarette and, in faltering English, asked if he had a light. He nodded, produced his lighter and looked at her as she sucked on the cigarette. Not bad-looking. Thirty-ish, a good bit older than him. Obviously alone and in need of male company. What the hell, he hadn't spoken to a decent-looking woman for well over a week.

He took the woman – whose name and nationality he never discovered – to a cheap hotel near Heathrow Airport. He told himself it was all he could afford and it was certainly all she was worth. It was all any woman was worth unless William Kaye International was paying. And his expenses had run out. It was ten o'clock on Friday evening when they checked in and eleven o'clock on Saturday morning when they checked out. The woman – was it Nina, Nana, something like that? – had been a natural but when she'd started making noises about going shopping in London and having lunch, he knew it was time to go. He thanked God her English was lousy and he didn't have time to get into any heavy discussions.

'My train leaves King's Cross at twelve o'clock,' he told her, and jumped into a very convenient taxi outside the hotel. Nina, Nana, whatever, stood on the pavement; a mixed look of confusion, distress and anger on her face. Well, he'd paid for the hotel, a meal, what more did the little bitch expect? His thin mouth tightened into a grim line and his small grey eyes screwed up. He suddenly felt sick to the stomach. Bitches, lousy bitches, every one of them ...

Chapter Eight

Brian was beginning to get a taste for what he called 'the good life'. The offices of William Kaye International were a stepladder from which he was raised to the dizzy heights of super salesman, globe-trotter and social celebrity. Thanks to the internationally acclaimed organisation, he was able to earn a good income, see the world, meet a variety of interesting people and explore the bodies of a variety of women. In short, he was having the time of his life. His working schedule not only included frequent trips abroad but also visits to companies within the United Kingdom, which meant spending many nights away from home. Sometimes in hotels, more often than not in ladies' apartments. He still claimed his expenses, of course. And he never saw the ladies again. Life was interesting, amusing, exciting.

Which made coming home to Greystones a rather depressing affair. The house itself depressed him. The 'mausoleum' as he'd baptised it. And the memories within its walls; memories of his beautiful, beloved mother; vague memories of his early infancy and memories of his shared childhood … his unhappy childhood … but life at Greystones now depressed him most of all. Although he loved his father and would have wished a more fulfilling, happier life for the elderly man, Brian had no joy in returning to Greystones. And after his trip to Bulgaria, he knew that he wanted and needed to get away. Permanently.

He was far too old to be living at home, anyway, at twenty-two. If he'd gone to university, as both his parents had wished him to do, he would have left home a long time ago. The academic life wasn't for him, however, and in spite of pressure from his family and his school, he'd opted out. He wanted to work, earn a living. And he'd obviously made the right choice. He'd made an early success of his professional life and now it was time to move on in other areas. Starting with the home. And yet a tiny feeling of guilt kept gnawing away at the back of his mind. Why should he feel guilty, for God's sake? He was only thinking of doing what thousands of young blokes his age did all the time. But they didn't have the same background, did they? They didn't have invalid, dependent fathers, and sisters called Melanie.

Melanie. *She* was the reason he felt guilty every time he opened the door on arriving home from Egypt, Bulgaria, France, Skegness, wherever. Her eyes and her increasingly spiteful tongue told him exactly how she felt about him; there was no need to spell it out. She hated him. She hated him because of the life he was leading and the life she was subjected to. She hated and blamed him because all her adolescent hopes and dreams had been crushed and she'd been condemned to a dead life. But somebody had to do it. Somebody had to stay at home, at least some of the time, and look after Dad and the mausoleum. The little brat could have found work if she'd really wanted to; a part-time job in Harrogate. But nothing was good enough for Melanie Jarvis. Melanie Jarvis expected to be on some kind of professional pedestal immediately, top dog – or rather top bitch – going places. Well, tough. If circumstances allowed only one Jarvis sibling to go places, it certainly wasn't going to be her ...

*

He told his father first. Vincent was sitting up in bed reading a hardback novel after a light dinner one Saturday evening. He called 'Come in' when Brian tapped on the door. Brian smiled at the thin, grey-haired-going-thin-on-top man in the bed.

'Hi, Dad,' he said, ambling across the room towards the bed, 'I'd like a word if you're not too interested in your book.'

Vincent smiled thinly and placed a red leather bookmark between the pages.

'I'm always ready for company, Brian. I get little enough of it. What's Melanie doing?'

Brian stiffened.

'She's watching some rubbish on television.'

'Will she be coming up soon?'

'No doubt.'

'Well, I do hope so. So, what did you want to talk about? Will you be going on your travels again?'

Brian cleared his throat.

'You could say that, Dad, yes. In a way. I'm ... erm ... I'm actually thinking of moving out of Greystones. Getting a place of my own.'

Silence except for a thin, blue-veined hand scratching at the eiderdown.

'Getting a place of your own?' When Vincent finally spoke, his voice was small. 'Why's that, Brian?'

'Because I'm ready for it, Dad. I'm not a kid anymore. I think twenty-two is a bit old to be living with ... I'd like my independence to come and go as I please and—'

'Don't you do that now, Brian?'

Yes, but not without being made to feel like a criminal every time I open the bloody door ... But there was no point in mentioning that to Vincent.

'Yes, Dad, but ... anyway, I've made my decision. I'd like a place of my own. I've got to make the move sometime and, as the saying goes, there's no time like the present. And, don't worry, I'll come to see you as often as I can, you know that. And Melanie will always be here, won't she?'

Vincent smiled at the very name.

'Yes, you're right there, Melanie will never leave me. She's a good girl, Brian. A good girl. What would I have done without her? I keep asking myself that, you know. What would I have done without her? My little treasure. My ... my life-enhancer.'

Brian gazed at his father. Even now, he could still make him feel inadequate, not needed, not wanted, surplus to requirements. Vincent continued.

'Well, it looks as though you've made your mind up to leave us. So, when are you thinking of going? Have you got a place fixed up yet?'

Brian slowly shook his head, grateful at least that his father had accepted his proposition.

'No, not yet ... I'm thinking about moving to Leeds...'

'Leeds? Why is that, when your work's in Harrogate?'

'There's a bit more life there,' Brian grinned, 'especially nightlife, and Neil and Linda live there, remember. And it's no distance to travel to the office. I'll just have to get up a bit earlier, won't I?'

Vincent's fingers abandoned the eiderdown and began to stroke his abandoned book and he let out a long, impatient sigh.

'Yes, son, I suppose you will. Close the door behind you when you leave the room, won't you?'

As soon as his son had left the room, Vincent returned to his story. He was so glad it was Brian hoping to flee the nest and not Melanie. He couldn't bear it if his daughter left him now. No, it didn't bear thinking about what would happen to him if Melanie left him now.

His sister was still watching television when Brian walked into the living room. She looked up as he opened the door and her eyes were apathetic. She wordlessly looked back at the screen.

'I've just been having a word with Dad.'

'Bully for you.'

Brian ignored the senseless remark.

'Look, I've made my decision and I'll be leaving home for good very soon. Getting a place of my own – in Leeds. Probably.'

'Leaving home?' Melanie's gorgeous blue eyes tore at his face. 'What do you mean "leaving home"? You left home two years ago, didn't you? You may as well have done for all we see of you. That's a good one ... leaving home.' She paused. 'And will Your Highness be gracing us with your presence after you've left home, Brian?'

'Yes, of course I'll be coming back from time to time. And I'll help you out financially—'

'Oh, big bloody deal!' Melanie was screaming at him now and the tears began to gush down her cheeks.

'And I suppose you'll be sending us your precious postcards and showing us your lousy photos, too? Well, don't bother, Brian, just don't bother. You're not wanted here, anyway. You're not needed and you're not wanted. The sooner you go, the better.'

Her screams subsided and she fled from the room. Brian heard a door slam upstairs. If his father had heard the silly little bitch yelling and slamming doors, he'd want to know what was going on. And it'd be Brian's fault. He closed his eyes, passed a weary hand through his fair hair and sighed. *You're not needed and you're not wanted. The sooner you go, the better.* Melanie was absolutely right. It was time for him to go.

He went to bed before midnight but it was almost dawn before he slept. His brain was busy, trying to plan out his life. He couldn't possibly stay at Greystones any longer; the house itself depressed him and the domestic circumstances nauseated him. His relationship with his father had never been ideal but recently, since the 'old man' had been bedridden, they didn't seem to have anything going for them. And as for Melanie, he literally couldn't wait to get away from her nauseating presence. She'd just have to accept and come to terms with her role in life. Her role at least until their father's death. After that, she could please herself. It was tough on the kid but life *was* tough. Brian already had a career that was blossoming; Melanie had nothing to give up except a lot of fancy dreams. Her whole life was ahead of her; a few years devoted to her dad would do her no harm. On the contrary. Brian tossed and turned and willed sleep to come but it refused. By the time a tentative light sifted through the curtain, Brian had come to a decision. He wasn't going to wait until he'd found a place of his own in Leeds. He had friends in the city who would no doubt put him up, give him lodgings for a while, until he got on his feet. He had to get away from Greystones at the earliest opportunity. For everyone's sake.

*

He left less than a week later. Neil, a lad he'd knocked around with for a while at school, and his wife, Linda, lived in the northern suburbs of Leeds, on Otley Road, and had said yes, they'd be happy to accommodate him in their spare room for a while. No problem. He wasted no time in explaining the new and happy state of affairs to his father and his sister. Vincent Jarvis was lying, as he very occasionally did, on the sofa in the living room, in front of a blazing fire. Melanie, sitting on the floor at his feet, was looking at a fashion magazine. Brian interrupted the not-very-companionable silence.

'Hi,' he said, sitting down in an armchair next to the fire and making a show of rubbing his hands together. 'Well, I've got some good news for you both.'

When he'd finished speaking, Vincent gazed at his son and said,

'I hope this doesn't mean we're never going to see you, Brian.'

Here we go again . . .

'Don't be daft, Dad. Of course you'll be seeing me. I'll come home as often as I can and I'll phone regularly. Out of sight doesn't always mean out of mind.'

Melanie continued turning the pages of her magazine; her eyes had never left its glossy contents.

'And I suppose you'll be sending us postcards from your travels?'

Brian sighed. Off on that old tack again. It was on the tip of his tongue to tell his sister to change the record, but he didn't want to get into any rows, not now. Not at this stage.

'Well, I'll have to keep your collection going, won't I?' he quipped. 'I'll

90

buy you an album for Christmas. Anyway, Dad'll be interested in where I am and what I'm doing, won't you, Dad?'

But there was no response from Dad.

He stood up, saying that he was going to start getting his things together; no time like the present ... Vincent looked up at him.

'You'll let us know as soon as you move into a place of your own, Brian? Send us your address and phone number, won't you?'

'Goes without saying.' Brian grinned briefly but his father's face remained deadpan. Melanie's head was still bent over the fashion pages. 'Right then, I'd better get a move on ...'

Vincent smiled and nodded and asked Melanie if she'd make him a cup of warm milk and honey. He was feeling sleepy and ready for bed when Margaret was ready to take him. His head suddenly fell forward and he began to doze. Brian left the room, noiselessly closing the door behind him. God, would he be glad to get out of this place; this mausoleum.

*

Brian arrived at the large, bay-windowed, semi-detached house on Otley Road on a cold, grey evening in late October. He was warmly welcomed by his old schoolmate Neil Johnson and his wife of six months, Linda. Neil took Brian into the living room and Linda went into the kitchen, to put the kettle on.

'I'm sorry about imposing myself on you both like this,' Brian said as he walked across the room to a chair near the fire. 'I promise it won't be for long. I just had to get away from that mausoleum. It drives me nuts, Neil. And Melanie's like ... like a spoilt kitten with claws that need cutting. Only ever thinks about herself. We couldn't have lived in the same house for much longer without killing each other. She's always been a thorn in my side, you know that. Anyway, I know I'm doing the right thing and I'm just sorry to ...'

'Don't you worry about it. Everything's fine. What's the point in having a spare room if nobody sleeps in it?'

Neil grinned at his friend and his fingers played with the gold rim of his glasses, a habit he'd had ever since Brian could remember. If Neil wore contact lenses, he'd probably try to fondle their frames ...

'I imagine that Melanie's not the easiest person to live with,' Neil was saying, 'but even so, I think it's a shame she's tied to the house like that—'

'She needn't be,' Brian interrupted, 'she could get a suitable job in Harrogate if she put her mind to it and still be able to look after Dad. He doesn't need her there twenty-four hours. His nurse, Margaret, she's more than capable. Look, because of Dad, Melanie doesn't have the choice. She has to live at Greystones, yes, but she could make a life for herself outside. The trouble with her is, she has too many big ideas ..... Modelling, for God's sake, and travelling ... so she thinks because none of that's possible that she can't try anything else. Silly little ... nothing else is good enough for her. Well, life's not a bed of roses and it's time she learnt ...'

The door opened and Linda, plump and smiling, brought in the tea.

'You don't take sugar, Brian, do you? I thought not. There you are. Drink your tea, warm yourself up and then you might as well do your unpacking and sort yourself out. I hope you'll be comfortable in that back room, Brian, it's not very big, you know ... not compared with what you've been used to.'

Brian sipped his tea. If he had to spend the next few weeks in a prison cell, it'd be ecstasy compared with what he'd been used to.

'It'll be champion, Linda. And this tea's like nectar.'

Chapter Nine

It didn't take Brian long to find a place. Within a couple of weeks, he had moved out of Neil and Linda's too homely semi-detached house into a second-floor flat in the swish district of Roundhay, overlooking the large park and its lake. The building itself was a huge Victorian house that stood in its own grounds and that in recent years had been converted into flats and bedsits. Brian saw the advertisement for rooms to let in the Thursday evening edition of the *Yorkshire Evening Post*. He wasted no time in using Neil's phone to call the landlord and make an appointment for the following evening. When the landlord, big-bellied, balding and with three days' growth on his chin, showed him the available accommodation, Brian opted for the vacant flat on the second floor, rather than the attic bedsit – he didn't relish the idea of sharing a bathroom and kitchen. Not after the comparative luxury of Greystones. Christ, it was bad enough having to resort to this. The flat was a decent size (he'd already seen quite a few inferior ones), containing a sparsely but adequately furnished living room, a double bedroom (at least that was in its favour), a kitchenette and a cubby-hole of a bathroom that was clean, if nothing else. However, beggars couldn't be choosers and he had seen a lot worse.

'And how much would you be asking for this?' Brian asked.

The landlord looked him up and down and ran a big, fleshy hand through the remains of his grey and greasy hair. His belly hung loosely over the top of his trousers, the belt of which was unfastened, and his slightly grubby shirt was unbuttoned to the waist. Brian could smell alcohol on his breath. Gin.

'Forty pounds a month inclusive o' rates and you're getting a bargain, lad. You won't find owt else in this area for that price. You can tek it or leave it.'

'I'll take it.'

'Right. When can you move in? I'll want a month's rent in advance.'

'As soon as possible. How about Saturday?'

'That suits me, lad.'

Brian ran his eyes over the lease, scribbled a cheque and followed the landlord downstairs. They walked through an impressive hall filled with plants in brightly coloured pots, an aquarium with brightly coloured fish and rather more sombre oil paintings on the walls. Brian was just about to shake the man's hand and take his leave when the landlord said,

'By the way, this is where me and me missus live – 'ere, on ground floor. An' I'm warnin' you, lad, we don't stand no funny business … you know what I mean, don't you? We don't tek students 'cos they're too bloody noisy, an' we don't tek them what's on dole, either. We like us tenants to be quiet an' respectable an' law-abidin'. We don't stand no nonsense – loud music, shoutin', swearin', annoyin' yer neighbours. D'yer understand, lad? An' if I 'ear any complaints about you, yer out, no questions asked. 'Ave I made mesen' clear? This is a respectable 'ouse an' that's 'ow I want it to stay.'

Brian was annoyed and amused at the same time. He objected to being spoken to as though he were a young thug, but as the landlord seemed such an incongruous character in this set-up, he couldn't help but see the humorous side.

'That's okay, Mr Gaunt.' He managed a laugh. 'I'm that bloody respectable I went to view a bedsit in a monastery last week!'

'I've told you, lad, no swearin'!'

They finally shook hands and Brian climbed into his company car and drove along Harrogate Road and back to the office. He was hoping that Sam hadn't got anything lined up for him before Saturday – the furthest he wanted to travel before the weekend was Leeds – but he needn't have worried. Sam Morrison's office was empty when Brian arrived, and Joan Little greeted him at the door.

'You won't be seeing Sam until next week,' she smiled. 'He's dashed off to France for a few days, an international sales conference in Paris. He was going to send you but decided you had other things on your mind.'

'That's true.'

'And how are you getting on, young man? Have you had any luck in finding a place?'

'Yeah, I've found a great little flat in Roundhay and I'll be moving in on Saturday. Will you be coming to my housewarming orgy, Joan?'

He winked at the middle-aged woman; she declined with thanks and a blush and he belted her backside as she walked past him with an armful of files.

94

'You'll be sorry, Joan, you don't know what you're missing.'
Oh, but I do, Joan shuddered, *that's why I won't be coming.*

*

A flat-warming orgy wouldn't be a bad idea, Brian mused on the Saturday evening, sitting alone in the barely furnished sitting room. There was no television, of course, and Brian hadn't thought to buy a radio as yet. The large old house was silent and Brian was beginning to feel morose and rather claustrophobic between the high and austere, silent walls. Yes, a few mates, a few drinks, music ... but not yet. There was no point in upsetting old Mr Gaunt; he'd get his feet under the table before he started taking liberties. Instead of organising an orgiastic party, he spent his weekend discovering the area he'd moved to; the local shops, the pubs and the spacious, pretty park. And he spent Sunday evening discovering Mary Gaunt. His landlady.

It hadn't been a warm Sunday by any means and as Brian wasn't one for enjoying too much of his own company for too long, he sauntered back to the flat in the late afternoon, fed up to the back teeth. He hadn't a clue what to do with himself that evening; he'd thought about giving Neil and Linda a ring but decided against it. He didn't want them to think him a nuisance. He might have to be a nuisance one day, if things in the new homestead didn't work out ... besides, he ought to have an early night, ready to give William Kaye International his best on Monday morning. Mary Gaunt was coming down the staircase and Brian, his mind on other things, almost collided with her.

'Good evening,' the woman smiled, and Brian immediately felt something stir inside him. Well, if this was his landlady and neighbour, he wasn't complaining ... Knowing his luck, she'd be visiting some other lucky sod.

'Let me guess, you're Mr Jarvis in Flat 2D. Our newest tenant.'

Brian grinned and held out his hand. They were now sharing the same step and the woman leant against the banister to support herself.

'I'm Mary Gaunt. Joe, my husband, said you were moving in yesterday. I hope you'll be very happy living here, Mr Jarvis. I must introduce you to some of our other tenants.'

Sod the other tenants ... how come Joe Gaunt, that bloated, balding, gin-reeking slob had managed to catch a prize like this? It must be his bank balance; either that or what he had inside his pants. Mary Gaunt was at least fifteen years younger than her husband. Tall, slim with honey-blonde hair that fell to her shoulders. She wore a lot of make-up, including painted-on eyebrows, but it suited her, enhanced her natural good looks. And her figure ... Brian wanted to get his hands on her, and the sooner the better. So much for the caricature landlady with her hair permanently in curlers under a net, a 'pinny' and the ubiquitous fag dangling from her mouth. The type of woman he'd have expected Joe Gaunt to be married to. He smiled at his landlady as she continued down the stairs, heading towards her home on the ground floor.

'I'd like to meet some of my neighbours, Mrs Gaunt, if you'd like to introduce me. I don't know many people in Leeds, and certainly not round here. It could get a bit lonely ...'

'Oh, you won't be lonely living here, Mr Jarvis.' Mary smiled and wrinkled her nose and Brian's body felt like melted butter. 'I'll see to that.'

*

Mary Gaunt was as good as her word. Brian was fixing his stereo unit later that evening, preparing to listen to a couple of albums followed by an early night, when there was a soft knock at his door. He jumped because it was so unexpected. Mary was standing in front of him, a friendly smile on her face, a bottle of red wine in her hand and the briefest of garments on her body.

'I know it sounds terribly corny, Mr Jarvis, but Joe's gone away on business for a few days so I thought it would be an ideal opportunity for us to get to know each other.'

She was right. It was corny. But Brian wasn't complaining. He took the proffered bottle of claret and told his unexpected but very welcome guest to sit down. She opted for the two-seater sofa rather than the single straight-backed chair. So, it *was* Joe's bank balance ... can't have been what he had inside his pants.

They talked for half an hour after which time Brian began to get bored. Mary Gaunt might be a stunner but she didn't have much on top; Joe must have married her for what she had inside *her* pants ... He stifled a yawn, put his empty glass down and turned to the woman sitting next to him. She smiled up at him and suddenly seemed like a silly, simpering schoolgirl.

What the hell had he thought about her half an hour before? He must have been mad. She was a female and all females were the same. No matter what they looked like, where they came from; underneath, they were all the same. Spoilt, silly bitches.

Mary's eyes weren't looking so good now. All that make-up was beginning to smudge and the wine had caused tiny, tentacle-like red veins to show on her cheeks. Brian suddenly couldn't bear to look at her. It was time for action. He slipped his right arm around her almost naked shoulder and, of course, there was no rebuff. He hadn't expected one. This was going to be so very, very easy. But weren't they all the same? After they had ravaged one another's bodies twice in the less-than-comfortable bed, Brian had had enough. He wanted rid of her. He felt physically satisfied, replete; it was very late and he had to be up early. But Mary Gaunt was in no hurry to go. She didn't like sleeping alone in their flat on the ground floor; she had a vivid imagination ... She looked imploringly at Brian with bloodshot eyes and he sighed. So, she was planning to stay the night. He shifted to a more comfortable position. So, he'd probably be late for work tomorrow. So what? It didn't happen often and Sam was in France ... he might as well make the most of this golden opportunity. Even if the lady was a tramp.

Joe Gaunt returned home from his trip on the same day that Sam Morrison returned from his, and this was a blessing in disguise in more ways than one. It put the insatiable Mrs Gaunt out of action for a while and it eventually sent Brian to Europe for several weeks. He paid his rent in advance for two months, sneaked a sullen kiss from his sulking landlady and gratefully disappeared for almost two months. He was looking forward to this trip. Sam had been busy at the international sales conference; he certainly hadn't wasted any of his time. There were new clients to visit in France, Cologne and the Scandinavian countries. Oh yes, he was looking forward to this trip. He intended to make the most of it, businesswise and otherwise. If he made all the sales he hoped to, he'd be able to live off his commission for several weeks and it'd keep him in Sam Morrison's good books, where he intended to be kept. And as far as 'otherwise' was concerned, he always enjoyed the food and wine in France, German beer was excellent and he'd heard a lot about Swedish women ... If everything went as planned, he'd be exhausted by the time he got home. Just in time for the Christmas break. He was actually ready for a break now; Christ, he'd be more than ready at the end of this trip. And then he suddenly thought about Greystones. He hadn't had the time to visit but he'd made a couple of phone calls, duty calls, just to make sure things were ticking over. Over the last few days, however, owing to his heavy workload and his illicit evenings with Mrs Gaunt, Greystones, and all who lived in her, hadn't entered his head. He really ought to pay a visit before he left the country but there simply wouldn't be time. He'd have to phone instead. Another duty call.

A telephone hadn't been installed in his flat yet. The local public phone box had been vandalised so that evening he went downstairs to beg the use of Joe Gaunt's personal phone. Joe Gaunt made a point of neither allowing tenants to make calls on his phone, nor to receive them. And he certainly wouldn't take messages. But he made an exception with Brian Jarvis. He liked the lad, the little he knew of him. He was quiet, clean-living, reliable with the rent.

'Aye, lad, I suppose you can use me phone this once. As long as you don't make a habit of it.'

Brian followed Joe into his apartment. The living room was large and square and the telephone stood on a glass-topped low table by the window. Mary was also in the living room, watching television. She glared at her young lover as he strode across the room. She neither spoke to nor smiled at him. His recently written cheque for £80.00 was lying on the coffee table in front of the gas fire, next to a large bottle of Gordon's gin and two half-empty glasses. Brian dialled the number and it was Melanie who eventually answered.

'Hello, it's me. Brian. How are things?'

There was a lengthy pause and then his sister's voice came down the line, loud and clear.

'Oh well, seeing as you ask, the house has burnt down, Dad's been dead over a week, Margaret's been raped at gunpoint and I've just taken an overdose. Apart from that, everything's fine.'

The blood started to pound in Brian's head.

'Look, you sarcastic little bitch …' He remembered where he was. 'Melanie, I'm going to Europe and I'll be away for about two months.' He was trying to keep his voice down. 'I'm just checking to make sure everything's okay before I leave tomorrow.'

'Oh, are you now? And if everything isn't okay, what are you going to do about it before tomorrow?'

'For God's sake, look, Melanie, I'm really trying to be—'

'Oh, go to hell, Brian. Where you belong.'

Brian left money for the call on the coffee table, mumbled his thanks and left the room.

Mary Gaunt watched him leave, sorrow and yearning written on her face; praying for the weeks to fly by until his return. She now lived for the nights and occasional days that she spent in his arms. He was a first-rate lover and she knew that, young as he was, he must have had plenty of experience. But she didn't care. She heard the glug-glug of gin falling into an empty glass and looked at the slob sitting at her side. He belched loudly and rubbed his belly, his face contorted with the pain of indigestion. Well, she'd certainly paid for her mistake. Affluence did not compensate for this.

She turned her attention back to the television but was unable to concentrate on the drama; the drama of her own life was gnawing at her insides.

Who was Melanie?

*

Brian spent the following two months working his balls off (as he told Sam Morrison) and, at the same time, having fun in Europe. And in that time two women were going out of their minds, for two very different reasons.

Mary Gaunt was in love with the man. At least, he was the object of her unhappily married woman's fantasies and desires. Her marriage to Joe had been on the rocks before the register was signed. Brian had been right, of course; she'd married the disgusting man for his money. And paid the price. Oh, Joe kept her well provided for. Their house in Roundhay was comfortable, and adequate rent from their many tenants helped towards an excellent standard of living. A standard of living that was devastated by the torture of marriage to Joe Gaunt. He was everything that Mary had feared he would be but, contrary to her pre-marital predictions, his provision of a comfy home, expensive clothes and jewellery did not make up for his basic vulgar character and total lack of sensuality. In short, he repelled her. He was not by nature an affectionate man, thank the Lord, but he was sexually demanding and in the beginning their marital bed was energetic with verbal warfare. Eventually, Joe turned to the streets and pornographic bookshelves for his satisfaction, and Mary thanked God for the gap in their bed. Although her marriage was sexually starved, Mary's nubile body hungered for the presence of an attractive, virile man and she found the answer to her prayers in Brian Jarvis. He wasn't the first young male tenant she'd propositioned but he was the first to comply. He was physically attractive, could be amusing, and was kind enough to make her fall in love with him. Too quickly and far too deeply. She kept telling herself that it was foolish and he was too young, too close for comfort and, well, there was something about him ... something she couldn't put her finger on, but it wasn't ... nice. And the way he'd conned Joe into thinking he was a decent, respectable tenant ... he was too convincing, too glib. After all, she didn't know anything about him, not really. He worked as an international sales representative at William Kaye International, a company in Harrogate. He grew up in a village near Harrogate and had good friends who lived in Leeds, on the Otley Road. Apart from those wispy facts, what did she know about him? Absolutely nothing. Nevertheless, she'd fallen hook, line and sinker, like a smitten adolescent; she couldn't help it. And now he'd gone away for a couple of months ... how would she live through those endless weeks? By constantly thinking about him, longing for his body and wondering who the hell Melanie was. That's how.

Melanie was going out of her mind because she could feel her character, her personality, slowly seeping away. Over the months, her virtual imprisonment at Greystones, her undesirable lifestyle as housekeeper and companion to her invalid father, her shattered hopes and ambitions gradually extinguished all insouciance, tenderness, sense of fun. Melanie began to see the shrinking world through a different pair of eyes. And it was all because of Brian. And Brian's life was so very, very different, superior. Hatred of her brother was growing like a cancer inside her.

She looked at the postcard. This was the second one this week; he was doing it on purpose. The only reason her brother would write so frequently was in order to flaunt his enviable life ... the life that should have been hers. She looked around the big, dismal kitchen and her eyes strayed to the damp, dreary late November morning outside. She looked again at the postcard.

Cologne, the Rhine, a top-class hotel, flying to Copenhagen tomorrow and then on to Stockholm. Hope to see you both at Christmas.

She felt the knot in her stomach tighten. Frustration was a deadly emotion. Absolutely deadly.

*

Joe Gaunt was away visiting one of his tenants who lived in accommodation in the south of Leeds, so it was Mary who opened the door to the beautiful but distraught young girl on that bitterly cold November afternoon.

'Hello. Can I help you?'

'Oh, good afternoon. I'm looking for Flat 2D … Brian Jarvis …'

Mary started. A cold shiver ran down her spine and she swallowed loudly before she replied. Her voice sounded high-pitched and unnatural.

'I'm afraid that Mr Jarvis isn't at home. He's working abroad and will be away for quite some time.'

The girl seemed to slump and looked as though she was trying very hard not to cry. This had to be Melanie. Mary remembered how Brian had spoken to the girl on the telephone. He'd called her a 'little bitch' and the look in his eyes had been, well, a bit scary. It was pretty obvious that their relationship was, or had been, a traumatic one. And she was such a beautiful girl.

'Oh no … no-o-o-, I have to see him …'

Mary suddenly felt a sense of foreboding. She opened the door wider and tentatively asked the visitor to come in. The girl sniffed, pulled a tissue out of her shoulder bag, wiped her nose and followed the older woman through the impressive hall. Mary pushed open a door and, forcing a smile, turned to the girl.

'I'm Br … Mr Jarvis's landlady and this is where I live – where my husband and I live. The tenants' flats are on the upper floors. Brian's flat is on the second floor,' she added, just for something to say. 'Please sit down. Would you like a cup of tea, coffee? You look as though you need one.'

She nodded, wiping her eyes, and Mary quickly and thankfully left the room. When she returned with a full tray, she observed the girl, partly in curiosity and partly in sheer, ugly jealousy. She wasn't bad-looking herself, but there was no way she could compare with this. She handed the girl her coffee, offered her sugar, which was refused, and they both drank in silence for a while. Mary was beginning to feel embarrassed and at a loss as to how to handle the situation delicately. She wanted and damn well needed to get to the bottom of this.

'Feeling better?'

The visitor nodded again. She certainly wasn't very talkative, whoever she was.

'Have you any idea when my ... when Brian will be back?'

Mary shrugged her shoulders and sucked her lower lip. If only she did ...

'All I know is he went away for a couple of months. But I'm sure he'll be home before Christmas.'

'Oh no, that's no good. I simply *must* see him before then.'

Mary hesitated for a second or two.

'Do you want to talk to me about it? I've no desire to pry but if you ...'

The girl looked at Mary with big, frightened blue eyes and with quivering lips she replied,

'Oh yes, if you don't mind. Yes, please. I've simply *got* to talk to somebody.'

She stopped and swallowed and then she poured out her heart. And Mary Gaunt sat and listened in stunned silence.

*

1973 was drawing to a close and it had been a hell of a year, Brian reflected sleepily, sitting on the train from King's Cross. And this last trip had shattered him well and truly; he was ready for the Christmas break. Christmas – no, he didn't know how he'd be spending it this year. In one way, he obviously wanted to go home to Greystones, where he belonged. Or used to belong. He knew that he didn't belong to Greystones anymore; Melanie had made that pretty clear on the phone. And, he had to admit, he hadn't visited as often as he should have done. Maybe he wouldn't be very welcome at the Christmas dinner table this year. Neil and Linda would be a better proposition ... if they'd have him. But of course they'd have him; they wouldn't allow him to be alone during the festive season. On the other hand, maybe his randy landlady had something in mind. He smiled to himself, settling more comfortably into his first-class seat. He was looking forward to seeing Mary; in his own way, he'd missed her. Not that he'd been short of women. But Mary was, well, very, very randy. He smiled again. And she was safe. She had a husband. He fell asleep.

The atmosphere of Christmas was all around as Brian climbed into a taxi at Leeds City Station. There had been a long queue; he'd had to wait nearly an hour and it was bitterly cold, the freezing snow glittering on the pavement. Brian cursed his frozen, aching limbs and numb extremities, but his foul temper began to mellow as the taxi circled the city with its Christmas trees and coloured lights and early revellers. In three days, it would be Christmas Eve. Brian closed his eyes. Yes, he was looking forward to this break, even if he didn't know what he'd be doing. It was eleven o'clock when the taxi pulled up outside the old house near Roundhay Park. The driver dragged Brian's suitcase and accompanying bulging briefcase out of the boot, cheerily wished him a merry Christmas and mentally cursed him when the expected seasonal tip didn't come.

Brian yawned as he strode up the path leading to the front door. He dropped the two heavy pieces of luggage and wearily felt into his trouser pocket for the front door key. But he needn't have bothered. The door suddenly flew open, seemingly of its own accord. Joe Gaunt then towered above him and Brian could smell the gin from where he was standing, in his inferior position on the bottom step.

'I'll give you exactly one 'our to get yer things together an' get out.'

Brian blinked. His landlord stepped back and Brian slowly moved into the hall, dragging his bags behind him.

'What are you talking about, Joe?'

Although Joe Gaunt had undoubtedly been drinking, he appeared to be more than *compos mentis* and his speech was articulate.

'I've been waitin' for you to put yer appearance in, Jarvis. I've been waitin' to give you this.'

He thrust a buff-coloured envelope into Brian's now-trembling hand; his name was typed in bold letters on the front.

'By God, you certainly 'ad me fooled, you did that. I'd 'ave sworn on me own mother's life that you were a decent bloke … I wouldn't 'ave thought you 'ad it in you.'

What the hell was he talking about? Brian ripped open the envelope with incompetent hands and pulled out a Notice to Quit. And the termination of his tenancy was dated three days before. Brian stared at the notification and then at his landlord.

'What's all this about? You can't do this … it's illegal. I signed a lease for three years. I'll see my solicitor.'

'You can see the Lord Chief Justice if you like, it'll mek no difference. I can do what I like wi' me own property, you 'aven't got a leg to stand on, lad. I want you out.'

The fight suddenly went out of Brian. He was tired, cold and hungry and he felt very drained. All he wanted was to climb into bed – alone, for once – and sleep for about a week. But apparently, he didn't have a bed to sleep in.

'Will you just tell me why, Joe? What on earth have I done to deserve this?' He rapped the Notice to Quit with his left hand.

And then he thought of Mary. Of course … he'd been too tired, his brain too sluggish for him to think straight … of course. Somehow, Joe Gaunt had found out about him and his wife. Well, he'd just deny it, for what good it'd do him. And that would be the end of him and Mary, as well. Oh well, you win some, you lose some. But he had no desire to lose his flat.

'You're a lyin', good-for-nothin', nasty bastard, that's why.' Joe leant forward and Brian reeled at the onslaught of gin on top of the verbal attack. 'I don't want any more poor young lasses cummin' round 'ere, cryin' and splutterin' and upsettin' me missus. She were nobbut a bairn, Mary said, an' could 'ave 'ad anybody wi' her looks.'

Brian felt totally bewildered. Joe Gaunt wasn't making sense.

'What?'

'Young lass that cum visitin' you 'ere a couple o' weeks ago. Long blonde 'air, pretty, accordin' to Mary, said you were shacking up with 'er before you cum 'ere an' you knocked 'er about and caused a lot o' damage to 'er home. Silly young devil said she wants you back so I reckon you'd better get yersen back there, lad, where yer wanted – cos yer not wanted 'ere. I've already told you, I'm particular who I 'ave in my 'ouse and I certainly don't want *my* 'ome wreckin'. Yer'd best get a move on.'

Brian stood where he was, unable to move. Was he dreaming all this? Would he wake up in his hotel bedroom back in Stockholm?

'Joe … Mr Gaunt, I honestly haven't a clue what you're talking about. I haven't been shacking up with any girl.'

Joe Gaunt grunted.

'That's not what Mary 'eard. Young lass upset 'er summat cruel. So, get a move on, lad.'

The landlord gave Brian one last, menacing look and then he disappeared into his own apartment. Brian realised he'd been fighting a losing battle. It was Mary. For some unknown reason, she'd decided she didn't want him in the house and had made up this cock and bull story ... Maybe she'd taken a fancy to one of the other tenants in his absence. What the hell. If it was his word against hers, he wouldn't stand an earthly. He kicked his case into the cold, empty flat. Well, at least this business saved him from unpacking. The lousy bitch. They were all bitches, every one of them. Women.

*

Neil smiled wearily when he opened the door to Brian and his belongings at one o'clock in the morning.

'I don't believe this. I thought you were abroad.'

'You'll believe it even less when I tell you what's happened. I've been chucked out of my flat.'

Linda, shuffling down the stairs in a quilted pink dressing gown and rubbing her eyes, asked her husband who it was at that time of night. Brian had the sense to look embarrassed.

'I'm afraid it's me, Linda.' He flashed her a smile. 'Begging your hospitality again.'

Linda looked from her husband to his friend and wordlessly went to make some tea.

'I feel rotten about this,' Brian murmured.

'Well, don't.' Neil shrugged, pushing his glasses onto his nose and fiddling with the frames. 'Just tell us what it's all about.'

Brian did tell them. And as he became more and more roused telling his story, as he began to describe the fictitious character invented by his fickle landlady, it seemed to strike the three of them at the same time. The character was no figment of Mary's fertile imagination. It was Melanie.

Brian's brain began to thud and his insides somersaulted. How could he ever return to Greystones without wanting to kill her?

Catherine

Chapter Ten

Catherine was exhausted; happy and fulfilled but totally exhausted. Sam Morrison, kind and paternal though he was, tended to live for his work and expected his colleagues and subordinates to do likewise. He was known at the office as a 'workaholic' and although Catherine had at first laughed at this seemingly absurd description of him, over the months she had to agree. Sam Morrison was, indeed, a workaholic. Catherine wondered how his wife put up with it; the poor woman hardly ever saw him. Or maybe it was one of those marriages that survived because of the infrequency of each other's company?

However, that wasn't Catherine's problem. She had too many of her own without worrying about Sam and his wife. No, that wasn't true; she didn't have problems, not really. She just wished there were at least ten more hours in a day so that she could work efficiently and still have time to sleep and relax. She was often required to work late at the office, and the number of times Sam invited her to be wined and dined with the foreign clients was on the increase. It sometimes included weekends when visitors had to be in Harrogate for two or three weeks and were at a loose end between Friday evening and Monday morning. Catherine enjoyed her share of entertaining these people, of course, and she enjoyed looking at her salary slip at the end of the month but, by the spring of 1975, she had to admit, it was beginning to be a strain. Other people were noticing, too. Her mother had kept her anxiety about Cathy's health to herself for several months. She knew her daughter too well and realised that if she asked how she was feeling, Cathy would say, *I'm well, Mum, really, really well,* or words to that effect. And Molly would be called a natterer, or something like that. So, she kept her thoughts to herself. However, when Catherine rang up for the third time in a week to say she'd be working late and not to worry about her dinner, Molly finally gave in …

'This is ridiculous, Cathy,' she blurted, 'you'll be runnin' yerself into the ground at this rate.'

As soon as the words were out, she knew she shouldn't have opened her mouth, or at least should have waited until Cathy got home before she spoke her mind.

'It can't be helped, Mum. I'm sorry, but work comes first.'

The phone went dead in Molly's hand. She sighed and replaced the receiver. The first time Cathy had snapped at her like that she'd been shocked and hurt but she was getting used to it now. Cathy snapped at the least little thing and it wasn't like her. It wasn't like Cathy at all.

Molly ate her dinner at the usual time, six o'clock. As she was finishing the last mouthful, the telephone rang and Molly smiled. That'd be Cathy, ringing to apologise for flying off the handle – again – surely the girl must notice how often …

'Hello?'

'Hello, Mrs Carter. Jean-Marc here. How are you?'

'Well, *I'm* all right, love, but …'

'Is Catherine there, please?'

'No, love, I'm afraid she isn't.' Molly sighed. 'She's workin' late again. It's the third time this week.'

There was a pause before Jean-Marc spoke again.

'Mrs Carter, have you noticed a change in Catherine over the last few weeks? Does she seem a little … well, irritable? Bad-tempered?'

Molly almost laughed.

'A little irritable? That's puttin' it mildly, love. So, you've noticed it yourself, 'ave you? I didn't think she'd be snappy wi' you, of all people.'

'I think she's working far too hard, Mrs Carter. She's too stubborn to admit it but I think she needs a break. A good holiday. What do you say?'

'I couldn't agree more, love. But you try telling our Cathy that!'

'I intend to, Mrs Carter. Tonight.'

*

Sam was still sitting at his desk when Catherine peeped round the door to say good night. One of the sales representatives was sitting opposite him and they were deep in conversation, so much so that Sam didn't notice his secretary standing there. Catherine looked at her watch. It was eight o'clock. Sam looked as vigorous as he had done at nine o'clock that morning.

'I'm leaving now, Sam.' Catherine managed a weary smile. 'Your letters are all in the tray for signing and these are the telex translations. They're both quite long, I'm afraid ... See you on Monday, and have a good weekend.'

Sam Morrison grinned at her.

'That's me girl, thanks a million, sunshine.' He looked at the wall clock above his desk. 'Eeh, is that the time already? *Tempus fugit* and not 'alf! Right, Brian, I think we'll call it a day, lad, an' if you're goin' t'same way as me secretary, I reckon you might give 'er a lift.'

The rep, whom Catherine had seen a couple of times around the office, immediately stood up and walked towards her, smiling. He had an attractive, cheeky smile, Catherine thought, absently.

'I'm driving to Leeds if that's any good for you.'

Catherine shook her head. 'No, thanks, it's out of your way. I'll soon get a bus. Bye.'

She saw the silver Peugeot as soon as she got outside, parked a little way down the street. Jean-Marc opened the door and she thankfully clambered in.

'Hello, you! This is a nice surprise.'

'Yes, I'm sure it is. Would you have been capable of walking to the bus stop?'

'What on earth do you mean?'

'I mean, my love, that this is the third time this week that you've worked till this ungodly hour. You look like death, you're unbearable to be with, quite frankly, and it's about time you had a holiday.'

Catherine sank back into her seat and closed her eyes.

'Holiday? That'll be the day. The work's piling up so much that I'll be taking my bed to the office soon.'

Jean-Marc didn't reply. An hour later, he gave her the airline tickets.

Molly Carter was delighted when Jean-Marc told her he was taking Catherine away for a couple of weeks – he'd been planning it for a while, as a surprise. When Catherine told Sam that she'd be taking two weeks' leave, he looked quite nonplussed. She was entitled to her holiday, of course, but

... and then he looked at her drawn face and heavy, red-rimmed eyes that no make-up could hide and that he hadn't noticed before.

'You do right, lass. You must mek most of it while you can. Where will you be goin'?'

'Jean-Marc's taking me to Paris. He has a flat there, as you probably know. But he's promised me I won't have to lift a finger there. He says it'll be just like staying at the Ritz!'

*

Vincennes is a suburb of Paris just south east of the city. A beautiful old town, complete with its fourteenth-century *château* and the 2,459-acre Bois de Vincennes, the largest park in the Paris region, with its racecourse, botanical garden, zoo, sports centres and four lakes. It also has the advantage of being the terminus for line 1 of the metro system. As well as its varied shops, restaurants and cafés, there are open-air markets there three days a week selling everything from fresh fruit and vegetables to fashionable clothes. Vincennes is also famous for its prostitutes, who operate in white vans around the wood. Jean-Marc's apartment was in Vincennes.

'*On arrive,*' Jean-Marc told the taxi driver as they drove up a tree-lined hill and pulled up in front of an elegant nineteenth-century building. '*Je vous dois combien, monsieur?*'

The driver told his passenger how much he owed him and Jean-Marc added a generous tip as the elderly North African man pulled their two suitcases out of the boot.

'*Merci bien, monsieur. Bonne soirée.*'

It *was* a '*bonne soirée*'; a warm, balmy Saturday evening in May. Catherine gazed up at the four-storey building as Jean-Marc carried the two pieces of luggage to the front door. He pressed a button, the door opened and he guided them through the entrance to the old gate lift that stood on their right, next to the concierge's domain. On the left was a wide red-carpeted staircase. The walls were lined with gilt-framed mirrors and a chandelier hung from the ceiling.

'Have you brought me to the right place?' Catherine breathed, 'or is this the Château de Vincennes?'

'I believe the *château* is much older and certainly much chillier than my

109

residence.' Jean-Marc smiled, pushing the button for the lift. 'My apartment's on the fourth floor – of course, I normally run up the stairs three at a time but, as we have heavy cases, we'll take the lift.'

'I'm quite happy to run up the stairs,' Catherine laughed, 'just don't expect me to be too athletic later, that's all.'

He pulled open the iron gates of the lift, and the look he gave her told her that was exactly what he *was* expecting. Catherine gasped as they walked into Jean-Marc's apartment.

'It's just like stepping into a Maupassant story!'

Catherine slowly moved around the large salon with its parquet floor, marble fireplace and heavy mahogany furniture. Beautifully framed reproductions by Monet, Renoir and Pissarro adorned the walls, and tall windows overlooking the Vincennes wood boasted thick brocade curtains with tassels that swept the floor. The window opened onto a tiny balcony now regaled with window boxes filled with scarlet geraniums.

'Jean-Marc, this is just perfect.'

He smiled and, taking her hand, led her into his dining room where a long mahogany table monopolised the room, accompanied by eight dining chairs in the same wood. More impressionist paintings hung on the walls and a dresser stood in a recess, filled with porcelain and crystal. Plants with trailing bright green leaves stood in corners, and a crystal vase containing yellow tulips occupied the centre of the table. Catherine asked her host who had put the flowers there and who cared for all his lovely plants. 'The concierge,' Jean-Marc told her. 'Maria. She's a Portuguese gem and all the residents are very grateful for her presence here.'

They moved into the kitchen.

'Oh, I love it!' Catherine cried, clapping her hands. 'You must let me cook for you this evening!'

Jean-Marc laughed, delighting in her enthusiasm.

'I'll think about letting you cook for me sometime but definitely not this evening.'

The kitchen, like the other rooms, was large, and all except the electrical appliances seemed donkey's years old. A rather ugly, cracked wooden table stood like a matriarch in the middle of the room, its elephantine legs firmly planted on the floor. The cupboards and worktops appeared to be of the same old time-decayed wood but proudly displaying earthenware pots, copper pans and other utensils, antique almost and well worn but obviously durable and packed with character. There was a stale smell about the kitchen, too, that somehow managed to be healthy.

'This place has got to have a history, Jean-Marc,' Catherine whispered, 'it's just got to have.'

She didn't notice the silence.

'Ah yes. My apartment has certainly got a history.'

Before Catherine could ask any questions, Jean-Marc caught hold of her hand and guided her into his bedroom. Old, ugly and beautiful like every other room. Another balconied window looking onto the wood, and in the far distance, a lake. A monstrosity of a wardrobe and double bed with a heavy blue brocade counterpane to match the curtains. Jean-Marc pulled them together against the now-dying day and the already dim light in the room disappeared. He pulled Catherine into his arms.

'And what does *mademoiselle* think of *monsieur*'s little pad?'

'*Mademoiselle* is very impressed. She thinks the bed looks very inviting, too.'

Jean-Marc lifted her into the air and carried her across the room, gently laying her onto the inviting-looking bed and unfastening the small buttons on her white blouse. Catherine smiled up at him, wrapped her arms around his neck and pulled him down to her.

'Have you any idea how much I love you, Catherine?'

Catherine's lips lightly brushed his dark, rough, five o'clock shadow, and her hands tore open his shirt and stroked his neck, his chest, his abdomen. The body that she now knew so well and worshipped so much. She heard Jean-Marc softly moan before he pushed her onto the pillow and pulled off her clothes. Oh yes, Catherine knew how much this man loved her.

Chapter Eleven

Paris in May was like an exquisite gem; colourful, sparkling, enticing – and completely out of Catherine's reach for two whole days. Much to her frustration. Jean-Marc bludgeoned her into resting, and he meant resting. The most energetic exercise they took was walking in the wood and taking a rowing boat on Lac des Minimes for an hour. In the apartment, he wouldn't let her lift a finger. He provided her with light and superficial French reading material while he cooked delicious and very French meals. He insisted that she go to bed early, no later than ten o'clock, and sleep late in the morning. Initially, Catherine had to admit that she was grateful for the rest but after forty-eight hours she was itching to get out and explore again the city she loved.

'Anyway,' she said, sulkily picking at her hot croissants on the third morning, 'if we stay here all the time, it's been a waste of money. You could have mollycoddled me like this in Russetlea.'

'Catherine,' Jean-Marc replied, gazing at her over his enormous yellow coffee bowl, 'the baker in Russetlea is excellent, but she wouldn't know a croissant from a Champagne cocktail. And I'll leave the "coddling" to your mum, whose name seems to fit the bill. I prefer to think that I'm looking after my best interests … and at the moment, that's your health.'

Catherine smiled at him, picking up the still-warm crumbs from her plate and licking her sticky fingers.

'I appreciate it, honestly, I do. But I'm feeling great now – honestly, look at me! No more smudges under my eyes and my cheeks are bright pink! And if I don't get into Paris soon, I'll have a relapse caused by frustration and …'

'Okay, *mademoiselle*, you win. Let's go out and get some excitement – and some good, unhealthy pollution.'

*

Catherine had thought she loved Paris before but it had been a dull, lifeless city compared with this. She was in love and it was obvious from every

112

glance, every smile, every touch that Jean-Marc was head-over-heels in love with her. And he showed her a Paris she didn't know existed. Small, interesting museums tucked away down unknown streets; tiny, antiquated shops that tourists never set foot in and restaurants that served mouth-watering food, heady wine and where Jean-Marc was familiar with the staff. They talked a lot and they laughed a lot. They took photographs and they bought each other silly souvenirs. They took the metro and leapt off at previously (as far as Catherine was concerned) unheard-of stations and explored the district they found themselves in. It was pure enchantment. Only one thing marred that first week for Catherine. It was obvious that Jean-Marc neither wanted to visit nor discuss his cousin Henri de Bergier and his wife, Véronique.

When Jean-Marc had first told her about the already-booked holiday, Catherine had taken it as a foregone conclusion that the de Bergiers would take priority on their mental list of things to do in Paris. She hadn't asked Jean-Marc questions or expressed her own desires; she hadn't thought it necessary. But when their third day in the French capital had come to an end and he still hadn't dialled his cousin's phone number, Catherine's mind had started to tick over. It was true, her own correspondence with the family had dwindled to virtually nothing over the couple of years she had been back in England. She put this down to increasing pressure of work and very little leisure time; at least not enough free time for writing lengthy letters. And the de Bergiers, she knew, were no great letter-writers, and they were also very busy people. So, correspondence had decreased to Christmas and birthday cards with a few friendly lines scribbled inside. Catherine, at the beginning of her relationship with Jean-Marc, had often brought Henri and his family up in conversation and had tried to ask questions, probe, prompt a little to find out more about the de Bergier family in general, and his relationship with that side of the family in particular. At first, Jean-Marc had seemed happy enough to reply to her questions and had shown an interest in her own relationship, as au pair girl, with his family in Paris. But, little by little, Catherine couldn't help but notice, his answers to her enquiries became shorter, less detailed, and his own initiation of the subject was nil. She noticed a certain look in his eyes that she couldn't quite fathom and was often on the point of cautiously letting him know that she'd noticed and asking if there was anything on his mind and, if so, would he please share it with her? Was it anything to do with Nathalie, that delightful little girl whom Catherine had often thought of as her own? Was Jean-Marc afraid of telling her of some … oh, she didn't know, she couldn't guess … So, she decided to leave the subject alone. For the time being. But now, Jean-Marc's obvious lack of enthusiasm for visiting his cousin had brought things to a head.

Catherine was lying on her stomach across the bed, a lilac and blue silk robe wrapped around her, watching Jean-Marc dressing for dinner. It was Saturday evening, the end of their first week, and he was taking her to a particularly stylish and elegant restaurant on the banks of the Seine with a view of Notre Dame. It was an appropriate way to thank a beautiful girl for a wonderful holiday, he told her, zipping his black trousers and carefully arranging his grey silk tie.

'That's a good one, *monsieur*. Shouldn't I be thanking you?'

Jean-Marc bent down, kissed her cheek and told her to hurry up or they'd be late. He'd reserved their table for nine o'clock.

'You don't have to thank me for anything, Catherine, please remember that. You've made me a very happy man.'

For a split second, the playfulness was gone from his face. Catherine tried to meet his eyes but he'd already turned away and left the room.

⋆

She wore green that evening; a deep emerald green halter-neck dress because she knew it was the colour that Jean-Marc thought suited her best. She let her hair fall about her shoulders and wore a fine gold chain that Jean-Marc had given her that morning.

'You're beautiful.' Jean-Marc kissed her cheek and Catherine felt beautiful, and she knew that the evening was going to be very special. She was right, it was.

They had a table by the window with a magnificent view of Notre Dame and the river. The cathedral looked majestic in the soft crepuscular glow and as the turquoise sky gradually became navy blue, the rose window shone like a special bright star, its timeless beauty reflected in the waters of the Seine. The duck was delectable, the Châteauneuf-du-Pape excellent, the service impeccable, and Jean-Marc had never been more attentive. Catherine knew that other women in the plush restaurant were far more sophisticated and glamorous than she was; but Jean-Marc made her feel like the elegant swan, surrounded by ugly ducklings.

'Thank you for bringing me here, Jean-Marc,' she smiled, at the end of the incomparable meal. 'It was always an ambition of mine; well, more a dream, really, to come here. So, you've made my dream come true.'

She looked around the elegant room and its equally elegant clientèle.

'You know, I expected to feel ... well, out of place here this evening, not being used to this ... this kind of thing. But you ... you always manage to make me feel special.'

'A very important lesson I've learnt in life, Catherine, is that being rich and glamorous does not make a person special. Glamour is superficial; it's the person inside that's important. Don't ever forget that. You have the kind of beauty that all the glamorous women in the world would give their high teeth for.'

'*Eye*-teeth, Jean-Marc. If women had high teeth, they wouldn't really be glamorous.'

Jean-Marc's English was almost perfect. His rare mistakes of grammar and pronunciation always amused Catherine. Their eyes met and the sparks that twinkled there put the illuminated cathedral to shame. Catherine's hand stole across the table and her fingers began to stroke the back of Jean-Marc's hand.

'Do you remember when we first met? Honestly, I can't believe you're the same man. Talk about Jekyll and Hyde! You were a real pain in the backside, you know, when I think about it. In fact, I don't have to think about it. You were arrogant, unbelievably sarcastic and ...'

Jean-Marc grinned and grasped the hand that was teasing his.

'I know, I know. I was arrogant, sarcastic – let's not forget bombastic – and no fun at all. And you, my love, took it all in like a sponge. You know, you were quite delightful when you bit me every time I barked. And you never saw through me at all, did you?'

'Saw through you? All I saw was a ...'

'Shall we go, my love? I think it's time to make a perfect end to a perfect evening.'

The perfect evening, however, was completely shattered when they arrived at the apartment.

*

'When are we going to see Henri and Véronique, darling?' Catherine asked, lying in Jean-Marc's arms and ready to sink into a deep, contented sleep. There was no response, only his body stiffening slightly.

'Jean-Marc?' It was a whisper.

'I don't think there's any hurry, Catherine...'

The tone of his voice said, *Subject closed*. Catherine's throat suddenly felt dry and the palms of her hands became clammy. Something wasn't quite right; of that she had no doubt.

'Does Henri know that we're in Paris?'

A pause.

'No. He doesn't.'

Catherine could feel unprecedented tension between them. She knew she ought to shut up but also knew she couldn't.

'Why on earth not? I thought you'd have let him know – written to him, or phoned. I want to see the family before we go back to England.' Her voice was becoming a whine and there was nothing she could do about it. 'I want to see Nathalie again. She was like ... well, she was like my own child and—'

'Oh, for God's sake!'

He threw back the covers and leapt out of bed, switching on the small bedside lamp, which gave out a dim blue light. He stood for a long time with his back to her, peering through the brocade curtains at the thick outline of trees on the horizon. Catherine was frightened.

'Okay,' he finally said, 'I ought to have expected this, I suppose. I'll phone Henri tomorrow and make arrangements to go and visit. But I think I should...'

He crawled back into bed without turning out the lamp. He lay on his back, his arms folded behind his head, looking up at strange shadows quivering on the ceiling. Catherine waited, her alarmed heart hammering.

'Yes?' she whispered.

Jean-Marc let out a long far-from-contented sigh.

'Nothing. Let's get some sleep.' He turned out the lamp and Catherine thought she would never sleep again.

The following morning, Jean-Marc telephoned his cousin, but Catherine didn't hear the conversation because she was in the bath. She knew he'd timed it that way.

'We're going to see the family tomorrow afternoon,' he told her without looking at her, spooning coffee into the percolator, 'and we'll be staying for dinner.'

Catherine replied, 'Oh, excellent. That'll be nice,' and silently watched him making breakfast which they silently ate. The visit, which should have been so exciting, so much anticipated, was becoming – unthinkably – something to dread.

That Sunday improved as it went along. The visit to the de Bergiers was not mentioned again (by unspoken, mutual agreement) and they spent the day walking in the wood, sipping wine on pavement café terraces and watching the world go by. In the evening, they returned to the apartment, played some Mozart on the stereo, made love and went out for a late dinner to a quiet, unpretentious bistro where they chatted about nothing in particular. They sauntered home towards midnight, holding hands, saying very little, loving each other a lot. And when they were inside the ancient, creaking lift, Jean-Marc pulled Catherine towards him and kissed her, almost violently.

'I love you, Catherine,' he whispered into her hair, his fingers running through the long red-brown tresses, 'I love you so very, very much.'

*

The following day, they stepped out of the metro station Odéon on the Boulevard Saint-Germain and a familiar surge of excitement and nostalgia swept over Catherine. The boulevard stretched in front of them, throbbing with life. The life that she had once been a part of and loved. The cafés, the boutiques, antique shops, restaurants and cinemas. The lively Latin Quarter, the heart of Paris. And she was back again. Yet, in a strange way she felt as though she'd never been away, as though this was where she belonged. As though she'd come home, to her second home. Jean-Marc slipped his arm around her shoulder and guided her, almost protectively, through the crowds. She smiled up at him but he wasn't looking at her and he certainly wasn't smiling. They turned off the busy boulevard and walked through some quaint narrow streets until they arrived on a short narrow street near the Jardin du Luxembourg. Catherine felt as though she were walking on a knife's edge; she knew she only had to say the word and Jean-Marc would turn on his heels and flee in the direction from which they'd come.

Catherine's mixed feelings of excitement and apprehension ballooned as they approached the building where the de Bergiers lived. How would they greet her, their au pair girl, after a period of two years or so? And what about little Nathalie, the child she'd cherished and thought of as her own? Would she remember her? *Oh please, please let her remember me,* she prayed. *I'll be mortified if she runs away and hides.* Catherine looked up at Jean-Marc again as they entered the vestibule and waited for the lift. For the first time, he almost smiled at her.

'Nervous?'

She nodded and he muttered something like, 'Me, too' under his breath. Catherine frowned but said nothing. The lift door opened and they stepped into the tiny no-room-to-swing-a-cat lift and wordlessly stepped out again on the third floor. Jean-Marc pressed the bell at the side of the double door that Catherine had passed through so many times. Several minutes passed before it opened.

Véronique de Bergier stood before them, as resplendent and chic as always. She was a woman in her mid-thirties, tall and thin with prominent cheekbones and slightly sunken cheeks. Her light brown hair was cropped short and highlighted with blonde streaks. She wore little make-up, cleverly applied, and a few pieces of good jewellery. Her short-sleeved maroon and white striped blouse revealed long, bony arms and beautifully manicured hands, and her maroon skirt showed thin but shapely legs, already tanned by the May sun. She pulled the door open to its full extent and gestured for them to enter her home. As they did so, a smile lit up the Frenchwoman's face, but it seemed as though it was intended for Catherine only.

'How lovely it is to see you again, Catherine,' she said in the French language. 'How are you?'

She bent and kissed both Catherine's cheeks and then, her right hand on Catherine's back, she led her into the unchanged, square, dark hall. Catherine caught Jean-Marc's eye and she could sense the tension in his body.

'I'm really, really well, thank you, Véronique. How are you and Henri? And how's my little girl? Where is she?'

Véronique de Bergier laughed and told her they were both fine. Henri was still at work and would be home at about seven-thirty. Nathalie was taking a necessary nap.

'She missed you for a long time, Cathy. In fact, it was quite distressing – and worrying – when she asked for you all the time. We thought she would never get over losing you.'

The lump in Catherine's throat made its presence strongly felt.

'I suppose she'll have forgotten me by now.'

'Nonsense. I'm sure she will recognise you immediately.'

It was at that moment that Véronique turned to her brother-in-law for the first time since they had arrived. She held out her hand but the smile on her lips didn't reach her eyes.

'Jean-Marc, it's good to see you again. How are you?'

'I'm ... fine, thank you. It's good to see you, too.'

His words were as stiff as his body and when he offered to kiss Véronique's cheek, the motion was mechanical and his lips touched only the air surrounding the woman's face. Véronique quickly moved away and walked into the salon on their left. Catherine was pleased to see the room hadn't changed one little bit. Two old and well-worn black leather sofas with huge red and black cushions monopolised the room; a glass-topped coffee table, holding pot pourri dishes and silver coasters, standing between them. An original print of a pretty coastal village hung above the fireplace, and other pictures, a mixture of old and very modern, adorned the cream walls. Their hostess told her guests to make themselves comfortable while she went to arrange for coffee and a snack to be prepared.

'I have an Austrian girl now,' she smiled. 'She's very sweet and efficient, but her French is still very poor. Conversation with Elfie isn't as easy as it was with you.'

Catherine grinned. What did her tutor think to that, then?

Her tutor was still standing and looking somewhat ill at ease. He smiled rather thinly at Véronique as she swept by him, but she merely indicated for him to sit down. He did, on the sofa opposite Catherine. She looked across at him, her expression a mixture of pleasure and confusion. She wanted to ask him so many questions but it was impossible. The silence between them was lengthy, uncomfortable and, for Catherine at least, agonising. At last, a young girl crept into the room with a copious silver tray containing a pot of coffee, cream, sugar and a variety of biscuits.

'Cathy, this is Elfriede – Elfie, my new au pair girl,' Véronique announced, following the girl into the salon and speaking slowly, enunciating every word carefully. Cathy immediately felt sorry for the au pair. She'd been living with the de Bergiers for only six weeks and Catherine remembered how shy, gauche and inadequate she had felt in those early stages of her life in France. Elfie smiled, muttered something inaudible and quickly disappeared.

'Is Nathalie very fond of her?'

The plaintive, obviously jealous tone in Catherine's voice was not lost on Nathalie's mum, and she laughed as she poured the coffee.

'Don't worry, Cathy, I'm sure you'll always be Nathalie's favourite.'

Catherine then felt childish and silly in front of Jean-Marc. She shyly looked across the room at him and he winked at her. It didn't help. Véronique sat down next to Catherine and took a delicate sip of her coffee. She slowly looked from one to the other.

'Nathalie adored Cathy, you know, Jean-Marc. Absolutely adored her. Cathy was her second mummy, weren't you, Cathy? When the time comes, I know Cathy will make some lucky children an excellent mother. I can imagine you with lots of children, Cathy, a very big, happy family.'

The expression on Jean-Marc's face was unreadable, unfathomable. He sat opposite the two women, his coffee untasted, clenching and unclenching his hands. Catherine suddenly had the feeling that Véronique's remark had been targeted specifically at Jean-Marc and was very silly as well as tactless.

'Oh, I don't know about that,' she smiled, 'at least not for a long time. Children are the last thing on my mind. I'm enjoying my work too much.'

'Tell me about it.'

Catherine didn't need asking twice. She talked eagerly about her career at William Kaye International, her wonderful boss, the interesting work, the translations, her friendly colleagues ...

'And she works too hard for her own good,' Jean-Marc added, smiling indulgently at her. 'Which is why we're here, in Paris. A pleasant break for Catherine before she kills herself.'

'*Mon Dieu*, I sincerely hope that's not the case!' Véronique spoke to Jean-Marc but her eyes strayed around the room and her fingers played with her coffee cup. 'How long have you been in Paris?'

'Nine days.'

'So long? I see.'

Their eyes finally met and a shiver ran down Catherine's spine. Before any more could be said or done, however, the door suddenly burst open and a little girl rocketed into the room.

'Nathalie!'

Catherine stood up and scooped the child into her arms. And it was so very obvious that Nathalie remembered and was as fond of the au pair girl as Catherine was of her. The remainder of the afternoon centred around the child, and when it was her bath and bedtime, Catherine pleaded with the mother to allow her to perform those wonderful tasks, just as she had done in the past. Nathalie's mum laughed and went into the kitchen to tell Elfie that, after she had finished preparing the vegetables, she could take the evening off.

Catherine was pleased to have time to herself with Nathalie, not only because she wanted to be with the little girl but because she sensed that Jean-Marc and his sister-in-law needed to talk. Véronique didn't approve of this relationship; that much was obvious. Catherine probably wasn't good enough for the Frenchman, who came from a totally different social class. Oh, she knew that Véronique liked her well enough in her place. A competent, hard-working au pair girl who'd adapted very easily to life within the de Bergiers' family circle. But that place didn't expand to being a possible member of the de Bergier family; Jean-Marc's wife. Of course not; how could she ever have imagined that it would? She suddenly felt extremely hurt, disillusioned, and she had to choke back tears as Nathalie happily splashed about in her bath. But more than anything else, she felt so sorry for Jean-Marc. His family would no doubt make him suffer for his lack of discrimination in choosing a partner. If Véronique's behaviour was anything to go by, Catherine felt sure he'd have to face the possibility of being totally ostracised by the family ... and she began to dread Henri de Bergier's arrival home from the office.

Henri de Bergier, however, was charm itself. As soon as he walked into the salon, he made Catherine feel like a long-lost and much-beloved relative. To his cousin, he was extremely polite and extremely cool. The dinner, which could have been a sumptuous and convivial meal, was ruined by lengthy and embarrassing silences. The host and hostess remained polite throughout, but their superficial civility didn't camouflage their evident disapproval of Catherine and Jean-Marc's relationship. By the end of the meal, Catherine was beginning to feel riddled with guilt, very near to tears and desperate to get away. No wonder Jean-Marc hadn't wanted to bring her back here; he'd known that they would never accept her as his girlfriend, lover, wife, whatever. No doubt he hadn't wanted to shatter her warm, loving memories of his family, hence his reluctance to get in touch with Henri and Véronique. Oh, if only they hadn't come here. If only she had listened to him instead of being so determined to have her own way. After dinner, cognac in the salon and then hopefully back to the peaceful apartment in Vincennes.

Henri de Bergier was a little shorter than his wife, quite plump and thinning on top. In the not-so-distant past, Catherine would have described him as 'cuddly', 'lovable' even, but those qualities weren't much in evidence that evening. His initial charm had quickly deteriorated into cold politeness and that, in turn, had become a palpable reserve. Watching the two men sitting side by side on one of the sofas, it was incredible to think that they were first cousins; strangers' behaviour could have been more congenial. Catherine tried to finish her drink quickly and inconspicuously. Surely, they'd be leaving when their snifters were empty? After some silence, Henri suddenly turned to Jean-Marc and asked when they would be returning to England.

'Next Saturday. We fly at noon.'

'Next Saturday.' Henri looked at the floor and nodded his head. 'And all your remaining days are spoken for?'

This was no ordinary question; that was pretty obvious. He wasn't about to ask if there were museums they intended to visit or films and shows to see. Catherine looked at Jean-Marc during the silence that followed and watched the cousins watching one another.

'Yes, Henri. All our days are very much spoken for.' A slight pause. 'Well, I think it's time for us to say goodbye.' He looked at Catherine. 'I hope you've enjoyed yourself, *chérie*. I know how much you wanted to visit your French family again.'

Catherine breathed a sigh of relief and ignored the stinging sarcasm. She smiled at everyone.

'Yes, of course I wanted to see my family again. And it was especially lovely to see Nathalie again and put her to bed and read to her. She's even more adorable than she used to be, if that's possible. I ... I love her *so* much. Please give her another kiss and a big hug from me, won't you?'

She stood up at the same time as Jean-Marc.

'And thank you for a delicious meal, Véronique. You're still a wonderful cook.'

Her words were clipped, artificial, so unlike her. She hadn't intended leaving this way. It wasn't what she wanted at all. Oh, why did there have to be such a thing as class? Why couldn't everyone be considered the same, no matter how much money or not they had, no matter what kind of family they'd been born into? Véronique offered her cheek to be kissed and Henri did the same. But it was standard practice, a French norm; there were no feelings behind the physical display of their affection. Jean-Marc then shook hands with his cousin and briefly kissed Véronique's cheek, but their farewells were less than fond.

'*Au revoir*,' they said and added something like, 'Have a good trip back to England.'

Jean-Marc looked steadily at both of them as he and Catherine stood on the landing on their way to the lift.

'I may call you before we leave Paris,' he murmured.

Neither Véronique nor Henri made a reply.

Chapter Twelve

Whether or not Jean-Marc telephoned his cousin before he left Paris, Catherine never found out. She didn't hear or see him using the telephone in the apartment and she certainly didn't ask him. She would have liked to, of course, but the truth was she simply didn't dare. Henri and Véronique de Bergier were a closed subject; Jean-Marc had made that quite clear the moment they left the apartment in the Latin Quarter. They had taken the metro back to Vincennes and Jean-Marc had marched towards the station, his fists thrust deep inside his trouser pockets, his face a complete blank. Catherine, angry and deeply hurt herself, realised the delicacy of the situation and accepted his silence. It wasn't until they were seated next to each other on the train that she ventured to speak to him. The ice had to be broken sometime and it would have been ridiculous to travel all the way home in total embarrassing silence.

'Jean-Marc?'

He didn't hear her and she gently tugged at his sleeve.

'Talk to me, Jean-Marc. Please tell me why ...'

As if she didn't know why.

'No, Catherine.' He patted her hand as though she were a much-loved but irritating child. 'It's actually none of your business.'

The callous words, curtly spoken, curdled Catherine's insides and bewildered her at the same time. Of course it was her business, for God's sake.

'Jean-Marc, please. I think it *is* my business. And even if it's not, I want you to share your problems with me and—'

'Catherine, please forget it. I didn't want us to visit Henri and Véronique but you insisted and you had a terrible evening. We both did. Let's leave it at that, shall we?'

It wasn't what he said particularly; it was the way he said it and the look he gave her at the same time. And Catherine didn't raise the subject again.

Apart from the obvious and unwelcome cloud hanging over their relationship now, their remaining days in France were nothing short of idyllic. They visited places known and loved by both of them and explored new territory. They always managed to find new ways to fill their time. They sometimes ate in ridiculously expensive restaurants and at other times cooked each other less-than- gourmet meals in the apartment. Catherine adored the ancient kitchen and would have loved to be set free in there one whole morning after shopping at the outdoor market; cooking a complicated, time-consuming but well-worth-it meal for Jean-Marc to tuck into and appreciate. But he put his foot down, very firmly. Catherine was there on holiday and she must rest as much as possible.

'I thought I was supposed to be resting?'

Catherine lifted her head from Jean-Marc's shoulder and looked into his eyes. They were exhausted after hours of love-making on the blue brocade counterpane on his bed.

'There is a time and place for everything, *mademoiselle*.'

They both laughed and Jean-Marc ran his fingers through Catherine's hair and down her naked back. She moaned. He pulled her towards him, breathed her name softly over and over and kissed her with the urgency that she didn't really understand and didn't want to understand. He loved her, of that she was so very, very sure, and as far as she was concerned that was all that mattered. She felt him pushing her down onto the bed, felt his lips moving slowly down her body and when she felt his tongue inside her she moaned and thanked God for Jean-Marc de Bergier.

*

It was a beautiful evening and their last in Paris. To say farewell to the city they both loved, they were going to see a cabaret at the quaint old Lapin Agile followed by a quiet dinner at a bistro in Montmartre. Although they were feeling rather melancholy at the thought of leaving their city, they were also looking forward to the evening ahead. It was going to be special. Catherine had heard of the Lapin Agile but had never had the opportunity to go there. While she was still getting ready – she wanted to look her very best this evening – Jean-Marc opened a bottle of Champagne and handed her a crystal flute as she came out of the bathroom. She did look her very best. The previous day, Jean-Marc had bought her a silk dress in aquamarine with a low-cut sweetheart neckline, huge puffy sleeves to the elbow and lots of swishy material that swung around her legs when she moved. She wore a matching aquamarine comb in her hair and the fragrance surrounding her was the 'Chantage' that Jean-Marc had also given her. He watched her walking towards him. He had never seen her looking so lovely.

'You are very, very beautiful, *mademoiselle*. Absolutely gorgeous.'

He kissed her lightly as he handed her the sparkling drink and Catherine laughed.

'I know your game,' she said, 'you're planning on getting me totally tipsy so you can have your wicked way with me during the interlude.'

'You always see through me, you wily northern wench. Cheers.'

Catherine giggled and sipped her Champagne.

'This is nice. What time will we be eating tonight, have you any idea? D'you know, I'm ravenous already. Honestly, I could eat a horse and go back for the saddle.'

Jean-Marc looked at the girl standing in front of him, sophisticated and very sexy in the silk dress and expensive perfume. He was proud of her, yes, for many reasons, but he was also grateful for moments like these when he realised that she was still a gauche, uncomplicated girl and perfect in her unworldliness. Her voice suddenly crashed into his thoughts again.

'I know I shouldn't bring the subject up again, but ...' Catherine turned away from him, unable now to look him in the face. 'You know what I'd really like to do before we leave Paris? I'd like to say goodbye to Véronique, Henri and Nathalie. Just a quick word ... you know, a quick *au revoir* ...'

The silence that followed was long and, no, not embarrassing, she thought, it was alarming. Not because Jean-Marc was angry with her; it would have been better if he had been. But she knew that she'd distressed him and that was painful to her. She didn't know why on earth she'd suggested such a thing; it had come to her in a flash, had just seemed like a good idea, a kind of finale before they went home. How stupid and tactless she'd been. She very quickly wished she could have bitten her words back but she couldn't and he had to answer her and she was terrified at what he was going to say; what she might have to be told.

'You know where the phone is, Catherine. You call them. I'll wait outside.'

And he left the room.

Alone and distressed herself now, Catherine stared at the phone. It seemed to stare back at her, willing her to pick up its receiver and dial the de Bergiers' number. And then she stared at the door that had been gently closed. She opened the door again and walked into the hall where Jean-Marc was standing by the lift gates, his head bowed and his eyes fixed at nothing on the ground. Catherine touched his arm as the lift clanked to a halt.

'Hello.' Her voice was a whisper.

He looked at her questioningly and she would have given anything to interpret the expression in his eyes. Oh, why did she have to go and spoil their evening? What an idiot. She'd only said it on impulse, without really thinking. Oh, she must learn not to be so impulsive, to think more before she opened her mouth. And did more damage.

'It was engaged.' She smiled and stepped into the lift.

*

In spite of the doubtful start, the evening was very successful. A taxi took them to the northern part of the city and dropped them outside the Lapin Agile, the pink house on a street corner which hosted, in a small and very basic room, traditional French cabaret; music, singing, French humour. Catherine was delighted with the place and applauded and cheered and laughed loudly at the puns and jokes. As she later pointed out to Jean-Marc, it wasn't really a touristy place, was it? Non-French speakers wouldn't have a clue what was going on and it would have been a total waste of time.

'And money,' added Jean-Marc.

'Did you notice the row of Japanese tourists?' Cathy said. 'They obviously understood nothing.'

'Yes, they looked absolutely deadpan. Exactly how I probably looked when I first arrived in Yorkshire and was invited to the Batley Variety Club.'

They dined in a bistro on a small, narrow cobbled street away from the lights and noise of Montmartre. The wall lights were soft amber, the pictures of local scenes painted by erstwhile artists and the few tables gingham-cloth covered. Edith Piaf sang soulfully in the background.

'What gastronomic delights shall we sample on this our last evening?' Jean-Marc smiled as the stooping elderly waiter handed them menus.

Catherine felt a stab of misery but quickly returned his smile. Their last evening in Paris. It sounded so ominous, so final. Would they ever come to Paris again? She had to swallow and breathe deeply before she could speak.

127

'I'm going to start with frogs' legs.'

'An excellent choice. I'd have the same just to keep you company but they're far too exotic for my simple taste. I'll be boring and try the soup.'

He ordered the meal and for a while they simply sat and watched the activity around them, holding hands across the table. They chatted about everything and nothing, laughed a lot and reminisced. When their meal and coffee were finished, a silence fell between them. Catherine could eventually feel Jean-Marc's eyes contemplating her face.

'What are you thinking about, Catherine?'

She looked at him and immediately knew what was going through his mind. But he was wrong; she wasn't thinking about the de Bergiers and her earlier regrettable gaffe. She wasn't even thinking about Nathalie.

'Well, I wasn't going to tell you,' she grinned at him, 'because I don't want you to re-become —'

'Re-become? What the …'

'I've just invented the word. Don't interrupt. I don't want you to *re-become* the arrogant pig you used to be. But I was just thinking that this has been the happiest evening of my life.'

Jean-Marc looked vaguely relieved and smiled at her.

'I'm very pleased,' he said. And then he leant across the table and whispered, 'And in that case, I do hope frogs' legs are available in Harrogate.'

The apartment seemed very quiet and still when they returned well after midnight. As though it knew they were leaving. Never to return? Catherine shivered and clung to Jean-Marc in the softly lit salon, their shadows dancing on the ceiling and walls.

'Thank you for giving me such a fabulous holiday,' she whispered. 'I don't want to go home.'

A warm tear rolled down her cheek and Jean-Marc tasted it on his lips.

'I just want to be with you,' she added, almost inaudibly.

Jean-Marc held her tightly, rocked her and kissed her and finally carried her into the bedroom.

'Our holiday isn't over yet,' he said.

And their shadows moved across the ceiling and onto the walls.

Chapter Thirteen

Molly Carter was pleased that her daughter had enjoyed her holiday so much and even more pleased that it had obviously done her so much good. She was looking like a human being again and for that Molly was thankful. But she wasn't prepared for the blow that Catherine delivered an hour after her return. And why hadn't that blinkin' Frenchman been man enough to come with her and explain himself?

'I can't believe what you're sayin', Cathy, I just can't believe it.'

Catherine sighed, rolled her eyes and tried to control her rising temper. Why hadn't she allowed Jean-Marc to come and talk to her mother, as well? He'd wanted to, had almost begged her, and she wouldn't hear of it. Now, she thought, she must have been mad. Did she think her mum would be highly delighted and congratulate her? As far as Molly was concerned, Catherine was still her little girl, not a young woman heading for her twenty-third birthday. But the world had moved on since Jane Austen's day.

'I can't believe what yer tellin' me.'

Molly sank into her armchair and sat staring ahead of her, and Catherine's patience was beginning to wear very thin.

'Oh, for goodness' sake, Mum, I'm not even moving out of the area. I mean, quite honestly, you didn't carry on like this when I went to live in Paris for a year …'

'Of course I didn't, you silly girl! You weren't goin' to live with a man then, were you? A foreigner who's too old for you anyway …'

'Oh, come on, Mum, you've never said that about Jean-Marc before. Never. He's always been "that charming Frenchman" and "mature", "responsible". Never a foreigner who's too old for me.'

Molly burst into tears.

'Oh, I'm sorry, love. I do like Jean-Marc, you know I do. But what will I tell folk? You know 'ow people talk. Me daughter's left 'ome – she's gone to live with a man.'

'You make it sound like one of the seven deadly sins.'

And it wasn't a sin at all. She was going to move into Jean-Marc's cottage so they could be together every day. Living together. He had suggested it

129

the evening before, their last evening in Paris. He had carried her, tearful, into the bedroom, made beautiful love to her and, afterwards, had asked her to come and live with him at his cottage in Russetlea. He'd asked her to think about it carefully and to talk it over with her mother – there would be so many things to sort out – and they would discuss it again in a week or two. But Catherine didn't need to think it over; she didn't need to talk things over with anybody, only him. More than anything else in the world she wanted to be with Jean-Marc, living with him, sharing every day with him. And no, she wouldn't 'talk things over' with her mum; she'd tell her. It wouldn't be easy; Molly had some very antiquated ideas about relationships and, although she held her tongue, Catherine knew she wasn't very happy about her spending nights and weekends at Russetlea. The holiday she'd overlooked; it had been a necessity. And, anyway, Molly had to realise sooner or later that Catherine was an adult with her own life to lead and she'd met the man she wanted to lead it with. And then Jean-Marc had begged her to let him talk to Molly – wouldn't he look like a real coward if he wasn't there? No, he could talk to her later, Catherine said, but she first had to speak to her mother alone.

'I'm sorry, Cathy,' Molly was wiping her eyes with an already almost drenched tissue, 'but it's not what I'd have expected of me daughter.'

'And what did you expect of your daughter, Mum? A big, fancy white wedding and marriage to a boring twerp in a semi-detached, two point five kids and a caravan in the front garden? That's not for me, Mum. I need my independence.'

'What d'you mean, you need yer independence when yer tekkin' off to live with a man?'

Catherine cringed. She managed to make it sound so ... so *unsavoury.*

'I mean that I need my own life, as well. My job ... my career.'

Molly leapt at the word and jumped forward in her chair, waving the wet tissue.

'Career! And that's another thing! How will this malarkey affect yer job, eh? What's Sam Morrison goin' to say about it?'

Catherine couldn't help but smile. It was absolutely nothing to do with Sam Morrison or anybody else. But, knowing Sam, he'd be as pleased as punch; he thought the world of both of them.

'If anything, it'll help my career. Just imagine, I'll have my tutor on call twenty-four hours a day!'

It was a daft thing to say but it brought a small smile to Molly's face. She sighed heavily and pulled herself out of the chair. She walked across to her daughter sitting rather stiffly on the sofa and took her face in her warm, chubby hands.

'If you think yer doin' the right thing, love, then I wish you both well. I would 'ave preferred that big, fancy white weddin' you talked about, I can't deny that. Anyway, you know where yer home is if it doesn't work out. Yer mum's always 'ere.'

*

Catherine moved into Jean-Marc's cottage on 14th June 1975, giving herself a month to 'sort herself out' and make preparations. Jean-Marc had previously had a long talk to Molly and convinced her that her daughter would be well looked after, loved and respected. That was what he guessed Molly Carter feared the most; that he would lose his respect for Catherine. A ridiculous, antiquated idea, he thought, but a deeply ingrained one passed down from previous generations. Jean-Marc and Catherine took Molly to the cottage, showed her round the home and the village, fed her, entertained her, and when they felt she was finally coming round to the idea, they took her home.

Sam Morrison responded to the news exactly as Catherine had anticipated.

'Well, lass, if yer sure yer doin' the right thing then I'm very 'appy for the pair of you. You allus seem as 'appy as two pigs in proverbial muck when I see you together.'

He leant across his desk and, with a twinkle in his eyes, winked and added,

'I'd like to know what 'appened in Gay Paree to spur 'im on to this!'

Catherine laughed.

'I bet you would. But I tell you what, Sam, I'll never tell you!'

Sam roared with laughter as Catherine closed the door behind her.

*

'As 'appy as two pigs in proverbial muck'. Sam certainly had a strange way with words, but he was always right on target. Catherine and Jean-Marc were as 'appy as two pigs in muck. It wasn't easy at first, of course, but neither of them expected it to be. When Catherine left home on that Saturday, Molly didn't exactly cause a scene but she certainly made her presence felt. She sat alone on the sofa watching her daughter preparing for her new life, unhappy in Catherine's happiness. Catherine, normally sensitive to others' emotions, surprisingly didn't seem to notice.

'You *are* quite sure yer doin' the right thing, aren't you, Cathy? I mean …'

'Yes, Mum, I'm quite sure. Would you pass me that little blue bag over there, please?'

'Well, if things don't turn out as you expect, you know you can always come back to—'

'Mum, don't keep saying that! It's like you're wishing it on us. Thanks – oh, I think I've left my jewellery box upstairs. I'm certainly not going to leave *those* worldly goods behind!'

She grinned at her mother and Molly said,

'Speakin' of worldly goods, d'you think 'e *will* marry you, one day?'

Catherine brushed past her and made some remark equivalent to '*Que sera, sera*', not wanting to prolong the subject. She skipped upstairs and came down with another boxful of belongings. Molly was sitting in the same position, the same expression on her face, not having moved at all in Catherine's absence. Catherine fell onto a convenient chair with the heavy box on her lap, and her fingers rifled through its contents. A lot of the stuff went into the bin and then she pulled out a pile of airmail envelopes tied with string. All Diana's letters and cards sent from Australia. She caught her breath. Diana. They certainly wouldn't be going in the bin; they'd be going with her to Russetlea. *Oh, Diana. If only I could write and tell you about all this. Or, better still, if only you were here to share all this with me.* She checked the date of Diana's last piece of correspondence, a simple postcard of the Sydney Opera House. But she couldn't write to her now. Too much time had elapsed; it was too late. Diana had her own life and, after not replying to a couple of Cathy's letters, it was pretty obvious that she wasn't interested in her old best friend's life anymore … And then Jean-Marc arrived. He had hired a small van for the day and together he and Catherine piled her things inside.

'Good God, woman, I didn't realise you had so much stuff. We may have to move into Mullion Hall before I intended.'

Catherine looked at him, ready to make a joke about his last remark and then noticed the expression on his face. Confusion mixed with regret and a little bit of humour thrown in. Before Catherine could open her mouth, Jean-Marc quickly asked, 'Where did you get that ridiculous teddy bear?'

'A ridiculous man bought it for me in Paris a few weeks ago. Don't throw him like that – he hurts!'

Molly watched and listened to them and tried to force back unwanted tears. They were so happy now and she was glad for them, oh yes, she really was glad for them. It was herself she was crying for, the selfish old so-and-so that she was. She ought to be thinking about her daughter and her happiness now, not her own loneliness in this great big house again.

Catherine was taking hold of her hand and she was saying something to her.

'... so I'll give you a ring tonight. Mum, did you hear me?'

'What, love?'

'I said we're off now and I'll give you a ... Oh, Mum, don't cry, please don't cry. I'm not going nearly as far as I went last time, am I?'

'No, I know, love. It's just me, I'm daft. You won't forget me, will you?'

'Mum, you definitely *are* daft! I'll be on the phone in about two hours, I promise.'

Molly waved them off and when the white Transit van had disappeared from view, she wept buckets until the telephone rang.

*

It was easy living with Jean-Marc; comfortable and, at the same time, exciting. They soon adjusted to each other's timetables, getting up together every morning in order to have a hurried breakfast with each other before Jean-Marc ran Catherine into Harrogate. Whoever arrived home first in the evening would prepare the dinner, and they always washed up together afterwards. They either washed up or crashed out in the two maroon leather chairs, to recover from their respective days.

They often worked together in the evenings. Not as a tutor and his student anymore; that aspect of their relationship had long since terminated. Jean-Marc no longer gave private French lessons at home – for him, it had been a way of fighting off loneliness, a pleasant and lucrative way of meeting people. But he didn't need the money. He'd made a couple of male friends through the enterprise and, of course, he'd met Catherine. And when Catherine moved in, the private lessons moved out. But he always had plenty of marking to do and lessons to prepare in the evening and he would sit and work quietly at his desk in the study/living room. And when Catherine had translations to do, which meant lots of overtime, she now took them home and worked in the study with her man. Sometimes, she turned to him for advice and help and he was always happy to assist, in spite of his own workload. Although Catherine was still working hard, at least she was in the comfort of her own home with the inexhaustible coffee pot at hand and nobody breathing down her neck. Weekend work was out; Jean-Marc made sure of that. Unless there were any college functions or work on his part that desperately needed to be finished between Friday evening and Monday morning, their weekends were reserved for pleasure.

The summer of 1975 was long and hot and perfect. Jean-Marc broke up from the college on the next to last Friday in July and wasn't to return until the second week in September. Catherine was due for another fortnight's holiday before the end of the year.

'We'll go to the South of France,' Jean-Marc told her, right out of the blue.

Catherine was delightfully stunned.

'Did I tell you my family have a house on the Mediterranean? A little place called Collioure, to be exact.'

His family? Henri and Véronique? He didn't have to tell her about the house in enchanting Collioure, she'd spent the summer there two years before; celebrated her twenty-first birthday there. It must be the same place but how could she tell him? How could she bear to see that look in his eyes again? But she couldn't *not* be honest with him, either.

'Well, actually, I've already been there, erm... with Henri and Véronique.'

She almost whispered the words, knowing that she was hurting him, but he had to know.

'We spent a month there. They gave a twenty-first birthday party for me there. In that house.'

'Well... would you like to celebrate your twenty-third birthday in that house, too?'

Catherine flung herself into his arms, loving him and wanting him to know that she loved him and would always love him...

'Jean-Marc,' she began, and didn't know how to continue, 'about Henri and—'

He pushed her away. Gently and compassionately but he pushed her away and he didn't look at her.

'Darling.' Catherine decided to persist, needing to talk to him, get this thing out into the open, discuss it, thrash it out and kill it. It was ridiculous and had gone on far too long. 'Look, I can accept it if Véronique and Henri don't think I'm good enough for you. It hurts, I can't pretend it doesn't, but I can accept it. After all, I was their au pair girl – a nanny-cum-cleaner, if you like – with hardly any money of my own. Even though they were really, really kind to me and we got on really well, I can understand they don't want their nearest relative to be . . . involved with me. I suppose it's normal. Don't take it to heart. If I can accept it, you can, too. Let's just—'

'Catherine, you haven't the faintest idea what you're talking about.'

*

Despite the seemingly immovable fly in the ointment, the holiday in Collioure, a charming small coastal town at the foot of the Pyrenees, was perfect. The house stood at the top of a narrow, winding incline with views of red-tiled rooftops, hills and, beyond, the sea. The house was also red-roofed with green shutters at the windows and an abundance of bougainvillea and other multi-coloured flowers in the window boxes and the small garden. The stone terrace at the back of the house sported sun loungers, tables, cushioned chairs and enormous parasols. Parasol pines shaded the house itself from all angles. Jean-Marc and Catherine spent long, hot days lying on beaches, exploring the old town, hiking in the mountains and taking boats around the coastline. They spent long, hot nights making love in the bed that two years previously Véronique and Henri had shared.

One night during the second week, Catherine woke up with a raging thirst. She rubbed her eyes, yawned and quietly got out of bed, not wanting to disturb Jean-Marc. She needn't have bothered. He was standing, a towel wrapped around his waist, on the balcony, leaning against the balustrade and looking out at the midnight blue sea. Catherine looked at the clock by her bedside. It told her it was just after three o'clock. She didn't know what to do, whether or not to speak. He must have heard her, however, or felt her presence, because he slowly turned round. Catherine was horrified to see tears in his eyes.

'Jean-Marc ...'

'Go back to bed, darling. I'm coming back now. I couldn't sleep ...'

What had happened? What was going on? Catherine couldn't just go back to bed not knowing what was troubling him ... She suddenly felt nauseous. Was it her? Something she'd said, done ...? But they were happy together ... He never made her cry and she could never, ever imagine making him cry ... What was wrong with him? Was he ill ...? A sudden panic soared through her and she rushed at him, trying to fling her arms around him and cling to him. He caught hold of her wrists and gently pushed her away.

'Catherine, for God's sake, don't you know when you're not wanted? Please go back to bed.'

*

The following day was Catherine's birthday and Jean-Marc gave her a gold watch by Tissot and a beautifully illustrated hardback book about Collioure. She was still lying in bed when he brought the gifts to her; trying to catch up on the sleep that she'd lost during the night. Her eyes were swollen and bloodshot, her skin sallow and pasty. She hiccuped loudly as Jean-Marc approached the bed, as though she'd been sobbing. Which she had. Jean-Marc sat on the bed, the same towel wrapped around his middle, and looked down at her. Was this the same man who had told her she wasn't wanted? His eyes seemed to be asking for her forgiveness but Catherine merely looked at him, her expression giving nothing away.

'Happy birthday, Catherine.'

Jean-Marc bent and kissed her and although Catherine accepted the kiss, she remained passive. Their eyes didn't meet and for a while there was a strange, unprecedented silence between them.

'Catherine.'

'You told me I wasn't wanted.' Followed by a loud hiccup.

'Yes, but, I didn't mean ... You know I didn't mean ...'

'Jean-Marc, I don't know anything because you won't tell me anything. How can you expect me to accept what I don't know? And I'm sure you don't expect me to tolerate the kind of treatment I got last night ... Surely

136

you know me better than that? If you want me to leave, if you're tired of me, then please be honest. Tell me exactly how you feel and I'll … I'll go. I've got my pride, please don't forget that.'

For a while, Jean-Marc said nothing, only sat looking at her with the same expression on his face.

'Look, I'm sorry for what I said last night. It was unforgivable. I didn't mean it, and you must know I didn't mean it. I love you and the last thing I want you to do is leave me.' He paused. Then he closed his eyes, opened his mouth and took a deep breath. Catherine waited. He exhaled and closed his mouth. Catherine slowly opened the gifts that under different circumstances would have delighted her. Jean-Marc kissed her slowly and gently and then made love to her over and over again, each time more urgently than the last, and he made Catherine feel very, very wanted.

Later, they strolled down to the marketplace, bought some fruit, a variety of cheeses and a baguette and took their picnic to the beach. They swam and played in the warm Mediterranean, ate their simple lunch and drank litres of ice-cold mineral water while they soaked up the sun. It was almost as though the previous night's drama had been a dream, or rather a nightmare.

*

September came and Jean-Marc returned to his teaching at the college, refreshed and revitalised and eager to meet his new students. He brought home stories about his lively days in the classroom; amusing, interesting and sometimes heartbreaking anecdotes about the young people under his guidance. And Catherine, in her turn, brought home stories about William Kaye International; the people she worked with on a day-to-day basis and the visitors whom she met once and whose paths she would never cross again.

'Sam's a killer, he really is,' she giggled one evening when they were relaxing in their chairs, drinking a bottle of rosé wine and listening to Chopin. 'He doesn't seem to realise, even after all these years, that foreigners don't always understand a broad Yorkshire accent. Honestly, he doesn't think to speak the Queen's English to anybody; he doesn't give a damn. And this poor German man this morning, he just stood in the office and looked totally bewildered. He thought he could speak and understand

English till he met Sam Morrison. I've tried to tell him, you know, to speak more slowly and more distinctly, and then he looks all hurt and I feel awful. He's a bit too old to change now, I suppose. Silly old sod.'

Jean-Marc poured more wine into their almost-empty glasses.

'You're very fond of the silly old sod, aren't you, Catherine?'

She laughed.

'I wouldn't change him for the world.'

Catherine loved the autumn so much that Jean-Marc bought her a camera so that she could capture the season on film. She screamed with delight.

'It's not a highly technical thing, is it, that I won't understand? I don't want to ruin my pictures!'

'Would I buy you anything that wasn't perfectly simple, my love?'

She playfully slapped his cheek and he explained that, although this was a bit more of an advanced model than the tin box she'd taken to France, it wasn't so highly technical that it would confuse her ... he knew how easily she got confused. She slapped him again.

The following weekend, they walked into the countryside surrounding Russetlea, Catherine delighting in the lovely season and Jean-Marc delighting in Catherine. They tramped through woodland, the amber leaves crunching beneath their feet, the gentle mists cool around their faces, the odd squirrel, hedgehog and numerous birds fluttering and chirruping around them. Catherine refused to go home until her film was finished, and when they finally arrived at the cottage, tired, cold and hungry, she announced,

'I'll buy another film next week and we can do the same next Sunday, somewhere else. Shall we?'

'Okay,' he groaned, 'but promise me – promise me, Catherine – that you'll buy a twelve exposure instead of a thirty-six. Please.'

Life was as perfect as life could be. They had their disagreements, of course, and their quarrels, and since Catherine had moved into the cottage, they both had adjustments to make to their lives. But, as she told Molly on her frequent visits home (or on Molly's less frequent visits to them), they were so compatible that they didn't worry about their occasional fights and squabbles; they just added a bit of extra spice to their lives. And when Molly asked, as she often did, if her daughter was happy, really happy, the answer was always the same.

'Yes, Mum, I've never been as happy in my life. Honestly.'

*

As the autumn days grew shorter and winter was obviously not long in coming, Catherine began to look forward to Christmas. Christmas in the cottage with Jean-Marc – and her mum, of course. She would bake her first Christmas cake and sod the consequences. Well, it would probably be a disaster but her two favourite people would eat it, anyway. And she was looking forward to putting up that gorgeous tree and the lovely lights and … oh, Christmas would be such a happy time this year. So perfect in her own home. Well, her and Jean-Marc's home, of course. And there was the office party, too; she was definitely looking forward to that. William Kaye International had booked a room at a big hotel in Harrogate. It was going to be a dinner and dance and husbands, wives or friends were invited too, which she was pleased about. It wouldn't have been the same without Jean-Marc. Nothing ever was. And, anyway, he was almost a part of the company, he knew so many people there.

Two weeks before William Kaye International closed for the Christmas holiday, Sam Morrison picked up the internal phone on his desk, rang Catherine's number and asked her to come into his office. No, she didn't need her shorthand pad, just 'erself.

'Could you give me a couple of minutes, please, Sam? I'd like to just finish typing this translation – the last short paragraph – and I'll be with you. Thanks a lot.'

Catherine walked into Sam's office smiling beautifully and she walked out weeping.

Brian

Chapter Fourteen

'Congratulations, young man,' said the managing director of William Kaye International, a man not renowned for lavish praise. 'This is indeed a great achievement. You're obviously following in Sam's footsteps. He was always a worker and he reaped his rewards. We're all going to miss him. He was a pillar in this company and he'll be a hard man to follow. You've got your work cut out but I think you're made of the same stuff as Sam, and I think you'll be a credit to the company.'

Brian Jarvis gave a short, suitable reply to this small speech and looked around the office that now belonged to him. He'd sat on the wrong side of this desk often enough and had known he'd be the one to inherit it one day. But he hadn't expected it to be so soon. He looked at the shining brass nameplate perched on the desk, identical to the one screwed onto the door.

BRIAN JARVIS: EXPORT MANAGER

Export manager of a large international company and him only twenty-four years old. Well, he'd have to work his backside off now, there was nothing surer, but work didn't frighten him. He thrived on it. That's why he'd got as far as he had in so short a time. He wouldn't be sitting at this desk, though, day in, day out, like Sam Morrison usually was, sending his reps to all corners of the globe. *He* would still be flying to all corners of the globe; meeting people, finding new clients, making big sales. It was in his blood, travelling, conquering the world ... it was his forté and he wasn't going to give it up. He turned to John Markham, the managing director, and grinned.

'I won't disappoint you, Mr Markham. You won't be sorry that Sam Morrison retired.'

Well, it was a great way to start the new year, 1976. And the year would get even better, he'd make sure of that. He was heading in the right direction; it was what he deserved and he'd carry on, working up the ladder. Although this promotion had come right out of the blue, he'd been expecting it for a long time, wondering when it would happen. Sam Morrison couldn't go on for ever and he'd been hinting for months that if Brian played his cards right ... well, he had played his cards right and it had paid off. The only thing that Brian regretted was missing Sam's retirement party-come-Christmas-Dinner-Dance on the evening that William Kaye International broke up for the holiday. He'd had a real send-off by all accounts and there'd been a lot of weeping and wailing and carrying-on. The staff had made a collection, of course, and bought him a gold watch. And Brian, Sam's successor, hadn't been part of it. He'd been in New York at the time, clinching a very unexpected sale and that was more important than any party. Including Sam's swan song.

Brian was alone in his office now. He moved around trying to familiarise himself with the place. Sam's stamp was everywhere; his reference on files, his name printed, typed, written, scribbled everywhere, his signature on various papers. Sam would be around for a long time yet, in spirit if not in the flesh. A man of his calibre wouldn't disappear into thin air. Not that Brian wanted him to; he respected and admired the old geezer too much to want to erase his memory completely. He sighed, grinned to himself and sat down in the black leather and chrome swivel chair that was now his. He picked up the nameplate and examined it. This was what mattered now:

BRIAN JARVIS: EXPORT MANAGER

Sam's memory might live for a long time, but Brian Jarvis was here in flesh and blood. And William Kaye International would know about it, by God they would.

*

Although Brian's professional life was successful, his private life was giving him many sleepless nights. Under the glamorous, worldly and successful exterior, he was an unhappy man. He enjoyed the high life he was leading, of course; the travelling, the money, the women. But he had no roots, nothing he could call his own. He would never dream of admitting it to anybody, least of all to himself, and on the surface, he appeared to be an enviable young bloke who had everything going for him. But he hadn't set foot inside his home for almost three years and, ever since that evening, many months before, when he'd been evicted from his flat in Roundhay, he'd drifted from one bedsit to another, never being able to settle down and not knowing if he really wanted to. On that fateful evening when, once more, he'd had to rely on Neil and Linda's hospitality, he'd promised himself to get even; have his revenge on Melanie, his sister, who could have been sired by the devil. But after he'd cooled down (or rather, after Neil had cooled him down) and he'd had time to think things over, he had decided not to give her the satisfaction of knowing how she'd ruined his impeccable reputation and pride. He just wanted to wipe her out of his mind, pretend that Melanie didn't exist. Unfortunately, he didn't feel the same way about his father, whom he would have loved to visit again. But his father had no thought for Brian. For him, it was and always would be Melanie, Melanie, Melanie ... No, Brian could never go back to Greystones. He occasionally sent substantial (in his opinion) cheques to his dad, more to absolve his guilt than for reasons of responsibility, and he'd sometimes picked up the phone and started to dial ... but that was as far as he got. When the telephone rang at Greystones, Brian was never the caller. Apart from the infrequent cheques, Brian had cut off all contact with his home. He didn't really have a home anymore.

*

He turned the key in the lock and thrust open the stiff, creaking door. He'd have to get this bloody thing fixed before it drove him round the twist ... and the window frame in the bedroom, the one that let water in. He'd have to speak to the landlord the next time he called for the rent. This Friday ... Christ, it soon came round. He'd better not let on to that old Scrooge about his promotion or the rent would be going up. That was one person he *wouldn't* be telling the glad tidings to.

The house stood in the centre of a long terrace of back-to-backs in the vicinity of Hyde Park, a stone's throw from the main buildings of Leeds University. It was therefore a district packed with student accommodation and, as such, not the quietest of suburbs. Brian climbed the badly lit staircase up two flights and into the attic, which was his bedroom. He opened the door and shivered. It was bloody freezing in here; just as well a mild winter had been forecast or he'd be dying of hyperthermia. He flung his briefcase onto a solitary chair with chipped wooden arms and threadbare green upholstery, and then flung himself onto the lumpy single bed. He closed his eyes. Christ, it was cold. He could go downstairs, of course, into the small, cramped living room and sit huddled in front of the gas fire, but Danny would probably come down 'just to keep him company'.

It was Danny who had advertised for someone to share the house with him. Danny was a Jamaican postgraduate, studying Medicine; very pleasant and polite and all that but a real pain in the arse at times. He was okay when he was in his room studying but when he was in a talkative mood or, worse still, when he brought his intellectual chums to the house, Brian wished he'd go back where he came from: the sunny Caribbean. He closed his eyes; he'd had a hard day; his first day as export manager. He smiled to himself. What he'd really like to do tonight was to go out and celebrate – a real shindig – but he had nobody to celebrate with. There was Danny, of course, but that wasn't quite what Brian had in mind. He wanted a woman and he didn't have one. Most unusual but it was only a temporary inconvenience and one that he'd soon remedy. Tomorrow, for example.

He hadn't met his secretary yet. Not officially. He'd seen her around Sam's office once or twice and they'd been briefly introduced a while ago, if his memory served him well. She hadn't been at the office today; she'd been ill over the Christmas holiday with a touch of flu or something. She'd been so ill, apparently, that she'd also missed Sam's farewell dinner and the old man had been very upset about that. Thought a lot about her and with good reason, or so Brian had been told. He tried to picture her in his mind's eye, from the few times he'd seen her. She was a pretty little thing, if he remembered rightly. Catherine. Cathy. Cathy Carter ... He heard the front door slam shut and Danny's slow, purposeful steps treading the stairs. Cathy Carter, a pretty little thing and, professionally speaking, she'd belong to him. He jumped off the bed, yanked his door open and yelled down the attic stairs.

'Hey! Danny Boy! Do you fancy going out for a few bevvies tonight? I feel like celebrating my promotion.'

He'd suddenly had a change of heart.

He wasn't late for work the following morning but he wasn't exactly on the ball, either. It had been a while since he'd been out on a binge and he'd really gone over the top. Danny didn't drink much, of course, him being into the physiological stuff, but Brian had never needed a partner to help him pour it down the hatch. He could manage quite nicely on his own, thank you. Besides, it worked out a lot cheaper, even if he did suffer the next morning.

He certainly suffered on that Tuesday morning. If it hadn't been for the new job, he'd have phoned to say he was ill; there was nothing surer. As things were, he had to make a big effort and prove himself willing and able. Instead of grabbing a slice of toast and a slurp of coffee, he bolted down a couple of paracetamol, tried to make himself look like a human being, and cursed having to drive all the way to Harrogate's environs. It was times like this when he wished he had a nice little place in Harrogate, but that would never be because he hated the place. Hated it. If anybody had asked him why, it wouldn't have been easy to explain. He hated Harrogate and its entire neighbourhood. Anyway, the rents and rates would be higher there and he wasn't paying out more than he had to. Not bloody likely.

By the time Brian pulled into William Kaye's car park, the paracetamol had done their job and he was beginning to come round. It was just as well – he had a busy day ahead and knew he had to be on his toes. He was going to make a success – a big success – of this job, and no lousy hangover was going to stop him. He pushed open the double doors of the imposing building, winked at the receptionist and headed for the stairs. He was now looking forward to the busy schedule ahead of him and he was keeping his fingers crossed – for more reasons than one – that his secretary would be back at her desk.

She was. Cathy Carter was sitting at her desk, opening the morning post. She didn't seem to hear him come in. Her head was bent over the pile of correspondence and the first thing Brian noticed was the silky, long red-brown hair falling around her shoulders. Nice. He coughed. Cathy Carter's pretty head shot up and she stared at him. You could tell she'd had the flu; her eyes looked puffy and swollen and she had a drawn look about her. Apart from those little defects, though, Cathy Carter was a little cracker. Brian grinned, walked to her desk and held out his hand.

'Hello, you must be Cathy, my – erm – my secretary. We've bumped into each other a couple of times, haven't we? How's the flu?'

Cathy had stood up and was shaking his hand. She had lovely hands, he noticed; soft, warm ... well manicured but no nail varnish or anything false like that ...

'Oh, I'm feeling a lot better than I did, Mr Jarvis, thank you. I'm so sorry I couldn't come in yesterday, it's not like me at all but ...'

'No, I know you're a real grafter, Cathy. Sam told me all about you.'

Cathy blushed.

'He never told me how pretty you are, though,' Brian added and, winking at her, disappeared into his own office and closed the door.

Chapter Fifteen

There was a lot to learn. A hell of a lot. When he had accepted the new position, Brian hadn't realised how much his work would change and the responsibilities he would have to shoulder. He had thought that, because he was an excellent sales rep and the export manager's blue-eyed boy, he could step into the export manager's shoes and start walking. Not so. He had to learn office politics, how to write and dictate business letters, deal with the workforce on a day-to-day basis, and it was all new to him. But Brian had never been a failure; he'd been a fighter right from the nursery because he'd had to be. And he wasn't going to be a failure now. For one thing, Cathy Carter was there to help him.

Cathy proved herself to be everything that Sam had described and more. She was always punctual, crisply efficient without being a pain, always pleasant and a perfect godsend as far as the many translations and foreign visitors were concerned. She was even prepared to take work home with her rather than work late at the office, which amazed Brian. He couldn't understand that; he couldn't understand why she preferred being tied up at home rather than stay over at the office for a bit and have her evenings free. It didn't seem natural somehow, and he often quizzed her about it. Her replies were always the same. Vague.

'I'd rather work in comfort, Brian, to be honest, and at my own pace.' Or words to that effect. Yes, Cathy Carter was definitely rather vague, and as the months wore on, Brian realised that he knew no more about her than he did that first January morning. And it wasn't for want of trying.

*

Brian still travelled but not as often as he used to do and certainly not as often as he would have liked. He found himself grudgingly sending out other reps to countries he either knew well or longed to visit, and to meet people with whom he was familiar or would have liked to be. He tried not to show his resentment when he asked his secretary to organise travel

146

arrangements and hotel bookings; although many a time he felt like snatching the airline tickets out of her hand and taking off himself. He did travel occasionally but now he was needed here in the office, needed to make big business decisions, some which could probably make or break William Kaye International. And he was determined to make it.

*

As well as his professional concerns, Cathy Carter was getting under his skin. It wasn't easy for him to admit, even to himself, but no woman had affected him the way she did. And the ridiculous thing about it was, he didn't know why. He couldn't put his finger on one damn thing and say, yes, that's the reason. That's why Cathy Carter makes me feel like I've never felt before. She was attractive in an unspectacular way, but so were a lot of women. She was pleasant and quite amusing and intelligent, but these weren't outstandingly rare qualities that he could shout from the rooftops. Christ, he'd been used to meeting women like that every week; women who had only to walk into a room and there was a kind of explosion. He'd wined, dined and bedded women like that and thought no more about them. But he thought about Cathy Carter a lot. On the boring drive to and from Harrogate every day. Sitting at his desk or alone in the house at night – she'd even started to invade his dreams. And he didn't know why, because she was just an ordinary, run-of-the-mill working girl. Even her name was nothing to write home about. Cathy Carter. Or Catherine, as she'd told him she preferred to be called. She didn't tell him why and he thought it was a bit odd; Cathy suited her, it was less formal and slipped off the tongue more easily. But he wasn't going to quibble. It suddenly occurred to him, though, when she insisted on his calling her Catherine, that after a period of six months he knew nothing about her. Not a thing. There lay his answer. Catherine Carter was a mystery and that was her big attraction. So, the best thing Brian could do, he decided, would be to solve the mystery. And then young Catherine bloody Carter would be just another female, another bitch, like the rest of them.

*

The end of June 1976 was a real scorcher. Brian went to an international sales conference in Milan for two weeks, worked like a Trojan, made the most of the pasta, Chianti and the nightlife and came home tanned and tired – to a sizzling summer's day. It was a Saturday evening when he touched down at Leeds and Bradford Airport, having taken a quick flight from Heathrow, and he spent the following day recuperating. He wanted to go to the office meeting on Monday morning refreshed and bursting with the sales he'd made and the eager new clients who were now desperate to sample the new machinery manufactured by William Kaye International. He was over an hour late.

The blazing sunshine had brought out the day trippers, mostly retired people who were careful drivers, and the main roads were crammed. This was a bloody good start. Wonder boys were supposed to be on the ball. Christ, he hated being late; it set him back for the day. He honked his horn at the snail in front, cursed all elderly and women drivers and perspired heavily.

He burst into the nine o'clock meeting at ten-fifteen and all eyes turned towards him. His was the only vacant chair. Nobody greeted him with any civility and he slunk into his seat, murmuring his apologies. John Markham was chairing the meeting and he told Brian that the Milan sales conference had been the first item on the agenda and had therefore been omitted, owing to Brian's absence. It wasn't what the man said; it was the way that he said it. And what he didn't say. Sam Morrison would never have been late for a sales meeting. Brian's heart was hammering and his throat had gone dry. The heat in the overcrowded room didn't help. It was times like this when he felt his comparative youth and inexperience. He was still a young pup being trained and he knew that any false move was being noted and discussed. Sod the bloody sunshine.

'Is it worth us going back to the sales conference before we continue the meeting?' John Markham suddenly asked, poker-faced, 'or have you nothing worth reporting?'

Catherine Carter was sitting on John Markham's right, taking the minutes of the meeting. Her pencil was still, poised above her pad, her eyes downcast, and Brian knew that she was embarrassed and feeling sorry for him. He cleared his throat, opened his briefcase and dropped his bulging file onto the long highly polished table.

'I was hoping we could have an extension of the meeting,' he said, looking John Markham straight in the eye. 'I've got a lot to report. And it's all positive. *Very* positive.'

Markham visibly relaxed and he smiled one of his rare smiles.

'In that case, everyone, shall we turn back to the first page?'

Brian breathed again and caught his secretary's eye across the table. She looked stunning today, positively stunning. That green tee-shirt suited her and she'd done her hair a different way; taken it back off her face, or something. Yeah, she looked stunning. He felt a sudden stirring inside him as he pulled out the long, lucrative list of sales.

Chapter Sixteen

'I thought I'd had it this morning,' Brian grinned, 'I thought I was for the chop!'

Catherine, coming into her office from her lunch break spent on the lawns outside, put her bag under her desk, sat down on her swivel chair and swung round to face him. She grinned back at him.

'Well, let's be honest, Brian, after the information you gave to the meeting, Mr Markham could hardly have sent you packing!'

She turned back to her typewriter and began to insert a fresh sheet of paper. She flicked through her ample notes of the meeting. Brian, however, didn't offer to move. He suddenly had a strong, unprecedented desire to spin her round, pull her into his arms and kiss her. His feelings had never been as strong as this before – but she'd never looked like this before. Sensual. Yeah, that was the word. Sensual.

'Catherine.'

She jumped because, engrossed in her work, she hadn't realised he was still standing there. She laughed.

'My nerves must be getting bad! Yes, Brian?'

He was, for the first time in his life, tongue-tied with a member of the opposite sex. He didn't know what to say – he had nothing to say to her – he just wanted to stand and look at her, for God's sake.

'Well,' he suddenly blurted out, 'if the meeting hadn't gone on so long, I'd have asked you to have lunch with me today. That ... erm ... had been my intention. To celebrate my success in Milan.'

Catherine's expression was ... nonplussed. He'd obviously taken her by surprise. Excellent. Brian began to relax and leant against the door between their two offices, smiling and not taking his eyes off her face. He waited for a reply, which wasn't long in coming.

'That would have been nice, Brian.' She began to turn back to her shorthand notes and her machine. 'Oh well, never mind.'

'Well ... erm ... how about dinner instead? This evening?'

Brian was on his own ground now. It hadn't taken long. He was used to seeing women like this, flattered and flustered by his attentions. This one would be no different underneath. He'd wine and dine her a couple of times, pay her a few compliments and he'd soon have her between his sheets ... just like all the other naïve and narcissistic bitches.

'Sorry, that won't be possible. Thank you for asking, though.'

She smiled and turned back again to her work, and Brian felt like he'd been slapped in the face. She'd said no; refused him. He was speechless and after standing and staring at her back for several minutes, he went into his own office and just about managed not to slam the door.

Catherine Carter had refused him. Two humiliations in less than twenty-four hours. He could feel the heat rising to his tanned cheeks and it was nothing to do with the interminable sunshine. He spent the rest of the afternoon trying to concentrate on his mountain of paperwork, plus incessant phone calls and cursing the lousy heat. He couldn't work in these conditions; there was no air. He couldn't think straight. Every time someone knocked at the door and walked in, he could see Catherine busily typing away, her head bent over her pad. Damn the silly little bitch. Well ... she wouldn't refuse him next time.

But she did. And the time after that. Twice the following week, in fact. The sun continued to shine gloriously and everyone continued to swelter, happily. The heat had addled everyone's brain except his own, Brian decided ... how could anyone work efficiently and keep smiling in conditions like these? Hell, he was used to it, more than anyone else in the company, all the places he'd visited ... At that moment, Catherine walked into the office following his authoritative summons. She sat on the leather chair opposite his desk and waited. Brian felt a kind of tremor surge through his body. She was wearing a deep yellow sleeveless dress and her skin had started to turn gold. Her hair was tied back from her face again. Today, it was decorated with yellow and brown combs and hung down her back ... red-brown and lustrous. That was the word, wasn't it? Used in shampoo and hair-colour adverts. Lustrous. He dictated a few letters, two of which had to be translated into French, and as she was standing up, he said,

'Are you doing anything tonight, Catherine? I don't fancy driving straight home when the weather's so good ... seems a shame ... how about taking a drive with me to a country pub? It doesn't have to be far ...'

God, he sounded corny ... where the hell was his usual wham, bam, thank you ma'am ...? He leant back in his chair, folded his cream-coloured trousered legs on top of his desk and lit a cigarette. He looked at her through the smoke.

'I'm really, really sorry, Brian, but I can't. Anyway, thanks for asking.'

Ten minutes passed before Brian shifted his position.

On the Friday evening as they were preparing to leave the office, he invited her out again. He gave her three choices: Friday evening, Saturday evening or how about all day Sunday? *Thanks for asking, Brian, but I can't.*

That weekend in mid-July, the temperature rose even higher and Brian spent the days lying half-naked in his tiny jungle of a garden and the evenings touring the local pubs with Danny. And thinking about Catherine. There must be a bloke. She must be spoken for. There was no other reason he could think of why she should keep saying no. He'd never come across this treatment before; he wasn't used to it and he didn't like it. The silly bitch was probably amusing herself with that old game, playing hard to get, teasing him. Well, if that was the case, she'd be sorry. Unless, of course, there was somebody else, a Mr Wonderful lurking in the background. No. It wasn't possible. She'd never mentioned a soul in all the months she'd been working for him. In fact, she never talked about her personal life at all. She could have been a recluse for all he knew. She really kept herself to herself, did young Catherine, your original Private Person. Well, he'd sort her out sooner or later. You couldn't work with a bod eight or nine hours a day and not get to know what made them tick, now, could you?

*

'What's wrong with you tonight, Brian? You're not the most scintillating boozing companion I've ever had.'

Brian swallowed a mouthful of lager and grinned at his West Indian friend sitting opposite him in the pub that was normally crowded with students. Students were few and far between in the summer months, however, so it was reasonably quiet. Danny never went home during the holidays; too far and too expensive.

'Sorry, old pal, I was miles away. Come on, let's make a move, I've had enough.'

The long hot summer showed no signs of ending. Nor did Brian's infatuation for his secretary. August sizzled and so did Brian's pent-up feelings, which he was determined to control. He was also determined not to let Catherine see the effect she had on him, and he made up his mind to bide his time ... he couldn't take another rebuff; he'd had enough. He contented himself with working alongside her on a daily basis, except on his rare trips, praising her work and paying her mild compliments. She always accepted the praise and the compliments politely, pleasantly, but with total indifference.

Catherine broke up for her summer holiday on the third Friday in August. Before she left the office, she handed several pages of French translation to Brian, which she'd been working on all afternoon. He smiled up at her and greedily cast his eyes over the telexes from affluent clients in Lyon.

'Hey, Catherine, this is great. Twenty more machines wanted for the late autumn ... that'll keep us all in work for a while. What would I do without you, Cathy? How did old Samuel cope before the angels delivered you?'

Catherine smiled and shrugged her shoulders.

'Oh, a very capable French teacher used to do the translations, Brian. See you in a couple of weeks. Bye.'

'Yeah ... see you, Catherine. Have a good holiday.'

After she'd left, Brian wondered how he was going to get through the next couple of weeks without her, and not for only professional reasons. He also wondered where she was taking her holiday and who with. As usual, his secretary had not been at all forthcoming about her plans.

Chapter Seventeen

It was while Catherine was away from the office that Brian decided to do some investigating. He didn't know who, if anybody, her special friends or confidantes were among her colleagues. He had never noticed her singling any of the women out and he'd never heard her mention anybody by name. Catherine never revealed anything about herself even within the limits of the office walls, for God's sake. But there must have been somebody, at least one woman, who had befriended Catherine; not just on a casual, working-day basis, but somebody to share problems and tittle-tattle with in the ladies' loo, or wherever women tittle-tattled. He'd never known a woman yet who didn't have a soulmate of the same sex, except his sister, of course, but she was an exception to every rule. Catherine seemed to be the kind of woman whom other women would turn to; the kind who'd be a good listener and all that rubbish. But he'd never noticed one female lingering longer than usual in her office, for a chat. And he couldn't broadcast to all and sundry what was going on in his mind; he couldn't start an official inquiry on Miss Catherine Carter. There was always the personnel office. They'd have all her personal details, wouldn't they? But, short of infiltrating the office at night and going through the filing cabinets by torchlight, there was no way he'd get any information from that department. Brian wasn't one to make a fool of himself – especially over a woman – and, hell, making 'discreet' enquiries about his secretary would be one sure way of making a fool of himself. He felt himself to be in a bit of a dilemma.

On the third day of Catherine's absence, Brian realised that his work was piling up and getting out of control. Owing to his inexperience, he'd been a bit lax, hadn't foreseen the need of a replacement during Catherine's leave. Why hadn't she thought of it herself? She knew the clerical ropes more than he did … He rang Personnel and James McMichael said he would organise a girl from the general typing pool to help him out for a week or so. Should have already been organised, he said, sorry for the oversight. Janet Bradley would be his temporary help. He thanked Personnel and breathed a sigh of relief.

Janet Bradley was in her late teens, small and slim with large breasts. Brian had previously noticed her about the building, as had most of the male staff, but had never made her acquaintance. Until now. She beamed at him with bright, glossy lips and happily fell into Catherine's chair. She somehow looked incongruous sitting there, at Catherine's immaculate desk. She didn't look the part. Brian inwardly squirmed; he had an uncomfortable feeling that this was going to be the most chaotic week of his working life.

The first morning passed fairly quietly with not too many mishaps, and Brian was just thinking he'd been wrong and done the girl an injustice when there was an almighty shriek from the office next door. He leapt out of his chair and flung the door open.

'What the hell's going on, Janet? Is there a mouse running up your ... chair leg? A spider crawling ...'

'Oh, Mr Jarvis, I can't type *this*. What am I supposed to do with it? Nobody said anything about—'

Brian snatched the letter out of her trembling hand. A scribbled note was pinned to it.

Please translate this and send suitable reply. BJ

He smiled down at the distraught young typist.

'Don't worry, Janet,' he said, as though he was talking to a frightened child. 'My secretary dealt with this last week. It only has to be filed.'

'Oh, that's a relief, Mr Jarvis. So long as you don't expect me to do everything *she* does, translatin' and all that. I couldn't do Cathy's job. She ...'

Janet burst into a fit of ridiculous, relieved giggles and Brian said,

'You know Cathy well, do you, Janet?'

'Well, aye, I've spoken to 'er a few times in canteen an' when she comes down to typin' pool. You know.'

She suddenly yawned loudly without covering her mouth and began to twiddle a pencil in her fingers.

'I see. Okay, well, you can get on with today's letters, and don't forget the filing, Janet.'

Later in the afternoon, Brian asked Janet Bradley if she'd like to have a drink with him that evening. She lived in Harrogate so Brian stayed late at the office, freshened up there and picked her up at eight o'clock. They went to a town centre pub in an alley off Parliament Street and they took their drinks outside. They sat at a rusty wrought iron table, wobbly because of the cobbles. Janet told Brian about her family in Bradford and why she'd left home to get a place of her own – a crummy little bedsit that she paid the earth for. She talked about her job at William Kaye International and the young typists with whom she worked. Brian pretended not to be bored stiff and tried very hard to laugh at the asinine jokes, and he paid her false compliments that she soaked in like a sponge. It was the longest evening he'd ever spent in female company – with the exception of his sister, of course. But she didn't count. When the pub finally stopped serving, he said,

'Okay, sunshine, are you going to show me this crummy little bedsit of yours?'

He knew she wouldn't say no.

Janet Bradley was right. It was a crummy little bedsit but at least it was clean, which was something in its favour. He sat on the lumpy single bed and thanked his hostess for the mug of too-milky coffee. They drank in silence and then Brian took Janet's empty mug out of her hand, paid a few more compliments he didn't mean, and made love to her the best he could. The poor kid did nothing for him. Afterwards, as she snuggled up to him, he could feel her gently dozing and her breathing becoming regular. Oh, no way, he hadn't gone through all this for nothing.

'Janet?'

'Hmm?'

'How well do you know my secretary? Do you talk to each other very often? I mean, about personal things … your families, friends, your love lives, you know, that sort of thing.'

'Well, I do, but then that's me. I'm one o' them girls who likes to be right matey wi' people and it sometimes gets me into bother.'

Brian could well believe it. He was getting impatient.

'Well, you're just naturally friendly, love. That's nice. And what about Catherine? Is she … friendly with you?'

'Oh aye, she's friendly enough. A bit … well, a bit reserved, I suppose you'd say. Don't get me wrong, she's not standoffish or owt like that but …'

'Do you think she's got … many friends?'

''Ow would I know?'

There was a short, heavy silence.

'Why are you askin' me all these questions, anyway?' Janet's now wide-awake eyes looked anxiously into his. 'I 'ope yer not goin' to get me into bother.'

Brian grinned.

'Don't be daft, love. Why would I want to do that? I worry about Catherine, that's all. She seems to be a very lonely young woman and I wondered—'

'Oh, 'ang on a minute, I've just remembered summat. A few of us were once talkin' about travel an' all that and she said 'er best friend had emigrated to Australia a few years ago. And she missed 'er a lot. Yeah, that's right. An' I know 'er dad died when she were a kid.' She paused and then added, 'I don't think she's very lonely, though. I've 'eard 'er mention a bloke's name once or twice. Can't remember what it were – it were foreign. But I suppose with 'er being into translatin' an' all that stuff, she'll go for that type. A foreigner.'

Brian stiffened. Janet fell asleep. Ten minutes later, he got out of bed and left the crummy little bedsit and its occupant. The following morning, he rang Personnel and told them that Janet Bradley was unsatisfactory and could they send someone a little more competent, please?

*

Catherine returned to work just as the long hot summer was beginning to die. She was beautifully tanned, brimming with health and vitality and obviously extremely happy. She walked out of her own office into Brian's, anointing his frustration with that lovely smile.

'Good morning! And thank you so much for the flowers. It's really kind of you.'

The bunch of golden freesias was standing in a rather inelegant pot vase beside her typewriter with a little note that said, *Welcome back. Brian.*

'It's a pleasure,' Brian grinned. 'You've been missed.'

Catherine laughed.

'I always knew my services were indispensable.'

'I'm not talking about your services.'

Brian, sitting behind his desk and swivelling slightly on his chair, looked up at his secretary, his grey eyes scrutinising her face. She had the decency to look a little embarrassed, which was exactly the reaction he'd anticipated. Her cheeks flushed pink under the golden tan and she began to look around the room, at nothing in particular. Brian was beginning to enjoy this and his eyes continued to focus on her face.

'Did you enjoy your holiday, Catherine?'

'Yes, I did, thank you … very much. It was … wonderful. Well, what would you like me to—?'

'I'm pleased to hear it. And are you feeling thoroughly refreshed or have you come back to work for the rest?'

Catherine smiled but avoided his eyes.

'No. I had a very lazy holiday and now I'm ready for the fray.'

She turned to go into her own office but Brian's voice halted her.

'And did your mother enjoy herself, too?'

She looked taken aback at first but replied, 'As far as I know,' which completely took the wind out of Brian's sails.

'I'm … erm … presuming, of course, that you did go on holiday with your mum? I think you once mentioned that she was a widow …'

Catherine's eyes were now twinkling at him but he failed to see the gentle chaffing there.

'Yes, Brian, my mum's a widow. Dad died when I was a little girl.'

Brian pulled himself out of his chair, rammed both hands into his trouser pockets and strolled to the front of his desk. He was now beginning to feel a little more confident.

'You must have got a bit fed up of each other's company after two weeks, I imagine. Mother and daughter on holiday together. Not the stuff of travel brochures' pics and parlance, is it? So, I imagine you're ready for a bit of male company now, eh? How about having dinner with me this evening?'

'I'm sorry, I can't, Brian. Unless there's anything else, shall we get ready for the sales meeting?'

She walked into her office and quietly closed the door.

*

It was Danny who suffered while Brian was analysing his feelings about his secretary. Danny, the innocent bystander who often received the sharp end of Brian's vitriolic tongue. Needless to say, he didn't know why. Brian wasn't one of those few-and-far-between men who could cry on another man's shoulder, especially over a woman. Danny lived from day to day, bewildered and wary, wondering what was happening to the bright,

158

happy-go-lucky chap who shared his home. He eventually put it down to pressure of work, knowing that Brian was taking on more and more responsibility and working much longer hours since his promotion. Privately, he thought that if the job was having such an adverse effect on him then he ought to do something about it before his health suffered, but his common sense told him it would be foolish to speak his thoughts aloud. In the months that they'd shared the same house, Danny had learnt that his mate wasn't the sort of bloke to take kindly to well-meant advice, especially as far as his work and his women were concerned. Danny had learnt from bitter experience that Brian was his own man. He didn't need a friend in the true sense of the word and he was only sharing the house to lessen his financial load – and for the occasional boozing partner when there wasn't a woman around. To a certain extent, this state of affairs suited Danny. He spent most of his evenings alone in his room, studying, and a noisy, garrulous companion was the last thing he wanted. Sometimes, though, it would have been good to have been able to call Brian Jarvis a close friend, especially as his own family was so far away. But he knew that Brian would never change and learnt to accept him exactly as he was, warts and all.

He couldn't accept him any longer, though, not as he'd been behaving in recent weeks. He'd expected the moods, the surliness and foul language to die a quiet death after a while but he'd been disappointed. If anything, the negative traits in Brian's character were swelling to intolerable proportions, and he was becoming impossible to live – or rather share – with.

'How do you fancy a night on the tiles this evening?' Danny suggested, one crisp autumn morning in early October. The new university term would be starting in a couple of weeks and, if Brian carried on as he was doing, Danny's studies would start to suffer. He had to do something. Brian stared at him before he opened the door.

'What's up with you? Wanting some instructions in the ways of the world?'

Danny smiled, more to himself than at Brian, and shrugged his shoulders.

'If you think you can teach me. I just thought it'd be a good idea to have an evening out before I'm back to hard studying. If you don't want to …'

'I never say no to a drink, Danny Boy, you know me.'

*

159

Catherine's tan was beginning to fade but she was still a little cracker. Brian watched her going about her work, talking with everyone who came into the office, laughing at their jokes, offering endless cups of coffee. He could feel the now-familiar stirring inside him, the quickening of his pulse when she came near him, the aching in his loins and the frustration of knowing he could never possess her. He'd stopped trying now, stopped humiliating himself whenever she said no, which was all the time. He knew there was someone in her life; and from certain things she'd let slip, either to himself or in conversation in her office or on the phone, Brian guessed that she lived with the bloke. But she told him nothing directly, never discussed her private life, never confided in him or asked his advice. So, the lucky bastard who shared Catherine's life remained unidentified; a mystery. Catherine never talked about her personal life at all and if he ever quizzed her, her replies were always the same: polite, vague and non-communicative. She was an enigma and Brian craved her. And, in spite of everything, he promised himself that one day he would have her. Her heart, her mind, her body. All of her would belong to him. He didn't know when, how long he would have to wait, but Brian promised himself. And Brian always kept his promises. To himself.

*

Danny suggested going to a quiet pub for a drink but Brian didn't fancy a quiet pub; he was in the mood for a lively evening. He felt like getting thoroughly drunk and to hell with everything. And sod the hangover. Danny didn't show his disappointment.

'Okay. Whatever you like.'

They walked to the local pub, which was full of students back in Leeds for the autumn term. The large bar was thick with smoke and the noise was deafening. Danny visibly squirmed and Brian grinned. He let Danny pay for the first round and went to stand in the middle of the big, unhealthy room, a position which allowed him a view of the bar and its clientèle. He fancied his chances tonight. Lots of pretty, young nymphets around ... Danny pushed a pint of frothy, overflowing lager into his hand, coughing and grimacing and with streaming eyes. He'd bought himself a tomato juice.

'Cheers.' Brian took a long drink and half the liquid disappeared. He licked the froth from his lips and looked around him.

'What d'you think of our chances tonight then, Danny Boy? Seen anybody worth getting the clap for?'

Danny sipped his non-alcoholic drink and his silence proved his disapproval. Brian laughed out loud, enjoying his mate's discomfort. He was a boring bastard sometimes.

'You know, Danny Boy, for a student you're a real wet blanket. I thought you lot were supposed to be a bit on the wild side? You're about as wild as a beakless budgie.'

Danny looked at him, his eyes still streaming.

'I'm a medical student, Brian, and as such I deplore the effects of too much alcohol, cigarette smoking and loose women on a person's health. Yours in particular. The way you're abusing your body, you'll be in your grave before you're forty.'

'Oh, you're a real barrel of laughs tonight, you are. I came out to cheer myself up, not—'

'Exactly. That's why I suggested it – I thought you might need someone to talk to.'

Danny, in order to lessen the severity of his words, grinned and showed his big, white, perfect teeth. He added that this den of iniquity was hardly the place and suggested another, quieter pub a couple of hundred yards away. Brian, at first on the defensive, bit back his angry words, swallowed the rest of his pint and banged his empty glass on the nearest convenient table.

'Okay, Danny Boy, let's go.'

The change of scene changed Brian's mood, and Danny was surprised and relieved that he appeared happy to sit and talk to him. He knew it would do no good whatsoever to lecture him on his unhealthy habits so he let that go. He gently explained how concerned he was about Brian's general attitude and if he had anything at all on his mind, did he want to talk about it?

'I know you've got a lot of responsibilities now,' he added, 'and that's bound to put some stress on you, but there must be a way of coping with it so that it doesn't affect your well-being.'

'What makes you think I've got problems at work? Are you saying I'm incapable of doing my job?' Brian was obviously on the defensive, his tone aggressive, and Danny, smiling, shook his head.

'I'm not saying that at all. I'm guessing, rightly or wrongly. But stressful jobs can affect your health and state of mind, and I know how hard you've been working.'

There was a few minutes' silence and Brian seemed to be turning things over in his mind. Danny watched him, mentally prompting him to spit it all out; to take Danny into his confidence and he would take it from there. At last, Brian spoke, staring into his glass of lager.

'I have got a lot of pressure at work but I can cope with that. And more.' He raised his eyes and looked into Danny's face. 'What would you say if I told you it was a woman?'

Danny was obviously taken aback. This was totally unexpected. Brian Jarvis suffering over a woman?

'Go on. I'm a good listener.'

Brian paused at first and then he plunged in.

'It's my secretary, Catherine. She's ... well, she's pretty special. Don't ask me why because I don't know. It's not her looks. She's pretty, attractive, but she's no Miss World. She's pleasant, amusing, all that crap. But no more than anybody else. I can't put my finger on it but she's got to me, Danny Boy, she's really got to me. And there's not a thing I can do about it.'

'Why not?'

Brian didn't reply immediately and Danny knew that this confession was killing him. But he didn't give a damn about Brian's image or his pride; at least he was getting it out of his system.

'There's a bloke in her life.'

Danny raised an ironic eyebrow. 'That doesn't usually stop you.'

'I know that,' Brian snapped. He looked apologetically at his companion, without apologising. 'It's just that I don't know anything about her – or him. She's one of those secretive – what's the word? – enigmatic types, who keeps herself to herself, even with other women. I don't know why. I'm not sure but I've an idea she lives with him. And I think he's a foreigner.'

'Why don't you find all these things out and then you'd be sure? At least you'd know one way or another and where you stood.'

'What am I supposed to do, Danny Boy, strap her to a chair and slap her around the chops till she comes clean?'

'Well, that's one way. On the other hand, you might be more subtle. Take her out to lunch; show a genuine interest in her as a human being instead of a sex object – or a prospective partner in life ...'

162

Brian's head shot up.

'Who said anything about that?'

'You don't have to say anything. You've fallen in love, Mr Jarvis, and it's shaken you up.'

Brian said nothing.

'Are you nice to her?'

Danny couldn't help thinking that if Brian spoke to his secretary the way he sometimes spoke to him, his chances of success would be rather on the thin side.

'Of course I'm nice to her. Christ, man, I even bought her some flowers when she came back from her holiday. She never even took them home. Left them on her desk. Can you imagine *me* buying flowers?'

'There's a first time for everything. She must be very special. I'd like to meet her.'

For the first time, Brian grinned and raised his glass.

'Danny Boy, one day you might even be a guest at our wedding.' He swallowed some beer. 'Hell, listen to me. I haven't even held her soft little hand yet.'

Danny laughed and slapped his friend on the thigh.

'Like I said, there's a first time for everything.'

Brian slept well that night, the first time for several weeks. The last thing he remembered thinking before he drifted into oblivion was that one day, Danny Boy would make one hell of a doctor.

Chapter Eighteen

The sizzling summer of 1976 had given way to a cool, crisp autumn. Most of the personnel at William Kaye International seemed to fade along with the dying summer. It seemed that while the sun was shining, their spirits were high and their ability and willingness to work were strong. As soon as the temperature dropped, they became inert, lethargic and ill-tempered. Strange. The season didn't affect Brian Jarvis like that; of course, he couldn't work to his utmost capacity in the heat. The cooler months invigorated him, spurred him on to better things. He was pleased to note that his secretary appeared to be made of the same stuff. She certainly didn't fade in the autumn months; she glowed. Her already pleasant personality blossomed; she was a joy to be with.

Unfortunately, he was with her only during office hours. In spite of Danny's well-meaning and, on the surface, sensible advice, Brian had so far been unable to establish anything other than a working relationship with Catherine Carter. And, of course, it was hardly for want of trying. He'd almost worn himself into the ground trying to impress her, invite her, make verbal love to her. He could only go so far without ruining their professional relationship and his own self-esteem, and he went home most evenings feeling drained, frustrated and full of hellfire. It was Danny again who suffered, more so now because his counsel had been to no avail and Brian quietly blamed him. Danny Boy had encouraged him to make a bloody fool of himself and it had got him nowhere. He took out his wrath on the helpless black student and on local girls who excitedly fell into bed with him, little knowing they would neither see nor hear from him again. Danny was the object of his mental frustration; the female population took the brunt of his physical dissatisfaction. And Catherine Carter, the cause of all this mayhem, hadn't the faintest idea what was going on.

It was a cold morning in early November and Brian was nervous. Three French businessmen were expected to arrive at the office at eleven o'clock and they had to be entertained for the rest of the day. A trip around the offices and factory, an expense-account lunch and business negotiations in the afternoon. Only one of the men spoke limited English, the other two none at all. Catherine was going to have to do her stuff, and how. He was relying on her one hundred percent. He felt nervous for two reasons. Not because Catherine couldn't do the job; she could. But because of his own linguistic inadequacies and because of his non-evolving relationship with her. This could be the opportunity he needed. *Would* be, damn it. He smiled to himself as he pulled into the William Kaye car park.

Catherine was already in the office when he arrived, sitting at her typewriter. Her head was bent over her work, her face invisible.

'Good morning!' Brian called as he breezed in.

'Good morning, Brian.' She didn't look up.

He walked straight into his own office and sat down. Five minutes later, he called Catherine in; there was a lot to be done before eleven o'clock. He did a double-take when Catherine walked towards him.

'What the hell's wrong with you?'

Catherine's face was a mass of pink blotches; she wore no make-up and her big brown eyes were red-rimmed and swollen. Her lips were making an effort not to quiver.

'Nothing's wrong, Brian.'

'What! Don't lie to me, Catherine. You've been crying, haven't you? In fact, you're still crying. Sit down ... look, just sit *down* and tell me what's going on.'

Catherine sat down but she didn't tell him what was going on. She merely said it was personal, she'd get over it, she'd pull herself together in a little while. Brian looked at her for a long time and sucked in his breath. It was a bloke, it had to be. A woman would only make herself look like that over a bloke. He lit himself a cigarette, stood up and walked to the window. He stood and looked at the autumn mist drifting over the lawns.

'Well, you'd *better* pull yourself together. Our visitors will be here in less than two hours and we've got work to do. We're also having a business lunch with them and I want you to look pretty. Okay? So, go do something with yourself and don't take too long.'

*

The Frenchmen were punctual and at eleven o'clock Catherine made coffee and took it into Brian's office on a tray. Brian looked at her. She'd done something with her appearance, put a bit of make-up on at least, but it was

165

pretty obvious that she wasn't really here this morning. Christ, if she ruined this business deal, he'd ... At twelve o'clock, there was a knock at Brian's door and he impatiently called, 'Come in.' A nervous and embarrassed office junior crept across the room, her blushing face partially hidden by a huge and beautiful bouquet of red roses.

'These flowers have just arrived for Catherine,' she murmured.

Catherine started, gasped and reddened.

'Oh ... oh, thank you. Thank you, Carole.' She held out her arms and cradled the flowers, her eyes scanning a short handwritten note.

Three of the men in the room were smiling at her. The fourth one said,

'If I'd known we were going to have an interval, I'd have booked an ice-cream vendor. Shall we get back to work now?'

Brian watched Catherine over the next hour. She was like a chrysalis, a dull brown caterpillar changing into an exquisite butterfly. Her conversation became animated, her smile natural and warm, her laughter genuine and infectious. Brian's head started to buzz, his fists involuntarily clench and unclench, his anger boiling inside him. Damn her, damn her, damn her. And him. Damn him to hell, whoever he was.

At one o'clock, Brian announced it was time to take a break for lunch. Catherine smiled at everyone, said that she would like to freshen up before they left, and walked out of the office. Brian quickly excused himself and strode into Catherine's room where the junior had left the bouquet. He caught hold of the card and cursed. It was written in French, with the initials JM scrawled at the bottom. So, Mr Wonderful was a native of France. JM. He cursed again for being unable to read the short but obviously affectionate (and maybe erotic?) note. He went back to his own office, followed by Catherine.

'Are we all ready?' she asked, smiling her incomparable smile. Brian wanted to wipe it off her face with one blow.

*

At about two o'clock, there was another knock at Brian's office door and, as there was no reply, the handle turned and the door slowly opened. A young woman walked in, looked around, looked at the clock on the wall and sat down. She sat for five minutes, became bored, got up and wandered around the room, picking up papers, putting them down, looking at the pictures and calendars on the walls and getting more and more impatient. Where was he? The receptionist had told her he'd be back from lunch at about two-thirty. Luckily, the said receptionist had a stream of visitors and hadn't noticed *this* visitor taking off on a tour of the building. An interesting place and luckily the export manager's door had been unlocked. How very careless. Suddenly feeling warm, she unbuttoned her coat, tossed her blonde hair over her shoulders and sauntered through another door into an adjoining office. His secretary's office by the look of it. A very neat and tidy office but Brian *would* have an efficient secretary, wouldn't he? The flowers were lying on the desk, monopolising the room, their stems stuck in a deep mug filled with water. She picked them up. She wondered what Brian's secretary must be like to receive flowers like this. From him, maybe? No, Brian buying anyone expensive bouquets was beyond her imagination. She looked at the incomprehensible message on the card. So, Brian's secretary, whoever she was, either had a foreign lover or a very happy client. What services did she provide to receive flowers like these? She glanced at the wall clock again ... where was he? At that precise moment, the telephone on the secretary's desk rang and after the third insistent ring, she slowly picked up the receiver.

'Hello?'

'Catherine? No, you're not. Excuse me. Could I speak to Catherine, please?'

A slightly foreign accent. Catherine must be the secretary.

'I'm afraid she's not in her office at the moment. Would you like me to give her a message?'

'Oh. Well, yes ... yes, please, if you don't mind. I won't be able to call again today. Could you please tell her that I've booked a table at the Old Windmill restaurant at eight o'clock this evening? It's very important that she receives this message. This is Jean-Marc de Bergier.'

'Wow! What a lovely name! Is it French?'

He laughed. 'It certainly is. You'll make sure Catherine gets the message, won't you?'

'Of course. The Old Windmill. A very romantic restaurant, or so I've been told. You must be a very romantic man, being French. I imagine the bouquet of roses on her desk are from you?'

Silence.

'Who am I speaking to, please?'

'Romantic men are so rare, unfortunately. The French have a reputation for being romantic, of course. Romantic and very, very sexy. Are you sexy as well as romantic? You *do* have a rather sexy voice, Jean-Marc.'

'Who am I speaking to, please?'

She put the receiver down and made a note of the message.

*

The lunch had been a success. At least as far as business was concerned. The three French clients were visibly charmed by the young interpreter and deals were made over steak, salad and bottles of full-bodied wine. Brian was pleased but his pleasure was overshadowed by what had taken place during the morning. He had put two and two together and guessed that Catherine and JM, whoever JM was, had had a row, she'd been upset and he'd sent the roses as an apology, a peace offering. Damn him. If he'd left things as they were, Catherine might have used Brian's shoulder to cry on. On the other hand, her improved state of mind had contributed to a successful business transaction even before they returned to the office. Maybe he ought to thank the bastard.

Arriving back at William Kaye, Catherine and the three visitors excused themselves and went to visit their respective lavatories. Brian went straight to his office; he needed to arrange a meeting with John Markham. Oh hell … he mentally reprimanded himself for leaving his door unlocked but this slight negligence was forgivable under the circumstances. He had a lot on his mind. He sat down at his desk and pulled out his pen and some notepaper to briefly jot down what had taken place in the restaurant, before dialling John's internal number. As he bent his head to begin writing, a shadow fell across his desk.

'Hello, Brian. You're late. You should have been back at two-thirty.'

'My. God. What the hell are *you* doing here?'

'Thanks for the warm welcome. I've come to pass on eagerly-awaited glad tidings.'

Melanie tossed her blonde locks over her shoulder and poised over the desk, her beautiful blue eyes boring into her brother's.

'Well, go on, I've got important visitors. I can't waste my time talking to you.'

'Dad's died. Last night. He went to sleep and didn't wake up again. I thought you might like to know.'

Brian's displeasure quickly melted and he suddenly felt nauseous. The fight and the life slowly drained out of him and he sank back into his chair, his face blanched, his hands shaking.

'Dad? No ... he can't ...' Brian's head was shaking, too. 'Was he in pain?'

Melanie shrugged.

'Do you honestly expect me to know? I'm going to phone his solicitor as soon as I get home. There's Dad's will to be sorted out – very important, wouldn't you say? I'll let you know as soon as I have an appointment. If you weren't interested in looking after Dad, I'm sure you'll be interested in his last will and testament. I know you'll want to know how rich you're going to be.'

Brian felt too shocked, too stunned, to absorb the unexpected news. His father had died and he hadn't been with him. He hadn't been near the old man for God knows how long ... and all because of this bitch who was standing in front of him now. He slowly raised his eyes to his sister.

'What about the funeral arrangements?'

'That's up to you,' Melanie smiled. 'I've done more than my fair share and I'm nobody's prisoner now. I'm free, just like you. Oh, for God's sake, Brian, don't get all theatrical and pretend to be sorry. You haven't been within spitting distance for months ... You're as glad to be rid of him as I am.'

Catherine chose that moment to come into the office, looked at the stranger, looked at Brian and quickly made her exit. Brian, his face broken, called her back. He needed a third party.

'Catherine, come in here, please. I want you to meet my sister. Melanie Jarvis.'

Catherine turned round, smiled, held out her hand and was about to tell Melanie that she was pleased to meet her when she realised there had been no response. The girl simply stared at her, obviously appraising her. Catherine started to fidget with her ignored right hand.

'So ... *you're* Catherine, are you? I've been wondering about you ever since the phone call.'

'What phone call?' Brian barked.

Melanie continued to look at her brother's secretary.

'A man with a foreign name rang about half an hour ago. He's reserved a

169

table at the Old Windmill restaurant this evening at eight o'clock.' Melanie paused, smiled and looked for a few moments at the wall clock. 'Well, at least you'll have plenty of time to spruce yourself up.'

Catherine was visibly startled and Brian bounced out of his chair.

'He sounds nice, your feller,' Melanie continued, slowly moving away from the desk. 'He's got a very sexy voice, hasn't he? I told him so, too.'

Catherine, speechless, could only stare open-mouthed at the young woman, but Brian didn't try to hide his fury. He grabbed his sister by the arm and spun her round.

'Don't you *dare* speak to my secretary like that, you little ... I swear to God, Melanie, one of these fine days, I'll swing for you.'

Melanie released herself, rubbed her arm and walked to the door.

'So you keep saying, Brian, and it's getting rather boring. I'll be in touch when I've spoken to the solicitor. Something for you to look forward to.'

She closed the door behind her, slowly. She walked down the corridor quickly, her high heels clicking on the shiny, polished floor. The employees who walked by her turned to have another look; the men appreciatively, the women enviously. She was smiling inwardly to herself. She had just discovered a secret of her brother's that he didn't even know he'd given away. He was besotted by, in love with, his secretary. It was written all over his face as soon as she walked into the room, and the way he leapt to her defence ... like a faithful little puppy dog.

When Melanie Jarvis arrived back at a quiet, sombre Greystones that afternoon, she picked up the telephone and dialled a number.

Chapter Nineteen

The Old Windmill was reasonably quiet that evening, but it was normal for a Monday. They had an intimate table tucked away in a corner but with an excellent view of the restaurant. Melanie smiled at the head waiter as he handed her a menu and she smiled at her escort. A man she disliked intensely; a relative of Margaret who'd occasionally visited the nurse at Greystones and who had 'taken to' the invalid's daughter. Melanie hadn't 'taken to' him at all but she could put up with him this evening. She could have put up with anyone this evening. She impatiently looked at her watch. They should be here any minute.

They walked into the room at precisely eight o'clock. Melanie recognised Catherine immediately; she recognised the red-brown hair that obviously came out of a bottle. Her eyes flashed from the girl to the man. So, this was – whatever his name was – she couldn't remember. Tall, slightly tanned, dark hair turning a little grey, well dressed. Nice. Very nice. His sexy voice had done him justice. They were shown to a table that Melanie could see quite easily and she was pleased that the girl had sat facing her partner, whose face Melanie could scrutinise. After a while, she looked across at her neglected companion, who thought that Melanie had invited him out in order to grieve her dead father. Nothing was further from her mind. She wanted to have a good time, enjoy her evening, and she was stuck with this boring fool. He smiled at her, compassion written all over his face, and she looked away, in the direction of the more interesting man sitting by the window. He seemed to be paying Catherine what's-her-name a lot of attention. His eyes had been glued to her face since they sat down. He was obviously very much in love with her – as was Besotted Brian, of course. She ate in silence, listening to her companion's voice droning on, his monotone falling on deaf ears and his gentle, probing questions receiving no reply. As soon as Melanie had finished her main course, she picked up her handbag and managed a smile at her date.

'I must go to the ladies' room,' she whispered.

She walked through the restaurant, a smile playing on her glossy lips, and stopped at the table by the window.

'Excuse me, I've been looking at you for a long time. I believe you're my brother's secretary, aren't you? We met in your office this afternoon. I'm sorry, I can't remember your name.'

Catherine, visibly startled, put down her fork, dabbed her mouth with the linen napkin and looked up at the young woman addressing her. Her gasp was quite audible.

'Oh yes, that's right. My name's Catherine and this is ... this is Jean-Marc de Bergier. Jean-Marc, this is Brian's sister ... Melanie?'

Melanie nodded, wrinkled her nose, but her smile was directed at Catherine's companion. Jean-Marc stood up and held out his hand. Their eyes held for a brief moment.

'Hello. We've already spoken, haven't we? I took your telephone message for ... her ... this afternoon.'

If Catherine's gasp had been audible, Jean-Marc's flinch was visible and he dropped his outstretched hand.

'Ah, the telephone message. Yes. Well ... nice to meet you.'

Melanie smiled and wrinkled her nose again, a mannerism she often practised in front of her mirror.

'Yes, we had quite a nice little chat, didn't we, while Catherine and my brother were out for lunch together.' She pulled her eyes away from him and projected her brilliant smile onto Catherine. 'I had the impression today that my brother's very fond of you.'

During the verbal emptiness that followed, it was Catherine's turn to look embarrassed and confused, remembering Brian's frequent and unwanted advances.

'And I wasn't a *bit* surprised. Brian's women have always been ... well, either filthy trollops or totally insignificant.'

She smiled, shook her blonde tresses over her shoulder and walked out of the restaurant, leaving the two diners sitting in stunned silence and her unsuspecting escort with the more-than- substantial bill. Outside, she hailed a convenient taxi and, relaxing in the back seat, decided that Jean-Marc de Bergier was definitely worth having. For herself.

Catherine

Chapter Twenty

———

There were two small but, to Catherine, significant clouds on her otherwise resplendent horizon. The first she hadn't exactly given up thinking about because it was always at the back of her mind; she'd just stopped talking about it. Even tentatively. Much as she would have liked to discuss and be in touch with Véronique and Henri de Bergier, she now accepted that they were a part of her past. Because of Jean-Marc's relationship with her, he'd been ostracised by his family and he refused to talk about the situation. Catherine felt hurt that the de Bergiers had taken this attitude, knowing them as she did, but she felt that Jean-Marc was losing far more than she was because he was losing his family. She wished he would talk about it, as she felt he needed to, but he wouldn't and she had to accept that.

The other small cloud was that Jean-Marc preferred to keep their relationship somewhat in the dark, or at least as much in the dark as was possible. They had a small circle of social acquaintances – some of her old friends in Harrogate and a couple of neighbours in Russetlea – and outside that circle, Jean-Marc preferred to maintain a certain amount of discretion. He spoke little to his own colleagues about his domestic life and asked Catherine to do the same. At least for a while, he'd said, in the beginning. Catherine couldn't help feeling hurt and rather angry. Was it a precautionary measure in case things didn't work out between them and, if they did eventually separate, no one would lose face? Was that how he saw their future? Or did he, like his relatives, think that she wasn't up to de Bergier requirements and he therefore preferred her to keep a low profile? When she vehemently put these questions to him, he had the good sense to look ashamed and deny the accusations in no uncertain terms. But he didn't offer an alternative reason for his request, only insisting that it wouldn't be for ever and it was certainly for the best.

So, Catherine reluctantly acquiesced and withdrew from office small talk about the home environment, how they spent their evenings, weekends, holidays, general chit-chat that helps the working day along and creates friendships. Being a naturally friendly person, Catherine was more than a little frustrated and knew that she'd earned a reputation at William Kaye International of being reserved. When she heard some of the women gossiping and backbiting, however, she told herself it was no bad thing.

Brian Jarvis was the most difficult person to deal with. Brian, for whom she'd been working for well over twelve months and who obviously found her sexually attractive. She couldn't imagine why because she certainly never encouraged him. She would have loved to be able to turn to him and say, 'Look, there's a man in my life, we live together and I'm very much in love with him. And we're very happy.' But she couldn't say that without betraying that man. He knew by now, of course, that there was someone. Little things she'd said, telephone conversations he'd overheard and the flowers that Jean-Marc had – very rashly, she'd thought – sent to the office after their tiff that morning. Brian had been furious; she could tell, although he'd tried very hard not to show his feelings. But at least he knew there was someone very special in her life and that was all that mattered. And Brian's sister, that dreadful glamorous blonde girl, had met Jean-Marc, and Brian must have heard about *that* little episode. Not that it made any difference, though; he still made a nuisance of himself in the office.

*

The headaches started around April 1978, although Catherine couldn't put her finger on the exact time. She just realised after a period of several weeks that the throbbing in her temple was becoming more frequent and definitely more acute. And then the dizziness started. She made an appointment to have her eyes tested one Saturday morning and spent at least half an hour, before the optician called her into his surgery, looking at frames and gasping at the prices. On the one hand, she was relieved when the optician told her that her eyesight was almost perfect, but on the other hand ... She walked out of the small old-fashioned surgery into the warm, rosy glow of a spring morning in Harrogate, and panicked. She made an appointment with her doctor the following Tuesday.

Brian was on the telephone when Catherine peeped round the door and he motioned her to come in. Catherine looked at her watch. She hoped he didn't want her to work late that evening; her head was hammering. Brian slammed the receiver down.

'I'm going to the Middle East next week, Catherine, and I'll be away from the office about sixteen days. Egypt and Jordan and then I'll be flying on to Saudi. It all sounds very promising – this client in Cairo, Abdul El Sayed, he's a ... Catherine? Are you okay?'

Catherine screwed up her eyes and leant against the door for support. Brian was already at her side.

'What on earth's the matter?'

She took a deep breath before she answered him.

'I've been having some really, really bad headaches, Brian, and I've been dizzy quite a lot. I've got an appointment with my doctor first thing tomorrow morning so I'll be a bit late. Sorry.'

'Don't worry about that. Have you any idea what's wrong?'

Catherine shook her head and the action made her wince.

'Well, it's not my eyes. I've just had them tested. To be honest, Brian, I'm worried. I'm getting really, really worried.'

Brian's arm was suddenly around her shoulder and he was gently squeezing her.

'Look, try not to worry too much. You'll probably make it worse. It's probably stress, love, you've been working too hard recently. You've probably been overdoing it. And you're *always* taking work home, aren't you? Maybe you need to let up a bit ...' Brian grinned as he hugged her again and Catherine, trying to smile, gently pulled herself out of his embrace.

'You're probably right, Brian. Anyway, I'll find out tomorrow.'

The surgery opened at nine o'clock and Catherine's appointment was half an hour later. It was difficult concentrating on ancient magazines while she waited. She walked into the surgery at exactly nine-thirty and when she came out, the previously empty waiting room was full. She hurried to the bus stop and arrived at William Kaye International at eleven-fifteen. Brian's head shot up when she opened the door.

'Hi. Well? Everything okay?'

Catherine nodded at him and smiled.

'Was my diagnosis right? Are you suffering from stress? Is it all my fault?'

'No, Brian, don't blame yourself. It's not stress at all. But it's nothing that can't be put right.'

Catherine decided to make a special meal that evening. She was living with a very special man in their very special home and she was in love and her lousy headaches would soon be a thing of the past. It was as simple as that. She bought flowers, pink carnations, for the centre of the table and lit two red candles. She'd made a lasagne and salad with ice cream to follow and had uncorked a bottle of Chianti. When everything had been prepared and the normally homely kitchen table looked quite lavish, Catherine went upstairs to prepare herself. For Jean-Marc.

He walked into the cottage at eight o'clock after a long staff meeting at the college and, although he was trying very hard not to show it, he was obviously exhausted. Catherine welcomed him home and she took him through to the kitchen. Jean-Marc's eyebrows raised a little when he looked at the elegant table, and then his questioning eyes trailed to Catherine. He kissed her.

'You look beautiful, the table looks very inviting and the aroma coming from the oven is tormenting my nostrils. Not to mention my stomach. Darling, are we celebrating? Is there something of the *utmost* importance that I've forgotten?'

Catherine laughed, hugging his neck and planting a kiss on his left cheek.

'Can't I spoil the man I love occasionally? Doesn't the man I love enjoy being pampered?'

'Of course he does! As often as the woman I love feels happy to do so.'

The meal was long, delicious and lively. They talked about their respective days; they made each other laugh; they became a little light-headed with the wine. And when the meal and the wine were finished and the candles burning low, Jean-Marc lifted Catherine into his arms and lay her down on the soft Persian rug in front of the dying embers of a crackling fire.

Jean-Marc didn't ask Catherine about her doctor's appointment because he knew nothing about it. She had never told him about the headaches because she hadn't wanted to worry him.

176

Two, or maybe three, weeks after that idyllic evening, Catherine had to work late, at Brian's special request. A question of entertaining foreign clients with cocktails in the office before Brian took them out for the evening. He had requested that Catherine join them in the bistro, too, but she'd firmly declined. 'It isn't necessary, Brian; the four Swiss gentlemen speak English perfectly, my interpreting services won't be needed; I'd be superfluous to requirements.' However, she'd happily agreed to stay late at the office, welcome the visitors, participate in the cocktails and then she was adamant she was leaving the office no later than seven-thirty.

So, it was Catherine who raised surprised eyebrows when she walked into the cottage an hour later and Jean-Marc greeted her with Champagne on ice.

'How lovely!' Catherine smiled at him, 'but what are we celebrating?'

Jean-Marc told her to sit down and he sat opposite her in the other maroon leather chair, twiddling his crystal glass around his fingers. For a while, he merely sat and looked at her.

'Well?' Catherine urged. 'What have you got to tell me, *monsieur*?'

'I have to tell you that we won't be living in Mullion Lodge for very much longer, my love.'

The bright, expectant smile slowly slipped away from Catherine's face. She had thought it was some kind of celebration, not the forerunner of disaster. She stared at him, trying to ignore the sudden rapid beating of her heart and the dryness in her throat.

'Why?' Her voice was barely audible. 'What are you talking about?'

Jean-Marc put his glass on a convenient low table, stood up and began to pace about the room, his arms folded in front of him and his right index finger rubbing his chin. Much in the same way he probably patrolled the classroom, Catherine mused. It was his academic stance and one that brought back a rush of memories.

'It's something I've never discussed with you for the simple reason that I didn't want you to get too excited in case my plans fell through. I think I vaguely mentioned it to you – oh, a long time ago – and I'm sure you've forgotten.'

His voice trailed away and Catherine sat very still, watching his movements, waiting for him to go on. He didn't.

'Go on.'

Jean-Marc came back to his chair, sat down, picked up his glass and finished his drink. God, he could be so ... so infuriating. Catherine waited.

'When Lady Faraday – you know of her, of course, the last of a long line of Faradays, and the owner of Mullion Hall. When Lady Faraday was alive, she and I became great friends for the simple reason that she was a very lonely old woman and I was a lonely ... man. I was living in a hotel in Harrogate and looking for a place to live in this area. I love it, you know that. One Saturday, I was taking a drive and came across Russetlea by chance. It was a case of love at first sight. I walked around the village and at lunchtime had a bite to eat and a drink in the Red Lion. I got chatting to the landlord who told me that Lady Faraday was looking for someone to rent the old lodge. For financial reasons. I didn't waste any time. I made an appointment with her and after she'd decided I was suitable, I moved in. She used to phone me when she was feeling lonely and ask me to spend an hour or so with her. She'd travelled extensively in France in her youth and she liked to reminisce with me. Mullion Hall is a magnificent edifice; a very beautiful exterior, as you know, and inside beautiful rooms which are extensive and full of character. Lady Faraday told me the Hall had known much happier times; when the family and servants were all living there, many years ago, of course. She often used to say that the Hall was wasted. It could have been put to good use and she hoped that, after her death, it *would* be put to good use. That started me thinking.

'I've never said anything to you before, Catherine, because I really didn't want you to be disappointed. But it's always been my dream, my ambition, to have my own language school. And now my dream is going to materialise.'

Jean-Marc began his tour of the room again. Catherine's bright eyes followed him.

'After Lady Faraday died, I immediately went to see my solicitors in Harrogate. We began negotiations for me to purchase Mullion Hall and open it as a language school, and as my own home, of course.'

He stopped talking, stood behind Catherine's chair, placed his hands on the two wings and whispered,

'It's taken a long time with many complications, but I've heard today that the sale has gone through. Mullion Hall belongs to me.'

Catherine let out a long squeal of delight, jumped out of her chair and flew into his arms.

'Oh, Jean-Marc, I can't believe it. You, the owner of Mullion Hall! Your own language school! It's unbelievable! It's ... it's like a dream! Oh, darling, it's really, really wonderful.'

Jean-Marc spun her round until she felt quite dizzy and they hugged each other and then he said,

'And, of course, Catherine, I'll want you to participate in my school. I'll need all the help you can give me.'

The following few months were dedicated to visiting lawyers, visiting Mullion Hall, communicating with accountants, academic institutions and suppliers and possible future employees and students of the Mullion Hall School of Languages. When Jean-Marc and Catherine weren't working, their time was spent making plans for their future. This new project. This new life. It wasn't easy. There were many problems to face and solve; there were long periods of frustration while waiting for replies or advice. Catherine spent most of her weekends at the Hall, deciding on new furnishings and decorations. Jean-Marc had given her carte blanche on this. He trusted her taste and he wanted the school to be as-near-as-dammit physically perfect before he opened its doors. Which wouldn't be for a while yet; maybe not for a couple of years, but that didn't matter. The property, the magnificent Mullion Hall, belonged to him, Jean-Marc de Bergier, and the rest would come later, when the time was right.

The time, therefore, passed quickly and during those months there were no real traumas, no dramas, nothing that Catherine could possibly have called a hiccup in her lovely life. As well as the impetus of the wonderful new project, her health had also improved, which added to her general feeling of well-being. She was in love, safe in the knowledge that her love was reciprocated. She had an interesting job, a dazzling future ahead of her and, thanks to several substantial and well-earned rises from William Kaye International, her personal savings account was more than adequate. She was also living with a very rich man; a rich man whose generosity knew no bounds and whom she frequently scolded for spoiling her. Therefore, in spite of one or two aspects of her relationship with Jean-Marc that occasionally niggled at the back of her mind, Catherine could easily describe her life as almost ... almost ... perfect.

The hiccup arrived in early August. It fell through the letterbox at eight-thirty, one Saturday morning, a white envelope carrying a French stamp. Catherine picked up the post and, not recognising the writing on this particular envelope, took it to Jean-Marc in the kitchen. She dropped it at the side of his coffee mug.

'*Voilà, monsieur,*' she grinned, kissing his unshaven cheek, 'if you have any trouble understanding the French, give me a yell. I'll be upstairs.'

Catherine loved her Saturdays with Jean-Marc. Sometimes, lovely, lazy days spent shopping and walking and reading and eating out; other times, frenetic and action-packed days at the Hall, labouring with love and going to bed very early. Today would be particularly enjoyable; Jean-Marc was taking her into Harrogate to buy her birthday gift (whatever was her heart's desire), although her birthday wasn't until the following week. He wanted her to have lots of time to choose something ... Okay, she was ready at last. She looked at her watch. Ten o'clock. There was no sign of life from Jean-Marc – was he still downstairs?

'Jean-Marc?'

No reply.

Catherine slowly descended the stairs and called out his name twice more. To no avail. She pushed open the kitchen door and looked at the man sitting at the table. In almost exactly the same position as she'd left him. A slow tremor ran through Catherine's body like a physical siren.

'Jean-Marc?'

Her voice was barely a whisper and as he still didn't reply, she moved forward and softly touched his shoulder. He jumped, as though he hadn't even realised she was in the room.

'Darling?'

Jean-Marc turned round very slowly and looked up at her and a sob caught in Catherine's throat. There were tears in his eyes. He couldn't speak. His mouth opened and closed but he couldn't speak. She knelt at his side, taking his large hands in her own and looked into his face, mentally pleading with him to tell her.

'What is it, Jean-Marc?'

She could see the envelope and the long handwritten letter out of the corner of her eye but knew she mustn't touch it. She desperately wanted to know the contents of those pages, the contents that had had such a devastating effect on this strong, normally self-controlled man. She gently squeezed his hand.

'Tell me, Jean-Marc. Please tell me.'

He gently released his hands and pushed them deep into his screwed-up eyes, so that the tears fell down his face. Catherine silently wailed, wanting to know what was going on in that complicated mind of his, in his heart; and yet knowing that this was his own private and, for some reason, un-shareable agony. She stayed for a long time in her inferior position at Jean-Marc's knee, silently wanting him to know that she was still there, would always be there. When his tears subsided but he still didn't move, Catherine stood up and, squeezing his hand, quietly left the kitchen, throwing a long last look at the white sheets of paper on the table.

'Forgive me,' Jean-Marc said, appearing in the bedroom. 'I behaved very badly downstairs. I don't know what you must think of me.'

His words were clipped, unnatural, as though he was speaking to a total stranger. Catherine, sitting on the edge of the bed, looked up at the man she would have given her life for and tried very hard to smile.

'Do you want to tell me?' she whispered, not wanting to hear his reply. There was no reply. Just a slight shake of the head and an unreadable expression on his face. He turned round and went into the bathroom.

*

Jean-Marc bought a gold bangle for her birthday. She told him not to be so silly; he shouldn't spend so much money on her. Jean-Marc completely ignored her and sent the bangle away to be engraved. He wouldn't allow her to read what he'd asked the assistant to have engraved and told Catherine it would be ready to pick up on her birthday, the following week. They came out of the jeweller's and into an old cobbled street bathed in the August sunlight. Catherine was delighted with her gift and couldn't wait to read the inscription inside; but there was no joy on her face as they walked, hand in hand, towards the Valley Gardens. Because there was no joy on Jean-Marc's. It was as though he'd just engraved his life away.

The day was beautiful but melancholy and Catherine was dying inside. She tried several times, quietly and gently, to penetrate Jean-Marc's thoughts, delve deep inside the abyss that was his tormented mind. She tried to make him laugh, but his smile was merely polite; she tried to make him talk, but his conversation was laboured. She tried to encourage him to include her in his thoughts, but the barrier between them was now too high and wide. Catherine felt like she was sinking in a deep, cold ocean with no limbs to help her surface and no voice to cry for help. Dear God, what was happening?

The following week could only have been described as a nightmare. Living with Jean-Marc was like living with a dummy; an object totally lacking in life and love. He shut himself off and out, and there was no battering down the door, no opening windows to look inside. Oh, she tried; she tried not only for his sake but for her own. A week had seemed like an eternity and Catherine's nerves were in shreds. If she didn't love him, if she didn't care ... but she did. Oh God, she did.

Catherine even tried to find the letter; the handwritten culprit that had been oh-so-carefully hidden away. Or torn into shreds, or burned. Normally, she would have been riddled with guilt at the thought of spying on Jean-Marc's post, but the circumstances were exceptional, she told herself. However, the letter was never found. But something would have to be done soon, for both their sakes. If she couldn't talk to Jean-Marc, she would have to confide in someone else. But who? There was no Diana to turn to as she would at one time have done. Not her mother; she couldn't bear being told *I told you so.* And there was no one else, which she found to be a very sad reflection on her life. In the end, however, she didn't have to confide in anyone.

On the Friday evening, Jean-Marc arrived home from the college looking tired, weary and as though the bottom had dropped out of his world. He was late, for some reason, and Catherine had been at home for over an hour. She had brought two long translations home with her and was sitting at the desk in the living room when Jean-Marc arrived. She tried to concentrate on her work, listening to Jean-Marc moving about upstairs and waiting, with a rapidly beating heart, for his appearance. The door opened very slowly. He stood for a brief moment in the doorway and then he walked towards her. He said nothing, simply stood looking with vacant eyes at Catherine. Her body stopped functioning.

'Catherine, my darling,' he finally said on a sob, 'I have something to say to you. And you'll never know how much it's going to hurt me.'

He beckoned her to sit in one of the maroon leather chairs and he sat in the other, pulling it forward so that the two chairs were almost touching. He spoke very slowly.

'I have to go back to France, Catherine. I have no choice. It may be for a long time and I can't take you with me. I must go alone.'

Time stood still. The earth stopped revolving. The glorious August evening turned to ice.

'I don't understand.'

'Oh, Catherine, if only I could explain. But I can't. Not now. I've left it too late. I should have ...'

Catherine suddenly came to life. She began to tremble. The blood rushed to her face and she flung herself into Jean-Marc's arms.

'Why? Why? Why? You can't do this ... Tell me ... Please *tell* me...'

The tears were streaming down her cheeks; tears of frustration, anger, love, hatred. All the emotions she had ever felt for Jean-Marc she was feeling a thousandfold now. This man was leaving her ... leaving her. The other half of her body and soul was going away. No, he couldn't. It wasn't possible.

'Talk to me, Jean-Marc. Tell me what's happened. You haven't been yourself for ages ... please. *Please.* I want to help you. I want to be with you. I love ...'

She was clinging to him now, her bewildered pleas turning to hysterical sobs. He couldn't leave her; he couldn't go away; it just wasn't possible ...

'Catherine, if I could take you with me, believe me, my darling, I would. But I can't. I'm going back to France to a lot of unhappiness and it's not part of your life. It's the life I should never have left and I should have been honest with you right at the beginning.'

He was cradling her now, rocking her backwards and forwards like a helpless baby. This was the old Jean-Marc, Catherine's Jean-Marc, the Jean-Marc she knew and loved. But he wasn't saying what she wanted to hear. For a long time, there was silence, broken only by muffled sobs. And then Catherine pulled away from him and stared at him with swollen, savage eyes.

'What about ... what about Mullion Hall ... your school?'

Jean-Marc briefly met her gaze and then his eyes moved away from her and his whole physical expression was one of hopelessness.

'I've been to see my solicitor this afternoon. That's why I was late home.'

He didn't offer to continue and Catherine opened her mouth to speak but no words came. She could see the beautiful old building refurbished with classrooms and a common room and teachers and students and Jean-Marc living and working there with her.

'And what about me?' The words almost stuck in her throat. 'What am I supposed to do now?'

He couldn't meet her eyes.

'Look, my love, this is the last thing I want for either of us. It will be best if you go back to Harrogate ... go back to your mum ...'

'No!' Her head was shaking and she didn't know.

'Yes, I'm afraid you have no choice under the ... these circumstances. You'll be better in Harrogate. You'll have your mum's company; you'll be closer to William Kaye. And I think it'll be best for both of us if you leave this evening.'

'What? This evening? You don't mean that, Jean-Marc, you can't ... I can't leave now ... I *won't* ...'

'It's for the best, Catherine. I can't tell you how very sorry I am, but ...'

Very sorry. Very sorry that he was throwing her away, sending her back in time, saying goodbye to their home, their life, their future.

'Catherine.' He'd grabbed hold of both her hands and was trying to look into her eyes. 'It's all for the best, believe me. We can't ... we can't go on living together anymore ... that's impossible. Believe me, Catherine, I love you as I always have and probably always will. I hate myself for hurting you like this and I'll never forgive myself. But there's no other way. I hope that one day—'

'Yes, Jean-Marc? What do you hope one day?'

He shook his head and held her close to him and Catherine pressed her wet face into his neck and wrapped her lifeless arms around him. Suddenly he let out a long moan and with one swift movement he lifted her and carried her up the winding wooden staircase to the bedroom that was theirs for the last time. He gently lay her down, kissed her tears, her eyes, her lips, and as they became one, their warm tears mingled together on the soft, downy pillow.

*

'Is it any good wishing you a happy birthday?'

Molly Carter pushed a small card and a gift-wrapped box into her

184

daughter's cold hands. It was almost noon and Cathy hadn't shown any sign of life. She turned over in the narrow single bed and looked up at her mother.

'No, I don't think it's any good wishing me a happy birthday. Not really.'

Molly felt helpless. It was like looking at her daughter as she had been twenty years ago, a six-year-old defenceless child. She didn't know what to say to her, what to do for her. She was beyond care. But she could feel for her daughter and, oh yes, Molly felt for her very much. She fumbled for a handkerchief and pretended to blow her nose.

'What would you like to do today, love?'

What would she like to do today? She'd like to lie in bed with Jean-Marc and be happy with him on her birthday. She rolled over and pushed her face into the pillow.

'I don't want to do anything. Thanks.'

Molly sighed, left the room and quietly closed the door. She felt totally confused. She hadn't a clue what was going on except that French feller was taking himself off to France without so much as a by-your-leave or anything else and poor Cathy had landed, devastated, on her doorstep the evening before. She'd tried to warn her a long time ago, hadn't she? Tried to give her some good advice but she wouldn't listen.

Catherine lay for a long time, her face thrust into the comfort of the pillow, her fists softly clenching and unclenching. Her mouth was dry, her limbs were wet and exhausted and she slept. When she awoke in the middle of the afternoon, she remembered the gold bangle. She was supposed to collect it today from the jeweller's. She wept fresh tears.

Chapter Twenty-One

A week went by before Catherine could bring herself to collect the bangle. The longest week of her life, during which time she went through every human emotion. She behaved like a rational human being on the surface but underneath, deep inside her, she was a corpse. She worked, she came home, she watched television, she read. But she may as well not have bothered. She didn't know she was doing those things or why, and if anyone had asked her about her activities, she would have given them a blank stare. Her mind, her body, her emotions were numb. Many was the time that she contemplated the telephone, wondering whether a call to Russetlea – because Catherine knew that Jean-Marc would still be at the cottage, he couldn't possibly have left his home and his work so quickly – would be beneficial. Two or three times she hovered near the telephone and once she picked it up and started to dial his number. But she only started; she didn't finish. And every time the phone rang at home, needless to say, Catherine was convulsed, and when it was never Jean-Marc, she dissolved into tears followed by subconscious inertia. And she never stopped asking herself one unanswerable question: why had Jean-Marc so suddenly shattered their near-as-dammit perfect life?

Molly offered to accompany her to the jeweller's on the Saturday morning that she steeled herself to pick up the gold bangle that she didn't really want anymore. Her beautiful birthday gift from Jean-Marc. Catherine said no, she didn't want company.

It was another hot, sunny afternoon when Catherine stepped into the rather old-fashioned family jeweller's, clutching the receipt. The polite assistant smiled the smile of the unaware and placed the piece of jewellery into a velvet box and then a beribboned little bag. She looked rather nonplussed when Catherine said no, thank you, she didn't want to read the engraving; but then, it was nothing to do with her. It was nothing to do with anyone, not even Jean-Marc now. She walked through the town centre and onto the Stray, where families, noisy children and happy lovers were picnicking and sunbathing. She sat down among the daisies and mechanically opened the leather box. The gold bangle glittered and gleamed in the sunlight. She held it for a moment in her trembling fingers. The engraving that Jean-Marc had requested was a quick moment away. All she had to do was flick the bangle into a different position. She swallowed. She looked around to see if anyone was watching. People would know. They'd know that something was terribly wrong, wouldn't they?

Je ne t'oublierai jamais. JM

Catherine dropped the bangle into its velvet home, dragged herself up and walked back into the town. She meandered slowly through the throbbing Saturday streets, bumping into passers-by without apologising, without really knowing. She walked home, taking the long way round rather than the short cut, just to waste time, give her something to do. It was late afternoon when she arrived at the old terraced house to which she had twice returned in her short life, and was thankful that Molly was out. The house was empty. Catherine poured herself a glass of cold orange juice and took it to her room. She released the bangle a second time and after a few moments, forced herself to look at the immaculate engraving once more. In spite of the orange juice, her mouth felt dry; in spite of the heat, her body was cold. Cold, stiff and devoid of life. Jean-Marc had known that he was going to leave her on the morning he bought her birthday gift. Her moist, tired eyes scanned the small lettering again.

I will never forget you. JM

*

During the next few weeks, Catherine's health began to deteriorate. There were no more headaches, they were a thing of the past, but she became immersed in a deep depression, waking up in the early hours of the morning and not being able to sleep again. There was a permanent lump in her throat and her eyes would well up with tears at the most unexpected and inconvenient times. She became a social recluse, not wanting to visit places that she and Jean-Marc had loved; not wanting to be with mutual acquaintances. During the long days, she tried as best she could to throw herself into her work; the work that didn't allow her to forget because she had to communicate with France oh-so-often. And then the nausea and dizziness started. She couldn't eat. Not because she wasn't hungry but because everything that went into her stomach came back again. She couldn't run upstairs or for a bus; she couldn't dash around the office as she used to because if she did, she stumbled and often fell. Her already drawn face became almost cadaverous, her brown eyes disappearing into their sockets. For several weeks, she tried to be brave and carry on; tried to pretend that she was coping with her loss very nicely, thank you. But by October she couldn't bear her mother's worried glances and silent pleas any longer. And Brian's occasional complaints about her work were becoming more frequent. She made an appointment with her doctor.

*

It was a cool, clear Tuesday morning; a perfect autumn day. A bright blue sky contrasted beautifully with the changing colours of nature, and a pale sun shining on amber leaves added a final aesthetic touch. A day Catherine would normally have gloried in, but not today. As she approached William Kaye International, she looked at her watch. Eleven o'clock. She'd spent almost two hours at the doctor's surgery. She walked through the double glass doors and was pleased that the chatty young receptionist was engaged on the switchboard. A light-hearted conversation with her would have been impossible. She ran past her own office door and disappeared into the ladies' toilet, where she locked herself into a cubicle and threw up.

Brian Jarvis, thank God, was more or less fully occupied that day. He had two meetings away from the office and an extended lunch break, so Catherine didn't have to face him very often. It was impossible to face him or anyone else. On the occasions he spoke to her and gave her work, she averted her eyes and prayed he wouldn't probe. He didn't because he was too preoccupied. Anyway, Brian wasn't her problem, not really. It was her mother. How could she tell her mother without shattering her life? She couldn't.

At the end of the week, on Friday morning, Brian was sitting in his office, preparing notes for another trip he was due to make to the Middle East. Catherine arrived at work an hour late and stood in the doorway joining their two rooms. For a while, she wordlessly watched him working. He finally looked up.

'Good God, you look bloody awful. What the hell's wrong with you?'

Catherine walked forward, swaying slightly, and then grabbed hold of the desk in order to support herself. Her skin was ashen, her eyes glazed and her hair lank and lifeless around her face. She sank into the chair in front of Brian's desk.

'Oh, Brian, I've got to tell somebody.'

The tears gushed out of her eyes. Brian stood up, walked to the door, closed it and dragged his chair next to Catherine's. He slowly encircled her shoulder with his right arm.

'Come on, gorgeous, there's been something bothering you for a long time. Don't think I haven't noticed. Spit it all out.'

Catherine blew her nose loudly and turned to face him.

'I'm pregnant, Brian.'

It was like watching a bloated balloon being pricked and bursting into lifelessness. A hundred and one expressions flitted across Brian's face in the next few seconds.

'I'd thought of everything but that.'

He pulled his arm away, stood up and strode to the window, for a long time looking out at the immediate world. And then he turned back to face Catherine, glaring at her almost, accusing her, and yet there was a certain amount of sympathy in his eyes, too. He came back to his chair, sat down, took Catherine's clammy hands into his own. His eyes searched her face and she suddenly had the impression that *he* was the baby's reluctant father.

'Tell me, Catherine, will you be getting married?'

She stared at him. It seemed an odd question. Married? Was it some kind of a joke in very bad taste? And then she remembered. Brian didn't know that the man she loved had left her, gone away. He'd known little – if anything – about him in the first place. He certainly didn't know her life had recently been turned upside down and inside out.

'No, Brian, I won't be getting married. I've got nobody to marry.'

Brian frowned and pursed his thin lips.

'But I don't understand, love. The father ...'

'The father's not here anymore. I don't want to talk about him.' Her temporary strong and resolute voice then broke. 'Oh, Brian, what am I going to do?'

The long silence that followed was broken by the telephone ringing. Brian took the call, cut his conversation short and then said,

'Let's have a cup of coffee and talk about it. No, sit down, I'll make it.'

Catherine took a sip of the hot liquid and it tasted foul; she felt nauseous but forced it down. They drank in silence for a while and then Brian looked into Catherine's distraught face and asked,

'Do you want this baby?'

She didn't reply immediately. It was as though she was thinking about the question, rolling it around in her mind, reflecting before she decided to answer.

'I really don't know. I've been thinking about it all morning. The emotional, physical part of me wants the baby very much. The practical part of me doesn't. I honestly don't know, Brian.'

He squeezed her hand and, after clearing his throat, brought his face closer to hers.

'Personally, I don't think it's wise to bring an unwanted child into this cruel world. Do you?'

'It wouldn't be unwanted. Not—'

'Only half of you wants it, Catherine. You just said so. What about the other half? The very important practical half?'

'I don't *know*, I'm confused. This is what I desperately wanted a few months ago but not now. Not like this.'

'What did you want a few months ago?'

Catherine sighed.

'Those headaches; do you remember? Well, they were caused by my birth control pill and my doctor insisted I stop taking it. Oh, at the time I was delighted. I-I was hoping I'd get pregnant and have Jean-Marc's baby.'

'Ah. And what's happened to … Jean-Marc?'

'He … he had to go back to France. I don't think … I'll ever see him again.'

Brian was about to say something but abruptly stopped himself.

'Well then, under the circumstances,' he said, 'I think the best thing you can do is get rid of it.'

Catherine visibly winced and coffee spilt onto her hand.

'Please don't say that, Brian. It sounds so … so cold and heartless.'

'I'm sorry, love. I didn't mean to sound so cold. An abortion then. A termination.' He was speaking slowly now, very deliberately. 'Under your present circumstances, I'd advise you to terminate this pregnancy, Catherine. Think of your future; think of … of *its* future. What sort of life do you think it'd have? No father … no financial support, or at least not much. Would you want to continue working … or be a stay-at-home mum?

190

Eh? All your talents gone to … anyway, think about it, Catherine. Think about it long and hard.'

For a long time neither of them spoke and Catherine could feel her boss's small grey eyes piercing her face. She lowered her head to avoid his gaze. At last, she sighed deeply and, pulling her hand free of his, she stood up.

'Maybe you're right, Brian, maybe you're wrong. At the moment, I just don't know. But I will think about it carefully, talk to my doctor again. I … I can't think straight at the moment.'

She walked away in the direction of her own office, not wanting to discuss this very private problem with her boss any longer; cursing herself for having confided in him – of all people – in the first place. Oh God, if only Diana had been there; a best friend to share her heartache and dilemma with. But there was no Diana; there was no best friend, not anymore. There was no Jean-Marc anymore, either. There was only her mother and her boss. What did that say about *her*? she asked herself. She could feel Brian's eyes following her and his voice halted her steps as she entered her room.

'Look, if you do decide to have an abortion, love,' he said, his voice soft and sympathetic, 'I'll be with you all the way. You're not alone. Please remember that.'

Chapter Twenty-Two

I n one respect, Molly Carter was delighted that her daughter had come home. Another human being in the house gave her things to think about, occupy her time. But the circumstances of Cathy's homecoming were so tinged with sadness that Molly couldn't help but feel it would have been better if she was still alone, and Cathy happy and contented with her Frenchman in their little cottage. Molly had liked Jean-Marc; she'd liked him a lot. She hadn't agreed with him living with Cathy like he did, no wedding ring and all that, but in spite of this improper way of going on, she knew him to be a kind, charming, quite wonderful man, and ideal for her daughter. Which made it so much worse, made his unforgivable behaviour so much more of a mystery. Taking off and leaving behind him a seemingly unmendable broken heart. Molly knew that it would be a very long time before Cathy got over the shock, not to mention the man himself, but she hadn't thought her health would suffer like this. Damn the bloody Frenchman. Damn and blast him to hell. Nice as he was. Cathy walked past the window and opened the front door. She looked like death and Molly's heart came into her mouth.

*

'Abortion?'

The evening meal was finished, the dirty dishes still lying on the table untouched. Molly's tea had gone cold. She stared across the room at Cathy, standing by the window, unable to look at her mother.

'What are you sayin', Cathy?'

Cathy told her again, in a tone of voice as though she were reading another person's script.

'You mean to say you told yer boss before you told me? I can't believe you'd do that, Cathy, I really can't. What on earth possessed you ... and who does 'e think 'e is, dishing out so-called advice like that? Who does 'e think 'e is?'

'He's trying to help me, Mum. He's being practical, which I can't be and—'

192

'Practical? An' will he be practical if it kills you?'

'Oh, Mum, stop it, I can't stand any more drama, honestly ...'

Molly sighed.

'Oh, I'm sorry, love. I've just 'ad a nasty shock. Two nasty shocks. I 'ad an idea you might get into trouble when you went to live with that ... that good-for-nothing French bloke. But I never thought it'd turn out like this ...'

'Don't talk about Jean-Marc like that. It wasn't his fault. I came off the pill and I didn't tell him ...'

'Then yer as much to blame as 'e is. Oh Cathy, I don't know what to say. Why don't you try phonin' 'im? He might still be livin' in Russetlea. Or write to 'im ... Write to 'im at that flat in Paris where you stayed ...'

Catherine had tried phoning Russetlea. She'd called that afternoon when she was alone in the office, knowing that even if Jean-Marc was still living in Mullion Lodge, he wouldn't be there at that time. But the phone, as she'd expected, was dead. He no longer lived there. She could write to him at his beautiful apartment in Vincennes. She could. But he had returned to France for a reason – and to a lot of unhappiness, he'd said. So, she couldn't involve him in her own unhappiness; it wouldn't be fair. And if he rejected her and the baby, she couldn't bear it. Catherine preferred to accept sole responsibility for her now unwanted pregnancy than risk another rejection from Jean-Marc.

'No, Jean-Marc and I are finished, Mum. I know I'll never see him again. I ... l never want to see him again. Not now. I've decided the best thing to do is have an abortion and put it all behind me.'

'Put it all behind you, lass? You'll live with this for the rest—'

But Cathy had left the room.

*

The doctor sent her away. The Allenby Nursing Home was situated in a quiet, residential and leafy suburb of Manchester, and her 'operation' was booked for the last Tuesday in October. Your pregnancy will have to be terminated very soon, Catherine, because after twelve weeks it can be dangerous. And you're past your eighth week now. Don't worry, dear, it's a nice, comfortable home where you'll be well looked after and you'll only be there twenty-four hours. You'll probably feel quite ill and weak for a while afterwards and you'll need to rest, of course, but you'll get over it. Everybody does. And remember, you can always change your mind, right up to the .... operation. Oh yes, and there should be someone with you to bring you home, needless to say, someone very reliable.

Thank you, doctor. You've been very helpful.

*

'I'll take you there and I'll bring you home. I'll stay overnight in a hotel – or B&B – or something, in Manchester.'

Catherine's head jerked up.

'No, you won't, Brian. I can't possibly let you …'

'You can and you will. I've made my mind up and once I make my mind up about something, I don't change it.'

'But it's not your responsibility …'

'I'm making it my responsibility. I want to help you, Catherine. I want to be your friend.' He paused, smiling down into her perplexed eyes. 'You haven't got anybody else to help you, have you, love? Not as far as I can see. The baby's father isn't anywhere around so he's not going to help you. Is he?'

Molly Carter met Brian Jarvis, her daughter's wonderful boss, on that last Tuesday morning of October 1977; a morning drenched in torrential rain. She opened her front door to him as she saw his car pull up outside. Her taut and tear-stained face welcomed him at the door.

'This is so kind of you, Mr Jarvis. I can't tell you 'ow grateful we both are. I don't know 'ow Cathy would 'ave coped … an' *I'm* not much good, I'm afraid …'

'I just want to help in any way I can, Mrs Carter, under these … very difficult circumstances. Is she ready?'

Catherine appeared in the living room, her blanched face free of make-up, her brown raincoat pulled tightly around her, her overnight bag swinging at her side. She smiled weakly at her boss and he led her gently through the pouring rain to his car. Molly stood watching them from the doorway, silent because she didn't have a clue what to say. *Good luck? I 'ope all goes well?* Afterwards, all that Catherine could remember about the normally breathtaking journey across the Pennines was the rain lashing on the windscreen and the wipers' incessant screeching on the glass. That and

194

the complete silence inside the vehicle. Brian located the Allenby Nursing Home without any problem. It was a monstrous red-brick building with net curtains hanging at the huge bay windows and a black iron gate bordered by two brick pillars. The *Allenby Nursing Home* black and gold sign that normally stood erect at the side of the gate was frantically blowing and crashing in the wind. For a long time, Catherine sat and stared at the thing through the car's drenched window.

'I'm scared, Brian.'

'Of course you are, love. That's normal. But we have to make a move now. Come on.'

Catherine had expected to be alone, a single victim of life's easiest error, awaiting her punishment. She was surprised, therefore, to find herself bustled into a lifeless room crammed with life-filled bodies. Women of all ages, sizes and backgrounds, hugging their meagre luggage and trying to look nonchalant and unafraid. Some with their men; most without. Brian sat beside Catherine and she blessed him for behaving like a surrogate father-to-be. Or rather, not-to-be. She suddenly realised that Brian was squeezing her hand and whispering to her.

'Danny, the medical student who shares my house, you know, he says there's nothing to worry about. It's a simple operation and not dangerous when it's done properly. Legally. And he should know, shouldn't he? There's nothing to be frightened of, love. And remember, you *are* doing the right thing.'

No, there was nothing to be frightened of. She was only going to lose her baby. Jean-Marc's baby. She was only going to have its life sucked out of her womb like a malignant tumour. What would Jean-Marc think – or do – if he knew where she was and why? She silently nodded at Brian. No, there was nothing to be frightened of, nothing to haunt her dreams for the rest of her life.

'Catherine Carter. Ward Nine. Come this way, please.'

She panicked. She squeezed Brian's hand and he returned the squeeze and wordlessly smiled at her. He carried her bag into the corridor where a young, pretty but unsmiling nurse was waiting for her.

'I'll come and see you this evening,' Brian said. 'Just think, it'll all be over by then. It'll all be in the past. And you're going to be fine.'

The next few hours were a nightmare that Catherine could not believe was happening to her. Scrubbing herself all over, being pushed and pummelled by strange hands, pills and needles being forced into her. Trying to rest, trying not to cry; trying to pretend that the little life inside her wasn't going to be sucked away ... *And remember, you can always change your mind, right up to the operation.*

There were twelve occupied beds in Ward Nine and Catherine was the second patient to be taken to the operating theatre. The first, a very young Irish girl, almost a child herself, was brought back to the ward and ungently laid on her bed, still unconscious. The two white-coated men wheeled the stretcher to Catherine's bed. She stared at them. They silently pulled her off the bed, placed her on the gurney and wheeled her out of the ward. Catherine lay watching the ceiling going by and the upside-down faces of the white-coated men, and listened to one of the wheels squeaking, all the time squeaking ... *And remember, you can always change your mind, right up to the operation.* Her tears were suddenly wetting and warming her marble cheeks and falling onto her mobile bed. She was pushed through a door marked *Theatre* and came to an abrupt halt. A smiling white-coated woman approached the gurney and bent over Catherine, needle poised in her right hand. The needle came towards her together with soft, soothing words from the white-coated woman.

'No! No! No-o-o-o ...'

Catherine screamed. The needle remained upright in mid-air.

'No! No! I want my baby. Please don't take my baby away from me.'

*

Brian arrived at six o'clock, visiting time, bearing a small bunch of mixed flowers. He asked the receptionist the way to Ward Nine but when he mentioned the name Catherine Carter, she showed him into the almost empty waiting room. Empty but for one person. Catherine was sitting there, small, pale and very tired, wearing her raincoat and clutching the overnight bag that she hadn't needed. She looked up with wistful eyes as Brian entered.

'Catherine? What the hell's going on?'

He looked bewildered, confused.

'I couldn't go through with it, Brian,' she said, slowly shaking her head as though to confirm her words. 'I want to have my baby.'

She stood up, still clutching her overnight bag, walked across to Brian and laid her head on his shoulder. She expected to feel his arm encircle her, support her; she expected him to whisper soft, understanding words of comfort and encouragement. But the hugs and the soft words were a long time coming. Catherine lifted her head and looked up into Brian's face; her boss who'd been so kind to her. She gasped. Why was he looking at her like that?

'Can we go home now, Brian? I'm so tired.'

He left the room and the building without answering, and she followed him through the still-pouring rain to the car outside.

Chapter Twenty-Three

Janine Carter was born on 1st May 1978, a healthy, screaming, wrinkled-but-lovely seven pounder.

'I bet she'll be spoilt rotten,' the nurse smiled, gently laying the baby in her mother's arms. The mother thought of her own mother and grinned.

'Yes, Nurse, I think you're right.'

Catherine looked down at the gurgling bundle in her arms and thought about the last few months of her life. How wonderful everyone had been; her mum, her few pals, her boss. Nobody had treated Catherine like she'd expected to be treated: a Fallen Woman. Well, it was 1978, not 1888. She and her baby were really lucky; they had everything. A comfortable home, a doting grandparent, more toys and baby things than either of them would know what to do with. They had everything. Except a father; a daddy for Janine. A Jean-Marc for Catherine.

There was no Jean-Marc but there was Brian Jarvis. Catherine felt that she couldn't have survived the last few months without him. As her boss, he'd been kindness itself; as her friend, he'd been perfect. Always there when she needed him, always willing to help in any way he could, sometimes forfeiting his shorter foreign trips to be with her. And when she'd finally had to leave William Kaye several weeks before the birth, Brian told her that her job would be left open for her whenever she wanted to come back. He didn't want another secretary; he wanted Catherine. He needed Catherine. He was used to her ways and she was used to his. They got on well and, as he kept telling her, they thought a lot about each other. When Janine was born, he sent flowers and a card and arrived at the maternity hospital with armfuls of gifts. Later, he visited the terraced house in Harrogate regularly, chatting affably with Molly, playing, albeit awkwardly, with the baby. And as the warm spring flourished into a gorgeous summer, taking Catherine and the little one out for walks during the day and taking Catherine out alone in the evenings. Catherine, with only her mother and her baby for company, began to look forward eagerly to his visits.

'Will you be coming back to work soon, Catherine? I need you.'

They were sitting in a shaded spot under a great oak tree, surrounded by wild flowers and the remnants of their lunch. Catherine was leaning against the tree trunk, Brian sitting at her feet.

'I'd love to, and I'm pleased that you've asked me. It's just that ...'

'It's just that you don't want to leave Janine. I can understand that. *Of course* I can. But we both know your mum would love to be in charge of her eight hours a day and you know she'll be in good hands. And I think your mum'll be pleased you're out in the big wide world again, doing what you do best. And meeting people. And making me very happy.' He paused. 'I need you, Catherine.'

Catherine went back to work for the export manager of William Kaye International in October, when her baby was five months old. Brian had been right; Molly was more than willing to take charge of her granddaughter during the day and she loved every minute. It felt good to fall back into her old chair in the office next to Brian's and slide back into her old professional life. It wasn't entirely the same, of course, not only because she had a little one to think about but because her relationship with Brian had changed. He wasn't just her boss anymore; he was her new best friend, her advisor, her mentor, her constant companion. He often drove her home after work, where a meal was always ready for him and, more often than not, a spare bed for the night. After a while, he began to leave odd personal items at the Carters' home; a toothbrush, spare razor, shaving soap. It was strange but Catherine found it quite comforting having Brian's things around the house.

*

The first snow of winter fell at the beginning of December. Brian had been away for a few days, visiting a newly opened factory in the Republic of Ireland, and Catherine had had a fairly quiet working week. But he would be back today and she was really looking forward to seeing him again. He always had amusing tales to tell after his trips away and he always made her feel that she was someone special to come back to. And today she had something special to ask him. She shook the snow off her coat, pulled off her boots and put the kettle on, waiting for Brian to come off the telephone. It would never stop ringing today; it never did on his first day back.

'Good morning, Mr Jarvis! Welcome back!'

'Hi, gorgeous! Have you missed me?'

'No, but my mother has. Not to mention my daughter. Have a cup of coffee.'

They chatted for a while, were constantly interrupted by the telephone and before Catherine disappeared into her own office, she said,

'Oh, Brian, there's something I want to ask you. I don't know what you usually do but – how do you fancy spending Christmas with the three Carter females this year?'

Brian blinked.

'Are you serious?'

'No, it's my welcome-back-to-the-office-Brian very bad joke. Of *course* I'm serious. Mum would love you to come.'

Brian grinned, his grey eyes crinkling at the corners with genuine pleasure.

'And you?'

'I'd be a *bit* disappointed if you refused the invitation.'

'Then tell your mum she's got herself a guest. And thanks a lot.'

*

Brian arrived on Christmas Eve loaded with parcels of various shapes and sizes. He arrived in time to see the baby before she was put to bed and gave her a kiss as Catherine carried her upstairs. He watched television with Molly and chatted to her about all and nothing and waited for Catherine to reappear. She seemed a long time in coming down.

Catherine was actually kneeling beside her baby's pink cot, watching the little one's eyelids droop and the comfort of sleep taking over. Christmas Eve. A very different Christmas Eve now that she had her own baby and she didn't have Jean-Marc. She had survived last Christmas without him but this year she had his baby, and she should have had him, too. She thought about her Christmases spent at the cottage; the little tree, the fairy lights, the incomparable ambience. There would be no more Christmases like them, ever again. No matter what the future held, no matter how many babies she had, those Christmases, those years spent with Jean-Marc in Mullion Lodge would always be very special. No one would ever replace him in her ... there was a tap at the door. Catherine jumped.

'Hi, it's me. I thought you'd fallen asleep with Janine.'

'I almost did.' Catherine smiled, dragging herself into the present. 'I'm coming down now.'

Brian looked at her. His eyes explored her face and for a split second they screwed up and his mouth became a narrow white line in his face. For a split second.

'Catherine, you know I'm in love with you, don't you?'

She stared at him.

'What?'

'I love you. I've always loved you. Oh, come on, you must know. You can't not know. I think you're very fond of me, too. Aren't you, Catherine?'

She turned away from him but he caught hold of her arm and spun her round. Janine gurgled in her sleep. Brian held Catherine's arm tightly until she gasped and then he gently drew her towards him and kissed her.

'Forget your past, my lovely. It's over, finished. You've got a bright future to look forward to. For God's sake, leave your miserable past where it belongs – in the past.'

Catherine blinked at him. He was so astute, so sensitive. He'd guessed why she'd stayed upstairs for so long.

'My past wasn't miserable. Not at all. I was really, really happy—'

She didn't finish her sentence because Brian's lips were suddenly covering hers and she surprised herself by responding.

It was a happy Christmas, filled with warmth and laughter, and for Catherine the knowledge that Brian was in love with her. Brian, her boss, her best friend, loved her. She had known all along, she supposed, right from the early days when he used to, well, *chase* her and ... when there was someone else in her life. He loved her baby, too, and that was just as, if not more, important. She couldn't possibly entertain a man who wasn't besotted with Janine.

On New Year's Eve, Brian invited Catherine out for a meal, somewhere special, he said. Molly was more than happy to babysit and waved them off through the living-room window.

'Where are we going?' Catherine grinned as they drove through Harrogate.

'It's a surprise. Wait and see.'

After a short drive, he turned left and pulled into the small car park of the Old Windmill. Catherine's heart leapt into her mouth and she could feel the goosebumps on her limbs.

'This is a restaurant that I don't know at all,' Brian told her. 'Never been here. I know it has an excellent reputation but it also has terrible memories for me. Memories that I'm going to try and kill this evening. With you. You see, my parents spent their silver wedding anniversary here and my ... my mother was killed in a car accident on the way home. A drunken driver. Dad was permanently crippled. Paralysed from the waist down. So – as you can imagine – I've never had the slightest desire to come to this place. But I think you can help me, Catherine. I think you can help me kill all those ... very difficult memories.'

Catherine was looking at him with compassion and sucking her lower lip. She buried her own memories deep inside her. For Brian's sake.

The evening was difficult for both of them, although they tried to disguise their respective emotions in the atmosphere of New Year's Eve. At midnight, they were sitting side by side in the small bar, drinking liqueurs, when a clock began to chime the magic hour. Brian gently took Catherine in his arms, kissed her and whispered,

'A very happy new year, my lovely. Together.'

'Happy new year, Brian.'

But Catherine's voice was muffled and the words came out distorted and inaudible. Brian didn't seem to notice. It was all wrong being here with Brian Jarvis. Or anyone else. This place belonged to her and Jean-Marc. She would never go to the Old Windmill again and that was a solemn promise she made to herself.

Brian slept in Molly's spare room that night and on the first, very snowy day of 1979, Molly accepted an invitation to visit an elderly neighbour. Brian insisted on driving her there (she couldn't possibly trudge through all that snow, now, could she?) and he was away about twenty minutes. Catherine spent the time with Janine, playing with her baby on the rug in front of the gas fire. On Brian's frozen return, she put the baby to bed for the afternoon and made two mugs of coffee; two mugs of coffee that never got drunk.

As soon as Catherine appeared in the living room, Brian took the coffees out of her hands and put them on the hearth. He took hold of her hand and silently led her upstairs. Janine was already sleeping. Brian pulled the mother away from the cot and took her into the spare bedroom.

'Brian...'

'Shh ... you're safe with me, my lovely. You'll always be safe with me. *I'll* never leave you. *I'll* never let you down.'

He slowly took the clothes off the body he'd hungered after for so long, stroking and caressing and kissing every part of it. Catherine clung to him; her boss, her best friend. Her lover. A lover she would always be safe with. A lover who would never leave her. Janine gurgled in the room next door; a happy, sleepy gurgle and Catherine's eyes searched her lover's face.

'I love you both,' he said, 'very much.'

And Catherine gave herself to Brian Jarvis.

Chapter Twenty-Four

Janine Carter was the most beautiful little girl in the world. Everybody said so. Everybody who mattered, that is. Catherine, Molly and Brian. On Thursday, 1st May, 1980, Janine's second birthday, Molly gave a small tea party for her beloved grandchild. Catherine was working, of course, so Molly prepared everything and told Cathy to bring Brian home, too.

'I intended to,' Catherine grinned. 'Do you think Janine would forgive me if I didn't?'

Janine scurried to the door when she saw the familiar car outside. Her round pink face filled with laughter, her dark hair bouncing around her tiny shoulders. She looked delicious. Catherine scooped her child into her arms, twirled her round and, after lots of kisses, handed her over to Uncle Brian. He gave her a huge honey-coloured teddy bear that she called Simon, and she went to show him to the few neighbours and their children who were gathered in the living room. They all managed to get through a rather disgusting tea of jam tarts, jellies and birthday cake and afterwards played silly games that left everyone exhausted and Janine definitely ready for bed. Catherine carried her tiny body upstairs, with the promise that Grandma and Uncle Brian would be up in five minutes to kiss her night-night and, yes, Simon could sleep at the foot of her bed. Janine was asleep before even Catherine had the chance to kiss her good night. She softly stroked a stray hair out of the sleeping child's eyes, smiled to herself and turned to leave the room. Uncle Brian was standing behind her, dragging Simon by the left ear. Catherine jumped and then laughed.

'You're too late, Uncle Brian, my daughter is hard and fast asleep.'

'I don't want to be Uncle Brian any longer, Catherine.'

She stared at him, her lips puckered; her mouth opened, but no words came out. She shrugged her shoulders in a lame gesture of acquiescence.

'Oh, right. Okay. Well, that's fine, Brian. I'll ... erm ... I'll tell her to call you—'

'Daddy.'

'What?'

An hour later, the chaotic children's party was transformed into a rather inelegant, very informal engagement party, and the happy couple were toasted with glasses of flat lemonade and leftover birthday cake.

Melanie

Chapter Twenty-Five

The offices of Messrs Heptonstall, Dunn and Jones were situated in a tall, narrow building on a street that ran parallel to Harrogate's railway station. Melanie Jarvis stepped out of the taxi and walked across the road, knowing that the driver's eyes were still fixed on her body. She looked at her watch; ten minutes to three. She was early. Their appointment was at three o'clock. Brian would probably be late out of spite, just to keep her waiting. She pushed open the swing doors of the solicitors' office, told the receptionist who she was and asked for the ladies' room. Once there, she gazed into the mirror and smiled at her reflection. Not only because she was pleased with her own image but also because of what was to take place in approximately ten minutes' time. She wasn't one hundred per cent sure, of course, but she would have staked her now-precious life on it. She hadn't lived a prisoner's life for three years for nothing; she hadn't suffered and stifled her life to see nothing at the end of it. She ran a tortoiseshell comb through her glossy hair and applied more dusky pink lipstick. And then she left the ladies' room to be told her fate.

Brian, thank God, had arrived and was sitting in reception looking nervous and slightly irritated when Melanie emerged. He didn't stand or acknowledge her in any way other than by spitting at her,

'For God's sake, Melanie, you've come to hear your father's will being read, not to a bloody debutantes' ball.'

Brian's eyes were travelling over his sister's body as she sat on the low, uncomfortable chair opposite his. She crossed her long legs and tossed her blonde hair over her shoulder. Even her brother appreciated her physically, although he'd never admit it. The ageing and rather unfeminine receptionist was watching them out of her eye corner.

'Yes, darling,' Melanie threw back, in a voice more than a trifle too loud, 'and I'm looking forward to it.'

Mr Howard Dunn, middle-aged, bespectacled and balding, stood up when his secretary showed the two Jarvis siblings into his office, smiled rather vaguely and held out his hand across the desk. He had known Vincent Jarvis well for many years, professionally and socially, but was only slightly acquainted with his children. He watched them both very carefully now as they sat in the two chairs facing his desk. It had been a strange how-do-you-do for a long time with this family; he'd never really known what to make of it.

'I'm sorry it's such a sad occasion that brings you here today,' he said. 'Your father was one of the most decent men I've ever known.'

Neither of Vincent Jarvis's children replied.

Howard Dunn offered no more platitudes. He picked up the document in front of him and hesitated. He was holding their future in his hands and he looked at both their faces, trying to elicit what was going through their minds. Brian Jarvis began to fidget and look uncomfortable. His sister crossed her endless legs, and the already short blue skirt travelled even further up her thigh.

'Is there something holding you up, Mr Dunn?' she asked, looking the solicitor straight in the eye. 'I'm sure you didn't invite me here just to gaze at my legs. Did you?'

Brian spun round, ready to verbally attack her, but Howard Dunn ignored the silly remark, threw Brian a placating look and began to read.

'Of course. Let's get on. "This is the last will and testament of me, Vincent Jarvis ... To my only son, Brian Jarvis, I give, devise and bequeath my house Greystones and all my personal chattels absolutely."'

The solicitor looked up. 'In other words, your father's home and all his personal possessions.' He continued. '"To my daughter, Melanie Jarvis, I bequeath my art collection. My residuary estate to be divided equally between my son, Brian, and my daughter, Melanie, absolutely."'

Howard Dunn raised his eyes again. 'Which means that the remainder of your father's estate would have been divided between the two of you.'

The two faces looking at him were bland, emotionless. Had either of them cottoned on to what he'd just said? He took off his glasses, wiped the lenses with a pristine handkerchief and observed the two young people.

'However, two months before your father died, he added a codicil to his will. You know what a codicil is, don't you?'

He watched Brian and Melanie exchange an impatient glance, coughed and continued.

'The codicil changes the will entirely.'

Melanie Jarvis inherited everything. Well, everything except £1,000.00 that her father had left to the nurse who'd taken care of him so well and for so long.

Howard Dunn finally stood up, walked around his desk and called his secretary into the office.

'Would you like to show Mr and Miss Jarvis out, please, Audrey?'

He solemnly shook their hands again and said that he hoped the next time they met would be under more pleasant circumstances. Brian, pale, shaking and obviously in shock, did not reply. His hand trembled in the older man's. Melanie squeezed the solicitor's hand and flashed her incomparable smile at him.

'Personally, Mr Dunn, my circumstances couldn't be any happier, could they?'

Howard Dunn winced and was relieved to close his door.

A biting autumn wind slashed their faces as Melanie and Brian walked into the street. Melanie pulled her jacket tightly around her and, without a word, began to walk in the direction of the town centre. Brian's hand on her arm arrested her. She looked at her brother with indifferent eyes; his face was white, his jaw stiff, his mouth a thin, tight line. The thin blade of his steely grey eyes slashed into her.

'You think you're very clever, don't you, you little bitch?'

'Correction. I know I'm clever. Why do you think I stayed all those years? You know I didn't stay for the love of Daddy, and you don't think I stayed because of you and your idle threats, do you? Do you honestly think I lived like a prisoner because I was afraid of you, or because I didn't have the guts to get out? Oh yes, in the beginning, yes, I admit...' She laughed in Brian's face and felt his grasp on her slacken. One or two passers-by glanced at them, probably thinking they were having a lovers' tiff. 'I admit I stayed in the beginning because I felt trapped and didn't know how to escape ... but I've got an active brain, Brian. A scheming brain; you seem to have forgotten that. I knew our daddy wouldn't survive for ever. I could see the decline more or less on a daily basis. I knew that if I stuck around and behaved like a caring, affectionate daughter and you never put an appearance in – I knew I'd win in the end. You reap what you sow. And I was right, wasn't I?'

Brian couldn't answer. His reply was a long, cold and questioning stare and a body that wouldn't stop shaking. Melanie continued.

'Well, I won't be around for much longer, Brian. But you've probably worked that out. Don't worry, though, I'll keep in touch. You certainly haven't heard the last of me.'

Brian started to walk away without a backward glance, and Melanie watched his defeated body moving towards his car. But she hadn't finished with him yet, not by a long chalk. This was just the beginning.

'Oh, by the way, Brian,' she called.

He slowly turned round.

'Did your secretary tell you we bumped into each other ... oh, a while ago now? At the Old Windmill? No? Oh, it must have slipped her mind. I seem to remember that she was with a very attractive man – the one who sent her the bouquet of red roses, yeah? They made a very attractive couple.'

She was now rubbing salt into Brian's already painful wound and he was suffering. It was written all over his face and his inert, dejected body. Melanie enjoyed watching Brian suffer.

And this was just the beginning.

*

Melanie saw a lot of Howard Dunn over the next few months. She needed him and he became her mentor, advisor, guardian almost. Under his guidance, Melanie was able to invest her new-found wealth wisely and when, at the end of twelve months, she began negotiations for the sale of Greystones, together with Vincent's private art collection and his own paintings, she knew that her years of deprivation and misery were finally over. During that time, she rented a small but adequate flat in the centre of Harrogate and devoted her time to planning and financing her future.

Howard Dunn tried to dissuade his beautiful, desirable and affluent client from leaving Yorkshire. What was the point in uprooting herself? he asked. Why didn't she wait a couple of years until ... but Melanie had waited long enough. And she knew by the look in Howard Dunn's eye that he didn't want to detain her in Harrogate for her own benefit. She hated the way saliva always appeared at the corners of his mouth whenever they were discussing business ... when she knew that business wasn't his primary concern. She couldn't wait to get away from him. There would be other lawyers, advisors, mentors in London.

She wasn't long in finding somewhere to live. A reasonably sized and furnished ground-floor flat just off the Tottenham Court Road. And right in the heart of things. Melanie went shopping. Clothes, shoes, cosmetics, jewellery, until she had a completely new wardrobe. She found a talented hairdresser and paid the earth to have her hair cut and restyled. A page-boy cut, slightly shorter at the sides than the back, with a deep fringe. A style that complemented her beautiful face, the male hairdresser complimented. And who was she to argue? When she was completely satisfied with her new self, she went to look for a job. Her first two interviews were failures. Her third was a roaring success.

*

The lavish and exorbitantly priced department store stood in the heart of the West End and the perfumery was on the ground floor, left at the main entrance. Which meant that Melanie Jarvis, sales assistant for Chantage, a popular French perfume house, was on view to the world.

Melanie worked hard, loving every minute. She was sent on a three-week training and induction course – not at the head office in Paris as she would have liked, but to a salon in a plush West End hotel. There she learnt, with two other young women, all there was to know about Chantage (blackmail in English, she discovered, but it sounded much more romantic in French) cosmetics and perfume, and the selling of both. What she learnt every day was fascinating, stimulating, her life's blood. She took her newly acquired knowledge home with her every evening; sitting for hours in front of the mirror, practising with creams, colours, powders; creating new Melanie faces, adopting hairstyles to match. Her already ample wardrobe flourished; her small bathroom overflowed with fragrances, lotions and bottles cluttering and clinking on the glass shelves.

The only aspect of her life that Melanie found unsatisfactory was her social life – she didn't have one. She was lonely. Melanie had never found it easy to make friends; she wasn't used to mixing with people of her own age

210

and girls especially were difficult to befriend. They never seemed to 'take to' her. The two other girls on the Chantage training course were a perfect example. Melanie had gone out of her way the first couple of days to be sociable with them, but they didn't want to know. They had already teamed up; three was a crowd. After a while, Melanie mentally shrugged her shoulders and put it down to jealousy, an idea that didn't displease her. In spite of this, she still felt a pang of something when she went home alone every evening and had to spend hours on end with her own beautiful, albeit lonely, image. But Melanie didn't spend sleepless nights worrying about her lack of social contacts. She couldn't afford to lose her beauty sleep and she knew that one day someone would come along and introduce her to London society and that would be her second beginning … and it wouldn't be a female.

*

In the autumn of 1977, a middle-aged but attractive and obviously affluent man walked into the main entrance of the West End department store. He stood motionless for several minutes and then, after looking around him, turned to his left and headed towards the perfumery. He saw the blonde girl standing behind the Chantage counter, and one glance told him she was just what he was looking for.

'Good morning, sir. May I help you?'

Even better. A radiant smile.

'Yes, my dear, I think you can. I'm looking for a model. Someone to sit on my new car and look sexy.'

Melanie stared at him. She had been warned on the training course about being propositioned by strange men. She wished she had the quickness of repartee to cope with this type of bloke … and the odd, obscene caller … she'd have to write a few lines down and memorise them … At the moment, however, all she could manage was,

'I'm sorry, I don't understand.'

At that moment, a woman laden down with the store's carrier bags approached the counter, wanting to be served. Melanie hoped the man would do a disappearing act but he didn't. She could feel his appraising eyes on her all the time. The woman took a long time deciding between Chantage toilet water and the perfume, and Melanie spent the minutes trying to ignore the man and willing him to go away. His words kept coming back to her. *I'm looking for a model. Someone to sit on my new car and look sexy.* Was he a pervert or had she totally misunderstood him?

The customer finally flourished her cheque, having chosen the perfume, and walked away with her purchase. The man smiled, almost kindly, at Melanie and this time she tentatively smiled back. She opened her mouth to say something to him but another customer was suddenly standing in front of her. Melanie, by now convinced that the man was not a weirdo, acknowledged the woman and threw the man a frantic look. He quietly indicated for her to serve and he'd still be there when she'd finished. The customer was difficult and Melanie found it a struggle to be polite. Not for the first time. She had the sense to realise, however, that this was one particular moment in her life when she certainly had to be on her best behaviour; the man was watching her every move and therefore she was charming. After what seemed like an eternity, the woman left and Melanie sauntered back to her visitor, doing her best to look nonchalant.

'I'm sorry,' she smiled, 'but the customer is king. Or, in this case, queen. What were you saying?'

He took a small plastic card out of his wallet and threw it onto the counter.

'My name's Jonathan Drew. I work for an American car manufacturer – Atlas Automobiles – you'll have heard of us, I'm sure. I'm the sales promoter for the UK and this month we've just brought out a new model – a beauty. Nearly as good-looking as yourself. On the 2nd of October, we're giving a cocktail party, an opening night at the Nightbirds discotheque in Piccadilly. I suppose you know it. I'm looking for a girl to pose and look pretty with our car on the photos. Will you be free on the 2nd of October?'

Chapter Twenty-Six

The Diadem was indeed a beautiful car. It stood, long, red and gleaming, in the centre of what was normally the raised dance floor at the Nightbirds discotheque. When Melanie arrived, wearing denim jeans, a blue sweatshirt and very little make-up, the various employees of Atlas Automobiles were busy giving the metal model her finishing touches. The employees of Nightbirds were busy arranging tables, organising the bars, the restaurant and the lighting. Melanie stood still for a moment; a brief, chill feeling of panic streaming through her body. This was it, then; this was the beginning. The real beginning. Jonathan Drew, also casually dressed but still attractive in a rather earthy way, suddenly noticed his human model looking lost and nervous and rather out of place among all the activity. He hurried to her side.

'Well, hello. I'm sorry you had to find your own way here tonight. I'd have picked you up myself but, as you can see, it's utter bedlam. At least you're in good time and *that* I'm grateful for. Okay, follow me, ducks, and I'll show you to your dressing room.'

Dressing room? Melanie's heart was going to burst ...

'There'll be a small band playing live here tonight and the girl singer will be sharing your dressing room. I hope you don't mind but needs must, you know. And she's a nice kid, you'll like each other. Here we are.'

Jonathan Drew knocked on one of the doors in the dimly lit corridor. A dark-haired girl of about Melanie's age, wearing only bra and pants, opened it slightly.

'Sorry to disturb you, Angie, but you've been expecting Melanie, haven't you, ducks? This is Melanie Jarvis, my model for the evening. Melanie, meet Angie, our lovely singer. Sounds like Diana Ross on a good night. Now, you remember what went on during rehearsals, don't you, Mel? You did just fine, so do exactly the same tonight and don't be nervous. You've got nothing to be nervous about. That's your wardrobe on the left; you'll have four different changes. Okay? Right; now look snappy.'

Angie closed the door and smiled at Melanie. Melanie briefly returned the smile and walked to the wardrobe on the left. She pulled open the stiff wooden door and began to inspect her four 'changes'.

'Do you do this sort of thing very often?' Angie asked, a friendly but curious note in her voice.

'What sort of thing?' Melanie didn't look at her, too engrossed in the look and feel of the exquisite garments.

'Modelling ... with cars ... that sort of thing.'

'Yeah ... yeah, I do. On and off.'

'And do you actually *enjoy* doing it? It doesn't make you feel a bit like a sex object ... you know, men ogling you and all that? Like they do with cars? Anyway, I suppose it's all very glamorous.'

Melanie threw the singer a swift look and went back to her wardrobe. She couldn't wait to get into some of these incredible clothes, even if they wouldn't cover much of her body.

'Oh, it's not as glamorous as people think. To be perfectly honest, it can sometimes be unutterably boring – like most jobs, I suppose. By the way, where's the bathroom?'

The Nightbirds was crowded. The public were not allowed access that evening; it was a private function for Atlas Automobiles and the promotion of the Diadem. And half the automobile world seemed to be gathered there; manufacturers and buyers, reps and salesmen. Wealthy, powerful men waiting to see what Atlas had to offer. There were long, tiresome, hilarious and sometimes incomprehensible speeches; toasts, thanks, encores. It was hot, smoky; the air was heavy and very unhealthy. Melanie stood in the wings of the raised dance floor, watching the entertainment. She could hardly believe that she was a part of all this; the main attraction, the grand finale. She clutched her still-sickly stomach, licked her well-glossed lips and tried to behave naturally. It was difficult. She looked down at her costume, her first of the evening. A sparkling midnight blue bikini top and flowing skirt that revealed her thighs when she moved. She looked at the large clock on the wall behind her; she would be on in five minutes; she would be sitting on the bonnet of that car, posing for all the world to see. No, she couldn't really believe it was happening ... Jonathan Drew, wearing a black evening suit and bow tie, was speaking into the microphone, his voice echoing around the packed room.

'And now, ladies and gentlemen, it's photograph time. The beautiful Diadem is going to be advertised in various national – and international –

magazines, not to mention television. And the car being such a beautiful model, we had to find an even more beautiful model to pose with her.'

Mild, polite laughter.

'Ladies and gentlemen, I'm always on the lookout for new, young talent, whether I'm working with car mechanics, sales reps or models for my photographs. Three weeks ago, I made a remarkable discovery and I know you're going to love our model for this evening – put your hands together and please welcome Miss Melanie Jarvis.'

At first, she couldn't move. And then, as the applause began to die away and the spotlight danced across the floor, she put one foot in front of the other and walked, tall, elegant and incredibly desirable, towards the Diadem. Jonathan Drew was holding out his hand to her, and he smiled as she took hold of it. The cameras began to flash. Melanie swallowed and screwed up her eyes against the bright lights. She panicked again. She looked into Jonathan's eyes.

'Smile, for God's sake,' he hissed.

Melanie smiled. The cameras flashed again. She walked to the car. She sat in the driving seat, on the bonnet, on the roof. She smiled, she waved, she blew kisses, she changed her costume four times. *She's a natural*, thought Jonathan Drew.

*

That was Melanie's beginning. When the photographs had been printed, Jonathan Drew sent the published results to Melanie's home address and she, in turn, sent copies to her brother's address. With a short, sharp note attached. Reminiscent of erstwhile exotic postcards. Jonathan Drew also called to see her again while she was working behind the Chantage perfume counter and asked if she would like to earn a few more pennies. A lot more, actually. At the Earls Court Exhibition.

The affair with Jonathan Drew lasted twelve months, during which time he showered Melanie with gifts; clothes, jewellery, bibelots for her home, and he introduced her to London society. He put her in touch with a relatively well-known modelling agency that he sometimes used himself, and was happy to finance a short, very intensive course for the 'mature' would-be model. While she was working at the agency, she met photographers, men who told her they knew talent when they saw it, and

215

who also told her they could make her very rich. And famous. If she'd allow them to ... Melanie allowed them to – and eighteen months after her move to London, she saw her face on the cover of a glossy monthly magazine.

Melanie Jarvis – Face of the Year

It was about that time that she started to get bored with Jonathan. And cars. He'd been useful – very useful – and as a sugar daddy she certainly had nothing to complain about. He had found her an unfurnished flat in South Kensington, furnished it beautifully, paid for her driving lessons, and when she passed her test the first time, he bought her a red Diadem. He took her abroad twice for mutual, much-needed breaks. He stifled Melanie with his money, his affection, his body; stifled and disgusted her. To the point where she wanted to throw up whenever he came near her.

*

Dinner at the Montego Moon hotel was at eight o'clock, in the elegant outdoor restaurant. The tables surrounded the dance floor and a calypso band played on a small stage. Melanie stepped out of the shower at ten minutes past eight, her naked body glistening with the tepid water, her hair tangled and dripping around her shoulders. Jonathan was sitting on the bed, already dressed for dinner. Melanie grabbed her towel and slowly began to pat herself dry. Jonathan sighed. This was becoming a ritual, a habit. And he knew why. It didn't take an Einstein's brain to work it out. Melanie Jarvis enjoyed making her entrance at dinner.

'Mel, sweetheart, we should have been in the restaurant ten minutes ago. This is the third time ...'

Melanie stood in front of him, her wet, naked body almost touching his face, her hands manipulating the bath towel. She tossed her tousled hair over her shoulder.

'What about it ... darling?'

Jonathan looked up at her and Melanie could see his lips beginning to tremble, his already rheumy eyes glazing over.

'Sweetheart, we're going to be late – again. Not that I really mind, but ...'

Melanie smiled at him, cocked her head to one side and wriggled her breasts. Water dripped onto Jonathan's hand. He groaned and his hand reached out, wanting to stroke, caress, give and gain pleasure ... Melanie laughed and turned away.

'We mustn't make ourselves later than we already are, must we ... darling?'

She walked to the mirror and began to perform, knowing that Jonathan was watching her; and not only watching ... He suddenly stood up and approached her from behind, his hands gripping her still naked shoulders. She saw his reflection in the mirror, the familiar expression on his face and she felt the familiar nausea rising.

'Let's forget dinner, sweetheart. Let's make our last night in Jamaica something to remember.'

He began to kiss the back of her neck, twisting the blonde hair around his fingers. Melanie cringed and clenched her teeth.

'I intend to make it something to remember, Jonathan. I intend to enjoy myself and that includes a delicious West Indian meal and as many banana daiquiris I can down before showing myself up. So, please, let me get ready, there's a love.'

An hour later, Melanie made her entrance. She walked through the restaurant to the music of the calypso band, her hips swaying slightly, her head erect, her thin, lacy ivory dress flowing around her tanned legs. Jonathan walked behind her, looking and feeling insignificant but proud, knowing that the eyes of the diners and those who served them were riveted on his woman. They sat down at their table in the centre of the room and, although Jonathan ordered, their young waiter never took his eyes off Melanie.

'Well, my love,' Jonathan smiled, when they were alone, 'I hope you've enjoyed your holiday and all my efforts haven't been in vain.'

Melanie stared at him and raised an eyebrow.

'*Your* efforts?' Then she smiled. She almost patted his hands and said, *Yes, you've been a very good boy, Jonathan. You can go and play now.* Instead, she said,

'I've had a wonderful time, darling, and I appreciate everything you've done for me.'

Paying for the holiday, buying her another complete, new wardrobe to come away with, hiring the car in order to visit the island. She supposed that was what he meant.

'I don't want your appreciation, Mel, I want ...'

Melanie's eyes flashed. The lobster in a mouth-watering seafood sauce arrived.

217

'Sweetheart, when I said I wanted our last night in Montego Bay to be something to remember …'

Melanie stiffened. She didn't want or need any melodrama, a scene; all she wanted to do was eat the delicious food, get a little drunk on the banana daiquiri and white wine, dance a little and go to bed reasonably early. There would be a long flight to London tomorrow.

'Mel?' Jonathan hadn't acknowledged either his food or his wine. He leant across the table and lowered his voice. 'When we get back to London; when we're back to our normal routine and we … Will you make me a very happy man and become Mrs Jonathan Drew? Will you marry me, Melanie?'

Melanie laughed, dabbed her lips with a napkin, and there followed a long and heavy silence.

'Marry you?' She burst into a fit of giggles that slowly melted into more silence. 'Oh my God, I think you're *serious*. You can't be … Jonathan, you're nearly old enough to be my father, for God's sake. Look, I'll be honest with you. I've absolutely no intention of marrying you … or anybody else, for that matter. A tedious, mundane marriage couldn't be further from my mind. I'm enjoying my life – and my freedom – far too much.'

She made that little speech while stabbing her lobster, not looking at him. Jonathan's slightly sunburned face blanched.

'Enjoying yourself? Yeah, I *bet* you are.'

He threw down his napkin, knocking over a glass of water, abruptly stood up, just avoided tripping over his chair, and strode through the restaurant towards the exit. Melanie calmly continued devouring the five-course meal and mildly flirted with the attentive young waiter. Towards midnight, much later than she'd intended, she strolled back to their room surrounded by the warmth and gentle sounds of a Caribbean night. She didn't know what would be waiting for her in the bedroom and she didn't care. In twenty-four hours, she would be back in England, in her lovely flat in Kensington. There would be work for her to do. Lots of it. She didn't need Jonathan Drew anymore. He'd served his purpose and was now superfluous to her requirements, professional and personal.

He was sitting on a wicker chair by the bed, a full glass in his hand, an empty rum bottle by his side. Oh God, this was all she needed – a pissed-up Jonathan Drew to make her last night in Jamaica something to remember.

He hit her. Twice. The second blow across her head sent her reeling backwards across the room; she slipped and her head slammed against the corner of the dressing table before she crashed to the white-tiled floor.

'You're a bitch, Melanie Jarvis. You're nothing but a selfish, conceited, greedy bitch. And one day some poor bastard's gonna swing for you.'

After a few moments, Melanie slowly and painfully pulled herself up. Her terrified and tear-filled eyes watched him; her carefully manicured hands moved towards the pain in her head. It was an echo from the past, someone yelling at her ... *I swear to God, one day I'll swing for you* ... She forced a mechanical smile at the man who'd attacked her. She had to spend the night with this drunken fool; there was no telling what he might do. And the glass was still in his hand. She improved the mechanical smile and held out a trembling hand as she slowly crawled towards him.

'I'm sorry, Jonathan, I didn't mean to upset you. You just ... well, you just took me by surprise. I didn't have time to think. Honestly. You know I wouldn't hurt you for the world ...'

All the time looking at the glass in his hand. It suddenly fell to the floor and shattered and Jonathan Drew was kneeling in front of her, clinging to her; groaning, tearing at her ivory dress, her body; his lips gnawing at her bruising face.

'I'm sorry, sweetheart, I'm sorry, I'm sorry. Oh God, I never wanted to hurt you. You know that, don't you? I love you, sweetheart, love you sooooo much ...'

Melanie screwed up her eyes, clenched her fists and fought back the nausea as her sugar daddy made her last night in Jamaica something to remember.

Chapter Twenty-Seven

Melanie had been right; there were jobs waiting for her on her arrival in London. The agency had a few small assignments for a relatively new cosmetic company, and Chantage, for whom she still worked on a part-time basis, kept her busy. Her beautiful, bewitching face could still occasionally be seen behind the French perfume counter, promoting its sales. She had had to fix that beautiful face, of course. The swelling and the bruise that Jonathan Drew had given her weren't exactly minor. But with clever make-up and a lot of know-how, nobody would have known. Nobody ever did know.

Jonathan Drew's unprecedented violence had been his undoing in the end. An ideal opportunity for Melanie to get him out of her life. He was dangerous. He'd attacked her; how could he expect her to carry on as before? She changed her locks, changed her telephone number and began a new life without her unwanted lover. A wonderful life, a life that had once been a far-off dream. A life mixing with all the right people; rich and famous people. A life working with luxuries; designer clothes, exquisite jewellery. A life posing for the camera; a life travelling and seeing places she'd only read about in brochures and on her brother's postcards. A life with a variety of men; rich, sexy, besotted men who fell insanely in love with her and always got kicked in the teeth. But Melanie was never battered again.

*

The invitation arrived in July 1980, the biggest shock of Melanie's life. Mrs Molly Carter requested the pleasure of Miss Melanie Jarvis at the wedding of her daughter Catherine to Mr Brian Jarvis, at the Register Office, Victoria Avenue, Harrogate. At first, Melanie could not for the life of her think who Catherine Carter was. Although she'd been efficient in corresponding with her brother, sending him professional photographs of herself and various postcards from her travels, Brian had been very negligent in keeping in touch with her. No prizes for guessing why. Only the odd necessary official correspondence from him came through her letterbox. And now, this had arrived, a most unexpected invitation to his wedding. How very odd. She didn't even know he had a woman in his life. Catherine Carter. The name rang a faint bell but she ... And then it dawned; the secretary, the one with the awful dyed hair. The one with the ... the rather delectable French boyfriend. A slow smile started to spread across Melanie's face. Oh yes, she'd 'fancied' him herself at one time, if she remembered correctly. At one time. She probably wouldn't look at him twice now. There were more fanciable men in her life than ... So, what had happened to Monsieur whatever-his-name was? She couldn't remember his name, of course. Brian Jarvis would be no substitute; that was for sure. She looked at the date of the forthcoming carnival and checked her professional and social diaries. Saturday, 20th September, 1980. Nothing booked on or around that date. She quickly wrote a short polite note to Mrs Molly Carter, accepting her kind invitation to her daughter's carni ... wedding. This was one bun fight she wasn't going to miss.

*

Melanie drove north in her scarlet Diadem on Friday, 19th September, the first time she'd headed for Harrogate since the day she left. After much heart- and soul-searching, she had finally reserved a room at the Heaton Brow Arms, rather than at a larger and more lavish hotel in the town itself. Melanie told herself she wanted to stay in her old neighbourhood in order to prove to those she'd once worked for that she'd 'arrived'. The young woman who would occupy the finest room the small hotel had to offer was no longer the same girl who'd helped out behind the bar and in the kitchen in order to escape a life-draining existence, albeit at Greystones, the most desirable house in the village. No, this Melanie Jarvis was a well-known celebrity, an international success, a phenomenon, and her return to Heaton Brow was in order to gloat. That's what Melanie told herself. But if she had looked deep inside herself and been totally honest, she would have admitted that her return to Heaton Brow was also a nostalgic excursion.

The receptionist who greeted the celebrity had only been employed at the Heaton Brow Arms for six months and, coming from the south west of England, knew nothing of the model's history. She had been told that Melanie had lived at Greystones with her family, had inherited the house, put it on the market, sold it and all its contents and moved to London. She had not been told any more because no one at the hotel knew any more. When the model telephoned to reserve a room, there was a lot of excitement, but the new receptionist, a middle-aged widow in dire financial straits, was not party to the commotion. Melanie Jarvis was a guest like any other and would be treated as such. Melanie parked her car in the small car park at the back of the hotel, pulled her Louis Vuitton suitcase out of the boot and walked to the front of the ancient building. She looked at her watch. It was six-thirty. She was early. She'd told the manager to expect her after seven. A little stab of annoyance and disappointment seared through her as she stood and looked at the hotel's unassuming façade. She had expected a reception committee and there wasn't one. *But there would have been if I'd arrived at seven-thirty, for example,* she told herself. She pushed open the door and walked into the short, narrow corridor that led to the reception desk at the foot of the staircase. There wasn't a soul in sight. She walked past the bar on her left where she'd pulled pints and entertained the clientèle, and the lounge on her right where she'd dusted the furniture and banked up the fire. Low voices and muffled laughter drifted through the closed door of the bar, and Melanie knew that the residents would be having their gin and tonics before scuttling into the dining room and an excellent Heaton Brow Arms dinner. How she had despised this hotel and its sedentary, predictable daily routine. The new receptionist, Mavis Brown, was bending over her register and wasn't aware that the affluent and influential guest had arrived and was about to check in.

Melanie, unaccustomed to unacknowledgment, dropped her suitcase onto the uneven wooden floor and Mavis's head shot up.

'Good evening,' she smiled, thinly. 'Can I help you?'

Melanie began to feel the stirrings of resentment mixing with disappointment and annoyance. *Can I help you?* This wasn't the reception that Melanie had been expecting. She didn't return the receptionist's wan smile.

'Yes. I'm Melanie Jarvis. I reserved a room for seven o'clock this evening. Where's the manager?'

'Oh yes, Miss Jarvis. We're expecting you. If you'd like to sign the register, please, and your room's on the first floor. Number Three. I'm sorry, there isn't a lift and it's the odd-job boy's day off. It's his task to carry luggage to the rooms so I'm afraid there's no one to help with your suitcase.'

'*Where* is the manager?'

'I'm afraid he's not here at the moment. He had to go into Leeds and he won't be back until very late this evening. He did send his apologies and said he'll see you tomorrow morning, Miss Jarvis.'

Oh no, the hotel's greeting wasn't at all what Melanie had envisaged. She looked around the reception area for a familiar face but there was none. Only voices humming from the bar and the dining room. Voices that, of course, she didn't know. She should never have come back here; she'd been a fool to even think of it. She would never be Melanie Jarvis, international model, to these people. She'd always be Melanie Jarvis, the poor kid whose life was a drudgery and who had occasionally worked at the Heaton Brow Arms just to get her out of the house and earn a bit of pocket money. Suddenly Melanie didn't want to face anyone. She picked up her case and headed towards the threadbare-carpeted staircase behind the reception desk.

'Will you be having dinner this evening?' Mavis Brown asked her, without looking at her, scribbling in the register at the same time.

'No,' Melanie replied, fighting back the tears that were pricking at the back of her eyes. 'I won't be having dinner. I'd like a bottle of mineral water – and maybe some fruit – brought to my room, please.'

Room Three was the finest in the hotel. A double room with a large four-poster bed and matching wardrobe and a huge chest of drawers, on top of which stood an old-fashioned lamp and a crystal vase of fresh flowers. An oval wooden-framed mirror hung over the chest of drawers and three paintings of Heaton Brow and its surroundings adorned the walls. All by Vincent Jarvis. A door to the right of the magnificent bed led to a small, relatively modern bathroom. The bedroom window was open and the net curtains were billowing slightly in the evening breeze. Melanie, the threat of tears now a thing of the past and only resentment burning inside her, moved to the window, pulled aside the curtain and looked out. Beyond the immaculately kept garden was the road, the crossroads and beyond them the woods and the lane leading to Greystones. No, Melanie should never have come back here. Whatever had possessed her? She unlocked her suitcase and gently took out the garment she had chosen to wear at her brother's wedding. She held it in front of her and it shimmered, creaseless in the fading evening light. A smile began to form on Melanie's face. Perfect. Yes, it was the perfect outfit to wear at her brother's wedding … As she was opening the heavy wardrobe door in order to hang up the dress, there was a light tap on the door. Melanie jumped and a sudden wave of excitement made its presence felt.

'Come in.'

A young unknown girl opened the door and brought in a tray, containing a litre of mineral water and a large bowl of apples, bananas and grapes.

'Put it on the table over there,' Melanie commanded, pointing to a low coffee table in front of the one chintz-covered chair in the room.

The girl smiled at Melanie and bobbed her head slightly.

'Everyone downstairs is right sorry that yer not 'avin' any dinner tonight, Miss Jarvis. We were all right lookin' forward to seein' you.'

Melanie turned away from the girl and concentrated on arranging her wedding outfit in the wardrobe.

'Well, it can't be helped,' she said. 'I won't be having breakfast tomorrow, either. I'd like some black coffee brought to my room. At eight o'clock.'

'Black coffee. Right-o. Anything to eat?'

'No. I just told you. No breakfast, just black coffee.'

'Right-o. Well, thank you. Thank you, Miss.'

She stood and waited but no tip came.

In spite of her negative emotions, Melanie slept well that night and it was another tap on the door that woke her at eight o'clock the following morning. She yawned, stretched and pulled on a red silk robe to cover her nakedness.

'Come in.'

She expected the same young face to peep round the door but this time the face was familiar. She had worked for Robin Jackson so many times in the past; the hotel manager who hadn't been able to greet her the previous evening. This morning, he'd brought her coffee himself. Melanie's sleepy but still beautiful eyes met his as he walked into the room.

'Good morning, Melanie … erm … Miss Jarvis.'

Melanie merely looked at him, waiting for him to continue. He strode across the room and placed the pot of coffee and the china cup and saucer on the low table, next to the almost-empty water bottle and the bowl of untouched fruit.

'I'm so sorry I wasn't here to welcome you yesterday, Melanie,' he said, 'I was disappointed but the meeting in Leeds was unavoidable. Anyway, how are you doing?'

He was talking to her as though she was still the young girl in his employ; he treated other guests with more deference, more courtesy. She'd heard him in the past, bowing and scraping to businessmen and ... Melanie didn't reply. She sat up in bed, the red silk robe hanging loosely around her shoulders, her blonde hair awry, matted. Robin Jackson, obviously not really expecting a reply, smiled at her across the room and began to walk towards her. The smile then left his mouth and Melanie recognised the old, familiar look in the ageing hotel manager's eyes; the look that she'd seen in so many pairs of masculine eyes. She pulled the bedclothes further up her body and at the same instant the hotel manager sat down on the edge of the four-poster bed. That old, familiar look in Robin Jackson's eyes was deepening and spreading to his temples, his mouth, his trembling hands that were tentatively reaching out to her ...

'Get out of this room,' Melanie murmured.

'Melanie, love, I knew your father ... Look, your father's paintings are all over the walls ... Your mum used to clean here, and so did you. You've cleaned this room more than once, haven't you? We're pals, Melanie, old friends ... almost family, you could say ...'

Saliva, that giveaway, was beginning to form at the corners of his mouth, and his eyes had taken on a glazed expression. His hands fumbled with the beige and cream duvet.

'Get out of this room,' Melanie repeated.

And, with his embarrassed managerial tail between his legs, he did. Three hours later, Melanie's scarlet Diadem roared out of the Heaton Brow Arms' car park in the direction of Harrogate. The hands that clutched the steering wheel were white and shaking, the glossy red lips rigid in her face, her heart hammering inside her. But the threatened tears had still not been released.

Unfortunately.

*

Saturday, 20th September, 1980, was a cool but fine morning. The Diadem pulled up several yards away from the Harrogate Register Office and Melanie sat for a while behind the wheel, watching the small group of people outside. Her facial features had finally relaxed and the trembling in her hands had calmed. However, her heart was still beating furiously and the bitterness, the rancour that had already fermented, was growing like a tumour inside her. She tried to identify a few faces in the little group but there wasn't one that she knew. Not one. And she suddenly felt a pang of … something she couldn't quite put a name to. Oh, hang on, there were Neil and Linda, Brian's lifelong buddies, huddling together like two peas in a pod. Well, at least she knew Neil and Linda, if nobody else. And Brian, of course, her dearly beloved brother. She pushed open the door and swung out of the car. And slowly, one by one, nudges, prods, turning of heads in her direction; some discreet and some not so. And then a casual turning away. As if Melanie Jarvis, international model, wasn't really there; as if she hadn't put her flamboyant appearance in. She moved through the small supporting cast that she didn't know and didn't care about, towards the principal boy, standing almost entirely alone, waiting for the star of the show. He looked nervous, bless him, just like a bridegroom was supposed to look. Maybe he was wondering if the star of the show would turn up or leave him standing centre stage, looking and feeling a right bloody fool. That would be a laugh. That really would make the day. He was cautiously watching her walking towards him. His grey eyes were darting from the flashy car to the flashy female approaching him, a gorgeous smile on her face and absolutely no evidence of the bitterness and venom in her heart. She held out her perfectly manicured hand and her brother stiffened. People began to stare. He took her hand briefly and released it, flicking it away like an irritating fly.

'It was so kind of you to invite me, Brian,' Melanie chirruped, the smile fixed on her face. 'Most unexpected, I admit, in view of our traumatic past.'

Her voice was far from low; she felt several pairs of embarrassed eyes glancing at her and away again. She nodded and waved at Neil and Linda, still huddled together like Siamese twins, and they both threw a small frozen smile back. Melanie continued.

'So, my clever older brother, you finally captured your secretary bird, after all. Tell me, how did you manage to drag her away from that delicious Frenchman?'

Melanie finally had her audience. A stiff, disbelieving, embarrassed audience. Brian made no reply but she knew he was shaking inside his smart grey suit with the white carnation. Then, when she turned away from her brother, Melanie caught sight of the big black man standing with Neil and Linda. She fixed her eyes on him; as his were fixed on her.

'Ah, I see we have an ethnic minority with us,' she quipped to her brother. 'Is he a friend of yours or the blushing bride's?'

Janine saved the moment. She skipped out of the car that had just arrived and ran away from her grandmother's arms, diverting the stunned audience from their entertainer. The little girl looked a picture; her shiny black hair in pigtails with enormous peach ribbons and a short peach cotton dress with white shoes and socks. Everybody cooed and made a fuss, grateful for the distraction, and Melanie now focused her attention on the intruder. Brian was bending down to kiss the child.

'Who's this little thing?' Melanie smiled at the black man and Neil and Linda. 'Anything to do with the bridegroom?'

Before they or anyone else could reply, the bride stepped onto the pavement. Catherine wore a long, flowing peach cotton dress with chocolate brown trimmings around the sweetheart neckline and the three-quarter sleeves. Her long hair fell around her shoulders and there were tiny peach-coloured buds scattered in her red-brown tresses. She carried a small bouquet of cream roses, and her only piece of jewellery was a gold bangle on her right arm. She smiled at everyone as she passed and Brian walked towards her. Melanie was forgotten. Temporarily.

The ceremony took place at midday and after photographs had been taken inside and out, the reception was being held in an elegant Edwardian tea salon that overlooked the Valley Gardens. Molly had reserved a special room at the back of the building, with a buffet and bar; a nice, intimate atmosphere for just a few close friends and relatives. Melanie got into her car and offered a lift to anyone who needed it and the black man gratefully, if a little reluctantly, accepted. He sat in the passenger seat next to Melanie and she could feel his eyes on her as she started to manoeuvre the vehicle.

'How does the kid fit in?' she suddenly asked without warning and without looking at Danny.

'The kid? Oh, you mean Janine. She's a little charmer, isn't she? A younger version of her mum. Catherine is—'

'She does belong to Catherine then? I wasn't sure. And the father?'

Danny looked away. He was trapped, alone in this fabulous car with

Brian's beautiful but vindictive sister. He'd heard a lot about her and was now beginning to regret accepting the lift she'd offered.

'Catherine was involved for a long time with a French—'

'Yes, I know. And he's the kid's father?'

'Yes. Yes, he is.'

Silence. Melanie was driving very slowly. She suddenly took her eyes off the road and flashed them at her passenger.

'Well, I'm not interested in kids myself. Tell me about you, Danny. Where do you come from? And please don't say Leeds!'

Danny grinned at her, happy to change the subject.

'Now, why should I say that? I was born in the West Indies. Jamaica, to be exact.'

Melanie braked hard at red traffic lights.

'That's interesting. I had a holiday there a couple of years ago.'

'Really? How fantastic; you must tell me about it. Where did you stay on my island in the sun?'

'In Montego Bay.'

'Lucky you. And did you enjoy your holiday – on my island in the sun?'

The traffic lights turned to amber, then to green.

'I had a wonderful time, Danny. I was raped.'

*

The reception was okay as far as wedding receptions go. The food was edible, the Champagne flowed and the company was ... well, the company. Brian the bridegroom and his blushing bride occupied a table at the far end of the room, with Neil and Linda (still looking like peas in a pod), Mrs Carter and the kid, and a couple of people that Melanie didn't know and didn't want to. Other, over-decorated tables were occupied by guests who, Melanie guessed, were employees of William Kaye International. Little cliques of people clustered together and then her and Danny. At a table for two near the kitchen. When Melanie was shown to the inconspicuous place, she thought there'd been a mistake. She should have been on stage with her brother, a member of the family. Not tucked away, almost out of sight ... this little arrangement had been done deliberately. The adrenaline began to flow again. Danny smiled at her and told her that, although he'd be making a speech after Neil, the best man, he'd been asked to sit next to

Melanie in order to keep her company; he and she being the only single guests at the wedding. He hoped she didn't mind? Melanie looked through him. She'd soon let them know if she minded or not.

Brian was talking, standing up in front of his friends and colleagues and telling everyone what a lovely new wife he had. How original, Brian. The lovely new wife was sitting there, blushing, of course, and smiling soppily at everyone. *Don't believe a word of it, sunshine, you don't know him.* The kid suddenly caused a commotion, spilt her orange juice or something, like kids do, and diverted everyone's attention. Nobody seemed to mind, least of all Catherine. The speeches finally finished, thank the Lord, or so everyone thought. But they were wrong. Melanie took a last sip of Champagne and stood up. She walked, in a cloud of Chantage, the length of the room, towards the bridal table, where she should have been sitting in the first place. She felt everyone's eyes upon her, inspecting the stunning, not-fit-for-a-wedding outfit that she wore. Watching the flesh of her tanned naked back and the gentle undulation of her perfect breasts as they swelled out of the low grey satin bodice. And the flash of her long, tanned leg through the deep slit of the satin skirt. Her silver sandals sparkled as she moved. She reached the table and turned to smile at the silence. She smiled at her brother and new sister-in-law and she smiled at the West Indian man who was darting glances between the other two. Janine clapped her hands.

'Ladies and gentlemen,' Melanie began, her Champagne-and-acrimony glazed eyes travelling around the small gathering. 'As the sister of the bridegroom and his only living relative – present company excepted – I think it's my duty to make a speech today.'

Silence. Janine giggled.

'I'm not acquainted with many of you. I've never met you in the past and I haven't been introduced to you today. However, I'm sure most of you will be familiar with my face.'

She paused and there were several embarrassed glances, shuffles, clinking of glasses. Janine burped.

'As I've been living in London for the past four years and travelling abroad, Brian and I have, unfortunately, almost lost touch. I say "unfortunately" not because we were very close – Brian and I have never been close ...'

Somebody said, 'Don't let her go on.' Somebody else said, 'She's drunk.' Nobody moved.

229

'I say "unfortunately" because if Brian and I had kept in touch, I could have warned the lovely Catherine here what she was marrying.'

Danny stood up and quickly moved towards her. He took hold of her arm. She shook him off. Molly Carter was frantically looking around for help. Melanie continued, her voice rising above the threatened commotion.

'Catherine, naïve as she obviously is, probably imagines that Brian will behave like a husband is supposed to behave, not to mention a father. That's a laugh, isn't it? Brian Jarvis wouldn't be capable of bringing his own kid up properly, let alone a sexy Frenchman's bastard.'

The speech was finished. The guests were speechless. Danny, the big black man from Jamaica, very gently put his arm around Melanie and quietly led her away from the bridal table and out of the room. Away from the frantic, incredulous audience. Away from Brian's voice, speaking to no one in particular, telling anyone who cared to listen that one day, may God forgive him, he'd swing for the bitch. And away from Brian's bride, silently weeping in her mother's arms. Not Brian's – not her husband's arms – her mother's.

Catherine

Chapter Twenty-Eight

When Catherine Carter became Mrs Brian Jarvis, she genuinely believed that she was marrying a man who loved and cherished her and would continue to do so till death did them part. She had no reason to think otherwise. Brian had always, or very nearly always, treated her like she was somebody special; as his subordinate in the office and as his friend and lover. She thought that they were compatible. She thought that Brian was a kind, compassionate man who would love and care for her and her child for ever. Disillusionment wasn't long in coming.

They spent their honeymoon touring Scotland; Brian's idea. Catherine had wanted to go abroad, somewhere exotic and romantic, a place unknown to them both that they would enjoy discovering together. A place in the sun. But Brian said no. He spent so much of his life travelling to foreign parts, he said, it would be a pleasant change for him to have a relaxing holiday on, more or less, home ground. And Scotland would be romantic, wouldn't it, he'd said. And cheaper. He couldn't pay for a honeymoon on William Kaye's expenses. At the time, Catherine had thought he was joking.

They decided to travel to Edinburgh early on the Sunday morning and, as part of their wedding present, Molly paid for them to spend their wedding night at one of Harrogate's plushest hotels. And she, of course, was looking after Janine. Owing to the unforeseen and distressing circumstances at the wedding reception, the few guests left much earlier than anticipated and each with their own excuse, everyone having their same obvious but undiscussed reason. Therefore, Catherine and Brian found themselves in their bridal suite early in the evening. As well as the fine décor, the management had also provided flowers and Champagne.

231

Catherine followed her new husband into the room and gently closed the door. Although the day's events were still fresh in her mind, she was hoping that now she and Brian were alone at last, and in such lovely and intimate surroundings, their mutual wound would be healed a little, and after a discussion about the unsavoury subject, they would put it behind them and it would be forgotten.

Brian deposited their suitcases on the thickly carpeted floor and looked around him. Catherine stood close by him expectantly, waiting for him to take her in his arms, comfort her, love her. But she waited in vain. Brian glanced at his bride and from her to the bottle of Champagne cooling in its ice bucket. He moved away from her, pulled off his jacket and started to unfasten his tie.

'Champagne's no bloody good for me. I need a whisky.'

Catherine watched him prowling about the room, the colour in his face deepening as his anger mounted. She'd never forgive herself for pleading with Brian to invite his sister to their wedding. He hadn't wanted to ... he'd been really adamant about it and his attitude had alarmed her. She knew a little of their history and she knew from her own experience with Melanie at the Old Windmill that she was far from pleasant. But Catherine had been very curious. Melanie, the sister of her future husband, intrigued her, especially now that her face was plastered all over magazines and occasionally seen on television. She wanted to meet Melanie again, maybe get to know her as a sister-in-law. Maybe even – stranger things had happened – become friends with her. She was fond of – loved – Brian but still missed a close feminine relationship in her life. Maybe Melanie, after a while, could fill that void? So, she hadn't listened to Brian; she had argued with him, pleaded with him, until he'd finally given in and Molly had sent a wedding invitation to Melanie Jarvis, at her address in London.

'She'll never accept,' Brian had told her.

But Melanie had accepted and Catherine was now paying the price of her small victory.

Brian took off his shoes and socks and, ignoring his wife, flung himself on the bed and lay for a long time looking up at the ceiling. He eventually closed his eyes and his already thin mouth became a tight line in his face. Catherine, rigid in her position by the door, stood and watched him for a while. She knew what – or rather who – was going through his mind and she could perfectly understand his fury but … she'd been hurt, too. And it was their wedding night.

'Brian.'

Catherine started to pull the peach flowers out of her hair and put them on the dressing table. There was no response from her husband. She started to finger the gold bangle on her wrist.

'Brian, let's talk. Please.'

She walked towards the bed and took hold of his left hand. Brian opened his eyes and Catherine waited for him to reach out to her, take her in his arms, love her. But she waited in vain. His hand, inert inside hers, slowly slipped away and fell onto the bed. He closed his eyes.

'We'll talk tomorrow,' he said.

They didn't talk tomorrow or any day after. At least they didn't talk about what they needed to talk about – Melanie. They needed to talk, discuss, fight, anything just to clear the air, get the wretched woman out of their systems. Catherine tried very hard but Brian wouldn't respond, wouldn't participate. He simply clammed up. And Melanie was a closed subject. Echoes of the past reverberated in Catherine's mind. Not talking, clamming up, a closed subject. Why were men so unable to open up, communicate, pour out their feelings, break the ice and maybe save a relationship?

*

The drive to Edinburgh was long and tedious because of lack of conversation and Catherine prayed that it wasn't a preview of what was to come. Surely Brian would start behaving like a newly married man very soon? It was raining when they arrived in the Scottish capital in the late afternoon. Their accommodation was just off Princes Street; small but adequate and inexpensive. It was a place that William Kaye used for their reps when an overnight stay was necessary. Catherine passed no comment.

As the week wore on, however, Brian's mood began to mellow and his love-making was pleasant if not passionate. The guest house was comfortable and friendly and when the newlyweds had explored the city, they drove further north into the magnificent Scottish countryside and took a couple of boats to the islands. Catherine fell in love with Mull but Brian was obviously bored there. They sailed on the lochs, explored ancient castles and bought dried heather to take home 'for good luck', Catherine said. She bought Brian a kilt but he failed to see the joke and admonished her for wasting her money. So, she bought him a bottle of Glenfiddich, a gift that she knew he'd appreciate. She felt rather disappointed but not surprised to receive no gifts from him. No silly but welcome souvenirs of their north-of-the-border honeymoon. The honeymoon which, as a whole, was pleasant, but that was all Catherine could say about it. Pleasant, like any other holiday.

*

Catherine had not wanted to move away from Harrogate; it was her town, her home and everything and everyone she cared for was there. It hadn't occurred to her that Brian wouldn't want to live in Harrogate.

'I can't stand the place,' he'd said, a few months before the wedding. 'Harrogate and its surroundings – I can't stand it. There's no way I'll ever live there again. No way!'

Catherine had stared at him.

'I didn't know that, Brian. You've never said anything before ...'

'I didn't need to, did I?' He'd shrugged and tried to smile at her. 'I have to work in Harrogate and that's enough. Leeds is my home now.'

'Leeds? You want us to live in Leeds? But I don't know anyone in Leeds, Brian, and ...'

Brian had grinned and kissed her.

'You'll know me. And you know Neil and Linda. Danny won't be here much longer, as you know. He's going back to the West Indies now he's qualified but ... anyway, you'll soon make new friends.'

'I'm not going to live in the house you share with Danny, it's too ...'

'Good God, of course not. No, I thought about looking for somewhere in Roundhay, that district. It's very nice, pleasant. Big park. I lived there for a while, you know. You'll like it.'

'Yes, maybe. I just didn't think we'd be moving away from Harrogate.'

'*You'll* be moving, love, not me. I don't live there, do I?'

*

234

Catherine had fallen in love with the house the moment she set eyes on it. It was a couple of streets away from the park – perfect for Janine – the end semi. But it was in far from perfect condition. An elderly couple had previously lived there and the house had become neglected over the years. But Catherine and Brian had great fun decorating the rooms, choosing furniture and trimmings and preparing the house for when they married and moved in. They disagreed on very little, which was a blessing. Catherine had heard lots of people complain that decorating a house together was one quick step in the direction of the divorce courts ... Well, they weren't married yet, were they? And their tastes and ideas were almost identical. Almost.

'This will be Janine's room, of course,' Catherine said, looking around the smaller room adjacent to the master bedroom.

'Janine's room?'

'Yes, of course.'

Brian slowly shook his head and smiled.

'I don't think so, love. I'll need this room for my bits and pieces. I'll be bringing a lot of work home, don't forget, and you won't want me to clutter our bedroom, will you?'

'No, but won't the boxroom be big enough for your things? This room's ideal for Janine. We'll paint it ...'

Brian shook his head again, smiled and kissed Catherine's cheek.

'Sorry, love. Janine will have to sleep in the boxroom. It'll do for her. This is my room.'

But they agreed on everything else.

They arrived back in Leeds on Saturday, 4th October at seven o'clock in the evening, after the long drive from Edinburgh. Brian was obviously tired and they had stopped a couple of times on the motorway, for him to rest.

'I feel helpless,' Catherine said as they turned off the motorway. 'I'm going to take driving lessons; I've made my mind up. It's something I intended doing ages ago and never got round to it. It'll be useful to all three of us if I can drive, too.'

Brian didn't reply and Catherine put his non-communication down to fatigue.

'Which driving school do you recommend for me?' she grinned at him. Brian kept his eyes on the road.

'I don't recommend any driving school,' he eventually replied, 'because you won't be taking any lessons.'

Catherine stared at him and felt the blood rush to her face.

'What do you mean?'

He meant that there was absolutely no reason for Catherine to take driving lessons; one driver in the family was quite enough and they certainly didn't need the unnecessary expense right now. He didn't look at her at all while he was making this little speech.

They were driving through Leeds now. Brian braked at some traffic lights and then turned down a long road lined with old Victorian houses, with long, narrow gardens. He began to slow down and the car almost shrieked to a halt in front of one of them.

'I used to live there,' he said, nodding towards the house, 'a long time ago. I had a very nice flat and ...' He paused and then he added, 'Ah yes, those were the days.'

Catherine turned tired eyes towards him. She didn't know what to say and said nothing. And then they arrived at their new address.

Brian got out of the car, opened the short wrought iron gate and wordlessly humped the two suitcases up the garden path. Catherine followed him. He dropped the cases on the doorstep and fumbled for the keys. Catherine, standing on his right and slightly behind him, gently tapped his shoulder and smiled up at him. He didn't look at her; he was still impatiently looking for his keys.

'I hope you're going to carry me over the threshold.'

She was still smiling at him, expectantly now. He still didn't look at her. He was turning the key in the Yale lock when he replied,

'The honeymoon's over, darling. I've enough carrying these suitcases over the bloody threshold. I'm afraid you'll have to carry yourself.'

Chapter Twenty-Nine

Molly Carter had had a beano. A whole two weeks with Janine to herself. She'd pay for this little treat later, of course; she wouldn't have her at all. She wondered how often she would see her family in the future. Anyway, Leeds wasn't exactly the other side of the world, was it, and knowing her Cathy ... Molly crept down the bedroom stairs, not wanting to waken the child she'd left sleeping upstairs. Probably for the last time. She turned the gas fire up and settled herself into her armchair. Nights were drawing in now and there was a definite chill in the air ... she sighed. Well, it would be nice to see the newlyweds tomorrow. She was looking forward to their homecoming and she knew that Janine certainly was – hence the overexcitement and early to bed. Molly frowned. She just hoped that ... well, that terrible performance at the wedding reception hadn't spoilt Cathy and Brian's honeymoon. They both took it badly at the time but that wasn't surprising. Fancy having your wedding day ruined by a cocky young madam like that. She hoped it wasn't an omen, a warning of things to come. Molly told herself she was being daft, picked up her library book and tried to concentrate on Agatha Christie's whodunnit.

The newlyweds arrived at ten o'clock the following morning, Sunday, both looking healthy and happy, Molly thought. She kissed them both with a tear in her eye and Janine almost fell over herself, not knowing who to kiss and cuddle next.

'Well, come in, the pair of you, I can't do with 'avin' this door open any longer. It'll be like an icebox in 'ere.'

Catherine and Brian stepped into the hall.

''Ere, let me take yer coats – Janine, let yer mummy tek 'er coat off, there's a good girl. Right, let's go in 'ere where it's nice and warm. 'Ave you both enjoyed yerselves?'

Catherine smiled, picked Janine up and twirled her round. She decided to keep her real thoughts to herself.

'Yes, thanks, Mum. It's been lovely. And how have you coped on your own with my daughter for two whole weeks?'

'Beautifully, thank you. I'll go an' put kettle on.'

Molly made a pot of tea and, while she was pouring, asked about the house in Roundhay. She'd seen it in its naked state months before but was aching to have a look at it again now that it was decorated and furnished.

'It's fabulous,' said Catherine. 'It'll be really cold at the moment because it's been empty for so long. But when we turn the central heating on ...'

Brian looked up from the television magazine he was flicking through. He spoke for the first time since his simple 'Hi'.

'Hold on a minute, love, it's only the beginning of October. We don't need the central heating on yet. Not for a long time.'

Catherine looked at him and visibly shivered just thinking about the cold house in Roundhay.

'I thought ... Just to warm the place up after it's been empty for so long. We don't have to keep it on.'

'I know we don't and we're not going to. We'll turn the central heating on at Christmas and not before.'

'But Janine's room – the boxroom – it'll be like ice.'

Molly, embarrassed and a little surprised at what she was hearing, laughed and sipped her tea.

'We're 'aving a difference of opinion already, are we? Let's get the honeymoon over first.'

Brian crossed his legs, leant back on the sofa and folded his arms behind his head.

'Like I hinted to Catherine last night when we got home. The honeymoon *is* over.'

A slow smile spread across his face.

They didn't stay late at Molly's because Brian said he had things to do, preparations for his return to the office the next day. And he wanted an early night.

'Yer new secretary'll be startin' tomorrow, I suppose, Brian?'

He nodded.

'Yes. Unfortunately. It'll be a drag training a new woman but it wouldn't do to have my wife working for me, would it?'

Catherine smiled – sort of – and started picking up toys and throwing Janine's clothes into a holdall.

'Well, 'ow d'you think you'll enjoy being a housewife, love?' Molly asked, thinking up new topics of conversation, anything to prolong their stay.

'It'll be a novelty, if nothing else. I'm going to buy myself a frilly apron and bake steak and kidney pies and chocolate cake every day! Anyway, it won't be for very long. As soon as Janine starts school, I'll be looking for a job.'

'You will if I say so,' Brian said. And smiled.

The ensuing silence was shattered by Janine's bursting into tears. She was confused; she hadn't a clue what was going on. Where were her mummy and Uncle Brian taking her?

'You're going to love your new house,' Catherine told her, hugging her little girl. 'It's really, really lovely. There are lots of rooms, a nice bedroom all to yourself and a big garden for you to play in. Aren't you a lucky little girl?'

Molly suddenly felt the tears pricking her eyes. No, she mustn't cry; she mustn't. They were going to Leeds, not Australia ... not like Diana and her family ...

'Look, love, any time you want me to babysit, you know you only 'ave to ask, don't you? I'll be there like shot of a gun. An' you can always bring 'er 'ere, you know that ...'

Brian started to rattle the car keys.

'Of course, Mum. You're the only one I'd ask to babysit. *You* know *that*. And don't forget – next Sunday, you're coming over for the day. Brian will pick you up in the morning. Won't you, love?'

Brian nodded and silently indicated for Catherine to make a move.

'We'll have to go, Mum. Thanks a lot for looking after my little terror.'

She saw Brian rolling his eyes and quickly kissed her mother.

'Next Sunday – don't forget.'

Brian mumbled goodbye and walked to the car. Catherine, struggling with the fractious Janine and the child's holdall, followed him. She could tell he was losing his patience. It wasn't like him at all.

Molly waited at the door until the car had disappeared and she was still waving when it was out of sight. She slammed the door shut and went back to her chair near the fire. Well, they seemed happy enough, she supposed. And she thanked the Lord that neither of them had mentioned the fiasco at the wedding reception.

*

239

How d'you think you'll enjoy being a housewife, love? Molly's words echoed in Catherine's mind quite a few times over the next few weeks. Three months after the wedding, she still wouldn't know how to answer the question. She enjoyed being a full-time mum. It was a long overdue, sometimes wonderful, experience having Janine to herself all day; playing with her, instructing her, praising her, occasionally scolding her. She was only sorry she'd missed out on the early days; her own mother had been the one to have that pleasure. But now she was making up for lost time and yes, she was enjoying her little girl. Very much. She also found pleasure in discovering her new home; the house and the city. She spent hours walking with Janine around the vicinity in which they lived and, she had to admit, it was rather lovely. She missed Harrogate but her new neighbourhood had a lot to offer. Good shops, good facilities, the park. Yes, she enjoyed her freedom to please herself during the day. To a certain extent. And she loved cooking, producing tried-and-true mouth-watering dishes for her hungry, overworked husband; creating new concoctions, waiting to be given the green light to cook this or that dish again. However, the green light very rarely came on. She was disappointed that Brian wasn't a very adventurous eater; he knew what he liked and didn't like and in no uncertain terms. In fact, he could be quite hurtful sometimes. If he'd counteracted his criticisms with occasional praise, it wouldn't have been so bad. But Brian was very slow to praise, about anything.

Apart from having Janine all day and trying her hand at cordon bleu cookery, Catherine didn't really enjoy being a housewife. Not if she was honest. She did her daily chores because they were chores and had to be done. She very often felt that her talents and her time were being wasted, and then she was riddled with guilt for having such selfish thoughts. Brian told her time and time again that, after the life he'd had, drifting from one bedsit to another, sharing his homes with unknown individuals, he appreciated his home comforts and a wife to come home to. Brian didn't want Catherine to work; they could manage. Could they? They managed to pay the mortgage and bills and buy their food but only because Brian kept a tight check on their outgoings and constantly talked about economies. There was never any spare cash left for pleasure, or for herself. Or Janine. And Catherine hated begging for money, especially when she was more than capable of earning her own.

Catherine finished her evening meal and watched her husband picking at the food on his plate. He was going to leave at least half of it, she knew he was, and then he'd say, *You know I only like ...* They hadn't spoken a word since they started their meal. Catherine knew it was useless to start a conversation until Brian had pushed his plate to one side.

'Brian, I want to talk to you this evening. Seriously.'

He didn't look at her. He was leaving the table and the dirty dishes for Catherine to clear.

'Go on, then. Talk.'

Catherine sighed. It would be lovely if, just occasionally, her husband would show a bit of interest in what she had to say.

'I want to look for a job. Even if it's only part time. I need to work.'

'No, you don't. I've told you. We can manage.'

'I know we can manage. The mortgage, bills, food. But what about me?'

'What do you mean, what about *you*?'

'I need an interest. I'm bored.'

As soon as the words were out, she knew she should have bitten her lip.

'Oh, are you now? After six months of marriage? That's good to know.'

He picked up the evening newspaper and walked out of the kitchen. Catherine sighed and followed him.

'You know what I mean, Brian. I'm not bored with you or our marriage. All I'm saying is I need to work, to have an interest.'

'You've got the kid.'

The kid. Over the past few months, Janine had become 'the kid', without a name, without an identity. Janine, who idolised her 'daddy' and showered him with her two-and-a-half-year-old love, didn't seem to be of any importance to him anymore. Sometimes, it was as though she didn't exist at all. For Brian, who had wanted to be Daddy.

'I can't hold an adult, intelligent conversation with Janine. What I need is—'

'A tanned backside from what I can make out. You're not satisfied that I'm working my balls off eight hours a day to give you a good home and a decent standard of living ...'

'I know you work hard, Brian, and of course I appreciate it. But I'd like to contribute ... Couldn't you bring me some translations home or ...'

'There's no need. Belinda's an excellent linguist.'

Ah. Belinda. Catherine felt a pang. She had been replaced so quickly, so easily.

'Yes, but, well ... if ever Belinda is overworked – like I often used to be – maybe I could help out. You could divide the translations between us.'

Brian accepted that this might be a good idea and that if the day ever arrived – but he doubted it – when Belinda couldn't cope, then he'd bring some translations home. Brian left the room and went upstairs and Catherine did the washing-up. They had been married a mere six months. She shuddered.

*

It was after about twelve months of marriage that Brian started going out a lot. Alone. Sometimes he wouldn't come home from work and Catherine would wait for the phone to ring. Sometimes it did; usually it didn't. Sometimes he came home later in the evening, usually in the early hours of the morning. Sometimes he told her where he'd been; usually he didn't. After a while, she stopped asking. Her interest in her husband's life and habits was well and truly on the wane.

Catherine had hoped and anticipated before their marriage that Brian's frequent trips abroad would lessen; she had thought that he'd delegate that aspect of his work to his subordinates. But he didn't. If anything, his foreign trips became more frequent and of longer duration. Catherine spent not only her days but her evenings and the long nights alone, with Janine tucked up in bed and only herself to amuse. There was the television, of course, but Catherine had never been an addict. There were limited programmes that she liked to watch and other than that, she never switched it on. She read a lot and invited the odd neighbour in for coffee, but that wasn't what she really wanted, wasn't the reason she'd got married. It was her husband's company she wanted. After a while, she noticed, people began to ask questions. *Where is Brian this evening? Is he working away again? No? Just out for the evening? Oh, I see.* Catherine couldn't bear the questions, the sometimes spiteful remarks, the knowing looks, the knowledge that her marriage was a source of general discussion and gossip. She stopped inviting the neighbours in.

Janine, in her young ignorance, worshipped Daddy, in spite of Daddy's

242

increasing indifference and, very often, verbal vindictiveness towards her. Daddy was a paragon who could do no wrong; he was idolised and adored in his presence and missed and fretted for in his absence. To Catherine, this was a constant source of wonder, grief and, yes, she had to admit, jealousy. Not that Janine was preferential in her affections; she loved them both equally. But Catherine couldn't help but feel that the Jekyll and Hyde character she'd married wasn't worthy of her daughter's love.

*

'When is Daddy coming home?' the little girl wanted to know for the umpteenth time that week. Daddy was in the Middle East again and the trip had been extended. Janine was missing him.

'Next week, darling. Daddy will be home next Saturday. Are you going to give him a big kiss when you see him?'

Janine nodded enthusiastically and grinned. Catherine's heart swelled. How she loved this child; how she thanked God for her birth, for not allowing her to ... She winced and shoved the thought out of her mind. Four years old, Catherine couldn't believe how the time had flown. Where had those four years gone? She kissed her beautiful daughter and stroked the dark hairs out of her eyes. Those eyes, so like ... another thought to be pushed out of her mind, along with so many more. She had hoped that Brian would have been home for Janine's birthday. He'd promised; he'd promised the child faithfully, if a little impatiently, that he wouldn't miss her fourth birthday. But he hadn't shown up and Catherine had had to make his excuses for him and invent a day when he'd walk through the door. Maybe he would arrive on Saturday, who knew? Maybe he'd even remember a birthday present. And maybe he wouldn't.

Molly Carter was watching her daughter closely. She had always made a point of never interfering but sometimes ... Cathy wasn't the same girl anymore; she hadn't been her Cathy for a long time. There was no life in her, no fire, no fun. She didn't seem to laugh anymore, or when she did, it was forced, like canned laughter on television. There was no enthusiasm in her. At one time, Cathy found enjoyment in almost everything; she would create her own enjoyment. These days, it was as though everything was such an effort for her. And her appearance. God forgive her for thinking those thoughts but her Cathy would never have looked like this once upon a time. She obviously had no interest in clothes at all; she seemed to wear the same drab outfits week in and week out. Gone was the lovely silky head of hair and those eyes that used to be so full of life. There was no shine, no lustre in her hair anymore, and her eyes were always tired, bloodshot. She certainly didn't give the impression of a happily married young woman. But Cathy never discussed her marriage. Maybe that was the trouble.

Janine suddenly skipped out of the room, bored with the two adults, and went to play in the garden. The 1st of May 1982 was a glorious day. Weatherwise.

'Cathy, love, can I ask you summat?'

Catherine looked up from the floor where she'd been playing with Janine. No, there was definitely no fire in those eyes.

'You don't 'ave to tell me if you don't want to but ... Look 'ere, love, are you and Brian 'appy?'

Catherine quickly looked away and her fingers began to pluck at the thick woollen rug.

'I suppose so.'

'You suppose so! What d'you mean by that?'

Catherine stared at her fingers playing havoc with the rug and she began to chew her bottom lip. She desperately wanted to talk, needed to talk, but didn't know what to say. She was still clinging on to the now dim hope that their marriage was still having teething troubles; that they were still adjusting to each other. She was still trying to come to terms with the fact that the man she was married to was not the man who'd wooed her so fiercely. She knew that something would have to be done, that she'd have to take her head out of the sand sometime and make a better life for herself. And, what was more important, for Janine. She had to admit that they both deserved more than what life was handing out to them at the moment. Or rather, what she'd allowed life to continue giving them. It had to stop. But talking to her mother wasn't going to help in the long run. She had to talk to Brian.

'No marriage is perfect, is it?'

'Well, of course not. But you look as though you've got all troubles of world ...'

'Maybe I have. No, I didn't mean that, Mum. Forget I said it.'

She stood up, walked to the window and watched Janine happily playing with a ball on the lawn. Molly looked at her daughter for a while, a frown creasing her face.

'D'you want to talk about it, love?'

'Talking to you won't help, Mum. I need to talk to Brian and I'm afraid he won't listen. Come on, let's go in the garden. There's a ball to be played with ...'

*

Catherine missed Diana more since her marriage to Brian than she had in the hollow years after her friend's emigration to Australia. As youngsters, Diana had always been there for Cathy and Cathy had always been there for Diana. They had seen each other through important exams, unrequited adolescent love and exciting first dates; embarrassing bouts of acne and excruciating period pains. All the failures, successes, tragedies and triumphs of late childhood and adolescence. Diana's exit from Catherine's life had been a traumatic experience and one that she thought she'd never recover from. There were other friends, of course, kids who were fun to be with, but they were mates rather than friends in the true sense of the word, and Catherine's relationships with them had always felt superficial, lacking in quality, and slowly but surely, they had disappeared from her life. As had her deep, intimate correspondence with Diana, which had ended up as affectionate birthday and Christmas cards. When Catherine and Jean-Marc had been together, she would have given anything to share her happiness with her best friend. The discovery of her pregnancy and all the emotion that went with it, she would have given anything to share with Diana. She had informed Diana of Janine's birth and received a pretty card in response but that, too, had seemed a bit superficial and Catherine had wanted more. And now, right now, Catherine would have given her right arm to have her still-best friend beside her.

When Brian introduced Catherine to *his* best (and since Danny's departure only) friend, Neil, and his wife, Linda, Catherine liked the couple immediately. Although rather pragmatic and down-to-earth, Neil had a deliciously dry sense of humour and Linda was a warm, homely, affectionate woman. They occasionally went out as a foursome, for a Chinese or Italian meal in Leeds, or sometimes just for a drink. From time to time, Neil and Linda would invite them for Sunday lunch, which was usually ruined by the time Linda served it because Neil and Brian were always late back from the pub. But nobody minded; eating charred beef and dried-up vegetables was a huge and familiar joke. And after the burnt offering, Linda and Catherine would giggle and gossip over coffee while their other halves slept off their Sunday drinking session. It was a kind of sporadic ritual and one that – at the time – Catherine didn't question.

But all that had been before 20th September 1980. Catherine had never really understood why their meetings with the couple had become infrequent and rather uncomfortable after the wedding. They were obviously embarrassed about Melanie's performance but so were the other guests and, in Catherine's opinion, the drama should have solidified their friendship rather than the opposite. At first, she was quite upset – another friendship disappearing into thin air – but as it didn't seem to worry Brian (and Neil and Linda were, after all, his friends), she tried to put it to the back of her mind. And as the months wore on, she sadly realised that she had other, more important things to worry about. And the phone calls and meetings with Linda and Neil became fewer and fewer.

*

On the evening of 1st May, after her mother had left and her daughter was in bed, Catherine started thinking about the conversation she'd had with Molly that afternoon. Her unhappiness and dissatisfaction with her life were becoming obvious to other people, but Catherine had been truthful when she'd told Molly that talking to her wouldn't help. Molly was her mother and therefore biased. And a little antiquated in her ideas, it had to be said. But Catherine badly needed to talk to someone; a good listener, a warm-hearted but sensible outsider. As she sat twisting a cup of cold coffee in her fingers and turning these thoughts around in her muddled head, she suddenly thought of marriage guidance. That's what those people were there for, trained to do; to talk to and help people like her. Desperately unhappily married people who desperately wanted to save their marriage. At first, she felt a warm glow inside her, saw a dim light at the end of her tunnel. And then she thought again. No, not yet. Marriage guidance was a last resort; it somehow seemed too final, grasping at thin marital straws. Surely, she and Brian hadn't reached that stage yet … and then she thought of Linda. She had always got on very well with Linda and whatever had caused the rupture surely had more to do with the husbands, the old friends, than their wives.

'Hello?'

'Hello, Linda. It's Catherine. Catherine Jarvis. It's ages since we've been in touch, isn't it? How are you? And Neil?'

There was a slight pause but when Linda's voice came on the line, Catherine could hear joy, relief there.

'Catherine! Oh, it's … it's lovely to hear from you. How are you?'

'Not too bad … thanks. Look, I was wondering if you'd be able to have lunch with me tomorrow. Just a sandwich, nothing special. I … I can meet you at your office any time you like.'

'Oh, Catherine, what a good idea! Yes … let's say twelve-thirty, shall we? I'll look forward to it.'

*

Linda worked as a claims assessor in an insurance office close to Leeds Town Hall, and Catherine was waiting for her when she stepped through the sombre brown door right on time. She had put on a little weight since Catherine had last seen her but she looked comfortable and contented in her rosy-cheeked plumpness. They smiled and briefly kissed each other and Linda made a great fuss of Janine.

'A new bistro's opened round the corner,' Linda said. 'Their pizzas are scrumptious – and it's my treat.'

Over one of the bistro's scrumptious pizzas, Linda chatted about Neil, her boring-but- reasonably-paid job and one of her colleagues who had just been threatened with the sack. Then she looked at Catherine, cocked her head to one side, and said,

'Right. Enough about me. What did you want to talk to me about?'

Catherine swallowed some seafood and looked at the woman who she hoped might become a close friend. She decided to plunge right in.

'It's Brian, Linda. I'm … he's … well, to put it bluntly, our marriage isn't working out. He's …' She began to fiddle with the napkin on her knee. 'Well, to be honest, he's difficult to live with; very difficult. He's … well, he's become very aggressive with me *and* Janine. He criticises me all the time about absolutely everything and now he's … he's started to go out a lot, by himself. I've tried talking to him, Linda, but he won't listen and *he* won't talk to *me*.' She briefly stopped and sighed. 'I've got to face it; he's just not interested in me or our marriage. At least, that's the impression he gives and it's not been a slow process, either. Even on our honeymoon, he ...' Catherine's voice trailed away and she pulled a forlorn face and shrugged. 'I'm sorry, Linda, I just wanted someone to talk to. Well, you. Someone who knows Brian well.'

'Oh, I know Brian well, all right.'

It wasn't what she said; it was the way that she said it. Catherine's head shot up and she stared at Linda across the table. She waited for her to go on. Linda hesitated and then she inhaled deeply, closed her eyes for a second, licked her lips and began speaking.

'I never liked Brian from the minute I met him. He was pleasant, quite good fun, but there was something about him, something I couldn't put my finger on. I never said anything to Neil, they were big buddies, you know, best mates from school. We often used to go out with Brian and his different girlfriends – for want of a better word – and the more I got to know him, the more I disliked him. He and his sister – the wonderful Melanie Jarvis whom I met a couple of times at Greystones – they hated each other. It was more than hate; it was something that nobody could really work out, not even Neil. But, you know, he and Melanie always seemed so much alike to me, both as bad as each other. Maybe that's why they never got on. They both seemed to have ... Look, I'm going to be honest with you, Catherine. They both seemed to have an evil streak in them. With Brian, I noticed it more when he was with women. Oh, he was always the perfect gentleman. But I used to notice how he looked at them and it made me ... shudder. And sometimes there were things he said to them; very subtle, clever things that made me shudder even more. But the women were usually too besotted with him to catch on.'

Catherine's mouth had gone dry and when she opened it to speak, no words came. She continued to stare at her companion and play with her napkin. Her seafood pizza was forgotten and so was Janine, who was struggling with her own food. Linda placed her knife and fork on her empty plate and wiped her mouth. She coughed.

'And then after Brian left home, he came to stay with us – twice. For Neil's sake, I accepted it but I wasn't really happy with the situation. The first time he was like a mouse, the perfect lodger, and everything was fine.'

She paused and her soft grey eyes wandered to the window and the busy street outside.

'The second time he arrived at one o'clock in the morning with a very strange story. His landlord had thrown him out ... and he'd cooked up a very clever little tale that Neil and I took in like two daft sponges. Anyway, we felt sorry for him, made him welcome again and everything was okay until the third evening.'

Linda suddenly stopped narrating and her eyes locked with Catherine's; she was gazing at Linda, trying to ignore the somersaults inside her stomach.

'Neil felt a cold coming on and went to bed straight after dinner, about seven-thirty. Brian and I sat up talking, about everything and nothing. I must admit, he made me laugh and we finished the bottle of wine we'd opened for dinner. He was sitting on the sofa and I was sitting cross-legged on a cushion on the floor, where I often sit. Suddenly Brian started paying me compliments; silly, untruthful things that went in one ear and out the other. Anyway, a warning signal started to go off in my head and I made a move to get up but Brian moved faster and got me in a clinch. I fell back onto the floor and he fell on top of me. He kissed me and ... and put his hand inside my blouse. Quite honestly, Catherine, I was repulsed. He did nothing for me physically but the idea that he could try to ... to seduce me when his best mate was ill in bed upstairs ... I managed to push him away and slapped his face so hard, the noise echoed. And do you know what Brian did? He laughed in my face, patted my cheek and said, "Well, love, you're not much of a catch but anybody's worth a try."'

Linda and Catherine were watching each other very carefully now.

'I was in turmoil because I didn't know whether to tell Neil or not. I wanted to but, on the other hand, it was his best friend, they'd known each other since they were kids. At the time, I couldn't do it. Brian soon found accommodation after that little episode and we didn't hear from him for a while. And then he met you. He rang Neil and told him he'd met this gorgeous girl – his secretary – and he wanted us to meet you, too. I liked you a lot, Catherine. But I felt sorry for you. I wanted to warn you ... strange, that's what Melanie said at the wedding, isn't it? She wanted to warn you. After your wedding and the commotion that Melanie caused, Neil and I talked for a long time; about you and Melanie and Brian. Neil told me how he'd really hero-worshipped Brian at school because he was the best at everything. And later he'd admired him because of his way with the girls.'

Linda managed a smile.

'I'm afraid my Neil couldn't be a lady-killer if he tried, thank God. Anyway, when we talked that evening, Neil confessed that as they grew older and he – Neil – grew wiser, he soon stopped admiring Brian. He realised that Brian was a user; he used people for his own ends, especially women. He was only interested in women until he ... let's say, conquered them. After that, he didn't give a damn. Brian never really grew up and his immaturity was bloody dangerous. I decided then to tell Neil that Brian had tried to ... to seduce me and what he'd said. He was furious, of course, but not very surprised. He said he'd have been more surprised if Brian had kept his distance. Not because he was interested in *me*; just to prove his own virility and fatal charm.' Linda paused and smiled. 'I can always rely on my husband to boost my ego, bless him. Anyway, the less he sees of Brian, the better, now. That goes for me, too. That's why we haven't been in touch.'

She called the waitress and ordered two coffees.

'I'm not a bit surprised at what you've told me, Catherine, but I'm sorry. Unfortunately, Brian met you at ... well, let's say a vulnerable time in your life and he took advantage of that. I don't like to mention this, Catherine, I know it's a delicate subject, but Brian did tell us that ... that you'd decided to terminate your pregnancy and that he finally persuaded you to keep your baby." She glanced at Janine and added, 'I suppose you've at least got that to thank him for.'

Catherine felt the sudden flow of blood to her cheeks and her head started to hammer. She silently choked back her tears of humiliation and the nausea that was rising in her stomach. Her mouth remained dry and words still wouldn't come.

'Brian fancied you like mad, I suppose,' Linda was saying. 'You were easy prey at the time and Brian jumped in. As Neil says, he's a user, a clever manipulator, and I'm sure most women in your difficult position would have been taken in. I'm no marriage guidance counsellor, Catherine, but if you really want my opinion, Brian's never going to change. And if he does, well, it won't be for the better but ...'

The waitress brought two coffees and the bill and Linda reminded Catherine that it was her treat. They silently walked out of the bistro and along the pavement towards Linda's office. Linda kissed and hugged Janine and squeezed Catherine's arm, attempting a smile.

'Look, work at your marriage if you think it's worth it, but personally, I don't. I think, in fact, I'm sure, that you deserve a lot better in life.'

*

Most women in your difficult position would have been taken in.
She'd been taken in and now it was time to take herself out.

*

By way of a miracle, Brian did arrive home on the following Saturday, thus putting an end to Janine's incessant questions; and he remembered a birthday present. An Arabian doll sitting on a furry, ferocious-looking camel. Janine was overjoyed, gave her daddy three of her best, obviously unwelcome, kisses and was happy to go to bed early, if she could take her new dolly. Catherine needed her child to go to bed early in view of the evening she predicted lay ahead.

Brian was watching television when she went downstairs and was yawning loudly. He looked tired and had said little since he walked into the house an hour before. And Catherine had said little to him. She didn't acknowledge him now as she sat in a chair on the other side of the room and picked up her library book. Suddenly she felt her husband's eyes contemplating her.

'What are you reading?'

'My library book.'

'Yes, my precious one, I can see that. What's the title of your library book?'

'*The Razor's Edge.* Somerset Maugham.'

Catherine continued to read, didn't offer to prolong her dialogue. The newsreader's voice in the corner of the room droned on without an audience because Brian's attention, surprisingly, was focused on his wife.

'So, my love, have you been doing anything wildly exciting in my absence? What did you do on Janine's birthday?'

Catherine allowed Brian's questions to well and truly sink in before she replied. She listened carefully and turned them over in her mind, mentally searching for sarcasm, hidden menace, but she couldn't find any. She slowly looked up from her novel and met Brian's eyes. He was smiling at her, his head slightly to one side as though he was scrutinising a mildly entertaining but annoying child.

'Mum came over for the day and I baked a birthday cake.'

'Ah. And did you eat it all or did you save some for me?'

'No point, it would have gone mouldy.'

Instead of the expected aggressive retort, Brian laughed.

'Yes, I suppose it would. And what else did you do while I was working my balls off for William Kaye, under a blazing sun?'

'I had lunch with Linda.' Catherine's voice was low and she spoke slowly. 'We went to a new pizza place near her office and she very kindly paid for me and Janine – knowing that I don't work and can't afford to pay my own way, I suppose.'

'That was good of her but she's not short of a copper or two, old Linda. How's Neil? Can't remember the last time we saw them. Why don't we invite them over for lunch one Sunday? Neil and I'll have a session in the pub like old times and you and old Linda can make another birthday cake for when we wake up.' He laughed at his own bad joke. 'How does that sound, sunshine of my life?'

'Absolutely wonderful. Why didn't I think of it myself?'

'So. You made a birthday cake and you had a pizza with old Linda. Anything else exciting?'

Catherine closed her book, put it on the coffee table and slowly returned Brian's unfathomable smile.

'Yes, actually. I applied for a job.'

'You what?'

'I applied for a job.' Catherine continued to smile at him. 'Well, I registered for a part-time job with a couple of agencies in Leeds. Bi-lingual secretary preferably; general secretarial work if not. They're going to let me know as soon as something comes up.'

'Are they now? We've been through all this before, Catherine. I don't want you to go out to work. I expect—'

'Quite honestly, Brian, I don't give a damn what you want or what you expect.'

She got up and headed for the kitchen, away from Brian's probing, accusing eyes and vicious tongue. She had taken the initial and oh-so-important steps towards her independence and an improved life for herself and her daughter. Without work, without money of her own, she could do nothing. But with even a temporary job and funds to fall back on, she'd now have no compunction at all in leaving Brian and the lovely but loveless house in Roundhay. But first things first; one day at a time ... As she was filling the kettle to make a probably unwanted pot of tea, she suddenly felt her husband's arms around her.

'And if you start working for some other lucky bastard, who's going to do all my translations?'

She jumped at the unfamiliar feel of Brian's lips on her neck. Water from the tap splashed onto her sleeve. In spite of herself, she felt sudden, unwanted physical arousal and turned round inside Brian's embrace.

'Well?' he whispered, his nose rubbing hers. 'Who's going to do my translations if you're too busy typing someone else's French letters?' He laughed again at his own puerile joke and Catherine, her desire gone, gazed into his eyes.

'Belinda,' she said.

Brian pulled away from her and made some kind of noise deep in his throat.

'Ah. Belinda. Belinda's a very busy lady, you know. That's why you sometimes have to help out. Actually, you'd have been very useful sitting at your old desk over the last two weeks, while Belinda was being useful to me.'

Catherine frowned.

'What do you mean ... being useful to you? Did she go with you to the Middle East?'

'Of course she did ... you know very well ... oh, maybe I forgot to tell you. I can't remember everything.'

He walked to the fridge, opened the door, took out half a lemon and sliced it. Then he dropped two large pieces into two mugs. 'It's William Kaye's latest policy. Secretaries must accompany busy bosses on business trips. And I couldn't agree more.'

That was a load of rubbish and they both knew it. He carried his own mug of tea into the living room and settled himself in front of the television again. But as there was nothing to hold his attention and as he was exhausted after 'working his balls off' for the past two weeks, he decided to have an early night. He leant across to Catherine's chair and she was taken aback when his perfunctory peck on the cheek suddenly turned into a lengthy kiss on her lips.

'Don't be too long,' he murmured.

And then, as he turned from Catherine to switch off the television, Melanie's face appeared on the screen. Advertising a certain brand of face cream, she smiled and pouted and told the nation that Melanie Jarvis wouldn't be Melanie Jarvis if she didn't use … And Brian's exceptional good humour and affection evaporated in front of Catherine's eyes. The colour visibly drained from his face and his body stiffened. He had seen his sister's face in Catherine's magazines and in certain tabloids but never on television before. He opened his mouth, the air turned blue and the screen went blank. He left the room in silence and Catherine sank back onto the sofa.

She sat for a long time in the gathering dusk and stillness of the late May evening, reflecting on the evening's events and remembering in detail her recent conversation with Linda. Who was this strange and totally unpredictable character whom she'd married? Was he really the misogynistic manipulator that Linda had described … and that she'd come to know herself? Or was he a man with deep psychological problems who needed support rather than rejection? If this was the case, Catherine would never be able to live with herself if she abandoned him, knowing that he really needed her and she could maybe have helped him. On the other hand, if she stayed with Brian out of misguided pity and a dim hope for a better future with him; in other words, if she was being taken in again, she'd never forgive her own naivety and downright foolishness. She eventually tried losing herself again in the pages of *The Razor's Edge* but was unable to do justice to the story. She put the book down, turned out the lamp and went upstairs. Brian was sitting up in bed, also reading, when Catherine walked into the bedroom.

'I thought you'd have been dead to the world by now.' She ventured a smile at him. But Brian didn't look at her; his eyes continued to travel down the page.

'I'll go to sleep,' he said, 'as soon as you get into bed.'

And, as usual, he did.

Chapter Thirty

The agencies that Catherine had registered with didn't succeed in finding her a suitable part-time job, but she always accepted their offers of temporary secretarial work in and around Leeds. She therefore spent the following months juggling sporadic job assignments, making sure that Janine was properly cared for in her absence, trying to build up financial resources from her negligible salary and playing amateur psychologist to her increasingly capricious husband.

The first time Catherine was sent out to work, as a typist in the debt-collecting department of a city centre solicitor's office, Brian threw a tantrum. It was out of the question; the hours were too long (nine to three); she didn't have a clue about legal work; how could she consider leaving her kid all those hours, etc., etc. But Catherine was prepared for this and had carefully rehearsed her replies. And on Monday morning she'd deposited Janine with an obliging neighbour, Judith Wainwright, who had a son the same age as Janine, and was sitting on the bus heading towards Leeds before Brian left the house. That evening turned out to be as melodramatic as Catherine had been expecting all day. She looked lousy; how could she do a decent day's work, look after a kid, run a home and cook a decent meal in the evening – and what was this garbage she'd just put in front of him? He'd never eaten frozen food in his life (not true, of course) and he wasn't going to start now. Catherine treated his remarks with humour and derision, determined to resist his petty arguments and to defend herself, yet all the time fighting back the resentment and anger that were building up inside her – and asking herself why he didn't want her to work. His attitude wasn't only ridiculous and archaic, it was also highly impractical, both from a financial point of view and as far as Catherine's sense of self-worth was concerned. But every time she asked Brian the simple question 'Why?', he always supplied her with the same unacceptable replies. Because the translations that William Kaye occasionally provided her with (translations that the 'efficient' Belinda was unable to cope with) were enough to keep her busy a few hours a week and paid enough to help towards the household budget. Anyway, he needed her to be there, to make a comfortable home, and he expected her to be a lively and sparkling hostess when he brought home important clients for dinner in the evening. The first time Brian threw that argument at her, Catherine raised her eyebrows in genuine surprise and said,

'Oh? And how often do you do that, Brian?'

And to prove his point, that Friday evening when Catherine had to call at the agency after work to collect her salary, call at the supermarket on the way home from the agency and call at Judith's to collect Janine on her way home from the supermarket, Brian had left work early, bringing home with him an influential American client for drinks and dinner. They were engrossed in commercial conversation when Catherine pushed open the living-room door.

'I knew you wouldn't mind, darling,' Brian said, the malicious light in his eyes obliterating the smile on his lips as Catherine stood, dishevelled and perspiring, surrounded by plastic supermarket bags, a screaming, turbulent child and various, seen-better-days toys. And only cook-in-the-bag fish and natural yogurt for dinner.

Why does he do it? Catherine continually asked herself. Why did he *really* not want her to work? After turning the question over in her mind many times, she could only imagine it was his immature and unacceptable way of trying to prove his masculinity and ability to provide. But why on earth did he need to prove his masculinity? And anyway, both partners were expected to provide these days. And then she turned more questions over in her mind and her initial anger and resentment changed to compassion and regret at her inability to understand a hidden and profound part of Brian's character; and back again to anger and resentment. If only she could, by some miracle, work out why Brian was the way he was. If she could only get him to talk to her about himself, his feelings, his hopes, his fears, maybe between them they could discover a base on which to start working and therefore save their more-than-rocky marriage. But it was always 'if only ...', a distant hope, a dream. And despite being unable to shake off the terrible feeling of failure as a wife in the deepest sense of the word, Catherine accepted that she couldn't build her and Janine's future on dreams. Her life was becoming a continuous vicious circle.

*

During the summer months, the agencies kept Catherine busy on more or less a weekly basis, although she sometimes had to refuse work if Janine was ill or if Brian brought home heavy translation work. In spite of her inexperience in legal work, she'd made such a good impression at the solicitor's office, being willing to try her hand at anything and a quick learner, that they always asked for Catherine in particular when they called the agency, and she was always happy to oblige. The more often she returned there, the better she'd get to know people, the more friends she would eventually make – almost as important to her as the work itself and the small financial rewards.

One evening, she arrived home from the office late owing to heavy traffic and at that particular time Janine was going through a 'playing up' period. So, when Catherine arrived home with a crotchety child, an armful of shopping and a hammering headache, she wasn't delighted to see Brian's car parked in the garage. On the two previous occasions when he'd arrived home early, he'd invited an unexpected guest for dinner, and this evening Catherine was certainly in no mood for entertaining. As she opened the front door, she braced herself for a hell of an evening, and also promised herself to talk to Brian about it after their guest – whoever he was – had left. Brian was doing it on purpose; his inexplicably cruel and childish way of making her look inadequate as a wife and mother. Well, it had to stop.

When she walked into the house, there was certainly no guest and Brian was nowhere to be seen.

'Daddy!' Janine yelled. 'We're home! Can I have a big kiss?'

Daddy didn't reply and then Catherine heard the sound of running water. Brian was taking a bath. Well, that would at least give her time to wind down and sort out their evening meal, not to mention Janine. Fifteen minutes later, she was in the kitchen scraping potatoes and didn't hear Brian approach her from behind.

'Don't make any dinner for me.'

Catherine jumped and whirled round.

'Oh! You startled me. You don't want any dinner? Why not? Aren't you very well?'

'Fit as the proverbial fiddle. I'm going out. Don't know what time I'll be home so don't wait up ...'

Catherine tried to concentrate on the potatoes, the smell of his aftershave still in her nostrils.

'Where are you going?'

'A Chinese restaurant. Important clients. Good contract.'

'I thought you liked to bring important clients home for dinner, Brian.'

'Ah yes, but the problem is, I have to make a more than usually good impression on these people, my love. So how on earth can I bring them home?'

It was well into the early hours of the morning when Brian quietly crawled into bed.

The following evening was Friday and Catherine had terminated her third week's work at the solicitor's office. When she arrived home, Brian met her at the door and again instructed her not to cook for him that evening. In view of what had taken place a couple of hours before, Catherine could only feel relief. She couldn't have faced her husband's company this evening, not without totally breaking down. And he would have demanded an explanation and she wouldn't have been able to give one. Brian left the house at six-thirty, Catherine fed Janine, who chatted about Judith and her little boy throughout the meal, and she was happy to go to bed early because she was tired. When Catherine was finally alone, she made herself a large mug of tea, sank onto the sofa and began to sob, violently.

'I'm afraid there's no work available for you next week, Cath,' her young supervisor, Joanna, had said to her, after handing over her payslip. 'We're coming to a slack period, you know, the end of summer. It's the same every year.' She was looking through her files. 'Unless ...'

Catherine waited eagerly, wanting to go to work on Monday morning.

'You don't drive, do you?'

Catherine shook her head.

'No, I don't,' and mentally added *not yet*. That was the next goal on her agenda.

'Unfortunately, Russetlea's a bit far to travel without your own transport. It's a small village on the other side of Harrogate ... No, it's no good for you. I'll have to send someone who has a car.'

Catherine was staring at Joanna, her heart pounding, her hands suddenly clammy, her mouth dry.

'Russetlea?' she heard herself croaking. 'What ... what company needs a secretary in Russetlea?'

There were no companies in Russetlea; there was a pub, a bakery, a church, cottages and an old manor house called Mullion Hall and ...

'I don't know if you know the village, Cath. There's an old house, a mansion really, called Mullion Hall. When the owner died, it was empty for a long time and then it was converted into flats and bedsits for students and visiting businessmen in and around Harrogate. Anyway, the estate agent's expecting to be busy over the autumn ... new college term, etc., and he's set up a temporary office in what used to be the lodge house. He's looking for secretarial help for a couple of weeks. Are you interested, Cath, or is it too far?'

It was a while before Catherine managed to reply.

'I'm sorry, no ... yes ... it's too far for me to travel by public transport. I don't suppose there's anything else?'

'Not at the moment, I'm afraid. Look, give me a ring first thing on Monday morning and ...'

'Yes, okay, I'll do that. Thanks, Joanna. Have a good weekend. Bye.'

She stood up and stumbled over the chair.

'Whoops! Be careful, Cath! That's before the pub crawling starts! Have a good weekend yourself. Bye ... eee.'

Mullion Hall, a residency for students and visiting businessmen and their ... their cottage, the Mullion Hall Lodge, an estate agent's office. Mullion Hall should have been their home, their school, their future. *Oh, Jean-Marc, why did you leave me? Why did you throw away our happiness, our almost perfect life? Where are you now; who are you sharing your life with? Why didn't I ask Joanna for the estate agent's name? I could contact him, get information about Mullion Hall and maybe ... No, it would do no good. There's absolutely no point in trying to go back. None whatsoever; I have to go forward.* Her sobs were finally beginning to subside when the telephone rang.

'Hello?' she hiccupped.

'Hi, Catherine, it's Linda. Can you talk?'

Catherine felt a welcome wave of relief and contentment surge through her. She hadn't really expected to hear from Linda again or at least not so soon.

'Yes, I can talk. Brian's gone out. How are you?'

'More to the point, how are you?'

Catherine sighed and smiled at the same time. Linda sounded genuinely concerned.

'As far as Brian's concerned, nothing's changed. Oh, he can be nice, Linda, he has his moments but they're few and far between.'

'Well, look, love, I hope you don't mind but Neil and I have been talking about you quite a lot over the past few weeks. In view of what happened with … well, you know, Neil's dead against seeing Brian again. He's given it a lot of thought and … well, let's say he's not the mate Neil thought he was all those years. Anyway, we want you to know that you mustn't stay with Brian because you think you've nowhere to go. You can always come and stay with us – and Janine, of course – we've got plenty of room. We'd love to have you both so, please, never think that you're stuck, that you've nowhere to go.'

'I don't know what to say, Linda.' Catherine could feel the tears bubbling again.

'You don't have to say anything. Think about it. I know it's not easy. Admitting your marriage has failed is difficult for anyone, I imagine, and especially when there's a child involved. But the offer's there, love. You just have to let us know and we'll get the spare rooms ready. Okay?'

Catherine was openly crying now.

'Catherine? Are you okay?'

'Yes, yes, thanks a lot, Linda. You don't know how much I appreciate it.'

'Well, love, keep in touch and so will I. Take care. Bye now.'

Catherine replaced the receiver and returned to the living room and the sofa, where she broke again into fresh tears. But this time, together with the wretchedness and despair of her life and the very recent reminder of a halcyon and irretrievable past, was the knowledge that she wasn't alone. She had friends who were willing to help her if necessary and it was good to know. But she knew that if she left Brian, she would want to be totally independent; she didn't want to have to rely on anyone, and she'd fight tooth and nail for that independence. That meant struggling to preserve her self-esteem, which Brian had continually and so cruelly tried to destroy, and it also meant her own financial support. Work with the agencies was going to be increasingly difficult to find now the autumn was almost here, and her next priority would be getting Janine settled in school in early September. She couldn't start thinking about full-time work until then. And, in spite of all this turning things over in her mind and planning for an independent future, there was still the very dim hope that if she kept chiselling away at Brian's imperfections, one day she would reproduce the kind, humorous, dependable man she'd worked for and, so very foolishly it now seemed, fallen in love with.

*

Janine's first day at school was a momentous event, not only for herself but also for other children of the same age in the neighbourhood and their young mothers. Janine was thrilled to enter this unknown and exciting world of which Catherine had spoken repeatedly with great enthusiasm, in order to prepare her daughter for the big day. They set off for the school, a couple of streets away, on the first Monday morning in September, Janine chattering away ten to the dozen; Catherine's initial enthusiasm and gaiety gradually changing to a sense of poignancy and loss at the thought of the only light of her life shining for the first time in a new, expanding and oh-so-important world. Their relationship would probably never be the same again. After she kissed her child in front of the school doors and quickly turned to walk away, the tears that had been threatening swelled into her eyes and she tried to inconspicuously blink them away. She turned for one last look at Janine before she disappeared into the classroom and to the care and discipline of another woman. And as she looked at her daughter, it was Jean-Marc's eyes that were gazing back at her, remorseful yet determined, the day he banished her from his life.

Janine adapted well into the new daily routine; enjoying most of her lessons, respecting Mrs Wilson, her teacher, and mixing well with her little classmates. Through this important development in Janine's young life, Catherine met other women on their way to school with their children; on their way home without them. Judith Wainwright was one of them. She struck up light friendships and a few of the mums decided to form a team so that they took turns in taking each other's children to school in the morning and picking them up in the afternoon. A seemingly excellent idea, as it gave most of the women more time to devote to themselves and their busy lives. Catherine, however, secretly deplored the plan. Her short excursions to the school and back were often the highlight of her day. She would also have appreciated Janine's coming home at lunchtime, but Brian decided it wasn't a good idea. It was better for Janine to mix with other kids in the lunch break. It wasn't good for her to be dependent on her mother all the time. If she didn't like the school meals, too bad; she had to learn to be a little stoic and take the rough with the smooth. Life was tough.

Janine had been attending school for two weeks when Catherine received another phone call from Linda. It was Monday morning and she'd just got back from her 'turn' at escorting several children to the school gates. The phone was ringing when she put the key in the lock. Linda invited her to have lunch the following day, if she could. She could.

This time, Linda suggested a tried-and-true pub that served an excellent ploughman's lunch and it was her treat again. But Catherine said no, and insisted that the lunch was on her. Well, maybe one of the agencies would have some work for her – she'd call in the office after she left Linda. If not, she'd just have to withdraw some money from her meagre savings. Whichever, today it was her turn to pay. They both ate hungrily for several minutes and then Catherine told Linda about Janine's starting school and the progress she was making.

'She enjoys reading and writing and yesterday I pinned her first masterpiece on the kitchen wall, complete with the artist's signature.'

Linda laughed. 'I can't believe she's a little schoolgirl already. Time just flies ...'

Catherine looked at her lunch companion and chewed her lip.

'It's our third wedding anniversary today.'

'Is it really? So it is – 20th September.' Linda pulled a face and added, 'Well, I won't say congratulations. What are you and Brian doing this evening?'

'Exactly the same as our last two anniversaries, probably. Nothing. Brian usually buys me some flowers but we don't go out. We don't celebrate. This evening won't be any exception. I don't know if Brian really doesn't give a damn or – well, you know his parents had the car accident on their silver wedding anniversary and his mother was killed. Maybe it's the association ... he doesn't like to be reminded.' She paused. 'Linda, did you ever meet Brian's family? Apart from Melanie, I mean.'

'I never knew his mother but she was a lovely woman by all accounts. Dutch, from Amsterdam, but you'll know that. His father ... well, he'd had the accident and was practically bedridden when I first met him. He was always very polite to me but, of course, he didn't have much to say for himself. Brian used to say he could be very aggressive and difficult after he left the hospital. I've no idea what he was like before the accident, but Neil got on well with both parents. Why do you ask?'

Catherine smiled vaguely and shrugged.

'To be honest, I've been wondering if … if Brian, and Melanie, too … take after someone in the family who … oh, I don't know … Is there any insanity in the family or…? Oh, it was just an idea, Linda, something for me to work on.'

Linda was watching her closely.

'You're really determined to work at your marriage, aren't you?'

'To a certain extent, I suppose I'm curious. I want to know why Brian sometimes behaves like a perfect bastard when he really can be a very nice man.'

'Is it worth going into so deeply when he's making you so unhappy?'

'I honestly don't know. I keep asking myself if he's ill, if he needs help, some kind of treatment. And then I tell myself I'm an idiot and I should get out … Maybe if I met Melanie and could talk to her, she'd throw some light on the subject.'

Linda laughed, mirthlessly. 'I wouldn't count on *that*, if I were you.'

'I suppose I'm grasping at straws, Linda, just to give him a final chance and to prove to myself I've done everything I possibly could before I make the break.'

Linda smiled at her, squeezed her hand and said,

'Take my advice and don't grasp at too many straws, love. And now I'd better be getting back to the office. Why are lunch breaks so short? Look, why don't you come into Leeds one Saturday and we'll have a look round the shops. Bring Janine.'

'That would be really, really lovely. Something to look forward to.'

'Good. Give me a ring in a couple of weeks. And *do* look after yourself.'

As soon as she left Linda, Catherine called at the employment agency but there was no part-time work available in the near future. Joanna apologised and promised to contact her when something suitable came in. Catherine walked the few streets to her bank where she withdrew the amount she'd spent on the lunch, plus a little extra so she could buy Brian a small anniversary present.

When he came home that evening, Brian placed a small bunch of mixed flowers on the kitchen table and a card on which he'd written *Happy 3rd Anniversary. Love, B.* Catherine thanked him warmly and gave him the blue and grey striped tie she'd found that afternoon and that she knew would match the dark blue suit he'd recently bought himself for work. She cooked a simple chicken in barbecue sauce that Brian managed not to criticise and after Janine had reluctantly gone to bed, they sat and watched an old film on television and talked about their respective days. Catherine told Brian about the ploughman's lunch she'd had with Linda in a city centre pub and Brian told Catherine about the lunch he'd had with Belinda in a plush Harrogate restaurant and the bottle of Dom Pérignon that they'd enjoyed with their meal. He scrutinised her when he said it; smiling, mocking, challenging, and Catherine knew. Her small back-of-the mind suspicions suddenly transformed into cruel certainty. Who was this woman, Belinda? *A not-quite-up-to-the mark bi-lingual secretary who's having an affair with her boss. My husband. And a happy anniversary to you too, Brian.*

*

Linda and Neil had kindly offered her refuge if she was desperate, and Molly would definitely take her back, of course, there was no doubt about that. But somehow Catherine couldn't bring herself to do it. She was grateful for Linda's generosity and blossoming friendship but she couldn't impose herself and a five-year-old child on a young couple's privacy. Nor could she return yet again to that comfortable terraced house in Harrogate, with her tail between her legs and her daughter in her arms. She had too much pride; in spite of the mistakes and bad choices she'd made in life, she still had a vestige of dignity that she intended to cling to. And that would, with a lot of determination and a little good luck thrown in, help her towards a better, if lonelier, life. No, correction. A better life. No life was lonelier than one spent with an indifferent, perverse and unfaithful so-called husband.

*

Catherine looked in her dressing-table mirror and examined the quickly-forming bruise on her cheek. How many more excuses did she need to leave Brian? Since the discovery of his infidelity on their wedding anniversary a couple of weeks ago, Catherine's relationship with her husband had become even more unsatisfactory; her vacillating feelings towards his behaviour becoming more rigidly negative. This evening, in spite of Brian's first physical assault, Catherine had gained a victory. She'd verbally fought him and she'd won the battle. She and Brian would go to London, to his sister Melanie's engagement party. Catherine deserved the break and maybe her long-term curiosity about the vicious international model would be put to rest and – more importantly – some light may be thrown on the strange and frightening relationship between the two siblings. While they were in London, on alien territory, Catherine would try yet again to talk to her husband, make him talk to her. And, if after all her efforts at reconciliation were in vain, if Brian still refused to behave in a way that would be worthy of the title 'husband', then she'd take the first difficult but necessary steps in making a new life for herself and her daughter.

The postman had called while Catherine was out walking among the autumn leaves. He'd left two envelopes. One was brown and obviously a bill; the other was a perfumed pink envelope from London. As it lay unopened on the kitchen table, Catherine had no idea that this was to be the second time an unsuspecting postman would have a devastating effect on her life.

Melanie

Chapter Thirty-One

The Boeing 747 touched down at Orly Airport, Paris, at seven o'clock on a hot Saturday evening in June 1983. A sleek black Mercedes was waiting to pick Melanie Jarvis up and take her to the lavish five-star hotel on Place de la Concorde, where a suite had been reserved for her. She slid into the back seat and closed her eyes, feeling thoroughly exhausted. She had been working for two months without a break and, just when she was expecting to take a much-needed holiday, this assignment had come up – one that she couldn't possibly refuse. The leading Parisian perfume house of Chantage, having recently discovered that the English model Melanie Jarvis had started her aesthetic career behind a Chantage counter in London, had invited her to be their new face. Melanie was thrilled and highly honoured; this was a chance in a million and one that she couldn't say no to. The holiday would have to wait.

Work was to begin early on Monday morning so Melanie had more than twenty-four hours to herself. And, she promised herself, at least sixteen of them would be spent sleeping. She ate an early, light dinner in the opulent dining room of the hotel, aware that, among many other celebrities, her presence didn't go unnoticed. She still experienced a shock, a thrill, even now, knowing that her face had been and still was her fortune and hers a household name. The excitement, the ecstasy of being an international, much-coveted model had never diminished. She had never become blasé about her fame, or her good looks, and this was probably the reason that she was still sought-after and idolised both in her public and private life.

It was hot in the hotel bedroom and Melanie turned the air conditioning to high. Did they expect her to sleep in this heat? She opened the window wide, stepped onto the small balcony and began to watch the world below coming to life in the dusk. The pavement cafés bustling with early diners and white-aproned waiters; the lights and the fountains in the Place and the commotion of the crazy Paris traffic. Melanie left the balcony door open and stepped back into the flower-filled, delicately perfumed and exquisitely furnished room. Her naked feet sank into the soft-pile, pale blue carpet as she walked to the mini-bar and poured herself a large measure of Perrier water, adding ice cubes and a generous slice of lemon. She swirled the contents around the glass before finally taking a sip; her thoughts simultaneously swirling around her head.

Paris was a beautiful city; she'd seen it several times but it wasn't a city to be alone in. It was a city to be shared, a city to fall in love in. And, as usual, Melanie was alone. Oh, over the next week or so she'd be meeting plenty of people from the exclusive perfume house. The artistic director and press attaché, photographers and all their entourage; people with whom she'd be expected to share her life on a very temporary basis. But, as far as Melanie was concerned, she was still alone. And lonely. And she had to acknowledge the fact that this life couldn't last for ever; in fact, it couldn't last very much longer. She was twenty-six years old and lucky – very lucky – to be modelling and as much in demand as she ever was. She didn't look her age but in four years she would be thirty and it would be time to rethink her life. She'd enjoyed the last few years. She'd certainly made the most of her physical charms, her wealth and, above all, her freedom. But there was something missing in her life. Or somebody. Melanie didn't know what it was to be part of a warm, loving, forever kind of relationship. Men had come into and got thrown out of her life when they'd outgrown their usefulness. The relationships that she'd had had been short but never very sweet. And over the past few weeks she'd come to realise, rather frighteningly, that she was desperately lonely. Her admittedly large circle of social acquaintances were superficial hangers-on; people who didn't care and whom Melanie didn't care about. She had no lover, no genuine, bona fide friends, no family.

No family. She had a brother, of course, and a sister-in-law and a step-niece, if that's what they were called. It was hard to believe that The Wedding had been three years ago. Three years and, even now, she still went hot and cold just thinking about it. And the dreams still came, every so often. She would wake up during the night, shivering and perspiring and unable to breathe. She'd paid for it; she knew she would. She'd neither wanted nor intended to cause a scene and make a fool of herself at Brian's wedding; she hadn't intended to ruin the day for him and his bride. It had been an accumulation of events and a compulsion, something deep inside her, something evil and enveloping that seemed to take over and manipulate her, so that she was always the one in the limelight, never her brother. It was as though this something deep inside her turned her inside out and maliciously cast aside any goodness that was there – although Brian had always been the prime victim of these subconscious proceedings, other people had suffered, too. Other beautiful women whose professional paths had crossed Melanie's; or men who might have, given the chance, put her down, suffocated her, demoted her to a nobody. Again. It seemed to be a sheer impossibility for Melanie Jarvis to establish a relationship with anyone, and over the past few months, as this flaw in her character had become more and more evident, she'd seriously considered having some kind of treatment. An analyst, psychiatrist, hypnotist. A miracle worker who would transform her into a nice lady before it was too late. Before the world became a totally alien place.

*

The photographic sessions, which took place in a studio in Montparnasse, lasted exactly a week. Melanie's face in this position, in that position; her hair in this style, in that style. And always a flacon of Chantage, elegant and sophisticated in its crystal-cut simplicity, prominent in the subsequent pictures. Pictures that were to be distributed around the world. Pictures from which the spicy, sensual fragrance of Chantage seemed to emanate.

Melanie returned to her hotel by taxi at eight o'clock on the Friday evening. She was looking forward to a long, warm bath, a light dinner and a very early night. Followed by a weekend alone in Paris and a flight back to London early on Monday morning. Followed by a long, well-deserved holiday. God willing. She unlocked the door of her room, slammed it behind her and was heading for the bathroom when the telephone rang.

'Allo?' Melanie had learnt how to answer the phone correctly without feeling ridiculous.

The caller was Madame Marie-Josiane de Marnay, the press attaché for Chantage, telephoning from her office in the west of Paris. After a few ritualistic pleasantries, Mme de Marnay said, in immaculate English,

'Do you have any special plans for tomorrow, Melanie?'

Melanie's eyes closed and she allowed a small sigh to escape her dry mouth. Now what was coming?

'Nothing very special, no. Do you have something lined up for me?'

Mme de Marnay's gentle laugh tinkled down the line. She was a woman in her mid-thirties, small, trim with short dark hair and an immaculately made-up face. Not a beautiful woman but certainly striking. And she had interminable amounts of energy. Melanie didn't know where she stored it all. When did the woman sleep?

'Yes, as a matter of fact, I do. I have received a telephone call today from La Foire Fantastique – you know, Melanie, the department store on Boulevard Hausmann. They've requested that you be present tomorrow afternoon, to sit at the Chantage counter, sign autographs and distribute small free samples of the perfume to customers. I took the liberty of saying you would be able to do it. And kept my fingers and toes crossed.'

Melanie sighed again but this time it was a pleased kind of sigh.

'Of course I'll be able to do it. It sounds fascinating and it'll be a pleasure.'

'Wonderful. Unfortunately, I won't be able to be with you – I'm flying to New York tomorrow morning, as you know. But maybe we could meet for dinner this evening to discuss it? Unless, of course, you've already eaten?'

*

La Foire Fantastique, a ludicrously facetious name for such a luxurious establishment, reminded Melanie not a little of the similar but slightly-less-grand department store in London where she'd sold countless flacons of the famous perfume. She arrived at one-thirty, ready to be on show from two o'clock. The June day was hot but the excellent air-conditioning system rendered the atmosphere pleasant, despite the many chandeliers that hung from the intricately decorated ceiling and no doubt giving out their own warmth.

There were two sales assistants working behind the counter. One, middle-aged and rather stiff, gave an instant impression of Parisian gentility and aloofness; the other, a girl in her late teens, reminded Melanie of herself when she had stood behind a perfume counter, waiting for her life to take off; obviously very pretty, fair-haired, enthusiastic about her work and slightly narcissistic. Both women, however, mellowed when Melanie Jarvis put her appearance in and they appeared to be putty in her hands.

Melanie, wearing a turquoise cotton dress with thin shoulder straps encrusted with pearls and diamantés, had brushed her hair back from her face and wore a matching wide, pearl and diamanté-studded black headband. Her eyeshadow was taupe and cream, colours that enhanced the blueness of her eyes, and her lipstick was a subtle shade of dusky pink. She poised herself on a high but comfortable stool behind the counter and at that moment a rather effeminate young male voice issued from the loudspeakers.

'*Bonjour, Messieurs/Dames.*

Today, we have the pleasure of welcoming to La Foire Fantastique the beautiful English model Melanie Jarvis, who, as from the end of this month, will be the new face for the incomparable perfume Chantage. If you would like to meet Mademoiselle Jarvis, she is now on the ground floor of the department store, at the Chantage perfume counter. There, she will be happy to sign her autograph and – if you speak English – have a chat with you. You'll also receive from Mademoiselle Jarvis's lovely hands a free sample of C-H-A-N-T-A-G-E.'

Faces began to turn in curiosity towards her and Melanie slapped on her professional smile. Danielle, the younger assistant, more open and talkative than her colleague, grinned at her and said in broken English,

'You are going to be very busy, I think!'

Women started moving towards her, some smiling and attempting stilted conversation, wanting Melanie to write her name on this, that or the other, with a special message. Usually in English, sometimes in French, when Danielle would offer to help her. The effeminate voice echoed around the department store several times during the afternoon, and as the place gradually got busier, Melanie was never short of admirers and autograph hunters. Her supply of free samples of the perfume she represented decreased very rapidly. Some of the customers were known to Danielle and her colleague, Mme Bizot; women who had been buying the well-established fragrance for many years from the equally well-established emporium. In this case, one of the two saleswomen would introduce Melanie personally to the privileged customer and would indulge in a little innocent gossip about that person after she left. Her

270

family, her work, the number of years she had been spraying or dabbing on Chantage.

'*Ah, regarde là-bas, Danielle. Voilà Madame de Bergier.*'

Melanie was signing her name on a novel newly purchased from La Foire Fantastique's excellent book department; and she was smiling at the customer as she handed her the free sample of Chantage bath oil. The supply of perfume phials had by this time expired.

'*Je crois que monsieur est son mari. Ils sont en train de regarder les bijoux de fantaisie, mais ils viendront nous voir, j'en suis sûr.*'

Melanie, not understanding a word of this exchange, looked at the two women enquiringly. Danielle discreetly pointed to a couple standing by the costume jewellery counter a few metres away.

'You see the man and the woman over there? Madame de Bergier is a very good client of Chantage. She always puts the perfume and make-up, too. You see, she's a very beautiful, very chic woman, but sadly she is always in a ... *fauteuil roulant*?'

'Ah, I think you mean a wheelchair.'

'Yes. Wheelchair.' Danielle pronounced the word slowly, making a mental note of it and Melanie cringed. 'Yes, it is a very sad story. Monsieur and Madame de Bergier were married many years ago, but Madame had a very bad accident in the South of France when they were taking their marriage holiday.'

'I think you mean honeymoon.'

'Yes, yes. The accident ... a moto ... a motorbike with a ... a crazy driver. It was very, very incredible because he was crying ... no, no ... he was *screaming*, shouting a name ... a *boy's* name ... I don't remember what but it was in all the newspapers and on television ... and he was laughing very crazily and he smashed ... no, he *crashed* into people who were leaving the market place ... Madame de Bergier was one of those people. So very sad.'

Melanie, however, was looking not at the disabled woman but at the man standing behind her, his hands holding the handles of the wheelchair, his face smiling down at his disabled wife. Melanie frowned. There was a familiar look about the man; she was sure she'd seen him before somewhere. De Bergier ... de Bergier ...

'Monsieur de Bergier went a little crazy at the time,' Danielle continued. 'He loved her so much. He bought a magnificent apartment so that his wife will be comfortable because she don't can work, of course. He wished to take care of her but Madame de Bergier became a little bizarre, a little crazy, too. They were very young and she say, her husband, he don't take care of her all his life. Not possible for her, it will be so selfish of her. She wished a divorce. But Monsieur de Bergier was very strong and wished to abandon his life to take … take care of her.'

Melanie felt a slow tightening in her chest. How could a handsome, virile and obviously prosperous man like him possibly want to sacrifice his own life in order to look after a handicapped wife? She suddenly felt a repugnance, a mocking scorn for this man, and with it came sudden and incredible recognition. Jean-Marc de Bergier. Yes, she had seen him before. The tightness in her chest began to give way to deep, excited breathing. At that moment, the couple turned away from the fashion jewellery and seemed to be looking in their direction. And then Monsieur de Bergier began to manoeuvre the wheelchair towards the perfume counter.

'And what happened?' Melanie asked. 'Has he spent his life looking after his wife?' Knowing very well that he hadn't.

'No. Madame became very depressed and insisted her husband was … er … losing his life on her. He's very intelligent and capable, you know. She finally convinced him that she wishes to live with her family in la Normandie and that he will have a better life alone. So, Madame went to her parents' home near Rouen and he went to live in England, but they never divorced. He teached French, I think. And now, I believe they live together again. But nobody knows why this is. It is a mystery.'

'But how do you know all this?' Melanie asked, staring at the girl.

'Madame Bizot said me. She knows Madame de Bergier since a very long time.'

Mme Bizot was greeting the couple now and Melanie took the opportunity of scrutinising the Frenchman, whose brief acquaintance she had once made. The man who'd once lived with her sister-in-law; the man who was the father of her step-niece. The man she'd once coveted and who, even now, she found extraordinarily attractive. An intelligent, handsome, virile man; tied to an invalid wife. Mme Bizot had turned her scarlet smile onto Melanie and was now beckoning to her. Melanie slowly stepped off the stool and walked to the other end of the counter, where a chic and disabled long-time wearer of Chantage was waiting to be introduced to her. Melanie smiled and held out a perfectly manicured hand. The hand was extended towards Mme de Bergier, but the smile was intended for her husband.

Chapter Thirty-Two

'**M**ademoiselle Jarvis.' Mme Bizot attempted her broken English. 'Allow me to introduce you to Madame de Bergier. A very important client.'

She gave a slightly apologetic shrug, intimating that the lady didn't speak English but would nevertheless like to make Melanie's acquaintance. The two women shook hands and a small frisson of repulsion invaded Melanie's body. It was involuntary; it was stronger than she. She briefly greeted Mme de Bergier in the same polite and professional way she'd greeted all her admirers, and proffered a small silky sachet of bath oil, which was graciously accepted. Then the woman turned her gaze onto her husband and they exchanged a few words in their own tongue. Her husband looked at Melanie and smiled.

'My wife apologises for not being able to speak to you, *mademoiselle*. She would like to have talked to you about your work. She used to work on a French magazine several years ago, in the fashion and beauty department. She has followed your career with interest – yours and other models, of course.'

Melanie was gazing at Jean-Marc, her eyes penetrating his, looking for some sign of recognition on his part. There was none.

'However,' he continued, 'she's very happy to have made your acquaintance, *mademoiselle*, and wishes you good luck in the future.'

At the end of this short, clipped speech, he began to manipulate the wheelchair, to turn it around, to move it away from the counter, out of La Foire Fantastique; to move himself out of Melanie's life again. Her sudden feeling of sheer panic took Melanie back several years to another Chantage counter in another department store in another city. Another man who mustn't be allowed to escape; another man who she'd instinctively known was essential to her existence.

'Monsieur de Bergier!'

The wheelchair stopped its motion and the Frenchman turned slightly, an enquiring look in his eyes. Mme Bizot and Danielle were looking at her quizzically too, but she didn't give a damn.

'Monsieur de Bergier ... you obviously don't remember me.'

The man would never know how much it hurt her to say those few words.

'It was ... a long time ago. But I believe you knew my brother in Yorkshire.'

He stared at her. He glanced at his wife, who was engaged once again in conversation with the elder sales assistant; and then his eyes locked with Melanie's.

'Your brother? I'm afraid I have a terrible memory, *mademoiselle*. What was your brother's name?'

'Brian. Brian Jarvis. He was ... he probably still is... the export manager at William Kaye International.'

Melanie watched the expressions on the man's face as they changed. He was obviously astonished, a bit embarrassed, absolutely overcome. She continued to smile at him but said nothing more.

'Brian Jarvis.' He whispered the name as though he was frightened to say it aloud. 'I ... I knew *of* your brother, *mademoiselle*, but I never had the pleasure of meeting him.'

He now looked at his wife and she smiled up at him, with an interested, questioning look at the English model. Melanie, however, ignored the woman and concentrated on talking to the confused Frenchman. She had to keep him there a little longer, she had to keep his interest, make him sit up and take notice ...

'You and I met one evening, very briefly,' she said, not knowing if she was doing the right thing in reminding him. Maybe in this case, Monsieur de Bergier's ignorance would definitely be bliss. But it was the only thread of their mutual history that she had to cling to.

'We were having dinner in the same restaurant – the ... the Old Windmill in Harrogate – and I ... erm ... I'm afraid I wasn't on my best behaviour that night. In fact, Monsieur de Bergier, I was unforgivably rude. I hope you've forgotten the awful incident.'

He had forgotten but she had just reminded him. His countenance changed in front of her. He visibly stiffened and his eyes seemed to glaze over with indifference. Or was it contempt?

'Ah yes. I remember the *incident* very well.' His hands were fumbling with the wheelchair. 'Well, as I said, my wife is very pleased to have met you but we're behind schedule and ...'

Melanie panicked. She'd blown it. She mustn't let him get away, and certainly not like this.

'Well, my work in Paris has finished now and I'm supposed to fly back to London on Monday. But I'm due for a holiday. A much-needed holiday, actually. In fact, I'm … I'm thinking about staying in Paris for a while.' She was babbling. 'Maybe we could meet again. The three of us … I'd like to have the opportunity to prove that I'm not as rude as I must have seemed the last time we met … I was going through a particularly bad patch in my life and … well, for a while I just wasn't myself.'

She smiled and held out her hand and Jean-Marc had no alternative but to take it in his own. But his touch was cold and limp.

'Goodbye, Miss Jarvis.'

'Melanie, please.'

Jean-Marc de Bergier acknowledged this with a slight bow of his head, releasing her hand at the same time. Melanie could feel a rising nausea, a mixture of shame, anger and despair. Mme Bizot and Danielle were both looking at her with anxious eyes, mingled with curiosity. Fortunately, it was almost time for the department store to close and the remaining straggling customers were merely eyeing the English model with polite interest, more eager to be on their way home than to receive samples of bath oil and an autograph. Just as Jean-Marc was about to take his leave too, his wife looked up at him and began to speak to him in rapid French, her eyes darting towards Melanie all the while. Jean-Marc looked rather uncomfortable and vaguely annoyed and after he'd replied to her, he turned his attention to Melanie and interpreted their conversation.

'My wife admires your work very much, *mademoiselle*. Apparently, you have often appeared in the magazine she worked for. And she's been wearing Chantage for a very long time. She's also interested to know – naturally – how you and I know each other. I explained that we don't really *know* each other; we met only once, for a very short time. However, my wife would like to invite you to dinner at our apartment – eight o'clock tomorrow evening, if that's convenient for you. It may be a little awkward, of course, as you don't speak each other's language, but I'm sure we'll manage. It will give my wife a great deal of pleasure if you accept.'

The nausea inside Melanie suddenly transformed into ecstasy.

'Oh, how kind! That will be wonderful. Tell your wife I'll be thrilled to have dinner with you … both.'

Jean-Marc produced a printed white card which he gave to Melanie and, after politely saying '*Au revoir*' to the three women, he pushed his wife out of the department store and onto the boulevard.

Melanie examined the card that she was holding in slightly shaking fingers. Mr and Mme de Bergier and the address was in Vincennes. Vincennes? Where the devil was that? Never mind, she'd soon find out. She looked up and two pairs of immaculately made-up eyes were studying her, waiting no doubt for some kind of explanation. But Melanie smiled, stifled a yawn and glanced again at the beautifully printed card. Tomorrow evening. Eight o'clock. At last, Melanie Jarvis had something to look forward to. Her third beginning.

Jean - Marc

Chapter Thirty-Three

Six years and where had they gone? What had he done with his life in that time? What had he achieved apart from age and a lot of unhappiness? Nothing. He had tried to play God, made a martyr of himself, probably ruined a lovely, innocent young life ... and for what? Self-gratification in order that he would go to his grave with an easy conscience? Or, at the time, six years earlier, had he really believed that he could rebuild a life for himself and make the last years of an invalid woman's life as happy as possible? Had he been so self-opinionated, so foolish? He should have given it more thought, of course; he'd been quick to come to that conclusion. He should have debated with his own conscience and he should have been honest and discussed this part of his life with that other, far more important, part of his life, who was now a part of his past. If he'd behaved rationally six years ago, he might be leading a very different life now; a far more satisfying, fulfilling, contented life with a woman he really loved. But it was six years too late.

And now this. What nasty turn of fate had suddenly dropped this unwanted, undesirable bundle into his lap? Jean-Marc closed the balcony door and walked into the bedroom, checking his watch. Seven-thirty, she would be here in half an hour, this beautiful but, if his memory served him correctly, venomous connection with his past. Sophie, for some reason that she wouldn't discuss, had been quite taken with her on their first meeting. She admired Melanie Jarvis as a model, she'd explained to Jean-Marc when he'd later asked his wife why she was so interested in the girl. But Sophie's answer hadn't satisfied him. Sophie's disposition was such that she didn't relate easily to strangers, especially at this traumatic time of her life, and she certainly didn't encourage visitors to their home, not strangers whom she would be expected to entertain and charm with her social graces. No, her feminine interest in the English model went deeper than that. Could she be jealous of the role Melanie had played in the chapter of Jean-Marc's life that she hadn't shared? Even that didn't ring true. Sophie had never been of a jealous nature and certainly not now in this final and indifferent stage of their relationship. Jean-Marc walked through his bedroom and slowly entered the salon, where his wife was being tended to by Amélie, her loyal and diligent housemaid. Amélie acknowledged Monsieur de Bergier's presence and wheeled her employer to a comfortable position by the empty fireplace. Sophie looked up at her, smiled her thanks and indicated for her to leave the room. She turned her attention to Jean-Marc.

'Well, our guest will be arriving in a few moments. It's a pity she and I won't be able to speak freely to each other. I'm sure I'd find her an entertaining companion.'

She smiled at her husband, a tired, giving-up kind of smile.

'Do *you* find her entertaining, Jean-Marc?'

There was no jealousy, no malice in her voice. She was asking a straightforward question and would expect a reply in the same vein.

'She leads an interesting life, no doubt, if a little shallow. Unfortunately, I don't know her well enough to make any judgements on her character.'

'How well *do* you know her? You never ...'

And then Amélie came back into the room and announced their guest's arrival.

The room seemed to come to life when Melanie walked in. She was wearing a very simple black dress with silver jewellery and there were black satin and diamanté slides holding her hair back from her face. She smiled as Jean-Marc walked towards her, his hand outstretched. Madame de Bergier welcomed her into their home and before they lapsed into an embarrassing silence, Amélie brought in the apéritif ... kir royale with pistachio nuts and olives. Fifteen minutes later, they moved into the dining room.

The dinner was delicious but the atmosphere constrained. Jean-Marc acted as interpreter between the two women; asking and answering their questions and modifying them as he thought necessary. Sophie did most of the asking. She was genuinely interested in Melanie's work and the people she met and the places she visited, and how on earth had she met Jean-Marc in England? Jean-Marc and Melanie exchanged a glance, as he obligingly repeated his wife's question.

'Tell your wife we were introduced by a mutual friend one evening – very briefly. Tell her that we didn't get to know each other very well at all in England but I'm so pleased I've been given a second chance. To get to know you both.'

Their eyes met and she smiled at him while he spoke to his wife in their own tongue. Jean-Marc watched Melanie, listened to her throughout the meal and wondered if this charming and gracious young woman could possibly be the same vindictive female whom he'd met at the Old Windmill several years before. She'd been younger then, of course; maybe time and experience had mellowed her, made a refined and captivating woman out of a spoilt little girl? Or maybe this beautiful charmer sitting at his dining table was an actress, a hypocrite? He didn't know and he wasn't going to make any rash judgements. His wife, from what he could gather under the difficult linguistic circumstances, appeared to be very impressed with her English guest, and Sophie was usually a good judge of character. Usually. Maybe in this case … Jean-Marc was intrigued. Melanie Jarvis was an enigma and it suddenly occurred to him that perhaps he would like to know her better.

Over coffee, Sophie enquired what Melanie's immediate plans were, when her photographic assignment for Chantage was finished.

'To be honest,' Melanie smiled, 'I'm so exhausted at the moment, I'm thinking of taking a holiday … a long holiday. I'm certainly ready for one.'

Sophie asked if she had anywhere in mind and, after Jean-Marc's interpretation, Melanie shrugged her shoulders.

'Not really. I wouldn't mind extending my stay here in Paris. I've briefly seen the city several times when I've been working but never as a tourist. I can't say I know the city at all.'

Sophie thought that was an excellent idea and if Melanie did decide to take a holiday in Paris, she must visit the apartment in Vincennes often. She would be very welcome. She looked to her husband for support and he quietly agreed.

'Well, that's very kind of you both. Thank you.'

Jean-Marc had to admit that he was intrigued by Melanie Jarvis. He was also intrigued by his wife's bizarre, as he thought, attitude towards her. When Amélie had cleared away the dishes, Sophie excused herself; she was very tired, she explained, and Amélie was going to take her to her room. She pulled Melanie down and kissed her guest on both cheeks, insisting that she visit again very soon. Jean-Marc kissed his wife in the same manner, their eyes met and, good God, she actually *winked* at him as she was wheeled out of the room. Dear God, so that was it; why on earth had it never occurred to him? Oh, but Sophie, you're so very, very wrong.

He guided Melanie into the salon and poured them both a large brandy. He needed one.

'I must apologise for my wife,' he said, 'but she gets tired very easily. She's very frail, I'm afraid, and now spends most of her days sleeping.'

He handed Melanie a snifter.

'Thank you. It must be very ... upsetting ... for you ... having a wife who's ... permanently ill.'

'Yes. It is.'

A short silence and then Jean-Marc looked up from the golden liquid and slowly, as though he was weighing up every word, said,

'And how is your brother, Brian, *mademoiselle*?'

'Please call me Melanie, I do prefer it. Oh, Brian and I don't see much of each other, I'm afraid. As you know, I live in London now, I travel a lot, and he's still in the north. And he's still with William Kaye International.'

Jean-Marc looked at her and they both knew what the other was thinking.

'I see. And ... do you have any information about his ... about Catherine?'

Melanie sipped her brandy and Jean-Marc would have given anything to read her thoughts. Catherine was obviously a painful subject for both of them but he couldn't for the life of him understand this lovely girl's hostility towards her. Catherine was never the type of person to warrant such obvious negative feelings. People usually warmed to her, or at least they used to do. When he'd been a part of her life. He was curious but he certainly wasn't going to pry. It was nothing to do with him. Now. Melanie finally looked up and met his gaze.

'I don't know about Catherine. I never really knew her very well. No doubt she'll have left William Kaye and moved on after all this time ... I really don't know.'

Jean-Marc said nothing because he couldn't think of anything to say. Melanie changed the subject.

'Tell me about Sophie. I didn't know you were married when you lived in England.'

'No. Nobody knew. It was my affair and I preferred to keep my past life to myself. It worked very well for a while, and then I met Catherine and we ...' He paused. 'I tried to tell her many times but somehow the time was never right and ... I'll be honest ... I was afraid. Terrified, in fact. I loved her. I loved her very much but she was much younger than I ... inexperienced in many ways – and I – I was afraid that she wouldn't understand my circumstances, that she'd be judgmental and that she'd leave me.'

Jean-Marc told Melanie the story of his marriage to Sophie. He told her about the house on the Mediterranean coast that belonged to the de Bergier family, where they were spending their honeymoon when Sophie had her almost fatal accident. Her exit from the market place when a speeding motorbike smashed into her and some other shoppers. He told her about his meeting with Catherine, how they'd fallen in love, although he'd tried very hard not to do so. He told her that he'd even brought Catherine here, to this apartment for a holiday. He told her that they'd visited his cousin Henri and Véronique, his wife, who was also Sophie's lifelong best friend and who had introduced her to Jean-Marc when they were all teenagers. Catherine had been Véronique's au pair girl in the past and the couple had been very fond of her ... and they were still very fond of Sophie, of course. As a result of this human, emotional jigsaw, his cousin and his wife had more or less ostracised Jean-Marc because of his – as far as they were concerned – unforgivable duplicity. He told her about their holiday in Collioure and how he should never have gone back there; and finally, he told her about the letter that had changed the course of his life. The letter from Sophie's parents in Normandy, informing him that his wife had been hospitalised for several weeks and had undergone various tests. The doctors had diagnosed leukaemia and Sophie had been expected to live no more than two years. This on top of everything else. At last, she was asking for her estranged husband and although by that time his feelings for Sophie had obviously changed – he felt a deep compassion but no passion, he was no longer in love with her – he considered it his duty to return to France and his dying wife and leave behind the woman he really loved. Oh, it hadn't been easy by any means, he'd had to fight with his own conscience, but duty and another woman's wishes, rather than his own happiness, had won.

However, owing to advanced medical knowledge and a seemingly determined Sophie, she had survived much longer than initially anticipated and Jean-Marc had been back in his native country six years.

'Our marriage isn't a happy one,' he finally confided. 'On the surface, my wife is a smart, intelligent woman but she's given up on life. She has been given a death sentence and, sadly, that's all she's waiting for now. Her own demise.'

Jean-Marc had been talking incessantly for over an hour and when he finally drained his brandy snifter and looked across at his guest, there were tears in his eyes.

'Why do you stay with her, Jean-Marc?' There was something in the English girl's voice that he couldn't quite fathom; something almost disrespectful.

'Oh, the usual story. I believe the expression in English is I made my bed and I must lie on it. I didn't have to come back to France, I had the choice. But I did what I thought was my duty and it was the wrong decision. It didn't make either of us happy. I wish I could turn back the clock but I can't.'

'And what about – Catherine?'

'Catherine? I think I'll always love Catherine – or at least the Catherine I knew. Of course, she's older now; she'll have lost that lovely innocence and naivety of youth that delighted me so much. And another man will have plucked that beautiful, blooming rose. I try not to think about Catherine.'

'Of course. I understand. It seems such a shame that you wasted both your lives ... but it's too late now – isn't it, Jean-Marc?'

Jean-Marc was suddenly overcome with embarrassment and shame at having opened his heart to this almost total stranger whose character he knew was questionable. What the hell had come over him? He wanted to scoop up all those very private feelings that had tumbled out of his mouth and tuck them back inside him where they belonged. What must this strange, enigmatic young woman think of him? Her face was bland, expressionless.

'Let's talk about your holiday, Melanie,' he suddenly said, grasping at a straw. 'Will you spend it here, in Paris?'

Melanie didn't hesitate.

'Yes, I've been thinking about it. It seems a shame not to grab the opportunity to get to know Paris better. Now that my work's finished, I'll start to make my arrangements.'

Chapter Thirty-Four

Two days later, a bouquet of white roses arrived at the apartment in Vincennes, together with a short, polite note. The flowers were for Sophie de Bergier, the note addressed to Monsieur and Madame de Bergier, thanking them for their warm hospitality. Sophie smiled languidly when Jean-Marc read the note aloud to her.

'She is a thoughtful young lady, your little English friend. You must invite her again. Or maybe you would like to take her out to dinner, Jean-Marc? It would be less stressful as you wouldn't have to do any interpreting, and I'm sure it would be more fun for her.'

Jean-Marc looked at his wife. Again, there was no vindictiveness, no sarcasm or jealousy in her voice; just a quiet acceptance, a gentle encouragement. If only he could love this selfless, compassionate woman again as he once had; but he couldn't. His sexual feelings, like hers, were dead; to the point where his wife was willingly pushing him into the arms of another, more vital, more physical woman. But the wrong one.

'I may take her to a few places of interest while she's in Paris, Sophie. Be her guide; and I might even use my professional savoir-faire and try to teach her some French. But I imagine she'll want to visit *you* again before she leaves. You two got along very well, didn't you? In spite of the language difficulty.'

'If she wishes, then by all means, invite her for dinner again. But please don't press her. You know I'm not much of a hostess at the moment, especially to foreigners whose language I don't speak. It's much too tiring for me.' She amended her slight frown to a mischievous smile as she added, 'And, before you offer, I don't expect English lessons from you, Jean-Marc.'

The following evening, Jean-Marc telephoned the hotel where he knew Melanie was a guest. He was in luck. Melanie Jarvis had just returned to her room.

'Hello, Mademoiselle Melanie. I'm calling to thank you for your kind note. And Sophie appreciated the flowers very much. She thought they were very beautiful.'

'My pleasure. I had a very enjoyable evening with both of you.'

'I'm glad. How would you like another enjoyable evening with only me?'

Melanie's laugh was soft down the telephone.

'That sounds very nice. But won't Sophie …'

'I have Sophie's blessing and she would like you to visit us again before you leave Paris. In the meantime, when does your holiday begin?'

'Officially next Saturday, 25th June – I can't wait!'

'May I take you out to dinner on Saturday evening?'

'Yes, you may, Jean-Marc. Thank you. I'm already looking forward to it.'

Saturday, 25th June was a sultry, warm evening. Jean-Marc sat in a deep, comfortable armchair in the foyer of the magnificent hotel, thinking about the woman who would be stepping out of the lift any minute. Melanie Jarvis fascinated him. Not on a sexual basis, although he had to admit she was more than a little physically appealing; but there was something else, something enigmatic, intangible, provocative. Had he met her for the first time at La Foire Fantastique a couple of weeks ago, he would have had no doubts. Melanie would have been a very beautiful, charming and interesting young lady and a pleasure to be with. However, his thoughts kept drifting back to that evening many years ago when he was dining with Catherine at the Old Windmill and Melanie had certainly made her malicious presence felt. Not to mention their prior telephone conversation, which had startled and repulsed him at the time but which was now only a misty memory. Which was the real Melanie Jarvis? He was fascinated, intrigued, wary … the enigma suddenly stepped out of the lift, causing a mild sensation in the foyer.

Jean-Marc stood up and walked towards the young woman who was to be his companion for the evening. Melanie was smiling at him and Jean-Marc could feel envious eyes looking in his direction. He knew he should be feeling proud but he was not. No, he wasn't proud at all. Merely intrigued, curious. Melanie wore a strapless lilac evening dress that swayed around her legs when she walked and had tied her hair up in a knot on top of her head, tendrils curling around her face. That supremely beautiful face.

The evening, spent at a small intimate restaurant on the Île Saint-Louis, was successful but for one detail. At the end of it, when Jean-Marc took Melanie back to her hotel and left her in the foyer, he still hadn't made up his mind whether this was the real Melanie Jarvis or a brilliant disguise for the rude and spiteful girl he'd met all those years before. If that was the case, then she was a very good actress; if, on the other hand, the other Melanie was dead and buried, so much the better. The girl he had been with tonight was a delight. In a strange, unexcited way, he was looking forward to meeting her again in a couple of days' time. He was tied up for two days but had promised to take Melanie to a show on the Tuesday evening.

At the end of that week, when Jean-Marc had entertained the English model almost every evening, he was just as beguiled by her as on their first meeting in Paris. On the surface, she was as perfect as a woman possibly could be; but there was something … Even if Jean-Marc had not already had a glimpse of her other, less savoury, character, he could feel a certain something that prevented him from saying, *Yes, Melanie Jarvis is a truly wonderful human being.* But he didn't know what that something was, and the finest word he could think of to describe his new friend was 'enigmatic'. The word could have been invented to describe her.

Something else was worrying Jean-Marc, but it was nothing to do with Melanie's character; it was to do with himself. And Catherine. This lady whose company he was enjoying so much was a reminder of his halcyon past. A connection with his past and, maybe, if their friendship developed sufficiently, Melanie would be happy to take him back into his past, introduce him once more, through Brian and William Kaye International, into Catherine's life. If her circumstances permitted it, of course. And her feelings. His own feelings were such that, knowing Sophie was encouraging him into relationships with other, in her eyes more suitable women, then their marriage had no hope whatever of survival. Sophie, unwittingly, was pushing him into the wrong arms, but that didn't matter. The fact was that she was pushing him, and the right arms might be closer than he had dared hope – if Melanie would be his friend.

*

Sunday, 3rd July, was a blazing hot day and Jean-Marc rang Melanie early in the morning to invite her for a picnic in the Bois de Boulogne. There was a pause before she replied.

'If you've already made arrangements, please don't worry about it. We can go another time.'

'No, no, I haven't made arrangements. Picnics aren't really my idea of fun ...'

'You've never had a picnic in the Bois de Boulogne with me. I'll ask Amélie to pack our lunch and I'll pick you up at eleven o'clock. Okay?'

Melanie laughed.

'Okay. It might be fun. Will we be alone?'

'Oh yes, we certainly will. I'm afraid Sophie has been feeling far from well this week and she's been sleeping most of the time. She's had a lot of excruciating headaches and ... well, vomiting. She's hardly left her room. I'm quite worried about her, to be honest. But I'll give her your best wishes.'

'Oh, please *do*, Jean-Marc. My *very best* wishes. Of course.'

It was a perfect day for a picnic. Jean-Marc guided his guest through the woods to a small clearing in the shade by the Lac Inférieur; surrounded by deep green foliage, an azure sky and a choir of birds. He dropped onto the grass and opened the lunch that Amélie had prepared for them. After dividing the bread, cold chicken, salad, cheese and fruit, he uncorked a bottle of Sancerre and handed a glass to Melanie.

'Amélie is like a mother to me. I don't know what I'd do without her.'

Melanie didn't reply. They ate in silence for a while and then Jean-Marc decided it was time to bring up the subject that was close to his heart, and the most difficult one to talk about.

'I've been wondering, Melanie. Will you be in contact with your brother when you return to England? It must be a long time ...'

They looked at each other. Jean-Marc would have given anything to read those eyes.

'Oh, I ... I don't know. It really depends on both our working schedules ...'

'Do you never go back to Yorkshire?'

Melanie didn't look at him and it was a long time before she answered. He couldn't even attempt to interpret the meaning behind her words.

'I went back to Yorkshire three years ago. I think it might have been the last time.'

'But you do keep in touch with Brian?'

'Not as often as we'd both like to.' She flashed him a smile and sipped her wine. 'We both lead such full lives, you know, our jobs take us to the ends of the earth. Which does make keeping in touch very difficult.'

'Yes, I can understand that.' Pause. 'And Catherine.' He coughed. 'You don't think there's a chance that Catherine may still ... still be working for your brother?'

Melanie moved into a different position, stretching her long legs in front of her. Her gaze seemed to concentrate on an insignificant blade of grass.

'I'm afraid I don't know anything about Catherine.'

She finally looked across at him over the rim of her glass. 'But I'll try to find out what I can for you. I promise.'

Jean-Marc watched the changing expressions on her face and he couldn't identify one of them. The smile on her lips somehow didn't match the look in her lovely eyes. And then it slowly dawned on him. Oh no, for God's sake, he hadn't planned it this way, not at all. He'd been kind to Melanie, an attractive English girl alone in his city, and he'd treated her, as he'd thought, like a pleasant acquaintance in need of company. Obviously, he'd thought wrong. Melanie was falling in love with him. She was infatuated with him. Oh, what a fool he'd been; a blind fool, imagining that he could have an easy, platonic friendship with one of the most beautiful, sought-after models in the world and expect her to play matchmaker to another female. A female who, if that evening in the Old Windmill was anything to go by, was intensely disliked by Melanie. How could he have been so foolish, so short-sighted? Jean-Marc suddenly felt very drained, as though all the life and enthusiasm had been pumped out of him. He was grateful to see unexpected dark clouds moving in front of the sun and he told Melanie that they ought to be making a move, before they were caught in a shower. Melanie wordlessly began to clear their things away.

When Jean-Marc parked the car in a side street near her hotel, he didn't attempt to get out and he told Melanie that he was going to be busy for several days but he would call her as soon as he was free. She merely nodded, thanked him for a pleasant afternoon and hurried towards the entrance in a sudden torrent of rain. Jean-Marc cursed himself. He wasn't handling the situation at all well; he was behaving like an adolescent and he wasn't proud of himself. But he'd genuinely believed that Melanie regarded their relationship in the same light as himself; he'd had no inkling that she was – or even could be – infatuated with him. And then for him to innocently throw Catherine in her face ... Anyway, he'd done the best thing. Not made any definite plans to see her again. Cooled it. There was no point in making arrangements to see each other and building up her hopes when there was nothing to build on. When he'd been hoping that somehow Melanie would light his way back into Catherine's life.

Three days later, the telephone rang in the apartment in Vincennes. Amélie picked up the receiver and then called Jean-Marc, who was with his wife in her room. Jean-Marc picked up the extension.

'Hello, Jean-Marc, it's Melanie.' Her voice was almost a whisper. 'I'm so sorry to disturb you at home but … well, to be honest, I'm … I'm a bit fed up and … well, I'm feeling rather lonely. I don't really want to cut my holiday short but even Paris can be boring when you've no one to enjoy it with …'

'I do beg your pardon, Melanie. My wife has been very ill over the past few days – barely conscious, in fact – and I've been spending all my time with her. She should really be hospitalised but won't allow me to make the arrangements, I'm afraid … and I have to respect her wishes. Look, I don't want to leave the apartment this evening but why don't you come to Vincennes? Shall we say eight o'clock?'

'Well … I don't want to be in the way …'

'Don't worry, you won't be in the way. In fact, it will be good to have your company.'

'Well, that would be very nice. Thank you so much.'

Melanie was charming company that evening; he couldn't have wished for better. She listened to his incessant talking about his life, encouraging him to confide in her, relate to her. She laughed with him and she sympathised with him and later, when he took her back to the hotel, he thanked her for a wonderful evening. She was, he had now concluded, a kind, unselfish, giving young woman, a woman whom he would always consider a good and worthwhile friend. And two days later, when Sophie peacefully passed away in her sleep, Melanie was the one to whom Jean-Marc tearfully turned.

Chapter Thirty-Five

'I go back to London on the 30th of July, but I'll do what I can before then.'

Jean-Marc was sitting in a chair on the balcony of Melanie's room, a large glass of whisky in his hand. He was pale and drawn and looked older than his years. Melanie was standing in front of him, leaning against the balcony railing, looking into the Parisian dusk.

'Thank you, but there's absolutely nothing you can do. All the arrangements have been made and Amélie, of course, has been wonderful. It goes without saying that she's extremely upset. She was devoted to Sophie for many years. But she's strong and can cope. I don't know what I'd have done without her. And anyway, you're here on holiday, Melanie, you should be enjoying yourself...'

Melanie tossed her blonde hair over her shoulder and smiled down at him.

'As I said to you once before, I've got nobody to enjoy myself with. Only you. I'd like to do whatever I can to help. Make you feel more ... comfortable, relaxed, relieved. Under these tragic circumstances.'

She held out her hand, still smiling at him, and he gently took hold of it.

'You're very kind, Melanie. We've known each other such a short time but you've been a real friend to me. Like we've known each other for years. Does that sound ridiculous?'

He felt her small hand stiffen inside his own. She slowly pulled her hand away and looked out again at the Paris evening.

'No, it doesn't sound ridiculous. We are ... friends, Jean-Marc. Anyway, as I said, I'm returning to London on the 30th of July. If you feel you'd like a break after all the stress, you'll be very welcome to come and stay with me. I'll extend my holiday.' She paused. 'And in the meantime, I'll find out what I can about Catherine. That's a promise.'

Jean-Marc sipped his whisky and concentrated on the taste. For a moment, he didn't know what to say.

'Catherine? What do you mean exactly?'

She smiled her enigmatic smile at him.

'I'll do my best to contact Brian. He'll probably know what her circumstances are, even if she's moved on. You'd like me to do that, wouldn't you, Jean-Marc?'

A shiver of anticipation and slight apprehension ran through his body. He could hardly take in what Melanie was saying, but saying it she was, and he couldn't throw this opportunity away. He couldn't reject Melanie's kindness and, he felt sure, her self-sacrifice, in her face. At the same time, six years had passed. Six years was a long time. Anything could have happened to Catherine. Anything. Would he be strong enough to face whatever truth came to light?

'Yes, Melanie, I'd like you to do that, if it's not going to cause you too much trouble.'

Melanie turned her face away so her words were barely discernible.

'I'll certainly do my best to contact my brother and ... take it from there, Jean-Marc. Will you be able to come to London during the second week of August?'

Melanie

Chapter Thirty-Six

———

She was in love. For the first time in her life, Melanie Jarvis knew what it was like to love someone; to be head over heels in love. And she had neither intended nor expected it to happen. She had anticipated Jean-Marc's falling in love with her and being happily seduced by her, followed by a short, one-sided relationship in which she came up trumps, as usual. But it hadn't worked out like that.

Melanie made herself an umpteenth mug of black coffee, took it into the living room and sank onto her pink corduroy sofa. The brilliant August sunlight filled the room with warmth. She'd been living in this flat in Hampstead for six months now and she loved it. It was smaller, more compact, than the flat in South Kensington and it contained furniture of her own choosing, not what Jonathan Drew or anybody else had provided. Jonathan Drew. That seemed like an aeon ago. What had happened to him? And all the others. All the grovelling, inconsequential men who had played such small parts in her life; men who had had their uses but who, in the end, meant nothing to her. Until now. Jean-Marc de Bergier had come to mean everything to her in a very short time, and she was determined to make him feel the same way about her, no matter how long it took. Even though, initially, he was coming to London as a friend in need and hoping to be reunited with his old flame.

Jean-Marc must not know that his beloved Catherine was married to Brian Jarvis; not yet. Not for a while. He must believe that she was well and truly off the scene, out of the way, a thing of the past. Totally unattainable. Only when Melanie was sure, perfectly sure, in her own mind that Jean-Marc belonged to her, would she then break the news to him, in her own inimitable way. Whatever that was to be.

Jean-Marc de Bergier arrived, as expected, at seven-thirty on that warm August evening. He stood in the doorway, pale and obviously very tired, a solitary suitcase by his side. Melanie smiled warmly at him, pecked his cheek and, slipping her hand through his arm, guided him into her living room. The sun still shone on the pink sofa and matching chairs, the maroon carpet and pale pink walls.

'I'm so glad you could come, Jean-Marc. You look as though you need the rest. The last couple of weeks must have been absolutely awful for you.'

He dropped into an armchair.

'Well, I can honestly say it hasn't been the happiest time of my life. Sophie's death didn't really hit me until after the funeral, I'd been too busy up to then. Then I cried, finally, and it was a great relief. Sophie should have had a very different life. *We* should have had a different life together and I should never have ... tried to play God. But I'm very happy that you invited me, Melanie, I do need a break. There's still a lot for me to attend to when I go home but for now ...'

Melanie poured a glass of what she knew was his favourite whisky, perched on the arm of his chair and handed him the crystal glass.

'For now, you're going to enjoy my scintillating company and forget all your troubles.'

She smiled when she said this, they chatted for a while, caught up on each other's news. Later, sitting together in the quiet evening dusk, Jean-Marc said, in a rather subdued voice,

'And Brian. Your brother. Have you managed to get in touch with him, Melanie?'

Melanie moved to another chair, opposite his. She turned her face away from him.

'Yes. Yes, I've been in touch with Brian.'

She could feel his eager anticipation across the room.

'Yes? And ... how is he? Still making millions for William Kaye ...?'

She stood up and walked to the window, looking at the lights that were coming on in the city.

'I'm afraid I have some bad news, Jean-Marc.'

There was no reply but Melanie could have sworn she heard his heart beating in the silence. A small smile played on her lips before she spoke again.

'Catherine left William Kaye three years ago. She's married now and she has a child. A little girl.'

When, several minutes later, Jean-Marc still hadn't replied, Melanie finally turned round and looked at him. Oh, why did he have to care so much, for God's sake? Catherine was well and truly in the past; she, Melanie, was the here and now.

'I see,' Jean-Marc murmured after a few moments. He looked up and their eyes met in the gloom. 'Did Brian tell you ... who she married?'

Melanie shook her head.

'No. He didn't want to talk about it. He ... erm ... he was very fond of her himself, you know.'

God forgive me. And may Jean-Marc forgive me when he discovers the truth. Please let him understand. And dear God, please don't ever let him find out the truth about Catherine's child. Not ever. Or at least not for a very long time. Not until he and I are a unit, an inseparable, happy-ever-after unit. By that time, Catherine and her illegitimate kid will be of no consequence to Jean-Marc. He will have other, more urgent, priorities in his life. Jean-Marc began to slowly nod his head.

'I should have known. Six years is a long time and Catherine was ... a very special lady. I wish her well; she deserves to be happy.'

'I'm sorry to be the one to tell you.' Melanie tried to smile at him. 'But you had to know some time. You couldn't go on thinking ...'

'No. Of course not. Melanie, may I go unpack my things? I'm really very tired and would like to sleep now. If you don't mind.'

Melanie once again slipped her hand through his arm as she took him into the spare bedroom. She wished him good night and gently kissed his cheek.

The following week remained hot and Melanie and her guest spent most of their time outdoors, sightseeing, visiting places that Melanie thought would interest Jean-Marc. On the surface, he was the perfect guest; polite, amusing, interested and interesting. But when Melanie looked closely into his eyes or caught him unawares, she realised that he was play-acting for her, pretending to be having a wonderful time when, underneath, he was thinking of another woman. And that woman was not his deceased wife – if only it were, she could have accepted that. Damn him, damn Catherine. Why hadn't she told him the truth; the beautiful, horrible truth that his precious Catherine was safely married to Melanie's brother, Brian? Because she didn't dare take the risk, that's why. She didn't dare take the risk that Jean-Marc would want to get in touch, to become a part, albeit a distant part, of Catherine's life again. She didn't dare risk rekindling a flame that wasn't quite snuffed. Not yet. Not until he belonged to her, Melanie Jarvis. And then she would introduce him to the world and his wife and not give a damn. Because the flame that burned for Catherine would be well and truly dead; murdered by Melanie. *Oh, dear God, make him sit up and take notice, please make him fall in love with me.*

At the end of the first week, the weather changed and on the Saturday afternoon there was a storm. Melanie and Jean-Marc stayed indoors, listened to music, played card games and made each other laugh a lot. *Is he finally coming round*, Melanie thought, *or is he still acting for my benefit?* She honestly didn't know. In the evening, she cooked an enormous amount of spaghetti Bolognese, Jean-Marc bought a bottle of red wine and they ate their supper on their knees while watching an ancient and corny film on television. When it finished, Melanie suggested an early night, as they were taking a trip to the south coast the following morning.

That night, the dreams came again. Melanie woke up in the early hours of the morning, her naked body perspiring, her wet hair tangled around her face, her throat dry, her eyes streaming. Oh, would they never stop? Would they never go away and leave her alone? She couldn't breathe ... she was gasping for air ... She flung the duvet aside and sat up. At the same time, the door flew open. Jean-Marc was standing there, a towel wrapped around his waist, his greying black hair falling into his eyes, which were dancing with alarm.

'What on earth is it, Melanie? You were screaming ...'

'Oh, Jean-Marc, I don't know. Nightmares. I keep having these horrible, horrible nightmares.'

Jean-Marc walked to the bed, sat on the edge and took hold of Melanie's trembling, naked body.

'What kind of nightmares? Can you tell me?'

'Oh, they're always different ... my dad ... his paintings ... the house ... men ... my family ... the wedding ... so many things ...'

He frowned, not understanding, pulled her towards him and stroked the damp, matted hair.

'Well, you're okay now. Everything is fine. Come on, try to get some sleep ...'

His words were muffled against her hair and Melanie pulled away and looked into his face, into his sad, aching brown eyes. They looked at each other for a long time and then Melanie gently touched Jean-Marc's cheek with the tip of her long fingers. It was her turn to comfort.

'Poor Jean-Marc. I should never have told you. It was wrong of me. You're so unhappy, aren't you, my love? So unhappy.'

A few hours later, when the sun peeped through a tiny slit in the cotton curtain, Melanie and Jean-Marc were lying in each other's arms, the duvet barely covering their bodies.

Jean – Marc

Chapter Thirty-Seven

Jean-Marc de Bergier was forty-five years old and, so far, hadn't made much of a success of his life. His school, for instance. The Mullion Hall School of Languages, Russetlea, North Yorkshire, should by this time be alive and kicking, a hive of international activity and learning; a home and an interesting life for himself – and Catherine. Instead of which, Mullion Hall, that magnificent, elegant, eighteenth- century house, was being tenanted by total strangers; needy young couples and single men and women who used the many and adequate rooms as flat and bedsits and the lovely grounds as a kind of communal park. Jean-Marc's agent in Harrogate forwarded the accrued rents on a regular monthly basis to Jean-Marc's bank, the BNP, in Paris. Over the past four years, since he'd been letting his precious property, he hadn't touched the money, still hoping that one day his long-standing dream of opening his own language school would materialise. At least he could live in hope.

And his personal life, also a failure. He sat up in Melanie's big double bed, watching the woman at her dressing-table mirror. Jean-Marc was forty-five years old and in all those years he hadn't succeeded in making one woman happy. Nor himself. He smiled at Melanie's reflection and she grinned back at him and blew him a soft kiss. She began to brush her long, blonde hair. Well, he had come to terms with his unsuccessful love life now. His wife, God bless her, was lying in her grave and the girl he'd loved so much and for so long was emotionally dead; non-existent for him, the best part of his past. The time had come for him to be realistic, matter-of-fact, practical, before, God forbid, he grew too old to care anymore. It was time to lock the door on his painful past and start thinking about his, hopefully, successful future. Difficult as it may be.

'Jean-Marc, are you getting up or are you planning on staying in that position all day?'

'Do you have any better ideas?'

'Right now, yes. Let's go get some sunshine while it lasts. The summer's on its way out, you know.'

Melanie walked across the room to the bed, sat down, wrapped her long, golden-brown arms around Jean-Marc and kissed him.

'You know you're a super bloke to be with, Mr de Bergier? You're the nicest guest I've ever had.'

Jean-Marc laughed.

'And you're a very lovely hostess.' He smiled at her. 'Do we really need all that sunshine today?'

*

September was the happiest month Melanie could ever remember. As she fell more deeply in love with her wonderful Frenchman, so she slowly began to feel his responding; and the slower the better, she thought, because that's the only type of love that lasts. *And Jean-Marc and I are going to last – for ever. We belong together. We're permanent; I just know that we're permanent.*

As the day of his departure drew nearer, Melanie began to feel a great melancholy, a deep sadness that was alien to her. She'd never felt like this in her life before and she didn't know whether to laugh or cry. But she also started to panic. Jean-Marc was going back to Paris. Home, to a completely different life, a life she wasn't part of, didn't belong to. And he hadn't actually said anything. He hadn't in the slightest hinted at his staying in London, or her returning to Paris with him, or keeping in touch or ... anything. It was as though they would say goodbye, thanks for a wonderful time, my pleasure, and that would be that. But surely that couldn't be Jean-Marc's intention? It *couldn't* be, damn it. Jean-Marc wasn't like that; their relationship wasn't like that. Their relationship was special; she loved him, for God's sake. And she was sure, almost one hundred percent sure now, that Jean-Marc loved her ....

Jean-Marc was due to leave London at ten o'clock on Saturday morning, 24th September. He wasn't looking forward to returning to Paris, he told Melanie on the Friday evening, before he began to pack. The apartment in

Vincennes would be like … like a museum now. He must move, find a smaller place; a place with no memories. Somewhere fresh to start a new life. And his teaching position at the lycée was no longer stimulating enough for his professional aspirations. There would be no joy in returning there. It would be good to be in his native city again but … and of course, he would miss her, Melanie.

'Will you miss me, Jean-Marc? Really?'

Her heart was pounding and her voice was barely a whisper as she tried to choke back the sobs. She couldn't bear the thought of never seeing him again, never touching him, never laughing with him. Oh, why the hell didn't he *say* something?

'Well, of course I will, my dear. I hope you'll miss me, too.'

They looked at each other and then Melanie was in his arms, weeping.

'Oh, please stay, please stay with me, Jean-Marc. *Please* don't go back to Paris.'

'I must, Melanie, I have no choice. I have a home there, and work to do …'

'But you've just said you'd have to move, find a different apartment, and your job's not … not what you really want and … you'd soon find work here, in London, teaching French.'

'Melanie, my dear …'

She pulled away from him and her tear-filled eyes danced over his face.

'Jean-Marc, do you have any idea how I feel about you? Do you? I've never … never … felt so close to anybody in my life, as I feel to you. I love you. I love you and I'm asking you to make a life for yourself here in London – with me.'

The old-fashioned carriage clock on the mantelpiece ticked loudly. The early autumn wind moaned softly and drifted through the slightly open window.

'If you stay with me, I'll make you happy. I promise, I'll make you a *very* happy man.'

Jean-Marc didn't reply. He looked for a long time into the tear-stained face of the woman sitting by his side and then he got up and walked into the bedroom where his suitcase was yawning open, waiting to be filled. He slammed it shut. He slammed shut the last forty-five unsuccessful years of his life. Here was his future beckoning him, offering him a new start, a chance of happiness. A chance to make at least one woman happy. Melanie

Jarvis was not a vindictive, malicious woman, nor was she an enigma. She was, he now knew, a warm and loving lady who wanted to share her life with him – a light at the end of his long, dark tunnel. He would really be a fool to throw this chance of happiness away ... Melanie suddenly appeared in the doorway, leaning against the frame, as if for support. Jean-Marc turned round and smiled at her.

'I sincerely hope you're going to make an honest man of me, *mademoiselle.*'

For a second, it didn't register. And then Melanie flew into his arms a second time, this time with joy. At last, someone loved her, someone cared for her. At last, she was able to love and be loved in return. And he wouldn't regret it. Melanie Jarvis promised herself that, thanks to her, Jean-Marc de Bergier would be the happiest man on earth.

Catherine

Chapter Thirty-Eight

How much is a person supposed to take before the final crack? How much suffering, self-sacrifice and humiliation is a human being capable of enduring before that certain something inside the head or the heart calls a halt? There are no rules written down, no book to which one can refer and then say, *Right, this is it, enough is enough – I'm going to snap.* Each individual has a different capacity of endurance. Certain people emotionally collapse when an almost perfect lifestyle shows the slightest sign of misfortune; others are able to persevere for years in the face of adversity, before the final last straw.

Catherine Jarvis was one of those people.

Catherine's breaking point arrived on a cool evening in late October, in an overly feminine flat in Hampstead, London. At a very early age, she'd had to get over the death of her beloved father; as an adolescent, she'd had to accept the departure of an irreplaceable best friend. She had, over the last few years, survived losing a man she loved, bearing his child, and subsequent marriage to an emotional sadist. She had suffered but she had survived, and her suffering and survival had recently given her the determination to better her life. And now this. Catherine felt that this was her breaking point. Would she find the strength to survive even this?

*

Brian was standing to her left, his right hand now limp at his side after releasing the fiancé's fingers. He was looking at him, a frown as usual on his face, but this time there was a reason for the furrowed brow. He was puzzled, uncomprehending. He didn't have a clue who Jean-Marc was –

the name hadn't registered with him. Not yet. He was trying to work out in his own mind why his sister had kept him such a secret, a mystery. As far as Brian knew, he wasn't a great celebrity; not an Oscar-winning film star, a regular in a TV soap opera. If he was a musician, Brian had never heard of him and he was certainly no politician. Although, he didn't know much about French politics of course … Anyway, his sister would never get involved with anyone in that particular field; she didn't have the intellectual … No, there was nothing special about this bloke, as far as Brian could make out. And then the Frenchman turned to Catherine. Their eyes met and held and Jean-Marc slowly held out his hand. Catherine snapped.

How dare he? That was her initial reaction. How dare this man who had in one way or another created chaos in her life, crashed her idyllic little world without even a kind word of explanation, stand by her side, look into her eyes and nonchalantly offer to shake her hand? How could he stand there, the fiancé of her oh-so-beautiful sister-in-law, knowing that he and she, Catherine, would be related by marriage – marriage to other people? What had he thought when Melanie had told him? What had gone through his mind when he found out that Melanie was Catherine's sister-in-law and that he and Catherine would be related? Hadn't he cared, for God's sake? Catherine didn't take the hand that was offered to her. She looked into those once-familiar but long-ago lost brown eyes and then she looked at his new fiancée, the spiteful sister-in-law who had sent that mysterious and very tempting invitation. She looked at her husband, the omnipresent frown on his face. They all disgusted her. They were all so unworthy of her wretchedness. She turned and walked away, pushing innocent people aside, causing drinks spillage and foul language, her eyes unable to see clearly because of the tears, her legs unable to move properly because of the trembling. She groped her way through laughing, oblivious bodies and pushed open the first door she came to. Melanie's big double bed greeted her, a port in her emotional storm. She lowered herself onto it, the duvet soft and warm beneath her, and thrust her fists deep into her eyes, trying hard to collect her thoughts, assemble them so that they made some sense. She hated him for leaving her, casting her off like a worn-out shoe; she hated him, unjustly, for the life she was now leading. But most of all she hated him for loving Melanie Jarvis; for wanting to marry Melanie Jarvis.

301

'Your husband has just discovered who I am.'

The voice was soft and so familiar. At first, Catherine didn't move and then she slowly lifted her head and looked up at the man she hated, the man who was in love with her husband's sister. He moved forward and Catherine flinched. She didn't offer to respond; she looked away from him. She wanted to stand up and walk out of the room and at the same time she didn't want to stand up and walk out of the room.

'Catherine, if I told you I had no idea you were married to Brian, would you believe me?'

He was standing over her, his physical presence making Catherine feel claustrophobic. She didn't want to be in a room alone with Jean-Marc de Bergier. Never again. She had nothing whatsoever to say to him; she didn't know what to say to him. She only wanted to tell him to go away, leave her alone; he'd already done more than enough damage, more than once. She still didn't look at him.

'Catherine, Melanie didn't tell me the truth. She lied to me and told me only that you were married and had a little girl.'

Catherine's head shot up and her breath caught loudly in her throat.

'But she didn't tell me you were married to Brian.'

She couldn't move and she certainly couldn't speak. She believed him. Some instinct deep inside her, together with her knowledge of the man and also of what Melanie Jarvis was capable of, told her she must believe him. There was a short silence and then their eyes finally met.

'Are you very happy, Catherine?' When he finally spoke again, Jean-Marc's voice was a whisper. 'I hope Brian is a good husband to you?'

That was it, the straw, and the camel that was Catherine could take no more.

Jean-Marc had crouched down in front of her, his arms resting on his thighs, his big hands pressed together as if in prayer. Catherine, through a fog of involuntary tears, looked down into those deep brown eyes and crashed her hand across his cheek.

'You fool!' she cried. 'No ... no, I'm not very happy. I'm not happy at all. I haven't been happy for six years. I'm a zombie, I'm only half alive. Brian *isn't* good to me ... he doesn't bloody well deserve me ... oh God. Jean-Marc, will you please tell me why you left me?'

Jean-Marc pulled himself into a standing position and then pulled Catherine's body against his own. He let her cry, stroking the lacklustre hair, feeling her breasts heaving against his chest.

'I left you because I believed I was God,' he told her, 'and I wasn't. I was a complete and utter fool.'

Catherine wriggled herself out of his arms and looked up into his face. She didn't understand; she wanted him ... needed him ... to explain himself.

'Do you love Melanie?'

Jean-Marc licked his dry lips and sucked in his breath before he spoke.

'I was very fond of the girl Melanie pretended to be, Catherine. I should have known better.'

The past tense. He was using the past tense.

'Have you known her very long?' she hiccupped. 'How did you meet her?'

'He met me in Paris and thought I'd be a suitable replacement when his crippled wife was laid to rest.'

Jean-Marc spun round and Catherine moved out of his arms. Melanie was standing at the entrance to her bedroom and she walked towards them. At the same time, doors began to open and close in the flat; muffled voices were still audible but the music had stopped. Cars began to come to life outside. Catherine gazed at Jean-Marc, bewildered, not understanding. What was Melanie talking about? Jean-Marc cleared his throat.

'That's not strictly true, Melanie, we were good friends. You helped me through a very bad time.'

'Friends!' Melanie screamed at him and no one would have guessed her to be a sought-after beauty at that moment. 'Friends! You're the only man I've ever cared about, Jean-Marc. Even though we knew each other for such a short time, you're the only man I've ever ... the only man I'd have given up my career for. The only man I'd have changed my whole life for. And you say we were *good friends*.'

She frantically pulled the diamond ring off her finger and flung it across the room. It landed on the soft grey carpet by the wardrobe. She turned to Catherine, her tear-filled eyes venomous and pathetic.

'Well, my dear sister-in-law, I hope you're satisfied. I hope that your revenge is very sweet. I managed to wreak havoc at your wedding and you've ... well, touché.' She paused and arranged one of her smiles on her unsmiling face. 'How *is* the Frenchman's bastard, by the way? Does she take after Mummy or Daddy?'

She walked out of her own bedroom, leaving the blue-white diamond twinkling on the carpet – and two people looking at each other, each knowing there was a lot of talking to do.

Melanie moved into the living room, empty now but for glasses and bottles and cigarette stubs and one body slumped in a pink corduroy armchair. Brian caught hold of his sister's arm and glared at her, his expression a strange mixture of hatred, defeat and complete indifference.

'You're a bitch, Melanie Jarvis.' His words were almost incoherent. He'd succeeded in getting rather drunk in a very short time. 'You're an evil bitch and one day you'll be sorry. One day, I swear to God I'm going to kill you.'

Melanie tugged her arm free with very little difficulty and stifled a sob. She would never cry in front of her brother. Never.

'I think in one way or another,' she murmured, almost to herself, 'you and I will kill each other, Brian. If we haven't already done so.'

She slowly, but with recovered dignity, left the room and at the same time Catherine entered it, from the opposite direction. She was alone, wanting the final combat with her husband to be without an audience. A few hours earlier, Brian had criticised her monotonous voice, not wanting to listen to it anymore that day. Well, he would never have to listen to her monotonous voice again. She looked at the supine body on the pink armchair, the legs stretched out and crossed at the ankle, the head lolling on the back, the right hand covering the face. A mixed vision of callousness and supreme indifference. This man was not and never could be her soulmate; he was an alien who did not belong in her world.

'Brian.'

Catherine's voice, clear and resolute, echoed in the smoky, silent room. She waited but there was no reply. Well, she would have to force him out of his apathy. She moved forward, repeating his name in the same tone, prepared for his verbal onslaught and ready with her own line of attack. Still the body didn't move and the verbal onslaught didn't come. Brian's mouth was moving slightly but there were no words, and Catherine couldn't see the rest of his face, which was still covered by his hand. And then she realised that not only his mouth was moving. His whole body was quivering, shaking uncontrollably, and then she saw the tears that were coursing down his face between his fingers. Brian was sobbing convulsively.

If Catherine was looking for revenge, she had found it. But she wasn't looking for revenge, only justice, and she had found that, too.

Epilogue

——————

Janine had gone to bed very quietly with hardly any fuss at all, that Saturday evening. Well, the poor kid had had a busy day, what with Molly dragging her round the shops and one thing and another. And she'd been really curious about the strange-looking envelope that was lying on the mat when they got home. She wanted her grandma to open it, show her its contents, put her inquisitiveness at ease. But Molly couldn't do that; the envelope wasn't addressed to her, it was addressed to Cathy. Janine was a good kid, though, never threw tantrums or anything like that, always a pleasure to have in the house. Molly smiled indulgently as she thought of the sleeping child upstairs. She was a little sugarplum.

The totally besotted grandma sighed to herself, walked to the window and pulled back the curtain slightly, looking at the dark world outside. *Eeh, it's cold and miserable, winter won't be long in coming this year.* She decided to have an early night and looked forward to the next day, Sunday, when she would have her gorgeous grandchild to herself again. She'd really enjoyed this weekend; she wished that Cathy and Brian had gone to London for a week instead of ... no, that wasn't very nice. She turned off the gas fire, turned out the light and went upstairs to bed.

Janine, as usual, was awake at the unearthly hour of seven o'clock the following morning, dragging her grandma from the depth of her warm blankets.

'You little tyke!' Molly grinned, rubbing her eyes. 'Sundays are for lying in! Come and get into bed wi' me ... come on!'

Janine giggled, delighted to climb between the sheets with her beloved grandma and doze in her soft, warm arms. They got up two hours later to a cold, grey, misty morning. Janine was happy to play on the rug in front of the fire while Molly read her Sunday paper and struggled with the crossword, and then she prepared her extra-special Sunday lunch for her extra-special granddaughter. Yorkshire pudding, roast pork, roast potatoes and veg, with her favourite chocolate cake to finish.

'Grandma, I'm full up!' Janine grinned, rubbing her tummy, and Molly laughed. She told the child to go and sit where it was nice and warm while she washed up and afterwards, they could play some games, if Janine wanted to. Ooh yes, please, Grandma! They spent the afternoon playing lots of games that Molly should have won but made a point of losing. They watched a children's programme on television and at five o'clock Molly made a light tea which they ate in front of the television set.

'Yer mummy and daddy'll be 'ome soon, Janine. I wonder if they enjoyed their party.'

Janine nodded her head abstractedly, her eyes glued to the cartoon on the screen. While she was occupied, Molly went upstairs and collected the child's belongings together. A small lump came into her throat. She didn't want Janine to leave … it had been a lovely treat having her here again … When she went back downstairs, she looked at the clock. Cathy and Brian would be here any time. At nine o'clock, Janine's eyes started to droop and Molly started to look out of the window. At nine-thirty, she decided to put her granddaughter to bed and at ten-thirty, she started to panic. At eleven o'clock, the telephone rang.

*

At first, she didn't recognise the voice, and the gentleman on the other end of the line had to repeat his name. She'd been expecting Cathy or Brian – or God forbid, the police – to speak to her.

'This is Jean-Marc, Molly. Jean-Marc de Bergier.'

It finally sank in and Molly slowly sat down on the bottom step – her telephone being in the hall – clutching the receiver as though it would suddenly take off and take this unexpected voice with it.

'I can't believe it,' she breathed, not knowing whether to tear him to shreds or verbally hug him. 'Are you in France? You could be in next room …'

Jean-Marc laughed down the line.

'No, Molly. I'm not in France.'

When Molly placed the receiver back in its cradle an hour later, she had to go into the kitchen and make herself a cup of tea. She needed one. Well, what a strange twist of fate this was. She didn't really understand, of course; she was a bit confused. No, damn it, she was a lot confused. But if Cathy was finally going to divorce that so-called husband of hers then that, at least, made her happy. As for the rest, time would tell.

Janine didn't understand. Why wasn't her mummy here? Where were her mummy and daddy? Molly gently tried to break the news that her daddy wouldn't be coming home but that Mummy was bringing a new daddy for her. But Janine didn't want a new daddy, so Molly tried to explain that this daddy was actually ... Oh, how could a five-year-old be expected to understand? This daddy was her real daddy, who should never have gone away. She couldn't tell a five-year-old that ... Molly gave up and silently waited for Tuesday morning when Catherine would be arriving with the new daddy ... waited with a mixture of apprehension and joy.

The train journey north from London's King's Cross was not easy. Only the knowledge that her miserable marriage was finally over and that Jean-Marc was back in her life pulled Catherine through what had been a very traumatic time. But the trauma was far from over, of course; it would take time. Divorce was painful even when highly desirable, and she also had to come to terms with the skeleton in Jean-Marc's cupboard. Not only come to terms with it but lay it to rest, forget about it and learn to trust him as she'd trusted him in the past – implicitly. It would take a while; it wouldn't be easy. The Jean-Marc who was now sitting beside her in the speeding inter-city train was a widower when she hadn't even known he'd had a wife, and a man who, as far as she could see, had quickly fallen in love with a scheming she-devil. Catherine judged him, yes, and recognised that their relationship certainly wouldn't and couldn't start where it had left off. But at least they both recognised this and were both willing to work hard together, after being given this incredible second chance.

Jean-Marc's tension stemmed not so much from his lamentable past as from the future into which he and Catherine were riding. He had a child, a little five-year-old girl whom he was now going to meet for the first time, and he knew that this child would be capable of making or breaking his new relationship with Catherine. Janine had suffered too much already for her years; Catherine wouldn't allow her to suffer anymore. If Janine wouldn't accept Jean-Marc ... And there were other practical, professional matters to concern themselves with, not least of these being the Mullion Hall School of Languages. He would give his tenants six months' notice and during that time he would wind up his financial affairs in Paris. In six months, he and Catherine would once again be able to start planning their language school and their home, and stabilising their future. He had expected Catherine to help him run the administration side of the school, the kind of work she was used to – secretarial with some translating. But no. Catherine had decided she'd like to do something completely different, develop her skills and talents. She really would like to teach English to foreign students at the school, at some later date, when the school was up and running and successful. So, there were many things to discuss, plan and hopefully look forward to. Together.

They hardly spoke on the journey north but each felt the other's thoughts. As the train sped through the early golden morning, Jean-Marc took hold of Catherine's hand and silently squeezed it. She smiled without looking at him.

*

After ringing the doorbell, Catherine walked into her mother's home and wrapped her arms around her. Molly was weeping and Catherine patted her back as Molly had often patted hers in the past, and encouraged her to let her tears flow. Molly finally withdrew from Catherine's arms and blew her nose, loudly. She made a show of pushing the handkerchief up her sleeve, sniffing a few times, and then she turned to the Frenchman. He looked uncomfortable, obviously not knowing how he was supposed to behave, not knowing what Molly's reaction would be after she'd had time to think. She smiled at him, a nervous, unsure smile, but there was more than a hint of welcome there.

'Well, Jean-Marc, it's nice to see you, after all this time. I ... I suppose you two have had plenty to say to each other an' sorted yerselves out?'

Catherine and Jean-Marc exchanged a smile. They followed Molly into the warm living room and the short, embarrassing silence was suddenly interrupted by a clomping of excited feet on the bedroom stairs and the appearance of a small body with an inquisitive face, balancing on one leg in the doorway and studiously sucking her thumb. Molly started to move forward but had second thoughts and sank into her chair by the fireside, unsuccessfully trying to avert her curious eyes. Catherine looked at Jean-Marc and watched a thousand expressions on his face. She gently pushed him forward.

'This is Janine,' she whispered, smiling at her little girl. 'Go and say hello to your daughter.'

While Jean-Marc was saying a long hello to his daughter, who had surreptitiously climbed onto his lap, Molly put an envelope into Catherine's hand. An airmail envelope, postmark Sydney, Australia. She and Molly exchanged a look. It contained a very short letter written on flimsy blue paper. Catherine's eyes devoured the once-familiar writing, more than once. She folded the paper and turned back to her mum.

'Diana's getting married,' she told her, 'in Sydney, and then they're moving back here, permanently. She doesn't say who her fiancé is; she hasn't even told me his name, but thinks we'll like each other very much. And this is an invitation to the celebration they'll be having in Harrogate. Just before Christmas.'

'Oh, right. Well, this is a bit out of the blue, isn't it? After all this time. Do you think you'll accept? If I were you, I think—'

'Yes, Mum,' Catherine interrupted, 'of course I'm going to accept, it goes without saying. Diana's coming home ... Oh, I do hope they'll want to live here ... well, in Yorkshire, not hundreds of miles away. Oh, Mum, I wonder who her fiancé is and ... why is she keeping him a secret? Anyway, I'm really, really looking forward to meeting him.'

She moved to the window, still clasping the precious correspondence, and through her tears looked out at the cool, crisp and russet autumn afternoon. The kind of afternoon that Catherine would learn to love again.

*

310

Milton Keynes UK
Ingram Content Group UK Ltd.
UKHW012046181023
430831UK00004B/62